This is for my parents, John and Ann, who would
take me and my sister to the Lake District every Easter.
This book grew out of every peak we climbed,
every rainstorm we survived and every last corner
of Kendal mint cake over which we fought.

A Cry in the Night

Also by Tom Grieves

Sleepwalkers

Tom Grieves has worked in television as a script editor, producer and executive producer, as well as a writer. *A Cry in the Night* is his second novel. Tom lives in Sussex with his wife and three sons.

A Cry in the Night

TOM GRIEVES

Quercus

First published in Great Britain in year of 2014 by

Quercus Editions Ltd
55 Baker Street
7th Floor, South Block
London W1U 8EW

A CIP catalogue record for this book is available
from the British Library

ISBN 978 0 85738 985 5
EBOOK ISBN 978 0 85738 986 2

10 9 8 7 6 5 4 3 2

Printed and bound in Great Britain by Clays Ltd, St Ives plc

Typeset by Ellipsis Digital Limited, Glasgow

PROLOGUE

Although the water is cold and clear, it still has its secrets. The pebbles in the shallows are easy to see, but beyond, a good mile from land where the wind buffets the surface, the water is so deep that the view below is impenetrable. From here, looking up and back at the shore, the steep fells rise majestically into tumbling clouds. Chunky rocks spew out from the slopes like angry welts, sheep dot the fields, and ancient stone walls cut and divide the land. The view remains unchanged over centuries.

It was the same sight that greeted the small village of Lullingdale in 1604. Its inhabitants were honest, God-fearing men and women who made their meagre living off the land. Among them was a pretty young girl called Catherine Adams. Catherine was the eldest daughter of seven and had inevitably grown up quickly. Her status as the eldest had led to her helping with children and then to midwifery. This began when she was only nine years old, and she soon became something of a good luck charm. Margaret Gifford, the skinner's wife, swore that she would never have survived the birth of her first were it not for Catherine, and, remarkably, no baby had ever died under her watch. Catherine would blush and stammer when praised, and it certainly wasn't her who mentioned miracles. But the word was used nonetheless and, in time, carried over the fells and across rivers until it reached the court of King James I.

King James was also a God-fearing man. Having survived a plot to kill him by some three hundred witches in 1590, he was determined to rid the country of their curse. This determination became an obsession, and the monarch was soon an expert on the subject. Witches, he decided, danced with the devil, and where one was discovered, more would be found. He also decreed that it was possible to discover them in actions that might initially seem benign. The act of healing might not be what it seemed. Nor, it could be assumed, might the ability to deliver babies without ever suffering an accident or stillbirth.

Catherine Adams would shrug bashfully when reminded of her feats. She had no idea that her good fortune and skill would speed John Stern into the village, with his team of men who watched her and every woman with mistrust.

Until John arrived, it had been thought inevitable that Catherine would marry the bashful shepherd Robert Cox. The village would have celebrated their union with a single, delighted voice. But John Stern was not fooled by a sweet disposition. Once he had set his eye on Catherine, it was only a matter of time before he exposed her.

Catherine was stripped naked, and although no mark of the devil was found on her, John Stern was undeterred. Witches, he told the cowed villagers, were cunning and deceitful. He then used his pricking stick, poking young Catherine in the back without warning. She did not react at first, and John claimed that this inability to feel pain was proof of her wickedness. Her fate was sealed.

The girl was dragged away, condemned as guilty. Now she was important only for one thing – to find and expose the others. John served the King and did God's work. He beseeched the villagers to help him exorcise this evil and save their souls from the danger that swirled invisibly around them.

Perhaps Catherine had danced too gaily at the May Fayre. Had her mother not been so distracted with her wayward brothers, she might have warned Catherine not to laugh so easily with the men. And had she been less pretty, then perhaps the villagers might not have let John drag her away.

The next morning, the mud-stained, beaten and bloodied figure was paraded in chains before the village. She was a harlot, a witch, a partner of the devil, and she had betrayed them all. It is not clear whether it was Catherine who mentioned Lucy Darwent's name or whether John had seen the girl staring at him, but his finger pointed to her. No one

3

stopped his men from throwing her to the ground, ripping her skirt up to her waist and declaring that the mole on her thigh was the mark of the devil. Angry and fearful, she spat in John Stern's face and screamed at the men as they shaved her head, cutting her scalp and breaking her teeth. Only minutes before, she had been rather beautiful, but in their arms she was branded dangerous, and her appearance proved their words.

A herd of sheep had died earlier that spring, and at the time it was blamed on bad fortune and the shepherd's foolhardiness – letting them graze too high on the fells when the weather was still so bitter. But now, with John's expert eye on matters, it became clear that the animals' deaths were a result of curses and spells. And the only woman who could have put such a hex on so many animals was Elinor Sibbell, a hunchbacked grandmother who had never spent a single day outside of the village. Elinor's age and physical weakness earned her no favours with John's men, and she was bound and broken with the others.

When he had six, John was satisfied. Some might say that his work proved unprofitable until he reached this number, but their voices are not recorded. Instead, John was able to rely on the fear of the male villagers, desperate to rid themselves of the wickedness among them, angry that they had not seen it themselves, fearful that their inability to spot it might turn eyes onto them.

4

It is unclear what happened that night. The witches were taken away to a hut at the edge of the village where they confessed their wrongdoing and repented of their sins. The husbands were told that they were not at fault. The devil was to blame and all that the men could do was pray to God that he would deliver them from the women's black hearts. The men took comfort from John's words. They agreed that a woman's guile was like no other and swore that they would not be fooled again. They retired in each other's company and felt safer for it. Perhaps it was the darkness that made this possible. Ghost, ghouls and gremlins are easily conjured against the eternal black canvas of a starless night.

The next morning, the witches were paraded before the village. They were spat at and cursed as brave John Stern delighted the crowd by announcing their confessions. They had admitted to the murder of farmer Francis Clifford's prize bull, which everyone had previously assumed to have died of old age. They had confessed to dancing naked with the devil by firelight near the lake while the menfolk slept, and admitted to future plans of evil. John Stern was good at his job and he controlled his crowd with the skills of a master showman. No one, it seemed, noticed that the women remained silent. But who would deny the words of good John Stern, servant of King James I and the Lord God Almighty?

5

Seven-year-old William Henshaw was only too happy to offer up his father's boat for the final proof and purification of the witches. The villagers came to watch as John and two of his men rowed the women out on the water. And there, with their hands tied behind their backs and their legs in hastily made shackles, the witches were thrown into the lake. All sank without a trace. This, good John said, was proof that their sins were finally purged. Had they floated and survived, then the devil's powers still flowed unabated through their hearts. The silence of the water was proof that good had won out. The witches were gone. The village was once again safe and John Stern could leave them to continue lives of prosperity and obedience.

While John Stern had stood among them on the land, the men had cheered with an impassioned zeal. Even the usually taciturn William Cox had shouted and spat against fair Catherine. But watching the action unfold out on the lake, the crowd's fervour faded. As the women plunged into the water, the men's voices were replaced with the tremulous wail of sisters, mothers and daughters who mourned their own with powerless, desolate grief. The men could not look at them.

Honest John Stern and his men stayed one last night, dining and drinking their fill at the inn. They left the next morning at dawn, hunting down rumours of a woman who turned herself into a magpie at dusk. They never visited the village again.

Once the noise of their horses' hoofs had faded, the villagers were left with the familiar sound of the wind in the trees, the murmur of cattle, the slap of water against the rocky shoreline. Nature remained unchanged. But the women looked at the men and the men looked at their women and neither could hold the other's eye. Once they had danced together, hands held, hips touching. The dance's steps would demand they did so again. Slowly, the memories receded.

But the lake was always the same, untouchable despite the ice, the rain, the sleet and snow. It swallowed it all, swallowed it whole. The villagers stared out across the water. Their children would stand in their place, and their children's children. The lake would always be there, guarding its stories for each new generation to tell.

PART ONE

PART ONE

ONE

Little Arthur Downing ran from the lake, tore into the woods and threw himself onto his belly among the long grass.

If I don't move, he thought, *if I stay dead still and don't make a sound, then maybe the witch won't find me.*

He lay amongst the bracken, his head pressed down against the mud and the moss, listening as keenly as he could for any noise. Although his little legs shook, he was sure he wasn't making a sound. But still, that might not be enough.

The Lake Witches come from the water and promise you presents. But under their coats are blades and a silver thread. And they drag you back down – deep, deep down where they play with you like a cat plays with a shrew.

The little boy's name was Arthur. It was his dad's dad's name and he was the latest in a long line of Arthur Downings. It was a name to be proud of. But when the woman had stretched out her gloved hand and said, 'Arthur Downing, is that you? Come with me, dear, I have something exciting to show you,' he had wished his name was anything but that. He'd known right away what she really was. He might have been only nine years old, but after seeing the news on the TV and hearing what people were saying, he knew that the witches were back. She made him feel cold. Like a rabbit must feel on the fells when it looks up and sees the kites circling. Maybe she had talons under her gloves that cut when she grabbed you so you could never escape. He wondered if her sharp claws had grabbed Lily. He didn't know where his little sister was now and he was torn between his worry for her and the stabbing fear that kept him pressed down in the dirt.

He listened again, raising his head ever so slightly to see, but the rocks obscured his view and all he could hear was the gentle lapping of the water against the shore. The witch had shouted after him as he ran, laughing as though it was all just a silly little joke. But now she would be floating above the trees, spying down on him, calling her sisters to rise up from the lake and join her. No child who'd ever seen a witch had lived to tell the tale. But Arthur Downing was going to be the first.

It was dirty and cold on the ground, but he stayed still for as long as he could. Once his mum had locked him out of the house and he'd been freezing all night. But they'd agreed not to tell a soul about it. Even then, in the dark, he'd been able to get up and pace about, but this time he had to lie still as a sleeping lion. Stiller than that.

The wet leaves nibbled at the back of his neck and soon he couldn't bear it any more. Arthur sat up as slowly and quietly as he could and looked around. He stared up at the trees and checked every branch. Two red squirrels twisted around a tree trunk and then scuttled off into the thick bed of autumn leaves. He sat and listened. Water, wind, a bird's cry, but nothing else. He finally stood up, his legs cramped and cold. He rubbed his dirty hands on the back of his shorts and tried to work out what to do next. The lake was somewhere down there, ahead. If he went right, he'd head back towards home. But that was where the witch would be waiting for him. If he went left, he'd go deeper into the woods, and Dad had made him scared of the woods and the boathouse that creaked and moaned. He didn't want to go there.

Arthur imagined them biting at Lily under the water, and his confidence failed him. Eventually he forced himself forward, heading right, towards home. The green, red and orange leaves hid the lake from view, but he knew it was there, just out of sight. He had to be careful. He stood behind the last line of trees, watching and waiting, his hand resting on a sycamore's trunk, its bark softened by lichen. There was no one there. All he had to do was slip along the pebbles, join the road and belt it back up to the village. Five minutes and he'd be home. Just five minutes. Easy.

He took the first step out from the wood and made his way along the shore. He glanced down and stared at the lake water – it seemed to creep towards his feet. He took a step away from it, but up it came again. The water should be still, he thought. He looked up – his eyes running over the surface of the lake. It was so dark and huge, it made him shiver. He half expected to see Lily there under the water, staring up at him.

He hurried, crablike, along the shore, his eyes fixed on the waves that lapped back and forth. He turned to run home and suddenly there she was, with that smile. When she put a hand on his shoulder, he felt his heart crumble.

The witch looked around and she definitely was like the kite. Her eyes moved fast, checking, checking, checking. Arthur started to cry. The witch dropped down so her face was close to his. She wore a long purple coat and it looked elegant and sleek, but Arthur could see leaves and a broken twig which had snagged on her sleeve. She'd been in the woods. Hiding in the trees, no doubt. Any minute now, she would drag him into the lake. There was no one around. He wanted to pee. He was crying, he wanted to pee and he knew that he was going to die.

'You mustn't be frightened,' she said. 'Nothing bad is going to happen. We're just going to play a game.'

She'll play with me, he thought, like the farm cats do in the barn. Leaving only the guts behind.

14

'Please,' he begged. 'Please, I want to go home.'

'Don't be scared. Your sister's waiting for you. And we're going to have such fun.'

She smiled at him and he tried to smile back, so she wouldn't expect it when he ran. But then her spell started to work on him. His eyes started to water and the magic was so strong it was like liquid black going over his eyes and nose and mouth. He felt dizzy. He saw that the witch had stopped smiling and that she was turning away from him. But he was powerless now. He wanted to scream, but the spell was too strong. Everything went woozy and dark. Her purple coat faded and clouded.

Soon he was like the water, quiet and still. Unknown and unknowable.

TWO

Zoe Barnes stared out at the water, rubbed her hands against the cold, and took everything in. She'd read up on the area before they'd set out from Manchester but the facts and figures now felt redundant as she faced Lullingdale Water. Yes, the lake was indeed big – two miles long from north to south – and the maps certainly showed the steep slopes' gradations with perfect detail, but nothing on paper could have reflected the sheer scale of the place. She took in the woodland to the left and the shale-strewn slopes on the right. The sky was blue but the sun had already fallen below the fells' peaks, making it feel like twilight, although it was still only mid-afternoon. A faint mist hovered above the water like a gossamer shroud, twisting with the currents. She felt silly for letting it distract her from the job in hand and turned her attention back to the shoreline.

'The boy's bike was found there,' she said, pointing.

Her boss, Sam, walked over to her and she felt tiny next

to his hulking frame. He looked to where she'd gestured and nodded.

'Bike there,' she continued, 'found by the mother at quarter-to-five or round about. Then there's a lot of shouting and running about and not much sense. Last known sighting of Arthur and Lily was when they left the school gates together at 3.30.'

'It's beautiful,' said Sam.

It was, and she was glad that he'd noticed it too. They always thought alike.

'What time are we seeing the parents?' she asked.

'Half an hour,' he replied and stretched, rolling his shoulders, now free from the confines of the car. It had been a long journey and he hadn't spoken much. While his silences made many of her colleagues uncomfortable, they didn't bother her.

'Okay, let's check in to the hotel first,' he said.

She reminded him that the hotel was actually just a room above a pub and made a joke about being 'strangers in these parts'. He just threw the keys at her.

'Bet your mobile phone won't work half the time,' she added. 'And all there is to eat is minestrone soup from a packet and rabbit stew.'

'DC Barnes.'

'Yes, DI Taylor?'

'Shut up.'

'Shutting right up, sir,' she said with a grin.

They walked back to the car, which was parked a small distance away from the lake, at the end of a road that looked as though it had just given up. When they got there, Sam stopped and looked back at the scene. Zoe did the same, seeing a thin line of clouds roll over the peaks to the left, illuminated by an invisible sun. A flock of geese flew low over the still water and she was struck by how quiet it was. There was no one on the water. When she was younger she'd visited the bigger, more popular lakes that were covered with sailing boats or jet skis. She remembered happy childhood days – splashing in and around the water by day, giggling in tents at night. But this lake was absolutely still.

Sam's hands hung loosely by his sides and she wondered how he didn't feel the cold. She tried to do the same, but after a few minutes she dug them back into her pockets.

'There's only one way down here,' Sam said. 'This road. It comes down to here, and stops here at the car park.'

They looked at the small gravelly square; room enough for two, maybe three, cars, plus the stile and nicely painted footpath sign nearby.

'There are no roads around the lake,' Sam continued. 'So if someone took them, they'd need to have parked here. Or carried them away – but that's more risky and would probably have been seen. We must make sure the local police checked all the CCTV that leads to here. If there is any.'

She nodded, cross that she hadn't spotted this herself.

'And I like minestrone soup,' Sam said with a wink. They got into the car and adjusted their seats – him pushing back, her coming forward.

'Good spot for running,' she said. He nodded, uninterested. 'How long do you think we'll be here?'

He just shrugged. It was a stupid question, really. Missing kids' cases were notoriously difficult to predict and she knew it. Sam had said that they were there to double-check it had all been done properly after the initial investigation had run cold, but she knew that anything could happen once they got stuck in. Something about the lake pulled her eyes back to it. The mist on the water had thickened and the far end of the lake was gone.

'You know this is witch country?' Zoe said, a grin on her face.

He looked at her. He had beautiful blue eyes, light and delicate. It was a stare that got people talking.

'Back in the old days,' she added to end the silence, 'sixteen something or other. There was meant to be some sort of witches' cabal here. It's in the guidebook.'

'You bought a guidebook?'

She shrugged – why not? – but felt silly and over-eager. She wished herself older and more hardbitten.

Sam said nothing, and she could tell his mind was now elsewhere. He was often like this. He would be talking and then something would take over, and he would disappear for a bit. It seemed to freak out some of their colleagues, but Zoe knew him too well for any of that. She guessed that he was thinking about his wife. So she let him be and turned the key in the ignition, reversing the car back and away.

Another glance at Lullingdale Water. She saw some birds fly into the mist and disappear, but they didn't seem to come back out. She would have stopped and checked it out properly if she had been on her own, but Sam's silence forced her hand onto the gears, turning the wheel and steering them towards the village.

THREE

Zoe was right. Sam was thinking about his wife. He was remembering the way she let her hair fall on his face as she lay on top of him, laughing when he grumbled. He stared out of the window at the tall hedging that lined the narrow road and tried to shake her out of his head. His mind found a new preoccupation: his meeting that morning with Chief Superintendent Frey.

Michael Frey was a tall, gaunt man who chose to keep his white hair cropped, giving himself a military appearance. He liked to look 'severe' and therefore smiled as little as possible. It was a decent enough performance and it only sagged when in the company of tougher men who would naturally smell the fraud. Then the Chief Superintendent would become a little too eager to be one of the lads. As a result, Sam loathed him.

'So we have an odd one,' Mr Frey said, patting Sam on the shoulder and offering him a seat. He returned to the other side of his desk and played with a paperweight as he talked. 'Two children have gone missing – you might have seen the reports. Brother and sister – Arthur and Lily Downing. Last seen near their local village up in the Lake District. It's been four weeks now and the local police haven't got anywhere. Press has got bored, thankfully, and moved on. But I wanted one of my boys to have a second look. I thought it was one for you.'

Sam wondered what this meant, unsure why this was coming from the lofty position of Chief Superintendent and not from his immediate boss, his DCI.

'You look well, by the way,' said Frey to fill the silence. 'Still pumping iron? Still boxing?'

'A bit.'

'Good for you. If it weren't for my knees . . . too many marathons.'

What a tit, thought Sam. He waited for the Chief Superintendent to continue, a blank stare on his face.

'Good, yes, right. So, pop up, stay for a bit, there's a local hotel that isn't too dear so we won't have the taxpayers muttering. See what you can find out. Never good when the little ones vanish, is it?'

'No, sir.'

'No. Few too many recently.'

Chief Superintendent Frey left his last comment hanging in the air. Sam had a good idea as to what he was talking about, but waited for his boss to continue. He watched the white-haired man play with the glass paperweight, the light throwing spectrums onto his desk.

'How are your girls?' was all his boss ventured after the silence had dragged on too long.

'They're doing well, thank you, sir. Stronger by the day.'

'Well, that's women for you,' Mr Frey replied. Then he reached behind him and dumped a large stack of thick manila envelopes onto the desk.

'Look at these, will you?'

'Sir.'

'I don't know if they're relevant to your case or not. Impossible to tell at this stage, but you should be as well informed as possible.'

'Yes, sir. Of course.'

'Good. And I'd be careful about how much you tell your young detective constable. What's her name?'

'Zoe Barnes, sir.'

'Barnes. Yes. She's very popular.'

'She's very good at her job.'

'Pretty little thing too. Just be wary of how much you divulge.'

The envelopes sat between them. The topmost was threatening to slip off and ruin the perfect order of the desk. Sam didn't move to take them, wary of the privilege of secrets.

'Keep me informed, yes?'

'Yes, sir.'

'Straight to me. Right?'

The meeting over, Sam stood, reluctantly scooped up the files, and thanked his boss again. Later he dumped them in the back of his car.

They were sliding around in the boot right now, as Zoe drove them into the village. They passed the medieval church and turned left before the pub, following the hand-painted sign to the patrons' car park. The Black Bull was a white, picturesque building with a pretty thatched roof. Around it were old, identical houses with black doors and window frames. The conformity gave the village a toy-town feel. A few doors down was a shop, then nothing – just a country lane with neighbouring fields filled with sheep. There were thirty houses in all – each one dainty and proper. The word 'sleepy' was irresistible. Once parked, they got their things out of the boot, Zoe waiting for Sam as he stuffed the files into a backpack. He saw that she looked at them with interest, but didn't ask him what was inside.

He felt guilty. He knew what they were, even without reading them. Everyone knew about them. They'd caused a frenzy of debate across the country; terrible tales about monstrous women. And he knew what Mr Frey had implied by advising him to exclude Zoe. That he should only trust men. It made Sam hate him all the more.

'Shithole,' muttered his partner.

'Fifteen minutes to check in and dump our stuff. Then let's go and meet the parents.'

'So, boss, how long do you think you'd last in a place like this? I'd go crazy after six months.'

He looked around at the quiet pavements, the pretty cottages and hedgerows. The fells rose up behind them, the darkening sky turning their browns and greens to purples and blacks. Even the leafless winter trees seemed pretty and bucolic.

'I'd last a week,' he said with a grin. Zoe's hard laugh seemed too loud for this sweet place. They grabbed their things and marched towards the pub.

FOUR

Tim Downing hung up the phone and turned to look at his wife. Sarah was sitting at the large wooden kitchen table, staring at a mug of tea. It was all either of them seemed to do. Make tea or drink booze, and stare at the table.

Sarah was beautiful. Even now, crumpled by grief, her eyes puffy and her face sagging without expression, she still looked incredible. He watched her thin fingers clutch the mug and felt like crying all over again. He fiddled with the shirt he'd ironed this morning and didn't know what else to do. He had always considered himself successful and the money he'd earned had seemed to prove this true, but all it had done was make him feel bigger and stronger than he really was. Arthur and Lily's disappearance had exposed the lie brutally.

'The cops are here. New ones,' he said.

She didn't reply. Her hands wrung the mug, slowly strangling it.

'Staying at the Black Bull.'

Still nothing from her. Not even the barest acknowledgement. Tim stared at his own mug on the black marble worktop. The coffee was untouched, stone-cold. He exhaled a weak, shivery breath and dug his hands into his pockets.

The thick curtains had been closed for days. The stagnant climate within seemed all the worse for it.

'Are you going to get dressed for them?'

It came out as an accusation, but it was just concern. She sat barefoot in a thin nightie and dressing gown, her long, lithe legs exposed to the thigh.

'What do they care?' she replied. Her eyes never moved from the mug.

That was all he'd get out of her. He went over and put his hand on her shoulder, leaned in and kissed her cheek. Her hand went to his, held it there, pressed hard to keep him close. He was so grateful for the contact, so desperate to feel needed.

The tears rose again.

FIVE

It was September 15th of the previous year, and Constable Eddy Pearson had only been in the job for five weeks. He was barely nineteen and as eager as a puppy. He was partnered with Alan Troughton, who was known by one and all as a miserable bastard. The hope was that he'd knock a little bit of the keenness out of Eddy before he did something silly.

Eddy and Alan had been called to a disturbance in Mapleside Avenue, a well-to-do leafy road in a posher part of Manchester. An elderly lady had been complaining about the noise from next door. She'd been grumbling for some weeks and this was one of many calls. Troughton thought this would be an excellent opportunity for young Eddy to try his diplomatic skills on the utterly uncharmable old woman.

They never got to see her. As Troughton rang on her doorbell, Eddy had wandered over to the neighbouring house, and was about to comment on the fact that there was no noise whatsoever when he saw a young girl throw herself at the first-floor window. She was soaking wet, but fully clothed. The glass cracked but did not break. Eddy and the girl's eyes met and he saw terror there. And then an arm appeared from behind her and dragged her out of sight.

Troughton saw none of this but he did see the cracked glass and paid attention to the yapping of his new colleague. Moving towards the house, he radioed in his concerns, banging loudly on the door. Eddy was frantic by now. As Troughton rang again and peered in through the large windows at the front of the house, Eddy ran to the back. He yanked hard on the back door. To his frustration, it was also locked. He could hear Troughton ringing repeatedly on the doorbell, clearly getting nowhere. He thought of the little girl again, her wet hair matted against her forehead.

He got inside without remembering exactly how. Evidence suggested that he had barged the door open. He ran through the rooms, calling out, until he saw a woman staring at him from the top of the stairs. She was about his age, with long dark hair that fell to her shoulders. It was the way she gazed at him that was most disquieting: the tilt of her head, the slackness of her mouth, the hint of a smile. Then he noticed that the sleeves of her jumper were dripping with water.

He ran at her and expected her to claw at him and fight, but instead she just collapsed as he shoved her and lay still where she fell, inanimate on the landing. Eddy ran past her, the doorbell ringing continually, the woman making no attempt to get up.

He found the girl in the bath. Her hair swam before her face like weed in a lake. Her eyes were open, no longer scared. A tiny bubble of air slipped from her lips. Her skin seemed so white. She was naked now and although she was dead, Eddy was embarrassed to look at her. The little drowned girl stared up at the ceiling, alone under the water.

Troughton found Eddy about five minutes later. The woman was still lying on the floor where his colleague had barged past her. Her cold, detached gaze echoed that of the girl in the water. Eddy was lying on the bathroom floor, the girl now in his arms after he'd failed to resuscitate her. His hand stroked her wet hair.

The woman was the nanny of a wealthy couple, Matt and Diane Parlour. The girl was their only daughter, Melinda. The evidence against the nanny was undeniable. The only troubling aspect was a lack of motive. As arresting officers, Eddy and Troughton were the first to interview her, although the case was soon passed on to CID. Eddie sat opposite her, unable to speak. Troughton asked the questions, but the nanny didn't respond. She just gazed at Eddy with that same curious, vague, unknowable expression. It was soon decided that she was unfit to stand trial and needed psychiatric evaluation.

Eddy was interviewed himself some days later. It was

partly a debrief, partly an examination into his own state of mind, and partly another box that Human Resources required ticked. He knew the answers he was meant to give – the reasons needed to justify forcibly entering a premises. He said exactly what he was meant to say and was commended for it. But when asked about the nanny and why he believed she had drowned poor little Melinda, his professionalism was derailed. He tried to sidestep the questions with a shrug, but this was not acceptable. He had faced something cruel and cold, without any comprehensible sense or reason. He had seen terror in the eyes of a little girl and he had seen her look to him for help. And he had failed her. He had watched that woman stare at him across the table in a police interview room without any sense of remorse or shame or any emotion that would make sense to him. And so, when pressed to answer the question, young Eddy Pearson floundered.

'She was just fucking evil. A fucking witch,' he stammered.

Witch. It was the first time the word had been used like this for years. The word would stick.

Sam snapped the case file shut. He had imagined the details too vividly. There were copies of photographs, but he chose not to look at them.

There was a bang on the door. It was Zoe.

'Come on then, we're five minutes behind already,' she said as she breezed in, checking out his hotel room. 'I take it all back. By the way, they've got wi-fi.' And then she noticed that nothing was unpacked, his bags lay on the bed, that he was still wearing his coat, with the closed file in his hand.

'What's that?' she asked.

'Nothing.' There was an awkward pause and he saw her eyes narrow, taking this in. She was a good cop, he reminded himself. 'Sorry for being late. Got distracted.'

'Yeah?'

'I'll tell you about it another time.'

That was good enough for her and her face brightened. 'They do loads of beers in the pub. Got proper pork scratching in bowls on the bar. Free pork scratchings! And there's this feisty barmaid called Bernie and she said tomorrow they'd have mini-Yorkshire puddings. None of that peanut bollocks. How cool is that?'

'Yeah. Missing kid.'

'All right. But come on, mini-Yorkshire puds! Sam!'

'Yes. Great. Now, stop smiling, you're on duty.'

He grabbed his coat and led her along the uneven corridor ('See, it's so olde-worlde!'), down the dark wooden stairs and out into the cold. They pulled their coats tighter around them; there was a real bite to the air now. Sam pointed to the small lane that ran away from the pub.

'Five minutes' walk,' he said, and set off. She was at his side immediately.

It was darker now and would be pitch-black in an hour

or so. The fells rose away from them and Sam thought he could see movement on the ridges, but the more he stared, the less sure he was. A cloud billowed above, and he noticed the branches shake in the bitter wind.

The village was dead quiet as they walked. Further ahead was a small gathering of buildings – a post office-cum-corner shop, next to a bakery and a grocer's. Sitting on three black benches in front of the shops was a gang of kids, hoods up, wrapped up against the cold. Two were mucking about on skateboards, doing noisy tricks to which the others paid little attention. Most were on their phones or gossiping, or both. They were a surprising shot of modernity in these pastoral surroundings. They looked up at Sam and Zoe as they approached.

'Five-Oh!' someone shouted and the kids looked up with hostile faces.

'Hey, kids!' Zoe said happily, as though she were the friendliest woman in the world. There was, unsurprisingly, no response to this.

Sam ran his eyes over each of them, checking for the tell-tale signs of guilt, drugs, abuse and shame. They seemed just like the kids he dealt with back in the city. Identikit youth with their everyday issues. He looked away, a little bored by their obviousness. As he did so, he spotted a girl, eighteen, maybe nineteen, a little taller and older than the others, watching him from further back. She was leaning

33

against a wall between two of the buildings, sheltering from the cold, he guessed. She wore a white bobble hat, a short white puffa jacket and white jeans. Her hair, as far as he could tell, was blonde. She watched him with a sneer. But when he looked at her, she didn't shirk his gaze like the others. Her stare was a challenge and it was Sam who broke contact first. They walked on, towards the Downings' house a few minutes further along the road. He didn't look back, but he imagined that the girl in white was still watching him with that aggressive gaze.

'We could pop back after and pull them all in for drugs,' Zoe said cheerfully. 'Give us something to do.'

Sam gave her a jokey cuff across her head. She replied with a sharp punch to his stomach. He was expecting it, though and slapped her hand away. It felt wrong to be this jokey so close to the house, and he glanced around, worried that they'd been seen. But the road was empty. So were the fields that stretched down to the lake. His eyes ran across them, reaching the water. He looked back down the lane where the kids had been but he couldn't see them now. He scuffed his boots against the floor, just to hear a noise that felt normal. Then he nodded at Zoe and they marched on.

SIX

Zoe let Sam enter first and do the introductions. She shook hands with Mr and Mrs Downing with a firm grip to let them know she was no patsy, but then stood slightly behind Sam with her hands behind her back.

She looked around – it was a nice house, they had money. Maybe money would be a factor in the case. Those curtains were thick and made-to-measure. It felt like they had a job to do: keeping peeping eyes out.

The mum, Sarah, was pretty. Zoe wondered why she hadn't bothered to dress before they arrived. She knew they were coming, after all. Maybe it was the grief.

The dad dressed posh. Bright cords and a checked shirt, a nice smile. His eyes latched on to hers when they shook hands, wanting to be liked, wanting her to be on his side. He's harmless, she thought. She's more interesting.

'I'm sorry to ask you to go through the details again,' Sam

was saying. 'But we'd like to hear it from you, first-hand. It's always better that way.'

Zoe watched the way Sarah played with the empty mug of tea before her. Nerves? Guilt? Grief.

Tim fidgeted with his wedding ring.

Sarah's other hand smoothed down her nightie against her leg.

'I was home, waiting for Arthur and Lily to get back from school . . .'

Her accent wasn't naturally posh. It had tougher vowel sounds. She would have talked differently once.

'. . . And then when they didn't come I went down to the lake. Arthur likes it down there and Lily always chases after him.'

Present tense. She thinks they're still alive. Okay.

Perfect nails, too. Despite everything.

Tim shifted his weight, uncomfortable about something. What did she just say?

'Down there I saw his bike, on its side. No sign of him. I went a bit mad after that. Ran about, caused a stink.'

Everything is very, very tidy. Where's the kids' stuff? Toys? Paints and pictures of their rubbish artwork like all parents stick up in their kitchens.

'We ran about for hours. Called the police first, then ran about. Got everyone looking. But they'd just vanished.'

Her voice was worn, but steady. There was no sign that she'd cry. She seemed oddly calm.

Sam knew when to shut up. He was sitting opposite her, his hands flat on the table. He waited, like a grief counsellor.

'That's all,' she said, withdrawing even further into herself. Tim looked away. They have things to hide. Things that might not help find the boy, but things that will get exposed anyway. Like always.

'When did you get home, Mr Downing?'

'Later on, the same time I usually get back from the office.'

'You're an estate agent?'

'That's right. The police checked − I was at the office, doing a ring around. You know, trying to drum up business.'

It was an attempt to make the cops smile and nod, be his friends. So they did what was asked of them. But Sarah stared at the table, unable or unwilling to join in.

'So you got home at . . . ?' Sam pressed, gently.

'Five-ish, I suppose.'

'We gave the other police photos of them,' Sarah said.

'We can get those back for you. We'll make copies and get the originals straight back.'

'He was the sweetest boy,' she said. 'And little Lily was so perfect.' Her voice cracked.

Zoe watched Tim go to her, take her hand.

She watched the way Sam looked from one to the other, saying nothing, letting the grief rise and then calm. He'd

37

wait patiently before continuing to ask his questions. He never wavered, never showed any expression that would betray his own thoughts. And Zoe watched them all the while.

They left as politely as they had arrived.

Sam and Zoe walked for over a minute before the discussions began.

'So?'

'They're hiding stuff,' she replied.

'Yeah.'

He had suspicions, she knew that, but he didn't like to share them until he was sure. She rather admired him for it. Whenever she started speculating at the beginning of a case, it always came back to kick her in the arse. So she decided to say nothing, to be a bit like him.

She lasted about a minute.

'Beer o'clock?' she asked.

'Let me call home first, check on the girls.'

It was properly dark now. Zoe looked up at the canopy of stars and felt tiny. She was reminded of Halloween. A little girl running around with skeletons and ghosts for company.

The kids were gone when they walked back. There was no one. No noise, no disturbances, not a thing. It was a relief to see the lights of the pub appear a little later. Zoe wondered why she'd felt so spooked. Maybe it was just down to it being somewhere new and unknown, and the way the night was so black. It was probably just the beginning of a new case and the feelings it dragged up to the surface. After all, this was just a dull, drab, boring little village, she reminded herself. There was no reason she should feel any fear at all.

SEVEN

Sam didn't rush to call home when he got back to his room. Instead, he sat on the bed and mulled over the meeting at the Downings' house. He thought about the mother, Sarah, and the way her hands stroked her arms so protectively. It made him consider his meeting with the Chief Superintendent again. Why should there be a connection here, with those crimes? He cracked his knuckles and picked up the original police report on the case. Everything tallied with the answers they'd got from the Downings, but Zoe had been right – there were secrets inside that house.

Secrets and lies. They were the currencies he traded in. He had prided himself on keeping them out of his home, and that was the reason he gave himself for delaying the call. He pulled a photograph of his wife from his wallet and stared at it, thinking about the twist on her lips in the morning as he would run his hand under the sheets, over her legs. He heard her laughter as they danced at his brother's wedding.

A prickle of heat stirred within him. He folded the photo and tucked it neatly away again. The room was perfectly pleasant – a carpet to hide the stains, a small kettle and instant coffee on top of a sturdy chest of drawers, thick curtains and that smell of industrial cleaner that made every hotel room smell the same. He sat on the edge of the bed and sagged. From downstairs he could hear the chink of cutlery and the dull murmur of polite conversation. Still, he didn't move. He pulled his fingers through his hair and closed his eyes. In the last few months, he had sat like this for hours. Finally he made the call.

'Hello?' His daughter's voice was slight and frail.

'Issy, hello love.'

'Hi,' she said without enthusiasm. Oh great, he thought, it's going to be like this then.

'How was today?'

'Rubbish.'

'Why?'

He heard her sigh and was flooded with guilt. He knew half of the problems, but didn't want to ask because he didn't want to have to rake everything up again. Instead, he tried to coax as much as he could from her, making it clear that he was listening, as he'd been told to, trying not to rise to the long silences. School, it seemed, wasn't going well.

'And how's Gran?'

'Alright. Made cauliflower cheese tonight.'

'Nice.'

'Dad, it was disgusting.'

He laughed. She didn't.

'I'm sorry I'm not there. I don't think this will take long.'

'You said already.'

'I know. I did. But it's true. I miss you, Is.'

'Dad, I gotta go.'

'Why?'

'Stuff,' she said.

'Sorry, I'm boring.'

'Don't be all dramatic.'

He apologised again and felt heavy on the bed. He could picture her, the phone cradled under her neck, one hand pulling idly at her long brown hair. At fourteen, Isabelle wasn't quite a woman yet, but each year seemed to widen a gap between them. Like the rings in a tree trunk, pushing out, pushing them further and further apart.

He asked about Gran and the nanny, but got short shrift. She muttered about how Jenny, her younger sister, was stuck in her room, 'always swotting,' and then she was gone. Sam fell back onto the bed and stared up at the ceiling. A weary sigh slipped from his lips, a low groan from deep down inside. Then he ripped the tie from his neck and went downstairs to find Zoe.

She was sitting in the corner, pretending to read the menu

as he slumped down opposite her. The bar was quite busy and he knew she would be watching the punters. It was a professional pastime. A pint was already waiting for him. He took a sip and nodded, appreciative.

'Anything new?' Zoe asked, referring to the case. He shook his head. 'Good. Are we allowed to enjoy ourselves?'

'How much attention are we getting?'

'Oh, loads.'

'Not too much then.'

'Roger that.'

They both ordered bangers and mash and chatted easily as they ate. Zoe joked about football and some of the guys back at the station, making Sam laugh with dead-on impressions of their posturing. But as much as he liked Zoe and her ebullience, he felt like a fraud. He nodded and smiled, but inside he felt grubby in front of her.

'So boss . . .' she said in that wheedling way she had when she wanted something that wasn't allowed. He cocked his head to one side – go on.

'There's a guy over there giving me the big eyes.'

Sam waited a beat before looking over. He saw a young, callow man at the bar. The pint looked big in his hands. He was chatting animatedly to the woman behind the bar.

'He could be a suspect.'

'I'm not going to do anything. Just play with him.'

He should argue more, he thought. He knew that Zoe

liked to mess about like one of the lads, but these games could get you into trouble and he should protect her from such things. But she was also giving him a way out. He chided her gently about being professional and excused himself to get some fresh air. As he headed for the door, he took another glance at the young man and caught his eye for a moment. The man looked away, staring down at the floor, then looked back at Zoe. Sam smiled at this shyness; his awkward stance. It reminded Sam of the moment he first saw Andrea, laughing with her girlfriends on the other side of the club. The memory stoked the heat and the itch inside. He wanted to turn back and watch Zoe, but he needed to move. The prickling urge drove him into the night.

Somehow he ended up down at the lake, his head spinning. He told himself he'd come down here because it was safe, but deep down he knew the truth. He stopped at the water's edge and bent down, unable to resist dipping his finger into the water. He listened to the rhythmic brush of water against the shore, then stared up at the clear night sky. A trillion stars gazed down at him. His eyes were drawn to the tops of the fells, to the silvery clouds, to the water that shimmered with the moon's dull light. Dwarfed, he felt as though everything was suddenly beyond reach, that there was no way out.

The girl in white appeared next to him as though his

thoughts had summoned her. She glared at him with the same confrontational stare. But now they were alone.

'Have I done something?' he asked lightly.

'People only come down to the lake at this time for one thing,' she said. Her accent was local and heavy. She allowed herself a small smile at her comment.

'What's that then?' he asked.

They were facing each other now, hip to hip. She must be nineteen, maybe slightly younger. A dangerous age, he thought. She wore little make-up, but her lips were ruby red.

'Witchcraft, of course,' she said with a tiny laugh. 'All sorts of naughtiness.'

Somewhere nearby, an owl hooted. Sam thought it must be contrived, its call was so perfectly timed.

'What's your name?'

'Ashley.'

'Hello, Ashley.'

Her stare was cool and confident.

'How come you're down here then, Mr Policeman? Are you feeling naughty?'

The darkness smothered them. He took a step towards her and she didn't move back. He could smell her cherry lip-gloss.

Her eyes were locked onto him, and he couldn't look away from the curve of her body.

'Yeah, you're feeling it, alright,' she said, leaning in closer.

She put a hand against his neck and pulled his mouth to hers. A moment later, she pulled away, and whispered in his ear.

'Got a condom?'

He nodded.

She unzipped the white puffa coat to reveal a pale-blue jumper and the curve of her breasts. The fire was roaring inside him now.

'I knew you'd come find me,' she said.

'How?'

'You're that type.'

He didn't know what she meant, but somehow it felt true.

'Where do you want to go?' he asked, his voice a little reedy with expectation.

'Here.'

He looked around and saw only pitch-black.

She leaned forward and her tongue sneaked into his mouth, then she bit his lip. He hated and loved the sting of it. Then she unzipped his flies, stepped back, took off her coat and lay on it, pulling off her jeans. She kept her white hat on.

It was cold and uncomfortable on the ground. He heard her breathing quicken but this was depressing, animal and bleak. He let his face fall into her neck and felt her head twist to move him away. He shut his eyes and imagined his wife watching from afar, her disgusted face as the girl squirmed below him.

46

He saw his wife dancing and laughing before his eyes.

He saw her car, mangled and wrecked at the side of the road.

Saw her broken body on the mortuary table.

He choked back a sob. *Andrea is dead. Andrea is gone. And you, you useless, foolish man, are all that is left. Oh my wife, my beautiful wife, my love, my life, where have you gone?*

The girl beneath him arched her back slightly and he came too quickly.

He stood up the moment it was over and tucked himself in. She didn't move, her legs still splayed, her eyes betraying amusement at his unease. He didn't know what to say, and when she offered him nothing, he simply walked away as fast as he could. The darkness shrouded him and he was grateful for it. He imagined it hid his shame.

He hurried back to the hotel expecting to feel the same as he always did: embarrassed, confused by the way his body's desire could control him so completely. He had been doing this more and more. In the city it was easy to be anonymous: there he could be busy and ignore the loss that smashed him apart. He could wipe away the taste of Andrea's lips when he woke, and ignore the murmurs that would invade his dreams because the job and his kids kept him busy and distracted. But still he was unable to hide from her shadow as it scuttled across his bedroom, or avoid her lilting laugh as he shopped alone in the supermarket.

But now he was away from home and the city's circus. Here, everything was silent and beautiful. He pondered how he'd slipped into the same depressing rut in this tiny village, just as easily as he'd done back in Manchester. He should have known it, really.

He imagined that Andrea would swoop back down on him as he got into bed. But instead, he saw the girl's face. He remembered her shallow breaths, her red lips and the touch of tender white skin. The memories stayed with him as he fell asleep, criss-crossing, muddling and jumbling with his wife and the Downing woman.

EIGHT

Zoe toyed with her pint for five minutes, but the man at the bar didn't come over to her table. So she necked the last dregs, stood and went up right next to him. As she ordered, he turned to her, a sheepish grin on his face.

'What do you want?' she asked.

'Sorry, nothing, didn't mean to bother,' he replied.

'No, what do you want to drink?'

'Oh. I'll . . .' he drowned the last of his glass. 'Pint of Little Gem, then. Much obliged.'

She turned to the barmaid, who was enjoying this, and pointed to her own pint – another, please.

He was handsome, his face had a ruddy glow. She guessed it was from outdoor work. He wore a thick jumper, jeans and brown shoes. It was the uniform round here. She stood out in her city clothes and felt both pleased and uncomfortable. She was often the outsider: too boyish at home, too feminine at work; too loud, too fast, too eager.

'So, you drink pints?' he asked.

'Please don't tell me I'm the only woman in the village who doesn't drink dry white wine?'

'Oh no, there are a few girls who love the beers. It's just they're all mingers.'

There was a roar of laughter from the men around the bar. Zoe knew they were all listening in, but she was surprised by how little any of them tried to hide it.

'So I'm not a minger then?'

'No. You're, you're . . .' and the bluster failed. She preferred them tougher. Her mum had been the same. Still, tonight was just a game. It didn't matter who he was, not really.

'I'm Zoe,' she said completing the sentence for him. She stuck out a hand, shook his with the same tough grip she used for all men.

'David. David Moore.'

The pints were placed in front of them. Zoe considered taking him back to her table, but she was enjoying the attention from the others. So she took a heavy gulp and waited.

'You're investigating little Arthur and Lily,' said David sadly. 'Any luck?'

'Just got here and couldn't say anyway.'

'Of course. Poor little mites. Everyone knew them. Great kids.'

There were solemn nods and murmuring assents to this.

Zoe knew that anything she said about the case would be chewed over and reinvented by the morning, so she shut up. Sam would kill her otherwise.

'It's nice to have a tight-knit community like this,' she said.

'Can drive you a bit mad. Coming into the pub and first thing you ever see is Brian's bald head.'

David got a good response from the gang for this. Zoe looked around and realised that she was surrounded by men. The other women in the bar had retreated to tables where they chatted away, seemingly happy. But Bernie was now the only female companion.

'Yeah, we're small and a bit backward,' David continued, 'but sometimes I think that's a good thing. You listen to stuff in the news, like down south in London, and you're glad you're not there.'

Zoe thought of the kids on the bench and of their bored, sulky faces. They'd be in London like a shot if they could.

A man strode forward. He was thinner, taller, a little better-looking than David, and she could tell that he knew this. He barged David out of the way and introduced himself as Al.

She shook his hand and clocked how David glared at the floor.

'Hello, Al. You a friend of David's?'

'We're all pals round here, love.'

'Al, sweetie.'

'Yeah?'

'Call me "love" again and I'll break your legs.'

The room rattled with laughter. She caught David's eye and enjoyed his blush. Another man called Jerry joined them, and she found herself, not unhappily, sandwiched between the three of them as they bought her more beers and vied for her attention with silly stories, excessive claims and fanciful tales. She let them wind each other up.

As they sparred, Zoe looked around at the pub. Wooden beams, painted black, ran across the ceiling, while the uneven white walls were littered with framed pictures and photographs of the surrounding countryside. Everyone chatted happily and easily. A coal fire burned and hissed, warm and inviting. She heard two men behind her collapse with a roar of confident laughter. It felt unchanged by time, or rather it was a battle against it, a hard graft against progress: no televisions, no dealers, no guys outside waiting to argue out a fight with their fists and blades. The men in here would die in different ways, she thought. Of boredom, most likely.

Another drink was placed in front of her. A shot of tequila. She saw the men's wolfish grins. She could be meek, she thought. She could demur. Instead she knocked it down in one and turned to Bernie as the men whooped with delight.

'Three more, please,' she said. But Bernie wasn't smiling.

Instead she gave Zoe a tiny shake of the head. A warning. Zoe felt it like a sharp stab. Her language had coarsened and her body language was more provocative, but she had felt safe in here, among the tiny china figurines and doilies. The three men were pressed tightly around her now, the jokes filthy. It was just the same in the locker rooms at the police station. She felt at home like this. She was acting, but somehow it felt natural. More natural than when she'd have to sit prettily with hands folded and her head bowed, a lovely little girl. But she wasn't at home, and she wasn't at work either. And Bernie's look stopped her dead.

'What time do you close?' she asked Bernie.

'She closes when we leave,' Al interrupted. 'Got to be some advantages to living out in the sticks.'

'You'll want to get home,' Zoe said to the barmaid.

'She's fine. Bernie's game for anything. Aren't you, honey?' Bernie looked down, a little flushed.

'Well, I'm going to head to bed after this,' Zoe said.

'Great, we'll come with you,' laughed Jerry.

'Behave yourself,' Zoe mocked, and Jerry's face fell.

The last customers slipped out of the pub, taking their glasses up to the bar before they left, wishing Bernie good night as they did so. One of them, an elderly man in his sixties, gave the men a patrician's nod before he went.

And then it was just them. The silence thickened in the room.

Zoe felt Al's hand on her shoulder, but she ignored the contact. Instead she finished her drink quickly and moved away from him. But another hand pulled at her arm.

'Guys, I have to go now. It's been fun, but I need to sleep.'

They began moaning, but she talked over them, a warning that she might see them tomorrow on a professional basis and that they shouldn't expect any favours.

'Oh, we weren't around when it all happened,' said David. 'We were over in Buttermere at the auction.'

'Good,' she said and placed her empty glass on the counter. She could see that Jerry was still smarting from her rebuff. And as she tried to get away, he stood in her way.

'Is that it?' Al asked, joining him.

Her voice was controlled now – the voice she used for work. 'What?'

'I just thought we might go back to one of ours. Have a bit of fun.'

'You go have fun, then.'

'Not the same without you, is it?'

'See you, fellers. Thanks, Bernie.'

She managed to slip past them before the mood could turn and moved quickly up the old oak staircase to her room. As she did, she heard them arguing downstairs.

In her room, she used the much-too-small glass by the sink to down as much water as she could until she felt bloated. Then she cleaned her teeth. She was about to undress when there was an uneven knock on the door. She opened it warily to find David standing there.

'Hi.' He was swaying slightly from all the booze.

She didn't reply.

'Oh come on, let us in, don't be boring,' he said. The shy lad from earlier was gone now. She wondered if he'd been pushed upstairs by the other two, egged on, but he seemed happy enough to be here.

'Alright' she said as he leaned into her, forcing her to let him inside. He ambled in and sat on the bed, then patted the space next to him, a leery come-on.

'God, I haven't been in one of these rooms since . . .' he fell silent thinking, then grinned, delighted. 'Since Julie Powis worked her way through the rugby team!'

'Nice. So you're quite the stud, then.'

'I know my way around.'

And to prove his point, he began to undress. He started humming the 'stripper theme', waggling his belt about in front of Zoe, oblivious to her folded arms and incredulous stare. He should have felt self-conscious and stupid, but if he did, it didn't stop him. His trousers fell to the floor and Zoe couldn't help but laugh. It only encouraged him.

He pulled off his jumper, and undid his shirt buttons. She could see he had a good body. But still she had said nothing to encourage him and his drunken arrogance angered her.

And so she nodded at him, go on. Soon he was naked.

'Not bad, eh?' he said, pointing at himself. This was all he had to do, just strip off and the women would come flocking.

'Come on then, stud,' Zoe said. 'Come and get me.'

David padded up to her and she undid the top button on her trousers to encourage him further.

'I'm going to fuck you till you're raw,' he said in a slobbery whisper.

She let him kiss her.

But he did not see that as he did so, her hand reached for the door handle and silently pulled it ajar. It was then that she drew away from the kiss and placed a hand gently on his chest.

'David.'

'Yeah?' He was almost breathless with lust now.

'In your dreams.'

His eager expression faltered for a second, but that was all she needed. In the blink of an eye Zoe's hands shoved him hard – far harder than he'd realised she was capable of – into the corridor.

And the door slammed shut.

Zoe stepped over the pile of clothes on the floor and went to brush her teeth. He banged on the door, cursing and whispering. More banging as she changed and got ready for bed, then a final, loud kick at the door and she knew he'd be scuttling back home, hiding in the shadows.

She folded his clothes into a neat pile and then left them outside the door, pants on top.

NINE

They met the local police early the next morning, joining them down by the lake. Sam made them walk there, so that they could get a better feel for the place. Zoe glanced into people's houses as they went. This was not a wealthy place. In fact, Tim and Sarah probably owned the nicest house in the village. Zoe clocked unfolded ironing boards, daytime television, dirty mugs in sinks, children's toys scattered on the floor. And then she would look up and see the fells swoop up and away into a pale-blue sky.

Two local cops were waiting for them by the water. Sam was professional as ever; thanking them for their work, apologising for the interference that he and Zoe inevitably brought, assuring them that he was there merely to make sure every last box had been ticked. They took it well. Everyone did with Sam. He had that way – that slow, stocky style of his that made him a man's man.

The detectives shuffled their feet as they dutifully repeated everything that was in the case file. They were remarkably similar in age and size, as if some sort of cop-processing plant had spewed them out: a decent height, neat dark hair, mid-thirties, friendly. They looked at Sam more than Zoe and directed most of their answers to him. She didn't care.

Everything that should have been done had been. The parents had been interviewed, checked and counselled. Their bank accounts showed no unexpected activity, and there was plenty of money there. The father was deemed likeable if rather wet, and his alibi checked out. The mother, however, was a bit odd. She'd married 'up', coming from a rougher background, but they seemed happy together. There were stories of her temper and of some heavy drinking, but nothing to make her a suspect. Her grief seemed genuine enough. There was something in the way they said this, however, that made Zoe suspicious. As if they didn't really believe in her grief at all. Pretty woman, rich man – it always raises an eyebrow, Zoe thought, even though it was nothing new.

'The teachers said they were lovely kids,' said Andy, the more talkative of the two. 'So does everyone. To be honest they're all so ripped up, you don't get anything more than that out of anyone. You know, fear of insulting the dead and all that.'

'I didn't know they were dead,' Zoe said.

The cops glanced at her, shrugged at Sam and carried on.

There was no CCTV down at the lake and next to nothing

58

in the village. Everyone had been questioned, including friends and relatives. David's parents had been abroad at the time, while Sarah's family lived miles away in a grim trailer park. Her brother, who had a string of petty convictions, had actually been in a police cell on the day. The woods had been trawled by long lines of volunteers, over and over. The lake as well – as much as it could be.

'Thing is, if someone goes down in the water, they could stay down there for months. Years sometimes. It's all about the water temperature, apparently.'

'You think they're in there?' Sam asked.

'Where else are they going to be? Kids round here don't disappear.'

'First time for everything.'

'Fuck, I hope not. It's special here. Sort of untouched, you know? If some lunatic really has snatched them then this place gets dragged into the present, know what I mean? I've been coming to Lullingdale Water since I was tiny. It gets under your skin. I'm hoping it's just a nasty accident, something silly. Bodies come up, we all grieve a bit and then life goes on.'

Zoe watched Sam, but his eyes were focused on them. They haven't worked hard enough on this one, she thought. They don't want to find out the truth.

'Me too, Andy,' said Sam and patted him on the shoulder. They all stared out at the cold water.

'Could they have got lost up on the fells?' Zoe asked, and they all turned to her as though they hadn't expected her to speak.

'Doubt it, love. It's a hell of a climb for little 'uns. Those slopes are murderous. Paul here's a fell runner, but for the rest of us mortals that's a painful climb. And why would they, anyway?'

'Maybe they were running away.'

'From what?' There was incredulity in his voice, which irritated Zoe. You don't shut down any angle just because it sounds unlikely. You voice it all, you follow every lead. That way you don't end up scratching your arse four weeks after the poor little sods have disappeared. She wanted to say something and back at the local station she would have, but she was wise enough to stay silent out here.

Sam asked about roads in and out of the village and Zoe listened to the standard line about the constant flow of tourists, here for the walking. The cops had managed to get lists of visitors staying in the local hotels and B&Bs, both here and in the neighbouring villages of Amblethwaite and Lannerdale, but little more beyond that. They managed to grunt out an apology at the end for the lack of progress, which Sam waved away.

'You've done a great job, guys,' he said. 'I'm sure we won't find anything you haven't already.'

Zoe admired the false camaraderie as hands were shaken and manly nods shared. The two detectives trudged off to their car and sat inside it for a bit before leaving. It was clear they were watching Zoe and Sam, so they turned their backs as they talked.

'They seemed lovely,' she said flatly, and Sam nodded in agreement.

'You ready to go over it all again?' he asked.

'Yes, boss. How was your night?'

'Quiet. You?'

'Same.'

Neither spoke for a moment. Behind them, they heard the car reverse and drive away.

'You think little kids really can't disappear,' Zoe asked, 'just because it's pretty round here?'

He didn't reply, his eyes fixed on the water. She followed his gaze and watched the silent lake as he did, wondering whether he had seen something she hadn't.

'It gets everywhere in the end,' he said quietly.

'What does?'

He didn't answer. Instead he started walking back to the hotel, where they divided their duties between them. No easy jobs for him, no obvious nasties for her. He patted her lightly on the thigh and headed out. Time for work.

TEN

Knock on the door, ring on the bell, show them your warrant card, introduce yourself, talk clearly, listen to every answer. Write it all down. Listen out for the pauses. Watch their eyes. Take everything in.

'Poor little angels.'

'Oh, he was such a lovely boy, that Arthur.'

'How's poor old Sarah coping?'

'I always used to watch Lily skipping down the street every day on the way to school. Always laughing. It breaks your heart, doesn't it?'

Keep nodding. Watch their eyes.

'Makes me cry every time I think about them.'

'I was out the whole day, pet – went shopping at the outlet store near Carlisle. Well, there's bugger all here, right?'

'The mum? Bet she's in pieces.'

'Loved him to death.'

'Some people said . . . No, I don't like to gossip.'

Push them gently. Everything helps, no matter how small. They're helping. It's confidential.

'It's just she got her claws into good ol' Tim pretty quick.'

'Soon as she saw how rich he was she had her hand down his pants, if you know what I'm saying.'

No to the tea, but thank you.

'That little angel, makes your heart shudder, don't it?'

Shake hands, make eye contact. Friendly but firm. They want to feel that you're in charge.

'Tim's salt of the earth. Proper decent fella. Good man. You know? Not a bad bone in him.'

'She runs rings around him, that Sarah.'

It's all gossip, but it keeps pushing the same way.

'You gonna find them, love?'

'She's got a temper on her, that Sarah. I tell you, a couple of drinks and that foul mouth shows itself quick enough.'

'She loved the boy, though.'

'Oh, yeah, loved him to death. Sorry, poor choice of words, honey.'

'You're a bit pretty for a copper, aren't you?'

'The mum? I never liked her, but I'm old-fashioned. My family's lived here for generations. Know what I mean?'

Frown and play dumb for more.

'Well, her family – not the sort you'd want to meet your mother, if you get my drift.'

Note it down.

Knock and smile. Ask and listen. More doors, more names ticked off the list.

'You know the witches have got him, don't you? You're wasting your time.'

'Go on, love, have a scone, tiny slip of a girl like you. You'll never find a man looking like that.'

Stop for lunch – sit alone in the room above the pub, stuff down a sandwich, catch up on Twitter. Then back at them.

'God bless their poor little souls. We pray for them at church every Sunday.'

'Never knew them really, or the family. Not my type. But she certainly got awfully stuck up once she had a joint bank account.'

Folded arms on a doorstep. 'Can't help you. Didn't know him, don't know anything.' The door slams.

More names ticked off.

The nursery school is nice. Cosy and safe. Lovely teachers who are all on the verge of tears. One holds up a painting that Arthur had completed the day he disappeared. A classic boy's picture of dragons and fire. No hints of any darkness or fear.

'They sit in the trees, you know. Watching and waiting for little children to come close. And then they drag them down to the bottom of the lake.'

What's with these stories? No one says them as though they actually believe them, but they tell them nonetheless.

'Oh there's always been witches in the lake, everyone knows that.'

'I just want to know what she put in his drink. One minute he's normal Tim, top bloke, next he's besotted. You women, I ask you.'

Walking from one row of houses to the next, the lake pops into view. The water glistens in the sunlight like a postcard.

'Poor little mites.'

'No, never saw nothing. Heard all about it, like everyone else. You sure you don't want a cuppa?'

Shake hands, watch their eyes.

'You're lovely, you are.'

Sit in a small, stuffy sitting room, staring at a set of china dolls, listening to the old geezer ramble on about anything but the case.

A second investigation has already started, twisting and rerouting everything to Sarah Downing's door, although no one will say as much. And why do they all talk about witches? Snap out of this, listen to what the man has to say. Stay focused.

'Little angels.'

Another name to cross off the list.

'Terrible, just terrible.'

Greet the first just the same as the last. Nod and listen.

Knock, smile, show your warrant card, smile and take it all in.

ELEVEN

Sam found the kids down a dirt track, sitting on metal beams in the eaves of a ramshackle barn at the edge of the village. They didn't see him coming until too late, so the smell of dope was still strong in the air. Sam stood at the entrance – a large, double-fronted expanse – and looked up at them, knowing he had them trapped.

He flashed his warrant card and introduced himself with a bored voice.

'I'm not interested in gear or anything else, just the missing kids, so you can all calm down,' he said.

The teenagers glared at him, then glanced nervously from one to the other, but no one said anything.

'Come on, come down from there, talk to me and then I'll be gone,' he said.

He heard a noise behind him and turned sharply to see the girl in white. She'd appeared behind him and when their eyes met, he felt a surge run through him. He hid it, looking back at the kids without acknowledging her. Sam called them down again, and after a pause they slowly made their way to the ground and stood facing him in a morose semicircle. He pulled out a file and read out a series of names.

'Daniel Boardman? Natalie Redpath?' He got a variety of grunts and nods in return. 'Ashley Deveraux?'

The girl in white behind him answered. 'Here, Miss.' And everyone laughed.

Sam smiled. 'Yeah, it is a bit like that, isn't it?'

He was greeted with scowls all round.

'Okay. So, you were all down at the lake when Arthur and Lily Downing went missing.'

'We didn't do nothing,' snapped one of the kids.

'I'm not saying you did. I'm here to find out what you saw. When did you get down there?'

There were various mutterings and arguments between them. Sam sighed. They'd been asked these questions before by the police and had given detailed answers. How could they be so casual and forgetful?

'About five? Maybe slightly earlier?' one of them – a spotty lad with a black beanie pulled tight over his head – ventured.

The others nodded in agreement.

'Okay, thank you. And what did you see?'

'Nothing. Not until Mrs D. came down with Tim and started screaming all over the shop.'

67

'What did she say?'

'She'd found Arthur's bike.'

'None of you had seen it?'

'Nah, but then we weren't looking for anything like that.'

Someone nudged the lad in the back and he shut up. Sam knew they were worried about drugs and he didn't want them to clam up, so he moved the conversation on.

'She was down there with her husband. Anyone else?'

'Bud.'

Sam checked his file. 'Bud. That's Matthew Bryden, yes?'

They all laughed at this.

'Is that his real name?' one of them said. 'Matthew? Epic!'

'That's what it says here. So he was with them?'

'Anywhere she goes, he's not far behind,' said a girl at the back with piercings through her nose, lower lip and eyebrow. The others nodded and grunted their agreement.

'Go on,' Sam said, but no one responded.

'Are they having an affair? Is that what you're suggesting?'

'Her and him?!'

The metal barn rang with their sarcastic laughter.

'He's more a pet.'

Sam wondered what this said about Sarah.

'What else can you tell me about that evening?'

Shuffled feet, a few sniffs.

'What are people saying about why the children disappeared? What do they think?'

More grunts, nothing about nothing. No one had a clue. These things didn't happen around here.

'And no one saw anyone that day that looked odd or suspicious or just out of the ordinary?'

They all just shook their heads, looking bored now.

'So, Mr and Mrs Downing came down with Matthew Bryden, saw the bike and started to panic?'

'No, he found the bike.'

'Sorry?'

'Bud. He found the bike, went and got them, and then they went all, you know, mental.'

Sam checked his notes. There was no mention of Bud in the notes. Odd. He circled the man's name.

'Why did you guys go down to the lake?' he asked the boy with the black beanie, who now couldn't meet his eye. Everyone was a little shifty. Sam assured them all, again, that he had no interest in whether or not they had been smoking weed. He was here to find the missing children and that was his only concern. The kids nodded at his words, but no one spoke. He pushed on, but if anyone started to speak, they were hushed by the others.

'Come on,' he urged them. 'Talk to me. This isn't a police station, I haven't cautioned you, nothing's being recorded.'

'We score down there,' said a kid whose jeans hung so low you could see 90 per cent of his flowery boxer shorts.

'Right. That wasn't so hard. Who from?'

'Piss off. And they never turned up anyhow. Totally un-reliable.'

'As always,' someone else added.

'Is that the place you always go to buy drugs?'

'Yeah. That's how we know Mrs D.'

There was a hiss from someone – shut up.

Sam's skin prickled.

'Sarah Downing used to score drugs down at the lake?'

No one spoke. It was so quiet that a horse's sudden neigh seemed deafening.

'Did she do this often?'

Silence.

'Okay. Just answer me this. Would she have done this recently?'

'Oh yeah,' one of the boys said. There was a knowing lilt to his answer.

Sam put away his file and looked around at them all one last time. He wanted them to see him watching them, clocking them, remembering them. They didn't like his stare. Except Ashley Deveraux.

'Thank you for your help.'

He dug his hand into his back pocket and pulled out a series of cards with his name and number on them. He passed them around the group, noting that Ashley made sure that she had one.

'If you remember anything more, please call me. I just want to find Arthur and Lily.'

He turned and walked away, his mind racing with this new information. He heard a moment's pause then a burst of breathless gossip and whoops of laughter. It was the same wherever he went, wherever he left. Silence, then laughter.

TWELVE

Sarah opened another bottle, filled the glass and drank down most of the wine in one. She placed the glass on the table a little unsteadily then started to refill it.

'What?' she snapped.

Tim watched her from the other side of the kitchen. She'd thrown a jumper over her nightie but had made no other concessions to the day's arrival. He looked down at his neat cords and stripy shirt and felt a twinge of irritation at her and a loathing of himself. You weakling, he thought.

'Say something, then,' she said, then knocked more wine down her throat.

'You'll kill yourself if you carry on like that.'

'I've barely got started.'

He turned away from her. She was loud and ugly like this and he couldn't bear it. He heard the glass land heavily on the table. She's going to finish the entire bottle in ten minutes flat, he thought. It was the cops coming back, that's what this was about.

He wanted to draw the curtains, to feel the sunlight on his face, but he knew she'd scream at him if he did. He saw Sarah sway in the chair, and for a moment he hated her. He hadn't expected it to be like this. The panic, the grief, the torment – all that made sense. But this new feeling of dirt and guilt, impotence and crushing boredom, these were new, cruel emotions that he hadn't been prepared for. The curtains stayed shut to keep prying eyes out, eyes that would see just how badly he was failing.

So this is what trauma does to you, he thought. It eats at you, from inside. At first it feels like an assault and it leaves you winded. But then it comes back, from deep in your gut, so deep you feel as though it's a part of you. It drags you down and mashes your thoughts and feelings into bits so nothing makes sense.

That's your wife, just there. Your beautiful wife. And she needs you. That's why she's drinking, you fool.

Tim turned back to Sarah. He saw her pour the dregs into the glass. He looked at her red eyes and saw her swallow painfully, holding back more tears. And his heart softened.

But then she caught his eye and he saw the sneer on her lip, and he had to turn away again to hide his anger.

He went out and smoked a cigarette. She opened another bottle.

73

He came back inside later, feeling no better. She knew he was there, he was sure of it, but she didn't look up. He was not worth looking at.

He watched her, stuck against the kitchen worktop, too exhausted to do anything else.

THIRTEEN

Matthew Bryden had always been known as Bud, but he couldn't tell anyone why. Zoe asked Bernie about him and she told him that he was a likeable, straightforward guy with no airs and graces. Reading between the lines, Bud sounded a bit thick, but Zoe would wait to meet him in person before making any judgements. A police check revealed repeated moves from one foster home to another.

Bud could normally be found in the pub, unless he'd run out of money, in which case he'd hole up at home, watching TV. He earned his keep through gardening and odd jobs, most of which he did for Sarah and Tim Downing – raking leaves, mowing their lawn and maintaining this and that for them. Or rather, for Sarah, as Bernie said with a lift of her eyebrows. It became clear that Bud had a soft spot for Sarah and trailed after her in a manner that suited neither of them. It made him a joke among the men, her a siren. Another reason to point at her, Zoe thought. She had her strategy in place as she rang on Bud's doorbell. Sam had let her do this one on her own, hedging that Bud was susceptible to a woman's charm. And although she appreciated his openness about the tactics, she still felt a little grubby.

Bud lived in a tidy run-down bungalow on the edge of the village. Tall evergreen trees robbed the building of light, and as she walked up the neat path she felt the air become colder. There was a green tinge of moss on the walls and around the white plastic window frames. A fire burned inside and logs were neatly stacked against a wall. But as tidy as he had made it, there was something functional rather than homely about the place.

Zoe watched through the bubbled glass as Bud approached the door. She saw his rippling silhouette pause in the hallway, clearly surprised by the unexpected call, before hesitantly unlocking the door and opening it. He was big but hunched, as though embarrassed by his own presence, and wore ironed jeans and a fading tracksuit top. His eyes flicked to her and behind her, nervous.

'Hello?'

She flashed her warrant card. 'Mr Bryden?' He nodded. 'I'm Detective Constable Barnes. I'm investigating the disappearance of Lily and Arthur Downing. Can I come in?'

He nodded and gestured for her to enter, before carefully shutting the door. She looked around, taking in the frayed carpet, the big muddy boots by the door, the lack of any pictures or paintings on the walls. He pointed to a door that led to a small, equally neat and equally dispiriting living room. It housed a big TV, a sofa, an armchair and a black Labrador panting in its basket.

'Has something happened?' His voice was surprisingly high for such a big guy.

'Just routine inquiries at the moment.'

He nodded, pulling nervily at his fingers. Zoe noted how big his hands were; thick and calloused from working outdoors in all weathers. She briefly imagined those hands on a small boy.

'So. You know the parents, Mr and Mrs Downing?'

'I do jobs for them. In the garden, mostly. Put up all that post-and-rail fencing at the end of their land.'

'They're good people.'

'I like them a lot.'

'Terrible thing to happen.'

'Awful.'

'Did you know the children?'

'Sometimes Arthur would kick a ball around on his own in the garden. I'd kick it back. But I didn't do it much. People get odd ideas.'

'Oh, I know. You pat a kid on the head and they do you for assault!'

He laughed, nodding. Eager to please.

'Did he seem lonely, then?'

'Huh?'

'Arthur. You said he was kicking a ball about on his own. Didn't he have many friends?'

'No, he was okay. Just, at home, it was . . .'

She watched him pause, saw him calibrating the lie.

'What was wrong at home, Mr Bryden?'

'Nothing.' His reply came out too quickly. 'Nothing. Lily didn't like football, is all. And you should call me Bud. I feel odd when people say Mr Bryden.'

'Bud. Please. What was wrong at home?'

'Nothing.' His voice was a pitch higher now, and Zoe felt a tingle in her neck. The feeling that she was about to break and enter.

'Bud . . .'

'There's nothing. They were good kids and that's that. She's very kind, Sarah is, so don't start stirring things up, okay?'

He stared down at the floor, still fidgeting with his fingers.

'Bud,' she said softly, and waited until he looked up. 'I'm here to find them and get them back to their mum and dad. We're on the same side, you and me.'

He nodded but was still withdrawn. He reminded her of her teenage nephew, when he'd been found with a stolen bottle of vodka under his bed.

'I know I'm just a girl and a bit goofy, but you need to trust me.'

'You're alright,' he said, and blushed. She knew she had him now. She told him how the case was like a jigsaw with lots of pieces, which don't seem to fit at first. But unless she could get them all, every single one, then no one would ever get the whole picture. And without that, they'd never find Lily and Arthur. Bud nodded, keen to help.

'So help me,' she said. 'Please. Even if it seems unimportant, help me.'

His foot twisted on the carpet. She urged him on with gentle, kind coaxing, keeping the conversation light.

He sighed. 'People don't like Sarah, that's the thing.'

'Why? She seems lovely.'

'They're jealous. Don't know her.'

'But you know her.'

'Yeah. We're special friends,' he said, and revealed a shy smile.

'That sounds great.'

He shrugged and blushed again. Zoe wondered what 'special friends' meant, but she also knew that she'd seen and heard too much to trust her imagination. So she pressed on, slowly loosening him up; flattering him, charming him, flirting a little when necessary.

Bud's face clouded with worry as she pushed for the truth and for a while neither spoke. But Zoe knew that she wouldn't leave without something. She was used to waiting.

'Just . . .' he paused again, then finally coughed it out. 'She got cross with Arthur sometimes. Really mad, and he'd run down to the bottom of the garden and cry. And sometimes he'd hide from her, but that was silly. She was just trying to teach him a lesson.'

'What did she do?'

'Nothing bad. Nothing at all, hardly . . . Just made sure he didn't do it again. But if other people had heard about it, they'd have said she was cruel, or worse. Leaving him out there for so long. People rush to judge round here.'

'I bet you knew how that felt,' Zoe said, and regretted it instantly. She was showing too much of her hand, that she'd checked up on him. But Bud didn't see the slip. He just nodded, staring down at the floor.

'I wanted to comfort him but I didn't think it was proper. A boy and a grown man.'

'So he cried all alone?'

'Not her fault. Sarah only got cross 'cos she cared.'

She moved a little closer to him and felt him squirm at the proximity. 'She loved him,' he added weakly. 'She's a great mum. People just don't see it. They all gossip but no one knows her like me. Not even Tim.'

He took in a quick, short breath, as though he'd said something he shouldn't have. Zoe wondered if his words had originally been spoken by Sarah, standing as close to him as Zoe was now. She pretended to look for something in her bag, giving him time to relax.

'I bet she never shouted at you,' she said with a laugh, her eyes still down as she rooted through her bag. She heard him chortle in agreement. She looked up and saw him grinning at her. Like an open target.

'Now, let me just tick you off my list and I'll be on my way. Was it you that found the bike?'

He looked as though he'd been shot. He nodded, unable to hide his unease.

'Okay, that's good. Now why isn't that in the original police report?'

He shrugged unhappily.

'No matter,' she said brightly and pretended to write something on the paper. She could tell his eyes were all over her.

'I think maybe there was some confusion ...' he stammered.

'Yes?'

'I found the bike and went and got Sarah and Mr Downing and then we all ran back down here.'

'How long does that take? From their house to the lake?'

'Five minutes or so.'

'Right, that's not mentioned here. The police seemed to think you weren't really involved at all. How did that happen?' she asked casually. He had no answer to this. She let the silence do its work.

'Bud?'

81

'It didn't seem important, that's all,' he said, his eyes rooted to the floor.

She asked him why he would think this, fighting the impulse to go in strong. Bud shrugged once again. The answer, she knew, was because of Sarah. When she asked him if this was right, he nodded, almost imperceptibly, as though the smaller the nod, the less the betrayal.

'So she told you not to tell the police that you were there?'

'We just thought it might confuse things.'

'How would it confuse things?'

She saw his eyes crinkle with confusion. The lie didn't come from him. Not originally.

'I just want the kids to come back.'

'Of course, and so do we. Don't worry, we're on the same side.'

He let out a breath of relief and gratitude, with no idea of the thorny trap ahead.

'The thing that concerns me is that you've told a lie. And there's normally a reason for that. Often it's to cover another lie. To hide something else.'

He was practically ripping his fingers out of his sockets now. And his raw panic made her nervous. She was alone in a house with a big man, a man who could hurt her easily if he so chose. But she was close to something here.

'Why did you pretend not to find the bicycle?'

He frowned, as if he was about to cry. 'They all want to hurt her!' he blurted.

'I know, they're jealous. They're idiots.'

'They are!'

'So this is about protecting Sarah, is it?'

He clammed up again. He veered between panic and brooding silences.

'Bud, please. Talk to me. Help me find the children.'

'People twist things. Cops twist things.'

'I won't twist anything. Look at me. I'm not clever like that lot. I just care about little Arthur and Lily.' She hated the exploitation of their names, but she was close now.

'People think she's not a good mum,' he said. 'They're cruel because she's happy. Was happy. If you'd seen her at the lake and seen how scared she was – if you'd seen that yourself, you wouldn't think anything bad nearly there.'

He nodded to himself, reminding himself how true his words were.

'She went totally crazy. And I was worried that it was my fault. Because I moved the bike. Maybe he was looking for it and maybe that's why he went missing. But I saw it on the ground and I thought, that's his. And I thought maybe he'd left it behind. I didn't want him getting into trouble. So I went to find Sarah.'

'You didn't do anything wrong. Okay?'

He nodded but his face was still creased unhappily.

'She said that too,' Bud continued. 'She was so kind and gentle. She said not to worry, even when she was scared. That's how kind she is. Thinking of me at a time like that.'

'She's great. I see that.'

'Yeah. And she could see how scared I was and so we agreed that I wouldn't say I found the bike or that I was around, just so I could stay out of it. So you lot wouldn't come and hassle me. 'Cos I'm no good when people come and bother me like this.'

'She just wanted to help you out.'

'Yes!'

'Well, that's nice of her.' He smiled at her and she almost felt guilty. 'So she lied for you.'

'Uh-huh.'

'And did she ask for anything in return?'

His mouth snapped closed again. It felt like he might bolt for the door.

'How about a glass of water?' she asked pleasantly. He nodded and turned away.

She followed him into the kitchen – a modest space at the back of the house with a single strip of Formica counter-top and battered units beneath. There was a dog bowl on the floor and big wellington boots by the back door.

He poured water in a glass and handed it to Zoe.

'I don't want to get her into trouble,' he said again, like a mantra.

'For what?'

'She's looked out for me. She's been a friend. Everyone else thinks I'm simple.'

'What have you done for her?'

'It's nothing to do with the children.'

'I know that. I trust you. So what was it?'

He shook his head. His eyes pleaded with her – don't ask.

'She didn't ask for anything. She's my friend.' The words seemed to restore some sense of control. 'What else do you want to know?' he asked, taking the glass off her.

She considered pushing him further, but the tone in his voice gave her pause, and for now she was satisfied. She doubted that Bud had anything to do with the children's disappearance. He had more to tell, but Zoe worried that if she pushed him too much now, it might backfire. He would go running to Tim and Sarah, she was sure of that. She remembered that he'd called her 'Sarah' and him 'Mr Downing'. Maybe he would only go running to her. Maybe Sarah kept her secrets safe with Bud and not Tim.

Either way, Bud had been 'removed' from the scene by Sarah. She didn't want the police questioning him and the reasons for that would have to be uncovered. But not right now.

She stuffed the notebook back in her bag.

'You're just trying to look after a friend, I understand,' she said, checking her watch a little theatrically. 'Thanks,

Bud. I know it's hard, and upsetting too. But we'll get there, I'm sure of it.'

'Are you going?' he asked, surprised that the torture was coming to an end.

'I am. Thank you again.'

He was confused by this.

'It's good to know that someone's watching out for Sarah. I think she feels very alone.'

He nodded, unsure whether she was friend or foe.

'Tell you what,' she added. 'If I hear anything, I'll come and find you, so you're the first to know.'

She could see how her words pleased him. Ten minutes and she had him on a plate. She wondered just what Sarah had been able to do to him, and what lengths he would go to for her.

It was dark outside. Zoe walked away fast, her speeding mind setting the pace. She could see why eyes inevitably turned to Sarah, but was also a little reluctant to hand this ammunition over to Sam without more detail. Out of context it looked bad, but something about this town and these men made her wary of jumping to any kind of judgement. Her mind was racing so fast that she almost didn't see David, sitting in his car, watching her as she marched past. She stopped to face him.

'Hello? What are you doing out here?'

He said nothing, just drove off. She watched the car turn a corner and disappear. She looked up. Thick clouds hid the stars and moon. She broke into a run to get back to the hotel. Not from fear, but to get away from the silence.

FOURTEEN

Cam and Lee had been teasing each other about it for months. It had gone beyond flirting to a single dare – they were going to fuck in the showers at Bennington Public Swimming Baths in Oldham just before closing time; just after the last person had gone into the changing rooms. They had nearly done it the week before but there was a man with two toddlers there, which had put them off.

The shower area had twelve nozzles sticking out from the tiled walls, six on each side. There was enough space for swimmers to walk between these showers, either heading out to the water or into the changing rooms at the other end. The showers themselves were a very public space, and that's what made the dare so delicious.

They chose a Thursday because that was always the quietest day of the week, though neither knew why. They changed as normal, entering near closing time, and swam separately for half an hour, never talking, just catching the other's eye and laughing to themselves, swollen with their bubbling desire.

There were just two other people there, a woman swimming with her son as the lifeguards came along and politely ushered everyone out. They got out of the pool and walked slowly towards the showers, their wet feet slapping against the tiles. It was the only noise. They saw the lifeguard glance at them, then check the pool, and then head out. Finally, incredibly, they were alone.

Lee leaned against one wall, pressing the shower button with his back, his eyes fixed on Cam. The warm water splashed onto him and they both laughed. She pressed the button on the opposite wall, then turned to face him, letting her bikini top slip to the floor. He pulled down his swimming shorts and they fell around his ankles. She stepped out of hers. Now they were both naked. The thrill hardened into lust as they stared at each other. They were only teenagers, their bodies still thin and unblemished, still deliciously half-baked.

'Quick, come on,' she whispered, glancing nervously at the changing-room doors. Lee took a step towards her, his heart thumping. He glanced towards the pool, not really looking, only interested in Cam. But then he stopped and looked again, and saw the woman's head at the far end of the pool. She was still in the water and when he saw that she was looking at him, he stumbled in shock.

'There's someone there!' he hissed at Cam, and they hurriedly threw their costumes back on. The shock quickly turned into hysterics at how close they'd been to getting caught. They giggled together, trying to make no noise, clutching each other. And then they looked out to the water. Yes, the woman was there. On her own, in the deep end, her mouth just above the water. Cam said later that the way she floated reminded her of a crocodile.

They would have just scarpered and got changed, but Lee thought it was weird, the way she was just bobbing like that, after everyone else had gone, after the guards had told her to get out. So they went over to her a little gingerly, suddenly feeling cold after the showers, feeling weird to be so skimpily dressed. They padded back along the pool's edge. Lee said that the woman watched him all the time. He couldn't see her mouth from under the water, but he was sure that she was smiling at him.

Cam noticed it first; the swaying shape beneath the water. It was so unexpected that she didn't really understand what she was looking at. She just noticed the gentle movement, the slow drift. It took a while to register that there was a body, held down by the woman who still smiled lazily at Lee. A little boy with bright red trunks. His face was turned away from them, pressed up tight against the woman's stomach.

They didn't know what to say. The woman just stared at them. Then Lee saw the body too and his legs started shaking.

He started cursing, then screaming. Cam ran, leaving him there, finding a young lifeguard who was as ill-equipped to cope with this as she was. He, in turn, called the police.

The woman never got out of the water. Eventually she was dragged out by two officers, clutching the boy to her as they did so. The two of them collapsed onto the side like the catch of the day. She just stared up and away from them, that terrifying smile locked on her face. Unblinking, delirious. The boy seemed so calm, it looked like he hadn't even tried to struggle.

The woman's name was Elizabeth Harrison. The boy, James, was her son. She was happily married to Duncan, a tall, muscular Scot who ran a successful business importing stone (for tiles) from Turkey, Greece and the Ukraine. She was a socialite and had also been a member of the local council's planning committee. When the police asked her friends and colleagues about her, they had all used the same words to describe her: 'bright', 'confident', 'determined' and 'normal'.

Elizabeth hasn't spoken since that day. She is in a secure wing at a psychiatric facility in Kent. She smiles but her gaze never reaches the person sat opposite her. It is as though she's somewhere else, she has escaped, she is safe and happy. And this brings a sense of rage and injustice to those who see her. They wish her damned to hell.

The fucking witch.

*

Sam put the file down. He rubbed his eyes, checked his watch, then placed the file on top of the others. Witches. The idea, the word, seemed so stupid. An image blinked into his mind of Sarah smiling up at him from the lake, clutching Arthur tightly to her chest. He dismissed it at once. He was a practical, logical man and fairytales were not a part of his world.

He rang his daughter, but there was no answer on her mobile or at home. He worried about this for a bit before stacking all the files in an even pile and shoving them in a drawer. But they didn't feel secure enough there, so he lugged them back to his car and dumped them in the boot.

As he slammed the door shut, he saw Ashley Deveraux standing there, watching him. It was as if she'd appeared from nowhere. He looked at her for a moment and then shook his head. A tiny, almost imperceptible no. He saw a flicker of irritation cross her face, but he didn't want to talk to her, to argue with her, to be seen with her. He turned his back, reopened the boot and organised the already organised files.

When he turned again she was gone.

FIFTEEN

Tim pulled the old-fashioned lighter from his pocket and stared at his engraved initials in the metal. It was a present from his father. He lit a cigarette, then started dragging the bins down to the edge of the drive. The sun was setting and the fells glowed with its dying light. He loved being up there, loved their colossal majesty. He wanted to go walking now, get to the top and breathe in the cold air like he did when he was little. His dad used to take him, just the two of them, and they'd stare down at the patchwork countryside below, hearing nothing but the wind, feeling wonderfully alone.

He lugged the last bin over the paving and dumped it down a little too quickly so that it nearly overturned. He grabbed and steadied it, then stood up straight and looked down the road. He saw his neighbour, Alby Kingston, walking over and he prepared himself for platitudes and sympathy. Alby's wife, Jenny, had always been disapproving of Sarah, and there had been plenty of sparring (some of it rather unpleasant) before the children's disappearance. Now, faced with a real-life, right-before-your-very-eyes tragedy, she'd become all eyes and heart, while Alby would skulk about behind her, unable to think of a word to say. He approached Tim and gave him a cheery salute.

'It's got warmer all of a sudden,' Alby said with a sad smile.

'It has,' Tim nodded.

'Jenny was asking after you,' he said, and pulled an apologetic face. 'Not that I'm not,' he added hastily. 'How are you, mate?'

'Oh, you know.'

'I see the police are back again.'

'Yes.'

'Different ones. Brought in experts this time, have they?'

'I'm not sure if they're anything more than just different, to be honest with you.'

He dragged deep on the cigarette, realising that he was stuck here with Alby until he'd finished it.

'Do you need any food? Jen keeps rattling on about bringing something over, but says she's not sure she's welcome.'

Tim wasn't going to rise to this. 'We're fine, but thank you.'

'It's easy enough to stuff in the freezer for one of those days when it's too much hassle. I've even managed to do it myself, and you know what I'm like in the kitchen!'

Tim thanked him again, and declined the offer once more. Alby just nodded but didn't head back to his home, seemingly unaffected by the awkward silence.

'So no news at all?' he asked after a while.

'No.'

'Oh dear. It's been a long time now. How's Sarah?'

'Up and down. You can imagine.'

'I can. You really must drag her out, though. It can't be good for her to be locked in that house with the curtains closed like that. Can't be good for you either.'

'We each cope in our own way, Alby.'

'I'm interfering, sorry.'

The cigarette was almost done. Tim saw Alby staring at his fingers and realised that he was timing their meeting by it as well. He waited for him to cut to the chase.

'You do seem rather trapped in there, matey. No one to talk to.'

'I have my wife.'

'Yes, of course. Yes, you do. But you don't seem to have anyone else. You know, like at the pub. A pint, a chat. A bloke's way to unwind.'

Another deep tug. Tim breathed out the smoke, dropped the cigarette on the floor and killed it with the heel of his shoe.

'God, I don't need to tell you this, do I?' Alby prattled on. 'You've lived here all your life. A proper local. So there's no reason for you to be on your own. And Sarah, well, she's got Bud.'

Tim caught Alby's eye and saw that he meant a lot by the phrase.

'He's hardly around here these days,' he replied gruffly.

'So we've seen.'

'You seem to see a lot,' Tim replied, and picked up the flattened butt, dropping it into the bin.

'Yes, we've seen an awful lot, Tim. But I'm on your side. We're all worried about you, mate.'

Tim felt that he was meant to press Alby on this, and drag the hidden meaning out of his words. But he was silent, his eyes fixed on the stupid green plastic bins.

'I'll get Jenny to pop some food over then,' Alby said and turned to leave. But he didn't go right then, he hovered, hoping for more.

'Thanks,' Tim muttered.

'Well then,' Alby said, as though pleased to have had his say but also disappointed not to have said more. He walked away and his words began to bounce about in Tim's head.

He watched Alby go and was embarrassed when he turned around sharply and caught him staring. He found himself fiddling with the lid of the bin until he was sure that Alby was back inside. He looked up again and the sun was lower, the peaks were no longer illuminated. He imagined his wife, sat at the table in that airless room, and for the first time, imagined her plotting about things he didn't understand. He looked up again at the peaks. Their majesty seemed tarnished. Right now they were just dirty silhouettes against a fading sky.

SIXTEEN

'Sarah Downing seemed nice enough when we met her,' said Zoe, watching Sam throw stones into the lake.

'Nice? Is that what you thought of her?' Sam said as he scrabbled amongst the rocks, discarding pebbles that were the wrong shape or size.

'Well, no, not "nice". But not a child killer.'

The stones hit the water and were swallowed up. She watched him lumber about before finally turning to her.

'You're unhappy,' he said. She shrugged an acknowledgement back at him. 'Okay, let's go through it again,' he said, and waited for her to take the lead.

'Arthur and Lily leave school but don't go home. Why?'

'Because of Sarah's temper, perhaps.' Sam said. 'Like Bud told you.'

'Maybe they just wanted to play.'

She bent down and scooped up a couple of pebbles herself.

'What was the weather like on the day?' Sam asked.

'Dull, but not rainy.'

She looked around. It was dull today as well. The kind where the cloud hangs thick and low. It was quiet and the lake was dead calm. The wind would cause tiny flurries across its surface, but the further you looked out, the more it felt like someone had placed a steel lid on top of it. She threw her stones and felt a little weak at how much further Sam's flew.

'I suppose it could have been both,' she conceded.

'Okay. But their mother was expecting them home.'

'That's what she said.'

'So they're a bit naughty and come down here . . .'

Sam walked around, trying to recreate the scene. It felt, to both of them, a little bit fruitless. Zoe tried to help out.

'So they come down . . . disappear . . . a bit later some of those teenagers come down looking to buy some drugs, and then Sarah appears and sees her son's bike. After that we have a lot of shouting and running about.'

'With the husband and Bud in tow,' Sam added.

'And for some reason, she then retells the story and tries to airbrush him out of it.'

'Stupid of her.'

'That's people for you,' she said. 'And the local police didn't pick it up. Hardly picked up anything at all, did they?'

But Sam wasn't buying. She threw another stone and was pleased as it skimmed across the surface, further than before.

'So the kids came down to score?' she asked.

'Yeah.'

'From who? We need to find the dealer.'

'They said there was no dealer,' Sam said. 'It was all a blowout.'

'We should still find out who they get their gear from anyway – it could be important.'

'You're right. Good thinking.'

Sam dutifully wrote it down and Zoe felt pleased with herself.

'Anyway, we all know that the witches did it,' she added.

'You got that too, did you?'

They laughed at the way that they were constantly mentioned; the way no one really believed a word, yet were unable to dismiss them entirely, like some form of voodoo. Sam told her the story he'd heard, having been collared by an old man outside the pub.

'Apparently there were a bunch of them, six or so women who got drunk on mead or wasted on mushrooms or something. Anyway, they went mad, off their tits, and led a bunch of children into the woods. They lit a fire and then started to roast them, one by one, claiming they were pigs for a feast or something. Fortunately one of the kids got away and some guy called John Stern, who was a farrier or something, he came down and saved them all.'

'What happened to the women?'

'They drowned themselves.'

'What?'

'Story is the women went crazy, like lemmings jumping off a cliff or something. They stole a boat, rowed out to the middle and threw themselves in.'

Zoe looked out at the still water, which stretched out for miles ahead of her. Somewhere, deep down, the women's bones rested at the bottom.

'What a crock,' she said. 'You believe that shit?'

Zoe imagined the screams and the splashing. She pictured the ripples that would have reached the land, and she saw how the lake would have sucked them down and kept them there. Sam threw another stone and the water gobbled it up. He made a joke about olden days and the locals worshipping crows, but Zoe didn't laugh.

'What's with you?' he asked.

She sniffed. It was just a story. She waved the moment away and agreed to meet him later for a drink. She wasn't angry with Sam – she couldn't be, she loved him dearly – but she didn't want to keep staring out at the lake, not after that. She walked back up the lane, past the small car park and towards the village. After a minute, she slowed: David was standing by a stile, hands in his pockets. His mood still seemed black, so she gave him a friendly 'hello' and kept on walking.

He caught up with her and walked beside her. 'So, I got my clothes back,' he said, after an eternity.

She just nodded and walked a little faster. David hurried along beside her.

'Guess you'll tell me I deserve it,' he added.

'Why, what would you tell me?'

'I guess I'd say you led me on.'

'Gagging for it, was I?'

'No, okay, fair enough, but, come on, I can take a joke as good as the next man . . .'

She gave him a look that said – *no you can't* – and instantly regretted it. Everything changed with that look. Oh, how men love to be flattered, she thought.

'You were out of order,' he said.

She shrugged and walked on.

'You know what?' he said. 'I was going to say sorry, I was going to bloody apologise and see if we could start over, but you're just so bloody stuck-up–'

He grabbed at her arm. Zoe spun around to face him, and her intensity made him step back.

She waited for him to say more, but he was still so wrought with hurt pride that she knew she was wasting her time.

'You were the one who pushed your way into my room.'

'You told me to come in.'

'I didn't tell you to take your bloody clothes off!'

'You invited me in just so you could make a fool of me.'

These were the version of events that would stick. His words, his mates, his story.

'Well then, I'm clearly a right cow and you should keep your distance.'

'I will.'

'Good. So fuck off then.'

She hadn't meant it to come out like that. But something about his self-righteousness and the stories about the Lake Witches pushed the words out too forcefully. Maybe it was the fact that those two children were still missing and she was miles from home. Maybe it was the cold and creeping darkness.

He didn't speak, so she just turned and marched on, annoyed with herself, her mind still spinning.

David didn't move. When, eventually, he did, he was stiffer and slower. He headed straight for the pub.

SEVENTEEN

Sam knocked at the Downings' door a little later that day. He'd clocked the green plastic recycling box stacked with empty bottles of wine, and his hopes rose that Sarah's boozing would keep her out of the way while he tackled Tim. However, he was disappointed to see a second car, a battered and scraped old red Audi, parked up in the drive. He made a note of the number plate and headed for the door, only for it to open, revealing Tim and another man heading outside. The man was shorter than Tim and dressed in a dull tracksuit and greying trainers. His thinning hair was cut short and Sam could see the edges of tattoos creeping out from under his sleeves. He stopped when he saw Sam, looked him up and down as a boxer might his opponent, then turned back to Tim, speaking quietly.

'Hello,' Sam said loudly.

A little embarrassed, Tim introduced the man to him as Sarah's brother, Jed. Jed shook Sam's hand with a shake so limp it felt as though he was scared of catching something from the contact.

'She's sleeping,' Jed sniffed. 'Popped by to check on her, like. But she's out of it.'

Tim took in a deep breath, but didn't say anything.

'Poor girl,' Jed continued. His accent was local, and Sam realised that he heard the same burr in Sarah's words, although her accent had been smoothed out. Jed was the life she'd left behind.

'It's a common reaction. A way to cope,' Sam said, as though he were just another onlooker, sharing bland, useless observations. Jed nodded in agreement.

'Do you mind if I ask where you were on the day that Arthur and Lily went missing?'

'That didn't take long did it?' Jed said.

Tim stared at his feet, embarrassed. Sam tried to imagine them sat across the kitchen table – they clearly had nothing in common beyond Sarah.

'I was in London,' Jed said. 'In a bloody custody cell. Told the last lot this. I bet you already knew it anyway, didn't you? Jesus.'

He turned to Tim and muttered words of reassurance, that he was sure the kids would be alive, that he'd pop by again. Tim nodded, and then there was a terrible moment when neither man knew how to get away. Jed went to hug him while Tim stuck out a hand. An awkward handshake-cum-embrace followed before Jed got into his car, glared once more at Sam, and reversed the car out of the drive.

'So that was Jed,' Tim said apologetically.

'My brother-in-law's an arsehole, if it helps,' Sam replied.

Tim nodded. 'Jed's alright, I suppose. Heart in the right place.'

At Sam's suggestion, they walked away from the house. Crossing the road, Tim pointed to a small footpath that led to the lake, heading through the wood. It took about thirty seconds before they were fully enveloped by trees.

'It's beautiful round here,' said Sam.

Tim grunted and nodded. He trudged forward with his hands stuffed in his blue parka jacket, staring down at his boots. After a while he sighed. 'I used to take the kids down here every Saturday. Sarah would have a lie-in and we'd come down, rain or shine. They'd run ahead and jump out at me from behind the trees.'

He stopped speaking and they walked on in silence. Somewhere nearby, a woodpecker's drill rapped out. Sam was pleased to hear it, but his focus was on the man next to him.

'It's too late, isn't it?' Tim said. 'For Arthur and Lily. You should have found them by now. Otherwise . . .'

'No cases are ever the same,' Sam said in reply.

Tim nodded, but he couldn't meet his eye. 'Jed says he's

sure they'll be fine. Bangs on about it, trying to be optimistic, but . . .'

They'd stopped in the middle of a path that meandered gently through the woods, down to the lake. The trees were old; tall and thick, and the light was mottled. Occasionally a bird's cry would break the silence, or the rustle of leaves as the wind picked up and then died. But beyond that, nothing. Tim seemed oblivious to its charms.

'I wanted to keep you up to speed with our investigation,' Sam lied. 'We've done the routine visits, talked to neighbours and locals, and gone back over all of the evidence.' He watched Tim carefully as he spoke. The man still didn't meet his eye.

'There have been some slight anomalies.'

Tim looked up at this.

'But they might be nothing.'

'Like what?'

'I don't want to waste your time, Mr Downing, not until we have a better sense of it all.'

'So what is there to tell me then?'

Sam put a matey hand on his shoulder as he avoided answering.

'You're very well liked in the village, if that means anything.'

'We are?'

'You are, Mr Downing.'

Tim walked on, muttering something under his breath.

'I'm sorry, sir?'

'I said "fucking oiks",' Tim replied angrily. 'They all hate her, don't they?'

'We've had some stories, certainly.'

'Saying what?'

'It's just gossip, it won't affect our investigation.'

'Good. I tell you, that lot would love it if she'd done it. Bloody savages. Just because she's not called Charlotte and doesn't get stuck in at the village fete. Just because she says what she thinks. Just because I chose someone different, someone with an ounce of spark and life in her, everyone thinks I've been drugged.'

'I didn't realise she was so different from you,' Sam said.

'She's not. Well, of course she is because her family have no money and I think there's a criminal conviction or two somewhere along the line, but who cares? You saw Jed. Smokes too much dope, wouldn't know a proper day's work if it hit him, but he's hardly a child abductor, is he? And me and Sarah, we're happy together, we're equals. Modern life, yeah? I bet you didn't ask your wife for a family history before you got hitched.'

'No, sir,' Sam replied. Andrea swept in, twirling around in her wedding dress as they danced in the small church hall, the rain battering down relentlessly on the corrugated roof. Sam had pulled her close, she'd pulled him closer still and they were both breathless, laughing, overwhelmed by how ridiculously, stupidly happy they were.

Sam turned his back on her, nodding towards the lake and following Tim along the path. Tim's hands were out of his pockets now and he looked around him as he walked. Sam noted that his boots no longer kicked at the ground beneath them, so he mentioned the kids again, and the routine of their walk down to the lake. It seemed to loosen Tim a little more.

'You should see it in the spring. Bluebells everywhere. A carpet of them all the way down to the lake. Magical.'

'I bet.'

'What else did they say about her?' Tim asked, a little hurriedly.

Sam had been waiting for the question.

'They think you were a better father to them than she was a mother.'

'Bollocks.'

'There were stories about fights between her and the kids.'

'Says who? Fucking hell.'

'It's hearsay. It's not important to us.'

'So she has a temper. Who doesn't?'

Sam kept walking. He made sure he didn't look at Tim, tried to make it seem as though he hadn't even registered the comment. A temper. Tim had to hurry to keep up with him. He put an arm out, pulled at Sam's arm.

'It's bullshit, it's impossible, she'd never, never, ever do anything like that. She's trouble in loads of ways but she adored them. Please don't listen to them.'

Trouble. Sam stored the word away and nodded politely.

'Can I ask you about Bud?' the policeman said.

He saw Tim stiffen and knew that he was tied into the lies too. Zoe had told him about how easily Bud was manipulated. Maybe Tim was cut from the same cloth.

'What about him?'

'He didn't have a bad word to say about Sarah, don't worry.'

'No, she's got him under her spell alright.'

Tim caught Sam's quizzical look.

'Oh, don't listen to me. Been cooped up in that house for too long. It's nice to stretch the legs. Get away from all those prying eyes in that shitty village.'

Sam looked around him. He could see the lake further down and the sparkling water, licking against the shoreline. It didn't feel shitty to him.

'What did Bud say?'

'He said that he was the one who found the bike. He alerted you to your children's disappearance.'

Tim just opened and closed his mouth, nodding uselessly.

'And this is something that wasn't in the original police report,' Sam continued, watching Tim fidget. He then turned and walked on, waiting for Tim to catch up. He stopped at the lake and took in its beauty and scale. It was easy to look distracted. He felt Tim standing by his shoulder.

'Why did you try to hide Bud from us?' Sam asked without turning to him.

'I didn't.'

'It was your wife's idea, then?'

'She didn't hurt our children. She couldn't.'

The avoidance was telling.

'Your children are missing and you're playing games with the police, Mr Downing.'

'I'm not. I swear. We want them back, of course we do, we're desperate!'

'She made you lie.'

Tim couldn't find a reply.

'People have also alleged that she's a drug user.'

'No!' Tim's face flushed with anger. 'No. No way. That was in the past. But not any more, not for years, not since the kids were born. I swear.'

Sam just stared at him and Tim began to flounder.

'She was wild before, she liked to party. Who wouldn't when there's nothing to do except fish and stick your hand up a cow's arse?'

'So why hide Bud from us?'

His reply was timid. 'I don't know why.'

'Come on, Tim, it's just us guys here. No one listening in. Say what you're scared of. Get it out, let's hear it.'

'Who said I'm scared of anything?'

'I'm going to find your children. And if it means steamrolling straight through you, then I'll do it.'

He could feel Tim wilting in his presence.

'You need to talk to your wife and then come and talk to us,' Sam said.

'She didn't take our children. It's just not possible.'

'You're trying to protect her and I appreciate that. You're a nice guy. But women can be . . .'

He shrugged. He didn't really know how to finish the sentence. He didn't have a view on 'women' in that sense. But now he was playing the 'man to man' card, he needed to keep it going. He could feel Tim's resolve weakening by the moment.

'What has she made you do, Tim?'

Again, the poor man couldn't find a reply. Sam left him there by the lake. There was a chance, he thought, that Tim would come running after him, but he wasn't expecting it. Right now, he imagined the man was staring out at the water, his thoughts scrambled and panicked. Soon he would run back to Sarah. And then, later, he would come and find Sam. The case was moving now, like a heavy train, slowly heaving itself forward, gaining momentum.

Sam walked through the wood. He enjoyed the crunch under his boots, his mood buoyed by his work and the progress he felt they were making. And then the moment was undone by the chirruping ringtone from his phone. It was Issy.

'Hi, love, what's up?' he said as merrily as he could. There was no reply, but then he heard her tearful sniff. 'Issy?'

'I hate it here.'

'Oh, love.'

'Magda's being weird.'

'Weird? How?'

'I don't know. I think she's on drugs or something. And Gran keeps going upstairs and not coming down for *ages*.'

Sam sighed inwardly and rubbed his tongue over his teeth.

'Issy. What's the matter, hon?'

'I just told you, didn't I? You should be here.'

'I'm sorry. It won't be long.'

She just snorted her derision back at him.

'Tell me about Gran.'

'She's just fucking senile, that's all.'

'Language.'

'She's ga-ga. Seriously, Dad. She's going to burn the house down or something. And she stinks.'

'Oh come on.'

'How would you know?'

'How's Jenny?' he asked, changing the subject.

'Yeah,' came the dull reply.

'Is she there? Can I talk to her?'

'No, she's doing more homework or something spoddy,' his elder daughter replied.

Sam made a laughing sound down the phone, but he couldn't tell if it was getting the right reaction or not.

'Look. Get Magda to call me and make sure she does it when Gran's around. I'll talk to them, okay?'

There was a long pause at the other end.

'Issy? Okay?'

'It's not the same,' she said quietly and then hung up on him.

He sighed and stuffed the phone deep into his pocket. He was about to head back to the hotel when he saw Ashley standing a little further up the path, watching him. The girl in white, her arms folded with a small smile on her face. His first instinct was to walk past her without acknowledging her presence. But the instinct was sucked down and drowned by more primitive, more powerful desires.

She led him deeper into the woods. It was warmer now, a sudden change in the weather which reminded you of the fading summer. She led him forward but didn't take his hand. And when they reached a spot that she thought suitable, she pushed him down onto his back and rode him, a tiny laugh slipping from her lips as he came. Her eyes pinned him down, merciless, and he felt like her prisoner. Neither moved. Sam felt a stick prod painfully into the small of his back.

'Your girl looks cool,' she said.

'My girl?'

'Yeah, the tomboy cop.'

'She's not my girl. I don't think she'll ever be anyone's girl.'

'Why? She's a lesbo?'

'No, I meant, she's too proud and strong to be . . . oh never mind.'

Still the girl didn't move. They were conjoined. She pushed some hair away from her face.

'Who do you buy your drugs off?' he asked.

She just shrugged.

'It could be important.'

'I don't buy them, I let the others do it, then get mine off them.'

'You don't even know the name of the person they score from?'

'No.'

'Well, you've been a great help, thank you.'

'Whatever.'

'Did you ever see Sarah Downing at the lake? Buying drugs like they said?'

'I've seen her down there, sure, but I don't think I've seen her actually scoring. You want to do it again?'

'No, talk to me about that.'

'I didn't nick no kid.'

115

She bit his ear. It hurt and he liked it.

He looked up at the tree branches above him and felt stupid and dirty.

'Get off, eh?'

She did, then pulled at her coat and threw it over her shoulders. Sam stood, pulling his trousers back up.

'You know the witches live in these trees?' she said, that same mischievous look on her face.

'I thought they lived in the lake.'

'Oh they do, but when they're out, they come and perch in the treetops, like birds waiting for their prey. When you walk through the forest, you need to look up, check they're not going to sweep down and rip you up. They can rip your stomach open with their claws.'

'What's with all this shit about witches round here?'

She burst out laughing. And then looked up and Sam found he was looking up too. And he saw how much this pleased her.

'Next time we fuck,' she said, 'we're going to do it somewhere nice. Not out in the open.'

'Who says there will be a next time?'

She sniffed at this and they both knew she was right. She gave him a little wave, the sort a tiny child does from their car seat, and walked away, already on the phone to a friend.

'Hiya, where are you? I'm coming now. Did you hear about Billy? I know! What a douche!'

Sam watched her walk away. His eyes slipped up once more to the treetops, and then he walked hesitantly behind her, keen for the distance between them to grow.

He needn't have feared. Within moments, she had disappeared.

EIGHTEEN

Zoe joined Sam in his room. She'd wandered down to the bar, seen David and the other men grumbling to themselves and hot-footed it back up the stairs.

Sam had laughed when she told him that the locals were revolting, and they agreed to eat in his room. He spread out the Downings' case files over the bed and together they talked through the dribs and drabs. All conversation inevitably returned to Sarah.

'But why would a woman kill her own kids? That's just not natural. And we've got no motive,' she argued.

'No. Not yet,' Sam said.

Zoe wondered why he said it like that. The case itself was fragile enough. They had nothing beyond gossip and the possibility that Sarah had lied.

'We know bugger all, don't we?' she said.

She wanted to press him about this, but there was a polite knock on the door and they turned as a waitress appeared, carrying a tray. She looked sixteen or so, no more, with tied-back dark hair and a mousy disposition.

'Dinner,' she said apologetically, though it was unclear as to whether she was sorry for her disturbance or the food.

'Great, thank you,' said Sam, clearing some space so she could put the tray down. The waitress glanced at the papers spread out all over the bed. Zoe stood between her and them and gave her a stern look. Cowed, the girl scampered away.

'They'll be talking about us, downstairs,' Zoe said. 'How long till this whole thing turns into the Wicker Man and they're burning you at a stake?'

Sam smiled and muttered something. She gave him a shove.

'Say that again, boss.'

'I said that I have a feeling it's not me they'll go for.'

For a woman who would tell you she was tough as fuck, Zoe felt strangely disarmed by the comment.

Downstairs, pints and chit-chat were downed in equal measure. The hearth burned warmly, and were it not for poor little Arthur and Lily, God would be in his heaven. The place hadn't changed in years and felt all the better for it.

There was a stir when Tim entered the pub. Heads turned and voices dropped, but he was soon welcomed in by one and all. There were pats on the back, warm handshakes and many offers to buy him a drink. He found himself leaning against the bar, enveloped by men he knew, but no one whom he would really call a friend. Tonight it didn't seem to matter.

Tim had watched Sarah open another bottle and had fled, wordless, into the night. The words from his neighbour, Alby, and from Sam had been spinning around in his head and had rendered him mute in her presence. They'd raised awful questions about Bud, and about that terrible day. He was scared of asking them, of the hurt he would cause and the answers he might hear. So he'd stormed out and then, stopping at the end of the road, realised he had nowhere to go but the pub.

'How's Sarah?' they all asked as a pint was poured for him. He repeated the well-worn phrases that gave them a sense of the truth, and of what he would and wouldn't speak of. He noted their kind responses and the way they hung politely on his words. He felt at home here. He found the beer loosened his tongue and he felt some of the crushing anxiety lighten a little.

He smiled as the conversation slipped to Duncan's sheep – a source of constant amusement in the village, as the hapless farmer seemed incapable of keeping them on his land. He joined in as they argued about football, about the RAF jets that roared so low over the valleys, about the cost of petrol and a first-class stamp. He drank a third pint with his old muckers and let the fug in his head settle and thicken.

*

On the other side of the bar, David sat at a table with Al and Jerry. He nodded to Tim when he entered and raised his glass to him.

'Poor bastard' and other similar phrases fell from their lips.

But soon, David was on about Zoe again. 'They're treating the case like it's a joke,' he spat. 'Like it's a holiday.'

They laughed at him, teasing him for the way she'd duped him. She wanted him, really, Al insisted. She was just playing with him, cock-teasing until she finally let him get in her knickers. He just needed to persevere. But David was still stinging from her brush-off earlier and their taunts only poked harder at his broken pride. He drank hard, the confusion and the embarrassment bubbling inside.

As the evening progressed, so the mood slowly twisted and soured. Sarah, who had been spoken of with sympathy, became 'the ball and chain' when Tim was invited out for an afternoon's shooting.

'Need to get a chit signed first?'

Tim clenched his pint glass hard and made all the right noises.

The chatter continued around him. He was surrounded by his peers, laughing aggressively, every comment a competitive pose, every joke vying for superiority. He listened to it all, secure in their presence yet utterly disconnected. He thought of his wife at home, vulnerable and alone, crying.

He felt the urge to run back to her, and at the same time a desperate desire to forget everything about her.

Someone mentioned Sarah again, but this time the question was more probing and less respectful.

'Still locked away in her dressing gown, is she?'

'You're a bloody saint, you know that?' came another voice as a hand patted him hard on the shoulder.

He felt the rage ripple within. He stared down at his empty glass and one of the guys grabbed it from him and replaced it with a full one.

David had drunk too much. He sat there, slurring angrily. His mates had tried to pull the conversation away from Zoe, but he wouldn't allow it and they were bored with the way he wallowed in it.

'She wants to fuck you, alright, but what she really wants to do is fuck you up there,' said Jerry, tapping his head. 'That's what women do, isn't it?'

'Look at poor old Martin,' said Al, idly tearing a bar mat into tiny pieces. 'It used to be the four of us here, didn't it? Now look what's happened to him – stuck with that miserable cow all the time, watching box sets of *Sex and the City*.'

'That's what they do to you,' Al nodded drunkenly.

David remembered the thrill he'd felt when he'd entered Zoe's hotel room. He remembered thinking that she was beautiful. He hadn't only wanted sex, he'd wanted her. And she'd mocked that.

'Fucking bitch,' he muttered.

His friends laughed at him.

Upstairs, Zoe and Sam pored over the documents. All roads led to Sarah. But there was never a reason. No sense of why something so cruel would or could have happened. Sam received a call from his elder daughter, Isabelle, and Zoe pretended not to listen in as her boss stammered into the phone, clearly unable to placate her.

'Women, Christ,' he said wearily as he finally hung up.

She winked at him, then cuffed him lightly over the head, again and again until he laughed.

Downstairs, Tim's head spun. He had to get out of there. The men were laughing and the words rebounded around his head, shapeless and senseless. He was grinning as best he could manage, but all he could think about was Sarah.

David poured more beer down his throat.

They pushed through the door at the same time, staggering out into the cold and the dark together. David felt awkward next to Tim, wanted to say something appropriate, but he was all too aware of his drunken, enfeebled mind. So he patted him weakly on the shoulder instead. Tim looked at him but said nothing, marching away. David felt stupid. He turned and looked up at the windows on the first floor. One of them would be Zoe's. He considered throwing a stone against it, breaking it. But then he too walked away and, like Tim, the darkness hid him soon enough.

NINETEEN

Cameron and Angus Farmborough dragged the dinghy down to the water and jumped in, ripping the off-board engine into action as they raced away from the shore and out towards the middle of the lake. The sun was up, but it wouldn't get over the peaks for a good hour yet, and Lullingdale Water was dark and somnolent. A mist hung over it, fighting with the warmer air. This brief respite would soon give way to the inevitable icy blast. It could be brutal here in the winter, and the two lads wanted to enjoy the last few days of good weather that the year would offer. They were athletic boys who were always outdoors. Winter for them was a dour purgatory.

As the elder brother by two years, Cameron steered the boat, heading into deeper waters while Angus attached floats and bait to each rod. They had some food, a six-pack of Coke, sunscreen ('like we'll need it!') and a big can of maggots. Today was going to be bloody ace.

Sheep wandered around the lower slopes of the fells, and Cameron watched Mike Ham's tractor dragging hay over to his cows on the far side of his land. He gazed back at the patterns the propeller made, the white foam and the twisting funnels of water that chased behind. A little later he killed the engine and let the boat drift. They were about halfway along the lake now, bang in the middle. He always used the same markers: the old stone wall on the east side and the dilapidated boathouse, half hidden among the woods, on the other.

'You don't think it's too deep?' Angus asked. Cameron just pulled a face, grabbed a rod and got down to it. Neither spoke and there was little noise except the waves against the boat, the sound of casting or reeling in, or a distant murmur of activity from the shore.

Two hours later they'd had little luck. They'd caught a few tiddlers but nothing to take home. The boys peered down into the deep, still water and watched for the shadows that slipped beneath; the big ones who were too old and too wise to be caught by mere children.

And then finally a shadow rose from the depths. It spun and twisted, a big one. But it wasn't a fish. It was Arthur Downing.

He rose with inelegant speed, breaking the surface with a slight hiss, and floated face-up, seemingly staring at the sun that now poured down from a cloudless sky. His body bobbed in the water, slipping back just below the surface as though he were now part fish.

Angus was sick and started to cry. The boys wailed and waved to the unhearing folk on land for help, but they knew it was in vain. Not sure whether they dared leave him there or not, Cameron eventually took the lead, tying a length of fishing line to his naked ankle and slowly dragging the poor little lad back to land.

Cameron made Angus drive the boat. He held tight to the line, watching Arthur the entire time, scared that the boy would slip off.

Later he told his friends that he was sure that the boy winked at him. But then he remembered that Arthur had no eyes, and he would fall silent, and no one around him could think of anything else to say.

TWENTY

Zoe and Sam stood amongst the chaos. A forensics team were already on site and a white tent had been quickly assembled, covering the boy's naked body. Locals had swarmed down to the lake, and after some brief, gentle questioning, the Farmborough boys had been released, emerging as local celebrities as they recounted their horror to everyone, over and over. Inevitably, their story lost nothing in the telling.

The shoreline was crammed as everyone looked for their own slice of tragedy. Sam stood amongst them, almost unnoticed, and listened to their conversations.

'Just rose up, from the deep.'

'How did he get all the way out there, then?'

'Underwater currents, aren't there? Drag anything down to the bottom.'

'Fish had pecked at him, Jack said.'

No one mentioned witches, but Sam knew that he wasn't the only person thinking about them; playing with the little lad on the bottom until they'd had their fun with him. He thought about the other cases – the drowned children – and he felt an involuntary shudder shake itself out of him.

But there was still no sign of Lily.

Zoe nudged him and gestured to the path – Sarah and Tim were coming down towards them. She was dressed in a long coat and her eyes stared bleakly and hazily before her, as though she were drugged. Tim held her arm. Sam watched as everyone fell silent.

'What's she doing here?' Zoe hissed. They'd visited the Downings earlier, explained that Arthur's body had been recovered and had arranged a private viewing later in the day when the boy's corpse could be made a less traumatic sight for the parents. Sarah had barely spoken when hearing the news. Tim's pained reaction had been more obvious, but Sarah had just closed her eyes and laid her head on the kitchen table.

Sam walked over to them, greeting them with a raised eyebrow.

'She wants to see him,' Tim replied tersely, and so Sam led them to the tent. He watched Sarah, saw her red eyes, her fluttering fingers and unsteady step. And then he looked to see the locals all watching her as well, all studying her in exactly the same way that he was.

Sarah stepped into the small tent and Tim followed. It was cramped inside with the other officials there, and as

Sam followed them inside, a photographer's flash blinded them all. Sam took a step back and came outside. He looked around and saw the wary, cool stares of the public. He went up close to Zoe and looked at her – What do you think?

'If it's a performance, it's a very good one,' she said, her hand covering her mouth so no one could catch her words.

'Yeah, but why is she here?' Sam asked, his eyes still scanning the crowd.

'She needed to see him. I'd be the same.'

Sarah's scream roared out from inside the tent and silenced everyone. It was as though this primal, gut-wrenching howl was a biting wind, such was its effect – the way everyone turned away from it, their heads ducking down into their chests, birdlike, their eyes closing, wincing in its wake. While quieter sobs could then be heard from inside, outside no one moved or spoke.

When Sarah eventually emerged, she needed Tim to help her walk. He practically carried her back up the path as someone ran over and offered to drive them the remaining distance. Tim thanked them with mournful politeness, but Sarah was engulfed in grief, unaware of anything around her.

All eyes were on the car as it drove off. The cops walked away, further along the shoreline.

'A bit spooky, eh? Him popping up out of the lake like that,' said Zoe.

130

'Not according to forensics. Apparently a couple of warm days is all you need – gets the bacteria going in his stomach and he pumps up like a balloon.'

'Nice.'

Zoe looked out at the water, towards the spot where he had appeared.

'She sure does know how to make a scene,' Sam said slowly, as though he was testing out the words. Zoe saw that he was staring at the forensics tent.

'Go on,' she said.

'Those kids saw her down by the lake when she claimed she found the bike. She started screaming. She made sure they all saw her.'

'She might just have been panicking – like any worried mother would.'

'Yes, but she was seen by them, all the same. Just like today. You think anyone's going to be accusing her of murder after that?'

'I guess not,' she said, making sure the lack of conviction was clear in her voice.

'Just run with this for a second,' Sam said, aware of her doubts. 'Is there a reason why she made such a scene down there? Is there something she's trying to distract us from?'

'Or maybe she was trying to distract the teenagers? From something down at the lake at the time?'

'Yes. Good. We should question them again.'

One of the forensics team, all white in a paper suit, had come out of the tent and was waving to them. They walked back towards him. They knew he'd probably have little to offer – the water would have washed away the killer's secrets and the temperature of the lake would make an exact time of death almost impossible to determine.

'I should deal with him,' Sam said. 'You okay with the kids?'

'Sure.'

They were closer to the crowd now and their voices dropped.

'Can I say something?' Zoe asked.

Sam stopped, and they turned their backs on the crowd so that they were shielded from them.

'What about a motive? You're acting like it's her that's done it.'

'She's a person of interest, yeah.'

'But there's no motive, no evidence, no link, nothing. And we still don't know what's happened to Lily. It's not like you, boss.'

'You think we're barking up the wrong tree?'

'No. Maybe. I don't know.' She shrugged, annoyed with herself. 'I just don't see why everyone's looking at Sarah.' She sighed. 'I'll go question the kids.'

'Thanks. I'll get divers organised – do a proper trawl of the lake.'

They were too close to the crowd to say more. Zoe strode back towards the car. Sam wondered about her for a moment. She was right, things were drifting towards Sarah without any proper motivation, but he didn't feel any impulse to push them in another direction. What other direction was there?

TWENTY-ONE

Sarah lay on the bed, face down. There was a knock on the door but she didn't seem to hear it. A little later Tim came in. He stood in the doorway then padded quietly to the edge of the bed and sat there for a while. But she didn't move and eventually he had to speak.

'That was Bud.'

No reaction.

'He was in a bit of a state. The police have been round.'

She turned over and stared at him, her eyes red.

'What did he say?'

'Not a lot. He wants to talk to you.'

She started to cry again. Tim wanted to go to her, but he'd been pushed away so many times recently, he didn't dare.

'Oh, my love,' was all he could say. He cursed his stupid, inadequate words and their failure to cut through to her. Their boy was dead and their little girl still missing. What words could possibly help with that?

'Get him back,' she said, and there was ferocity in her voice. It surprised him. 'Get Bud here.'

Tim had never been sure about Bud. He'd watched Sarah flirt with him in the garden and then seen her face fall to a stony blankness when she came back inside. He'd thought that these were silly, personal jealousies that he should ignore. But then his neighbour had caught him at the bins and that big cop had pushed his way into his head, and now he wondered all sorts of things.

'I don't think that's a good idea,' he said.

'What would you know?'

It's just the grief, he thought, it's just the grief coming out. This isn't the real Sarah, not the Sarah you know. This will pass.

'Honey, we need to be strong together now,' he said. But somewhere deep inside, he wanted to slap her.

'Go get Bud, get him here and make sure no one sees.'

'Why?'

She didn't answer.

'What have you done, Sarah?'

He stared at her. This isn't you. This isn't the woman I married.

'The police don't trust us,' he said. 'There's stuff they won't tell me and I don't know why.'

He waited for the response, the acknowledgement, at the

135

very least an admission that they were still together, still fighting for each other.

But she said nothing. She was a stranger to him.

He was about to leave her, about to scream, but suddenly she was there, with her arms around him and her cheek pressed against his. He felt her hand stroke the back of his neck. He hadn't seen her move from the bed. It was as though she'd just appeared next to him.

'I'm sorry, Tim, I'm so sorry,' she whispered. Her lips kissed his mouth. It felt as though he was being pulled gently into velvet sheets. He closed his eyes as she hugged him tighter.

'We've lost our baby,' she said. And they cried as one, locked together, forgetting all about anything and everything else.

He could have stayed like that, wrapped in her web, for ever.

TWENTY-TWO

Zoe's search for the teenage gang was laborious. Eventually she managed to find a spotty boy called Ian Popper who was munching his way through a family-size packet of crisps outside the convenience store. Ian, however, offered nothing of use ('yeah', 'no', 'no idea') and his dull idiocy jabbed at her until she was so angry that she virtually charged back to Bud's house. He wasn't there, but it didn't take her long to track him down. He was working on a long line of post-and-rail fencing at the far end of the village. A small brook gurgled over moss and rocks nearby while he lugged heavy, rough lengths of wood into position. The fencing joined the end of an old stone wall, which felt as though it had existed for centuries; as though some ancient immortal had laid the rocks there at the dawn of time. Bud's Labrador sat panting in the passenger seat of his Land Rover Defender.

He saw her and straightened, the wood clasped in his hands like a medieval lance.

'You heard about Arthur?' she asked.

'Yeah. Awful.'

'Dead. Not missing. Dead. Where do you think Lily is?'

'I don't know. Why are you talking to me like this?'

'Because I can't be arsed with your secrets any more.'

'Is Sarah okay?'

'Why do you mention her when I ask you about secrets?'

He looked at the floor and she went in close and kicked the wood out of his hands. He looked up, startled.

'You're going to talk to me. I'm not leaving till you do.'

Bud snorted angrily and Zoe had to hide her unease. If he had a hand in the kids' disappearance, and in Arthur's death, then she shouldn't be here alone with him. But she was angry herself and she wanted someone to shout at.

'You're a liar,' she said.

'You can't talk to me like that!'

She threatened him with arrest, telling him how she'd drag him to a nearby station and let him fester in a cell. She saw his shoulders hunch and knew that his memories of foster parents were giving her words extra weight. It wasn't difficult to imagine his fear of institutions. She saw him crumbling.

'Bud. Stop lying to me.'

'I don't want to get her into trouble.'

'Did she murder her children?'

'Of course not!'

'Then spit it out.'

'I promised I wouldn't.'

'Matthew Bryden, I'm arresting you on suspicion—'

'No, don't, please!'

'Tell me. Tell me everything.'

'She just, oh shit.'

'Tell me!'

'She had some drugs in the house. She had drugs in the house and she was scared that the police would search the place and find them. And then they'd think she was worse than she was and do all the things that you lot do.'

'What do we do?'

'You twist things, you screw things up. Just because people don't fit into the way you want them. I'm not right like that and you're always after me. Council, cops, always the same.'

'And Sarah?'

'Yeah. She's different too. It's why we get on. We're rejects.'

He said the word with a bitter sense of pleasure. Again, she wondered if he'd worked this out on his own, or if Sarah had spelled it out for him. But either way, the words made sense.

'She didn't do anything,' he said again, his voice stronger now the truth was out.

'Thank you for telling me this. I'm sorry I was so angry. But you mustn't hide things from us.'

He just nodded back at this.

'Now. For me,' Zoe continued. 'One last time. You went down to the lake . . .'

'I went down after work to walk Meg,' he said, gesturing to the Labrador. 'And I saw Arthur's bike and I took it up to the house. And Sarah was there. And Mr D. And they ran down with me and we looked everywhere and called the police. And it was then, after we'd searched and searched and got home, that Sarah remembered she had some stuff on her. And she got even more scared. She was in bits 'cos of the kids, see? She was frantic. And so she asked me to take it and get rid of it. Do you see? It's bad but nothing like . . . you know.'

'What were the drugs, Bud?'

'I don't know.' He saw her disbelief. 'I don't! I'm not into any of that. She just said it would get her into trouble and she asked me to dump it.'

'And did you?'

'Yeah. Of course. Burnt it on the bonfire.'

She winced inwardly; the evidence was gone.

'We already knew she took drugs,' she said. 'We found that out almost as soon as we got here. You've wasted our time.'

'Sorry,' he said without much conviction.

'You've made us suspicious of her for all the wrong reasons.'

Bud just sniffed and picked up the wood and began

his work again. Zoe wanted to say something else, but his answers made perfect sense, and in so many cases the truth was just dull and depressing. Sometimes the job felt equally messy; digging up the dirt and shining a light on it. But on this one it felt as though too many people were already peering and pointing.

Sarah was no murderer, and Bud no accomplice. It didn't matter what everyone said, she needed to look elsewhere. In the field opposite, two sheep had wandered over and stared at her, chewing hard like teenage brats. She headed off without bothering to say goodbye to Bud. She needed to talk to those bloody teenagers.

TWENTY-THREE

Sam found Ashley sitting alone in a small brick shack that passed as a bus stop. She was smoking a cigarette, her feet up, headphones on. Sam could hear the pumping bass as he approached her. She saw him and didn't move, just blinked slowly and looked away. He stood in front of her and waited. Eventually she turned off her music and looked at him.

'Now?'

'No, I want to talk to you.'

'Well I want to fuck.'

'Jesus, Ashley.'

'What? Come on, you like it too.'

'This is about the case. About the boy.'

'I heard he turned up without his eyes, but his skin was still perfect.'

'I'm sure there are all sorts of stories going around.'

'I know you want to.'

'I want to talk to you about Sarah Downing,' he said, ignoring the tease. 'Can you go back through everything you saw on the evening when Arthur and Lily disappeared?'

'Everything? God, I've already done it for the last coppers.'

'Ashley, it could be important.'

'Are you saying she did it?'

'No. I'm not saying anything like that at all.'

She shrugged, bored, then reached out and grabbed at his belt buckle. He took a step back.

'The time. Come on, girl, the time.'

'I don't know, whatever time I said before. Five? I don't know.'

'Did any of you go down to the lake earlier?'

'No, we all went down together.'

He sagged, hoping for more.

'Are you hard?' she asked. He feigned boredom at the crudeness of the question, but his pulse was racing. 'There's a back way into the pub,' she said. 'You can go in the front, I'll come the other way, see you in your room.'

'Are you sure about the time?'

'God,' she tutted. 'Like I said. Whatever we said to the cops before. You're being very boring.'

He didn't understand how this brat of a girl could have such a hold on him. The sex was meant to make up for his loneliness and help him keep his mind straight, but now this stroppy young woman had got under his skin and he found himself thinking about her all the time. He didn't even like her.

'You're in room four, aren't you?' she said. 'End of the corridor. Shit carpet but the view is nice.'

He looked at her and knew he couldn't resist. So he nodded – a nod that was small and embarrassed considering his big frame – and walked away. He knew he'd be with her in less than five minutes. And his heart pumped wildly in his chest.

When it was over, she spun around in the sheets, wrapping her naked body in them like a shroud. She looked at him and giggled – young and flirtatious, and he was thrown by this intimacy. He got dressed as quickly as he could while she continued to writhe on the bed, enjoying his awkwardness.

'You've got a great body for an old bloke.'

'Thank you, I think.'

'Yeah, you're not saggy at all, are you?'

'Come on, you need to get dressed.'

'Oh but honey,' she said in a bad Southern drawl, 'I can't leave you yet or my little old heart will break.'

'Ashley. Sod off and get dressed, eh?'

Her coquettishness vanished and the familiar glower returned. But she didn't move from the bed.

'How come you were asking me those questions before?' she asked.

'I can't. You know that.'

'I know what everyone's saying, but I don't think she did it.'

'If I ran my cases on what everyone thought, I'd never get it right.'

'Yeah, but if you'd seen her down at the lake when she was looking for him. Running about. Her make-up was all smeared and her dress was falling off her shoulders. You'd be so on her side if you'd been there.'

'I'm not on anyone's side. This isn't the playground.'

'I'm just saying. If you'd seen her, you'd be more sympathetic.'

'Hey, I'm as sympathetic as I need to be. Now, please put some clothes on.'

He stopped, and turned to look at her.

'We could do it again, if you wanted,' she said, her eyes wide and beckoning. 'I've got time.'

'Say what you said.'

'We could do it again.'

'No, not that, Jesus, about Sarah Downing.'

'What? Which bit?'

'You said she was wearing a dress?'

'Uh-huh. And it was riding up her legs and the strap hung off her shoulder because she was running about like crazy. You could see her tits.'

Sam grabbed his bag and pulled it open, rifling through the pages of a file. The girl stared at him, curious. He found the pages he needed. A witness statement – and a description of the clothes that Sarah was wearing that day. No dress. Jeans and a dark-blue jumper. No dress.

'You're sure about this?' he said.

'Yeah.'

'But you didn't say this in your witness statement. None of you did.'

'We said we saw her. We said she was in bits. What's the problem?'

Sam no longer cared if Ashley had clothes on or not. He needed to see Zoe. He grabbed his bag and walked out, hurrying down the corridor. And then he stopped and thought about the naked girl in his bed. A girl with the key to the case. A girl who could compromise him. He walked back to the room slowly, each step feeling heavier.

She was still lying on the bed, just as she had been, when he came in. She looked up at him – what? He sat down next to her and she ran her finger along his arm.

'You all saw Sarah, right?' Sam said. 'In her dress, running around?'

'Well, I saw her first. And then maybe the others saw her later.'

'You said you were all down there together.'

'Did I?'

The frustration roared up inside and he tried to hide it.

'You said that you all went down to the lake together.'

146

'Oh, yeah, I did. Well, I was a bit before them.'

'So why didn't you say that?'

'Well, it was only a bit.'

'Right.' He took a breath and continued. 'So you saw Sarah Downing. And then the rest saw her a bit later.'

'Yeah, probably.'

He scratched at the back of his neck, trying to keep calm.

'And did you notice, when the other guys saw her, that she wasn't in a dress any more?'

Ashley looked at him blankly, as though she didn't have a clue what this old man was on about.

He pressed on as gently as he could bear to, pointing out that while the teenagers had happily admitted to seeing Sarah Downing, Ashley hadn't mentioned that she'd seen Sarah earlier until that moment. He pressed her for a time.

'I don't know. She was just running around. Can you calm down, please?'

'This is very important.'

'I didn't lie, if that's what you're saying.'

He felt her hackles rise and recognised the silly teenage petulance within her.

'I'm not saying that, I'm not saying you've done anything wrong.'

''Cos I'm not a liar, you got that?'

He put a hand out and took hers, and she squeezed his

hand back. And as he did so, he knew that he was playing this wrong, but he didn't know what else to do.

'You saw her, she ran off and then when your friends came back, she was there again?' he asked gently.

She nodded.

'And you didn't notice that she'd changed her clothes?'

She frowned, thinking about this, and then shrugged.

'I like it, when we do it in your room,' she said, and grinned at him.

'Yeah, me too,' he said. 'Listen, we're going to question you again, I'm going to get my colleague to come and talk to you. And you need to tell her what you told me. About the dress.'

'Will you be there too?'

'No.'

'But you'll have told her, so why do you need me?'

He felt a net tighten around him.

'Are you not going to tell her?' she asked.

'If she knows about us then it makes things tricky.'

'How?'

He wondered about the expression on her face; so thoughtful and so sweet. It felt put on.

'If anyone thinks that I could have influenced what you say, then your evidence becomes invalid.'

'What evidence?'

'You could be the key to this investigation, Ashley.'

She sat up straighter at this, thrilled by the news, and the bed sheets fell away, revealing her nakedness. He looked at her and felt a rush of attraction and desperation in equal measure.

'I'm important?'

'You are.'

'How?'

'Will you just tell Zoe Barnes what you told me? And say it in the same way so it doesn't sound rehearsed?'

'Like how?'

'Like with all of that bolshy shit you normally give me.'

She laughed at this, a delighted cackle.

'Alright, no probs.'

She fell back onto her back and he let go of her hand. But she grabbed his and held it, placing it onto one of her breasts.

'Tell her about the dress and the stains. Yes?' he said.

She nodded but she was smiling and teasing. She wanted him again, now.

'I can't, Ashley. And we can't. Not again. Not now. Not with this.'

But she didn't let go of his hand.

'But I don't want us to end. If I tell her, then we're over, aren't we?'

His stomach turned over. A cold, icy spike ripped around inside him.

'This is more important than us fucking.'

'But I really like you. Can't we just carry on in secret?'

She sat up and kissed him on his lips. He didn't respond, but he didn't pull away either.

'You want more of me too. I know it.'

'When she comes to talk to you, will you tell her about the dress?'

'Maybe. Are you dumping me? Yes or no?'

He sighed and stood up, fed up with her childishness and angry at his own failings and the trap he'd jumped into. But she didn't move, waiting for his answer. The case was dead without her.

'No. Of course I'm not dumping you, Ashley.'

She jumped up and kissed him and then, with a sudden matter-of-factness, started to get dressed. He turned his back on her as she did. A wasted, useless gesture of fallen morality. She was dressed in the blink of an eye. She walked to the door.

'See ya,' she said, and somehow, despite the tenderness, it felt like a threat.

TWENTY-FOUR

Zoe answered Sam's call after one ring.

'I hate teenagers,' she said without waiting for him to speak. 'Can't we arrest some for crimes against fashion? Or haircuts. Or hygiene.'

'No luck then?' Sam replied. He was sitting on the shore, staring out at the lake, forced out of the hotel by nervous energy and unable to settle anywhere else. The forensics tent had been struck and the body taken to the local morgue. Without the horror show, the lakeside was quiet again.

'No. Dipshits,' Zoe said on the other end of the phone.

'How many more to go?'

'Two. Seriously, boss, it's like talking to the living dead. Only half of what they say makes any sense.'

'Stick at it.' He heard her sigh at the other end. 'You okay?'

'Sarah Downing got Bud to hide some drugs she had at the house. That was his big secret.'

'When?'

'Later that evening, after they'd called the cops.'

'What sort of drugs?'

'He doesn't have a clue, he's too thick.'

'Okay. Well done, that's good to know.'

'I thought it would be a lead. But it doesn't get us any closer to Sarah Downing, does it?'

'That doesn't, no.'

The silence on the end of the line was palpable.

'Alright,' she finally said. 'Well, I'd better go find the last two.'

She hung up. Sam placed the phone on a smooth, round rock next to him. He had to wait for Zoe to find Ashley and then they could get moving again. He wondered about Zoe's discovery – if Sarah already had drugs then she wouldn't have been down at the lake to score. The dress proved she was down at the lake earlier, probably around the time the children vanished. More than probably. So if she wasn't there for a score, then why?

He thought about little Arthur and imagined the shock for the two lads when the corpse had floated to the surface. He'd seen the body close up, seen the way it had been scratched and beaten against the lake's rocky bottom, the bites and nibbles from the fish. But he'd also noticed how alabaster-white Arthur's skin was, preserved by the icy depths. It had made him into a chilling spectacle.

Why would Sarah Downing murder her own children? There was no motive. Aware of Zoe's doubts, Sam's mind was pulled back to the other cases where those women had drowned their little ones for no reason at all.

Blame the witches, that's what everyone would be saying, he thought as he stared out at the dead-calm waters. The witches had been playing with Arthur, playing with him in the dark, teasing him and twisting him over and over before they began to feed. And finally, bored, they cast him away, spun him back up to the surface. But they remain below, dark shadows, cursed centuries ago by those on land and always hungry for their revenge.

He stared at the woods, at the treetops where they waited for their prey. You would know if they were there by the water that dripped down from the high branches. You'd hear the patter of water from up high. And if you did, you had to run. Run, run and never turn back.

He imagined a group of children, sprinting from the woods, screaming with laughter and fear, spooked by a sudden shower of rain. And he remembered himself, sprinting through a torrential downpour, his eyes stinging. Zoe was shouting at him from the car while the traffic cops tried to hold him back. They stood no chance though and he burst through the cordon, running to the accident, running to his wife. Too late.

She shouldn't have been there, she should have been far away, miles and miles from this world of violence. He stopped in front of the mangled car, wanting to pull her from the wreckage even though he knew it would do no good. He wanted to howl down the heavens, but his lungs betrayed him and allowed him only a sob before his legs went, and he had to be helped back to the car.

She shouldn't have been there. It wasn't her fault. The driver of the truck that hit her had been on the road for over twenty hours, having falsified his logbook in order to make up time and money. He'd fallen asleep at the wheel and his vehicle had veered across the road, ploughing into her car. She never stood a chance.

He should not blame her, but the crash hurled splintering glass and metal into their home and the scar-tissue would not heal. It exposed his fragile grasp of parenthood, it ripped his girls' confidence to pieces, it turned their home into a hollow, shadow-filled, memory-stalked cavern. It made him pace the streets at night, unable to sleep in the oh-so-big double bed, unable to talk to friends and family about his loss. It made him debase himself. It gave him excuses for his behaviour.

He imagined Andrea, right then and there, rising up from the water as Arthur had done. He pictured her bobbing, lifeless, just under the water's edge, released by the witches after their playtime. He imagined her eyeless sockets and felt sick.

When he looked away from the water, he was startled to see that Sarah Downing was there. She was also staring out at the lake, her coat wrapped tight around her. She'd just appeared there and his mind, still ragged from the memories of his wife, momentarily imagined that she'd appeared from the water. Sarah showed no sign that she'd seen him, hugging herself tight for warmth. Her face looked peaceful and at that moment he felt a connection, their proximity and their losses binding them together. But then she looked at him and he saw her expression change, becoming closed and guarded. She should have seen him as an ally, as someone who would help her. But the way she turned from him and hurried away made him more and more certain that what he had seen was not grief, but guilt. Whatever Zoe thought, he knew he was right to have primed Ashley and set in motion the inevitable chain of events that would catch Sarah and prove her guilt.

And then his phone rang.

'I might have something,' Zoe said. Her voice sounded tight.

'What?'

'There's a particularly annoying girl called Ashley Deveraux who all of a sudden seems to remember that Sarah Downing was wearing a dress when she saw her at the lake.'

155

'A dress?' Sam said. He wondered if Zoe would see through his fake surprise and was glad of the distance of the telephone.

'Yeah. So either she's dippy and unreliable or Sarah was down there twice.'

'And why change?'

'That's what I was wondering.'

'We should—'

'I've got her with me. I'm going to take her down to the station at Penrith and get a formal statement.'

'Pick me up on the way will you? I'll be outside the pub.'

'Still doesn't mean Sarah Downing did it.'

He thought of the way Sarah had just looked at him and of the hatred in her eyes. He was about to say something when he realised that Zoe had hung up.

TWENTY-FIVE

Zoe drove to the pub, found Sam sitting on a small bench outside, and let him take the wheel. He barely acknowledged the girl in the back as they drove to the station in silence. They needed a proper station to do a formal witness statement like this, and Penrith, although twenty-five minutes away, was the closest. Zoe thought the silence was odd, but didn't say anything until they reached the station. A uniformed officer took the girl to a 'soft' interview room (a formal space for victims and the public who were not suspects in a case) and they got a chance to grab a coffee and catch up. She explained what she'd found out.

'It could be nothing,' Zoe said. 'Apparently the dress was virtually falling off her, so maybe she got fed up and changed into something more practical.'

'How practical would you be when your kids are missing?' Sam asked.

'No idea,' she conceded, adding that the girl was vague

157

and unreliable. 'She comes across as a bit of a bitch, to be honest.'

She handed him a cup of coffee. He tried it and winced.

'God, that's disgusting.'

'You're in the country now, boss.'

He just nodded, and she wondered what went on behind those calm blue eyes of his. She wished she could shut up like he did.

'You want to run it?' she asked, to fill the silence.

'No. You talk to her.'

'Really? I think she'd respond better to your Alpha Male routine than me. She's got quite the potty mouth.'

'You do it,' was all he said and started walking down the corridor.

She hurried after him and was about to make a joke about getting back to the city and enjoying a flat white, but he was already at the interview room, his face creased in thought. He opened the door and ushered her in before she could say any more.

Sam knew that it would be better for the case if Zoe asked the questions, but he also knew it would look odd to have a silent Senior Investigating Officer and, worst of all, he had no idea what Ashley might do. The nerves made him jumpy and he worried that Zoe would notice. He said little in the corridor as he tried to imagine various scenarios and how he would deal with them, but in the end he decided to brazen it out.

He'd avoided looking at Ashley and only paid attention to her now that she was in front of him. She'd changed since she'd been in his hotel room. Her white attire had been replaced with a baby-blue cashmere top, skinny jeans and cowboy boots. He introduced himself to her and she made him shake her hand. He could tell she was enjoying this game and it scared the hell out of him.

'How long would you say you were down at the lake before your friends joined you?' Zoe asked pleasantly. Ashley looked at her with a withering scowl and turned her attention to Sam.

'Are you just colleagues, you two? Or do you fuck as well?'

'Please, miss, just answer the question,' Zoe said. 'We'll be through with this soon enough and then you can get back to your homies.' Her tone was just about friendly.

'Ten minutes,' came the sulky reply.

'Great. And could you describe the dress?'

'Flowery. Green and red. Pretty. Summer dress. Like you'd wear to a party. But she always dressed a little slutty,' Ashley replied, her eyes never leaving Sam.

Zoe picked up on this and glanced at him, but he just stared at the table. So she carried on.

Ashley answered her questions with grumbles and moans, and Sam wanted to reach across the desk and grab her, shake some sense out of her, but he knew that he couldn't, and he knew that she knew. And he worried that Zoe would wonder why he said nothing. He wouldn't normally take such shit.

Finally it was over. Her statement had added nothing more – just that she had been at the lake earlier than the others and that, from her vague recollections, Sarah had also been there; twice that day. The first was around the same time that Arthur and Lily Downing had disappeared.

They left Ashley in the room, promising to return in a few minutes to drive her home. After they'd stepped outside, he felt Zoe pat him warmly on the shoulder.

'Well done for keeping your cool in there, skip. I wanted to slap the silly cow.'

Sam shrugged as best he could.

'We need to find the dress,' he said gruffly, and felt cross with himself for not faking a laugh.

'You think she'll still have it?'

'Depends on whether or not it's incriminating. We should hunt for it anyway,' he said. 'You did well in there,' he added, trying to soften his tone.

He saw the pleasure that this gave her and felt winded by his own deceit.

In the car, again, no one said much. Sam drove and would glance occasionally at the girl in the back seat. And whenever he did, he found that she was staring right back at him.

*

The cops returned to Sam's room and his heart lurched as they entered and he saw the unmade bed; dirty sheets twisted and ruffled. He could almost see the imprint of the girl's body upon them. He feared that they stank of sex.

'How come they didn't make your bed?' Zoe asked casually. 'I'm sure they did mine.'

Sam hurriedly straightened the sheets and dragged a cover over them. Zoe sat on the edge of the bed and kicked off her shoes.

'My feet pong,' she laughed.

Sam tried to bury his unease with questions about the case. Ashley's information felt like a breakthrough, but, as with Bud's revelations, it offered little concrete evidence. And Zoe was still unconvinced about Sarah.

'Does Mr Downing know about Sarah being down at the lake?' she asked.

'That's what we need to find out. He said that Sarah is pretty drunk by eight most evenings. I say we wait till she's conked out and then go talk to him. Get him alone.'

Zoe nodded. As she thought about this she ran her hand over the bed cover absent-mindedly.

'She was odd, that girl, the witness,' she said.

'How come?' His stomach spun as he waited for her reply.

'She remembered it pretty damn clearly. All of a sudden.'

'What are you saying?'

'Maybe she was primed. Set up.'

'By who?'

'By anyone who doesn't like Sarah Downing. Like all the men there.'

'You don't believe the girl's statement?'

'I don't know. I think I do. I just don't like being played and the way I found her.'

And with that she looked at him and he could feel the accusation that he was hiding things. He knew, for Zoe, that this was unforgivable.

'Shall we go question her again?' he offered, and prayed she wouldn't expose the bluff.

She considered this for a moment, then blinked and the tension vanished. 'No,' she said, then sniffed her shoe again and then chucked it at him. He caught it and threw it back at her, as he knew she wanted. One of the boys.

'So, we kick back for a bit?' she asked. 'And then take him apart.'

He nodded and she left him with a soldier's salute.

Sam wondered about the water. He imagined the little girl in the bath and the boy drowned by his own mother in the swimming pool. He imagined little Arthur floating in the icy-calm lake, all alone. And he wondered whether Sarah Downing would herself fall into that strange, emotionless, blissful haze that had affected the other women. Maybe it was a disease of some sort, a virus that would strike at any time.

He remembered Andrea's cold body, lifeless on the tarmac, soaked by the rain, and then he thought again about Ashley's cool stare in the car mirror.

Outside, the sun battled with tumbling clouds above the austere fells. Sam tried to find some solace in their beauty.

TWENTY-SIX

Zoe went back to her room, sat on the bed, untied and then retied her shoes, and stared at her perfectly pleasant and inoffensive surroundings. She lasted another thirty seconds before she changed into her running gear and headed downstairs. Bernie at the bar gave her some brief directions with the understated warning that *it can get a little steep up there, pet*, and with that, off she went.

The run through the village was fine. An old man gawped at her Lycra but said nothing and soon she was out in the fields, following the footpaths' signs – up, up and further up. Her lungs burned and legs ached but she loved feeling like this. When she was younger, she'd been a keen athlete and had competed at a high level – four hundred metres was her preferred distance. She used to break the opposition. A set of injuries had stopped her going further, but she still had the same hunger and desire when she ran. She pushed hard against the slope, exorcising the frustrations that swamped her. No bloody hill was going to defeat her.

Inevitably, the fell won. She reached the peak with a scrambled, desperate lunge and collapsed onto the rocky peak, breathless, staring up at the clouds that raced above her. She finally found the strength to sit up and stared out at the incredible, magnificent view and felt very small. Zoe enjoyed noise, clutter and chaos, but she found herself unusually still up there. She shivered as her sweat cooled. The wintry gusts never stopped. It was just her and the wind.

She thought about Sam's silences and his odd avoidances over the past few days. He had turned away from her during their time here and she didn't understand why. She didn't understand his preoccupation with Sarah, just like everyone else in the village.

The lake shone below her like a glistening liquid silver bean. When they'd first arrived and stood at its edge it had felt mysterious, even a little creepy with the mist and fading light. But from up here, it was majestic.

She let out a roar, screamed as loud as she could and was delighted by the way that the wind stole it and threw her voice away. She'd always imagined her cry would echo across the hilltops. But it went nowhere. She was just a dot.

She made her way back – a mixture of sliding and staggering down the steep slopes of grass and shale. Her calves were sore by the time she reached the bottom. In fact, she was dog-tired, but pride forced her to jog the last half-mile into the village. She wondered again about Sarah Downing and why she might hurt her own little boy. Then she thought again about the girl, Ashley Deveraux, and the way her evidence had appeared out of the ether. It smelled wrong and she didn't like the way the girl had stared at Sam. There was history between them, and Zoe worried about what this meant. Sam was a good guy, she believed that beyond anything else, but she didn't know how long she could last without mentioning it again. She found she was constantly watching her words in this village and longed to get back to wide streets, bright lights and the reassuring cacophony of the city. She resolved to give Sam the rest of the day and then confront him in the morning. Hopefully both their heads would be a little cooler by then. She was full of such thoughts when David was suddenly in front of her.

'Hi,' he said without a smile.

She gave him a curt nod, then moved to step around him. But he blocked her path again.

'What?' she asked.

'What happened?' he asked.

She was tired, her legs were heavy from the run and she just wanted to get back inside and flop into a hot bath. She caught his angry stare and couldn't stomach such childishness.

'You embarrassed me,' he said.

'Shit,' she said, and then, a little too flat: 'Sorry.'

Again she tried to make her way past him, but this time he pushed her back – a hard shove against her elbow. It was the act of a kid in the playground. Next would be a scuffle. And then a punch. And she was all alone.

'Okay, stop that now, David,' she said, but the next shove came too quickly and now she could see just how angry he was, pumped to the brim. He didn't meet her eye. His gaze was trapped on her chest, her neck, her clothes.

'David. I'm a cop, think about it. Stop. Okay? Stop.'

But he didn't. He pushed her again. And then he raised his hand to strike her.

She had to move quick.

As his hand came powering down, she used his weight against him to send him tumbling to the ground.

'Okay, stay there, just—'

But he went for her again and she had to force him back, jamming the heel of her trainer hard into his neck. He coughed and spluttered, unable to breath.

'Shit. I'm sorry,' she said. 'Sorry, just . . . I'm a bloody cop, you idiot!'

He looked up at her with rage in his eyes and she knew that she mustn't let him get up. And so, as he pushed himself to his feet, she punched him hard in the kidneys – another apology slipping from her lips as she did so.

Winded, he fell back to ground on his front. She grabbed his right arm and pulled it behind his back. David yelled out in pain. She pressed herself on top of him, pinning his arm behind his back. He was powerless now.

'You stupid prick,' she shouted, angry and upset. Although he was bigger and stronger than her, her hold on him was such that he was utterly powerless. He wriggled for moment before he realised his pitiful position.

'I could arrest you,' she said, holding firm. She felt cold and tired and the man below her now looked pathetic. 'What were you thinking?' she asked, but he didn't say a word.

She stood quickly, spitting angrily at the floor. He didn't move.

As she began to walk away she saw him sit up from out of the corner of her eye. And then she heard him speak.

'You fucking bitch.'

She looked at him, sitting on the floor, with grit stuck to his cheek from the road, and she felt like kicking him in the face. But she also felt ashamed. She rearranged her clothes and jogged away, slowly enough for him to catch up. Part of her wanted to continue this and end it properly, but she reached the pub alone.

TWENTY-SEVEN

Sam walked around the village for ages, but he couldn't find Ashley anywhere. He trudged around the back roads with high hedges, peered over farm gates and stiles, and followed meandering footpaths, but to no effect. Everyone had hunkered down inside, sheltering from the cold. The warm days had vanished as quickly as they'd come. Soon it was dark and he knew that Zoe would be wanting to go after Tim Downing. But he needed to find the girl first.

He saw them before he heard them. It was a flicker of flames through the wood that caught his eye as he trudged miserably along the lake's shoreline. He followed the flames and soon realised that there was a party going on. He hung back, sheltering in the trees so he could take it all in.

Fifteen kids, some in their mid-teens, some maybe in their twenties, danced and cavorted around a fire. There were cans of cider and beer in their hands and someone had brought along a stereo which played rabidly tough, discordant music that seemed violent and crude. The kids loved it. They danced around the fire, whooping to the music, twirling and laughing: stoned, smashed, drunk, out of their tiny minds. He saw Ashley, all in white again, laughing and frolicking with two girls as they drank fiercely. Her face was lit by the flames, and as the others partied around her, so she swayed to the music, revelling in it.

Sam watched from a distance, shrouded in the night. He saw the kids jumping over the flames, pushing and fighting with each other, smashing bottles against trees. It was primal, a fight against rules and limits that was danced by each new generation in defiance of the old one. Sarah Downing would have done this herself, twenty years ago, Sam thought. And, in the middle of it all, the girl in white laughed and joked with her mates.

And then Ashley caught his eye.

He didn't even know how she could see him from there, but her eyes hunted him out, somehow, and she left the others and found him.

'You want me?' she asked, starting to unbutton her top.

'No.'

Behind them, the bonfire suddenly roared as one of the lads poured petrol onto it and the kids cheered and howled.

'Jesus, you can't pour petrol onto a fire like that. They'll burn their faces off,' Sam said.

Ashley laughed at him. She took his hand and held it like a girlfriend would.

'I need some cash,' she said softly.

'I want to talk about what you were up to today. You can't mess about like that. And we need to work out what you'll say when the police come and ask you more questions.'

'Not tonight, baby,' she said and he faltered. Unexpectedly, she kissed him on the cheek.

'Wasn't I good today then?' she asked.

'No. You know you weren't.'

The music thrashed through the trees. Its bass line was like a merciless stick that beat at him.

'I did what you said, though, didn't I?'

Sam looked at her, licked by the fire, her smile so sweet and so cruel. She knew she had him and he knew that this would play out in whatever ways she wanted, whatever he tried to do.

'How much do you need?' he asked wearily.

'Fifty. Costs a bloody fortune in the club,' she said with a sigh, as though she expected him to sympathise.

He dug into his wallet and handed her the money.

'Thanks, babe.'

He didn't know what to say. He heard another bottle break, and felt the heat of the fire as an idiot stoked it even higher with petrol.

'You should go,' she said. 'This can get a bit crazy and you don't want to be seen with us when it does.'

Her giving him advice. Her trying to protect him. He was powerless now.

The kids partied on. Sam backed away, tripping on invisible roots as he fled from the madness. She would be with them now, he thought, dancing and drinking and probably screwing.

He staggered to the lake, spooked by the whole thing. Its stillness was no comfort.

TWENTY-EIGHT

Sam seemed even more withdrawn when he finally came out of his room and marched ahead of Zoe, out of the hotel. He muttered stuff about his daughters and she knew well enough not to press him about it. But as they trudged through the dark, she felt compelled to talk.

'Boss. You alright?'

'Sure.'

'No, I mean, are you alright for this, for Mr Downing?'

He looked at her, a glance of irritation, but he nodded. 'Don't worry, Zoe, I won't fuck it up.'

'Course not. Sorry.'

He walked on and she shuffled along next to him. A little later, he let out a long, slow sigh and stopped.

'Sorry.'

He looked exhausted. She wanted to give him a hug but didn't know how to bridge the gap. She chose a shit joke instead. 'I'll give you twenty quid if you make him cry,' she said.

173

Ahead they could just make out the lit windows of the Downings' house and those of its three neighbours. But other than that there was nothing. Clouds overhead masked the stars. Somewhere out there, the fells rose above them. Somewhere to their right, the land slipped gently away and led to the lake. But in this pitch-darkness there was nothing. Zoe imagined someone switching on a light and revealing that none of it existed at all.

Tim answered the door. He was wearing his usual outfit; this time his cords were lime-green, with a chequered blue shirt tucked in neatly by a brown leather belt. His shoes shone, perfectly clean. He nodded warily at them.

'May we?' Sam asked, and Tim reluctantly gestured for them to come inside. He closed the door quietly behind them.

'I'm afraid Sarah has gone to bed. If you were hoping to talk to us both . . .'

He let the words drift in the hope that he'd be interrupted, but the two cops stared at him without offering any help. He looked at them, his mouth slightly agape, his shoulders tensing as he sensed the changing atmosphere in the room. Zoe waited for Sam to speak and stared grimly at Tim for effect.

'How are you, Mr Downing?' Sam made it sound as though his words were a criticism, not a question.

'Same as ever.'

'You should sit down,' Sam said, and he walked to the kitchen table. Zoe followed him and clocked the confusion on Tim's face. He sat down at the head of the table, where Sam had indicated, and the cops sat either side of him. He glanced nervously from one to the other. Neither smiled or offered him any solace.

'Look, what's going on?' He voice sounded strangled.

Sam placed his big rugged hands on the table, calloused and scarred. Zoe watched as Tim stared nervously at them. Her heart was beating faster now.

Tim swallowed involuntarily. 'Have you found something? From the autopsy, maybe?'

'We've found something, yes.'

'And?'

Neither cop spoke. Zoe watched Tim's hands slip off the table and dig into his pockets.

'Look, really, this silent treatment, it's not appropriate. I'm the bloody dad, remember?'

'We need to talk to you about your wife, sir.'

Zoe loved the way Sam would do this, with men like Tim – the tougher he'd be, the less he'd say and the more polite he would become.

'There's nothing to say about her.'

'Can we talk about your movements from the moment you returned home that evening, please?'

'Oh, I'm a suspect now, am I?'

'No, sir. Your movements, please?'

'For the millionth time: I got home. Sarah was there. And then Bud came up with Arthur's bike. And that was when we started to panic.'

'Bud.'

'Yes, okay, well done, we didn't mention him before to you, but it's nothing. It doesn't change anything. Our children are missing and we don't have anything to do with that.'

'What else?'

'I'm sorry?'

'What else happened, after you'd searched for Arthur and Lily?'

'Nothing. We called the police, we searched some more, we ... I don't know what to tell you. We've been stuck in here, praying for the phone to ring. For some news, something. And all we've got is Arthur's body ...'

He started to cry at this. Twenty quid to Sam then. He had his head down. He could almost have been praying.

'My wife hasn't done anything and I'm fed up with this shit,' Tim said, the tears turning to rage. 'I'm so fucking bored with all of your pathetic innuendos and nasty little games. We've done nothing wrong.'

But Sam was impervious.

'When you got home, that evening, after your children disappeared, after you'd searched around the lake and the village, did Bud come back home with you?'

'He, I think, yes, yes he did. But only for a moment. Why?'

'What can you tell me about that?'

Zoe saw Tim blink, his tongue touching his lip.

'I can't. They talked about something, I don't know, the kids, I imagine, and then he left.'

'You didn't hear what they were discussing?'

'Look, stop asking me all these questions. What do you know?'

'Do you trust, Bud, Mr Downing?'

'He's a simple soul but he's no harm. Are you saying he . . . ?'

'We have collected various witness statements during our time here, Mr Downing. And they paint a different version of events to the one you and your wife have given us.'

'I don't understand.'

'I believe your wife is a drug addict, sir.'

'What? No. That's crazy. In the past, sure, she dabbled, but not now, not since the kids were born.'

'Are you sure of this?'

'Yes. I'm absolutely . . .' but he faltered. And swallowed again.

'I don't believe your wife has been honest with you about this.'

Tim didn't reply. But he sagged slightly. To Zoe it felt as though something had been confirmed – his demeanour was one of a sad acceptance rather than denial.

'Does your wife own a summer dress – it has a floral print, green and red?'

'Why?'

'Please, sir.'

'She . . . yes.'

'May we see it?'

'No.'

'Why not?'

'It's gone.'

Sam shifted his weight in the chair at this news. Zoe's eyes were locked on Tim. She could feel his pulse rate climbing.

'She was seen, Mr Downing, in that dress. She was seen at the lake, in that dress, around the time that your children vanished.'

Tim faltered, his mouth opened and closed, as he tried to take this in.

'No. She was at home. She'd been at home all afternoon.'

'Is that what she told you, sir?'

'Yes. And so that's the truth.'

'Just as she's told you the truth about her drug intake?'

Sam waited. Zoe watched and hardly dared breathe. Finally the words pushed themselves out Tim's mouth.

'She was wearing that dress?'

'Yes, sir.'

'Are you sure?'

'Yes, sir.'

'Oh . . . oh fuck.'

His head fell into his hands.

'Where is the dress, Mr Downing?'

'I . . . I got rid of it.'

'You did? Why?'

'Because it was ruined. Because I was so cross with her and . . . oh shit.'

He was breathing faster and faster.

'You see,' he spoke between uneven breaths, 'I bought it as a present. And she looked amazing in it. She looks amazing in everything but it was special. It was an anniversary present. And I saw it about two days, three days after the kids went missing. She'd shoved it in the back of the cupboard. It was covered in grass stains. And mud and stuff and I was so angry because it was so wasteful. She can be so careless like that. She throws money away like . . .' he threw a hand in the air to make his point.

'And so I destroyed it. It could probably have been saved – dry-cleaned – but I was angry. I was in a state because of Lily and Arthur and I was spitting and upset so I burned the fucking thing. To teach her a lesson. We shouted at each other and said stupid, terrible things. All about a poxy dress.' He fell silent for a moment and then looked up at them, finally reaching out: 'But you said she was wearing it, that day?'

'That's right, sir.'

179

Tim fell silent again, his chest heaving with emotion. Something new was rattling through his brain.

'She said she was home all day. She said she'd fallen asleep. That's why . . . oh fuck.'

He gasped and Zoe thought that he might be sick.

'What is it, Mr Downing?'

'She was in the shower. When I got back. She was in the shower and when I asked her why she said that she'd been asleep and felt groggy. But she was scrubbing herself. Really scrubbing at herself. And when I commented on it she snapped and screamed at me. And then, when Bud appeared with the bike she went crazy. I kept saying that we shouldn't panic, that there was probably nothing to worry about, but she went crazy. Why would she be crazy like that? How could she have known?'

'She was scrubbing herself clean, sir?'

'Yes. Oh fuck.'

He stood, unable to control himself, and Zoe and Sam were instantly on their feet as well.

'Please, sir, sit down, let's go through this again.'

'No, no. Oh God.' Tim dragged his hands across his face. His voice was a wail, now. 'She was in the dress. And it was covered in shit and blood.'

'Blood?'

'Yes. Blood, definitely blood. And she hid it and scrubbed

herself clean. And then she did stuff with Bud and made us both lie for her.'

And then he was sick, retching and pulling away to the kitchen sink.

'I lied for her. I lied for her,' he wailed.

'Why did she say the dress was dirty, sir?'

'She didn't, she just shouted at me. Oh my God, my little babies.'

His legs went and Sam had to hold him up. And then Tim was sick again.

'My children, oh God, what did she do?!'

They heard a bump upstairs. Sam looked at Zoe.

'Call in two cars. One for him, one for her.'

'Yes, boss.'

She watched him hurry up the stairs. Tim was crumpled over the sink, each breath was a sob. She helped him back into his chair and he sat there, unsteady, tears pouring down his face.

Sam took the stairs, three at a time. When he reached the landing, the door at the far end was ajar. He spied a tiny flicker of movement and walked quickly towards it, but as he got there, Sarah Downing pulled the door open. He was so much bigger than her and she looked especially frail, wearing nothing but an oversize black T-shirt, but the sight of her stopped him in his tracks. She looked at him, confused.

'Sarah Downing. I'm arresting you for the murder of Arthur and Lily Downing. You do not have to say anything but it may harm your defence if, when questioned, you do not say something which you later rely on in court.'

Her mouth opened and she started to smile. He felt the dread pour through him, but then she spoke.

'No. You've got it all wrong. You can't.'

The smile flickered and faded.

'There will be a police car outside soon. You need to put some clothes on.'

She stared at him, dazed. Her head tilted as she looked at him but she seemed strangely emotionless.

'Mrs Downing, you must put some clothes on now.'

She didn't reply. She just turned and walked into her bedroom. But before she got there, Sam grabbed her arm.

'Where's Lily?' He was desperate. 'What have you done with her? Please. Your own daughter. Please. Tell me!'

Sarah just gazed at him and shook her head, almost as if she were talking to a child too young or too stupid to understand anything. He released his grip and she entered the bedroom.

Sam shouted for Zoe and she raced up the stairs.

'Watch her, will you? I can't go in there while she's changing.'

Zoe nodded and went into the bedroom.

Sam listened out for any conversation. But there wasn't a sound.

TWENTY-NINE

When the two police cars arrived it took a while before Sarah was brought out, and in that brief delay, the villagers came to gawp.

Their faces were illuminated by the police car's flashing blue lights – a repeated, syncopated rhythm. They would appear and vanish, reappear and vanish again, like ghosts. The crowd thickened with each flash. Soon there were dozens of people, all standing silently outside the house, all watching and waiting.

Tim appeared first, with Zoe next to him. He didn't speak to her or acknowledge the people around him.

The shame, the shame.

Finally, Sarah Downing was led out of the house with Sam next to her. There was a reaction from the crowd when they saw that she was handcuffed; whispers and cries. The story was fully told now. Someone shouted something – a cry of despair – but the words were lost in the night. Sam led her to the second car and gently helped her into the back seat.

Sam looked up before he closed the door and saw them all watching. He scanned the flashing crowd for Ashley's face but he couldn't see her. He heard a woman's laugh and it sounded just like his wife. His head whipped around, trying to find her, even though his brain was already shouting down the possibility.

Before he closed the door, a voice cried out from the darkness.

'Witch!'

There was a gasp from the others. It was as though this word had a special power. The word was muttered again. The invisible crowd rolled it around in their mouths, spitting it back out.

Witch.

The police car drove off and Tim was led to the back of the other vehicle by Zoe. She got in next to him and nodded to the driver, who did a swift three-point turn and then shot back along the unlit lanes.

Zoe looked over at Tim. He looked small and frail, and as they drove away from the village, he started to cry again. Zoe was glad to be out of there.

It was much later when Tim asked the question that taunted her.

'Why did she do it? I don't understand. Why?'

Zoe didn't answer. She looked out of the car window, unhappy and unsatisfied. The moon had a clawed a hole through the clouds and the fells were lit by its cold blue light. They had turned their backs on her now.

Why? The answer was as biting as the wind that blew relentlessly across their peaks. It was as cold and as unknowable as the depths of the lake. As the car sped away towards a more familiar, urban landscape, Zoe wondered if the answer would ever slip to the surface.

PART TWO

THIRTY

Slowly, the darkness faded. At first it was the intrusion of an oncoming car's headlights on a narrow road; blinding, then fading to two red dots in the rear-view mirror. Later, as they joined the motorway, heavier traffic adjusted them further, and Zoe was glad when she finally saw the orange haze that heralded the city. A billion lights, fighting against the night.

They reached the police station late, and after a quick medical examination of the prisoner, the custody sergeant deemed her fit for interview and Sarah Downing was led to a small room, found a solicitor (although she refused to acknowledge the need) and sat in front of Sam and Zoe once again.

Sarah hadn't spoken in the back of the car and Sam hadn't played the radio, making it an uncomfortable ride. And now, staring down at her feet, Sarah continued her silence, despite the myriad questions that Sam shoved at her. He asked, he demanded, he cajoled and urged, but the woman ignored it all. Away from her home, Sarah seemed a more fragile, pitiful figure, but her silence was impenetrable. The cops stared at her as though she were a grotesque exhibit, entranced by her beauty and the monstrosity of which she was accused.

'Where is your daughter, Sarah?'

The questions continued, but none were answered. The barrister would occasionally complain about the police browbeating his client, but as long as she said nothing, he had no real role to play.

'We just want to find your daughter. Don't you want that too?'

She was surprisingly still, Zoe noted. Her hands didn't twitch, her fingers didn't play with the edge of the chair or the cuff of her sleeve. It was as though there was nobody inside.

'Why did you change your clothes on the day your children disappeared?'

The only noise was the scratch of the solicitor's pen.

'Why won't you try to help us find Lily?'

Sam would lean forward, trying to catch her eye, trying to break through, to no avail.

'If you didn't do this, then you have a perfectly reasonable explanation for your actions. You could explain what you were doing down at the lake at the same time that your children vanished. You could tell me why you lied about being there. You would tell me why you hid your clothes and why you lied to your husband. And then we would be able to investigate other avenues and move closer to finding Lily. Please, Sarah, talk to us.'

Sam's voice was calm and measured, but Zoe knew that he'd be bursting inside. She would have talked if she'd been Sarah. The silence was baffling.

'You loved your children, didn't you?'

Not a flicker of emotion.

'Why won't you even answer this? Why won't you say that you loved your children? I don't understand.'

The solicitor looked up at Sarah, as though even he expected something, but the woman gazed down, head tilted slightly, saying nothing. Sam let the silence stretch, his eyes fixed on Sarah, urging her to come to the surface, to come back out and face up to what she'd done. But such tactics were fruitless. A knock on the door brought it all to a sudden close.

A nervous constable slipped inside and muttered an apologetic message in Sam's ear. Zoe saw him stiffen as he heard the young man's news, then nodded and let him go.

'Interview terminated; it's 11.23 p.m.'

He stood, glared down at Sarah, who didn't move, then marched out of the room. The solicitor looked around, confused. Not having any answers, Zoe sped out after Sam.

She found him in the corridor, marching away.

'Boss, what's happened?'

'She's dumped her brief,' he replied with a shrug, but Zoe could see the tension in his body.

Two constables hurried past, and she greeted them with a cheery nod. Their radios crackled and coughed as they passed. The corridor itself was tired and battered with a thin, industrial blue carpet which was pockmarked with stains. A male detective in his twenties – baggy suit and colourful socks – winked at Zoe as he slipped into the interview room opposite, carrying a cup of tea. It felt like home.

Zoe looked back at the open door of the interview room. 'How did she manage to do that when she was in there with us?' she asked.

'Quite.'

'And who has she dumped him for?'

Considering this, Sam led them back the other way, passing two recalcitrant teenage prisoners who jostled with the policeman who pulled them forward. One of the lads broke free and sprinted back the way he'd come, and a chase ensued. Zoe and Sam caught up with the melee in Custody, where they found the young man lying on the floor, kicking and screaming. He spat at the cop who somehow managed to keep his temper before subduing him. With the help of three others, he dragged the kid off to a cell to calm down.

Because of this furore, Zoe didn't notice her at first. The woman sat patiently on a bench, so polite and still that it was easy to miss her. But as the chaos died, so all eyes were drawn to the stranger in their midst. She didn't move until Sarah was led into custody by her solicitor. At this point she stood and went over to introduce herself.

Sam approached as the woman spoke hurriedly to Sarah, her voice too quiet to be overheard. Sarah listened and then nodded. It was the first normal, human behaviour she'd exhibited since they arrested her back in her house.

'Hello, I'm Helen Seymour,' the woman said, offering her hand to Sam and then to Zoe. 'I'll be representing Sarah Downing from now on.' She was small, and Sam towered over her, but this seemed to cause her no discomfort. At first glance she looked a little dowdy, and the eye slipped easily past her onto more interesting things, but Zoe found herself drawn in by her calmness. When she shook Zoe's hand, the grip of this fifty-something-year-old woman was surprisingly firm.

'I'm afraid it's been a bit of a wasted trip for you, Graham,' she said to the solicitor, who stood open-mouthed at her arrival. She offered Graham her hand, just as she'd done with Sam and Zoe, and he was simply dispatched. Then she turned back to face the cops.

'If it's okay with you, I'd like to have a quick chat with my client and then I'll come and find you. Shall we meet in the canteen?'

She looked at them and waited, hanging on their reactions as though their happiness really, genuinely mattered. But at the same time, she'd just strolled into a police investigation and derailed an interview. Zoe noticed the simple jewellery, gold hoop earrings, no wedding ring, and the smart leather bag that she carried.

'Yes, no?' Helen ventured when Sam didn't reply.

'Sure, no problem,' Sam replied, but didn't move. In reaction to this, Helen, whose hand had never left Sarah's side, gently guided her client away from them, talking quietly and earnestly throughout. Somewhere, someone started screaming; a man, wailing and roaring. Other voices rose to meet his cry but Helen seemed oblivious as she led Sarah out of sight.

Sam turned at once and he and Zoe walked out, heading for his office.

'Where did she come from?' Zoe asked. Sam shrugged, as per-plexed as she was. 'Well, I'm stuffed if I'm waiting in the canteen,' she said. 'Let's go back to CID and let her find us there.'

Pleased by this petty rebellion, they walked on, soon reaching the main staircase that lay in the centre of the building. Built in the 1970s, everything felt archaic and drably utilitarian. Warped wooden wall tiles were uneasy partners to a mosaic on the floor in garish cyans and aquamarines, all lit by harsh strip lighting which reminded those inside that this was a place for work, and work alone. Zoe liked it like this and felt comforted by the lack of pretension. She was buoyed by her return to the noise and the clutter, and bounded up the stairs happily.

But Sam followed more slowly. He was tired, they were making little progress and this woman seemed like she was going to make things slower and harder. All around, policemen and women shunted their duties before them. He saw a big, bulky skinhead who was being led down the stairs, flanked by two uniformed officers. The skinhead had tattoos that crawled up from his chest and wrapped around his neck.

'Don't touch me! Don't touch me!' he snapped, over and over. One of the men held his arm tightly, chatting calmly to his colleague throughout.

'Don't touch me!'

'Yeah, so we'll ask his mum. She'll be back around ten.'

'Don't touch me!'

'Fancy a curry tonight? Me and Charlie are going for something cheeky.'

'Don't touch me!'

Sam checked his watch. He had wanted to call home and let the girls know that he was back, but it was too late now, and if this carried on much longer, he worried that he'd be sluggish and grumpy in the morning. It made the stairs even steeper.

At the top a WPC had dropped a stack of files and was desperately trying to reclaim them as feet hurried past. Sam trod around her as delicately as his big feet would allow and then moved on up. The paintwork on the stairs was flaking and the last ten or so steps were sticky. There used to be a series of wall-mounted lights here, but they were constantly broken by prisoners (or frustrated police) and so they were taken down and now there were ungainly holes with wires jutting out, their tips wrapped in masking tape. The higher you got in this place, the more it felt like it was slowly crumbling away.

Sam pushed through a set of double doors that led to CID: a large open-plan space, littered with desks and computers. At either end were offices for more senior officers (like Sam), while the rest of the team all mucked in together in the middle – fifteen or so detectives who personalised their desks with football scarves, photos of their wives and kids or magazine snaps of semi-naked women. The room was rarely empty and it was hard to have a private conversation in here. Last month, DC Darren Heath's divorce had come through and he was the last person to know about it. Since Andrea's death, Sam had noticed that the gossip reached his ears a little more slowly than the others'.

He went into his office, passing a bored DC who was listening to someone on the phone while playing solitaire on his computer. He sat down at his desk and checked his in-tray, noticing the usual mountain of dull bureaucracy. There were framed photographs of the girls on his desk, plus a separate one for Andrea. It was of him and her together, taken the year before by Issy when they were on holiday. It sat behind the others, as though it was wrong for it to grab too much attention. Elsewhere, he had pictures on the walls. Buddy shots of him and the guys on golfing trips, of him receiving a commendation, certificates and congratulations.

Zoe burst into the room. 'So this is weird,' she said. 'I just asked Adam about Helen Seymour. And guess what? She's a silk. Not even a duty brief. A bloody barrister.'

The news was a jolt. 'A QC?'

'Uh-huh. What's a QC doing turning up in person to intervene like that?'

Sam went to the door and called out to Adam Brown – a misanthropic DS in his late thirties. His skin was pitted with acne and he was constantly rubbing his teeth with his tongue. Everything seemed to leave a bad taste in his mouth.

'Yes, Guv?'

'You know this new brief – Helen Seymour?'

'Of her. Seen her in action in court. She defended that mad bird six months ago – the one who stabbed her kid.'

Sam knew the case well – it had been one of the files that he'd taken with him to the lakes.

'Did she win?' Zoe asked.

'Always wins, apparently. She on your case?'

'Yeah.'

'Unlucky.'

'Alright,' Sam nodded, dismissing him, 'cheers.'

'No worries, Guv.'

Adam headed back to his desk and Sam shut the door again. His fingers drilled a rhythm on the door frame.

'Let's go to the canteen,' he said. 'I want her thinking we're utterly professional, thorough and respectable coppers.'

Zoe raised an eyebrow at this.

'Which we are,' he added.

'If you say so, boss.'

At that moment there was a sharp rap on the door, and when Sam turned he could see Helen Seymour waiting patiently outside. He opened it hastily.

'We were just heading down,' he said, a little too defensively.

'Oh, I'm sure, but I thought I'd come find you anyway. Save us all the bother. Shall we do this in your office?'

She stood there, smiling politely, waiting for him to let her in. He saw that all eyes in the office were on them, so he stood aside and gestured for her to enter. Zoe decided not to sit but leaned against the wall, stuffing her hands deep into her trouser pockets. The pose was designed to be unfriendly, but when Helen registered her, it was with a friendly nod. Sam went back behind his desk. The small office now felt bursting with the three of them inside it.

'So?' he asked.

'So,' she echoed politely. 'I'd like you to release Sarah Downing immediately.'

Sam laughed and she smiled, as though her words were indeed a comedy act. But Zoe saw the steel in her eyes. As much as she shuffled and shrugged, there was a ferocious tenacity underneath.

'Talk me through it,' Sam said genially.

'Sarah doesn't like cops,' Helen said. 'She's had bad experiences in the past. That's why she won't talk to you. She's a very fragile figure. I feel awful for her. I'm not blaming you for that, I hasten to add!'

She said the last line to Zoe but got no response. It didn't seem to bother her in the slightest and she continued with her same thoughtful, professorial manner.

'Now then, here's what happened. Sarah went down to the woods to get away from her husband. They're not happily married and haven't been for some time. You know this, I think. Anyway, she goes to the woods, gets stoned as she is wont to do and passes out. When she wakes up, she's covered in moss and grass and panics because she's ruined a rather lovely dress. So she hurries home, scared that her husband will flip out when he sees the mess she's in. Apparently there's a more unpleasant side to him that he reserves for her in private. Sarah then hides the dress because she thinks he'll go mad, and that's the end of it.'

'She told you all this?'

'She did.'

'In, what thirty seconds?' Sam leaned forward, his hands spread out on the desk before him. 'How long were you actually with her for? I'm amazed she even got to say her name in the time.'

'Well, once she felt she safe, she seemed very keen to unburden herself. Unless you're implying that I've made up her testimony. You're not implying that, are you, Detective Inspector?'

And there was the steel again. She sat primly in her chair but all the pressure was on Sam. He brushed it aside with a casual wave and mutter – 'Of course not' – then sat back and watched Helen, who waited for more.

'I don't believe her story,' he said when her eyes drifted to the framed photographs on the desk.

'I understand why you consider her a suspect, but you have no evidence.'

'We believe that there was more than just moss on the dress. We believe there was blood.'

'But you don't have the dress.' She said it a little sadly, as though she were embarrassed at his fruitless labour. 'Really, you have a lot of innuendo, but that's your lot.'

And then she turned to Zoe. 'What do you think?'

Zoe couldn't hold her eye and so Helen turned back to Sam.

'I understand your actions, there will be no follow-up, you don't need to worry about any civil cases for wrongful arrest—'

'Hey, hang on—'

'But you have to let her go now. You do understand, don't you? It's best for everyone.'

She felt so much older than either of them. It felt like they'd been playing at being detectives now she was in the room. Zoe had seen tough men squirm in that seat when Sam had gone for them. Helen, however, was unflappable. Sam seemed so too, but Zoe knew that he would be seething beneath the facade. She had absolutely no idea what Helen was thinking or feeling.

'Let her go, Sam. Please. Come back when you've got something concrete.'

She was carrying a file, which she placed into her fine leather case. She zipped the case shut, placed the bag on her lap, rested her hands on top, and waited.

'Who called you?' Sam asked.

'I'm sorry?'

'It's not normal for a barrister of your considerable calibre to be called to the station like this. This is the work of a duty solicitor.'

'You're flattering me now.'

'My question, Helen.'

'I was interested in the case. That's all.'

'Why?'

'That's all.' She glanced at her watch and waited.

'Does Sarah have any idea where Lily might be?' Sam asked.

'Of course not. She didn't do it.'

'I think she did.'

'No. She's their mother.'

Sam shook his head as though the comment were somehow risible. But that was all he could do.

'I'll let the duty sergeant know,' he said. 'She'll be released within the hour.'

'Thank you.'

Helen stood up and then looked back at Zoe.

'I'm surprised you don't say more,' she said as she passed. It was a simple, throwaway comment and there was no obvious bite or rancour in the tone, but Zoe felt the barb sure enough. Helen looked at her again, her head tilted slightly as though she was trying to work something out.

'Until the next time, then,' she said, shutting the door quietly behind her.

Something smashed before Sam stormed out.

THIRTY-ONE

Two hours later, Sam turned the key in the lock and was greeted by the familiar smell of home, a sensation rather ruined when he then tripped over three school bags, dumped by the door, and nearly broke his neck. Clambering over them and whispering curses, he slipped up the stairs, hoping that his noisy arrival might have woken one of the girls and given him a chance to say hello. But the house was deathly silent. He carried his bags into the bedroom and closed the door before turning on the light.

The room was just as it always was. Tidy, pleasant, marked by Andrea's eye and female touches. Sam put his things away, not really looking at any of it. It had felt fine when he'd shared it with his wife, but now he felt too big in here. He pulled the powder-blue throw off the bed and chucked the red velvet cushions onto it. When the girls wake up, he thought, I'll make them pancakes. I'll surprise them with tea in bed and then drive them both to school. Pleased with the idea, his mind drifted back to Sarah and then to Helen Seymour. He wondered again what had summoned a QC to a police station at that time of night. Would Sarah's husband have called for her? It seemed unlikely, especially if Tim had turned against her.

He tried to think of other things, but the loss and embarrassment of the collapsing case poked at him. He checked his watch. He'd need to be up in just over three hours. He rolled onto his side, where he was skewered by a photo of Andrea with the girls when they were toddlers. He rolled onto his other side to hide from them.

Sarah Downing said nothing for hours, didn't move, barely blinked, and then suddenly this stranger appeared and opened her up. It felt unnatural.

He worried about it some more, his eyes screwed shut to avoid the painful reminders around him. He should move some of the pictures, he thought to himself. But that would upset the girls. How would he get Sarah Downing to speak to him if and when he returned to Lullingdale? He wondered if there was any maple syrup in the cupboard and what Helen Seymour charged for a visit at such hours. He'd waited for Sarah to be released and had watched her for clues as she'd stumbled into the back of the police car. God, maybe Issy was being funny about food again and would only eat something like muesli or dry toast. And what about those other women and their terrible crimes? Was Sarah one of them? Is that what Mr Frey was suggesting? And how would he know?

He scolded himself for such thoughts. He was tired, he'd not slept well during the stay at Lullingdale and clearly wasn't thinking straight. He would get the girls to school, take the fallout from the case on the chin, and then work it all out on the back of a good night's rest.

Helen's polite nod and smile chided him. He wished he'd been better prepared for her. God, no doubt there wouldn't be any eggs downstairs.

He opened his eyes. It was light. He must have slept, but it felt like he'd been arguing and ruminating all night. Still, it must be early, as the house was quiet. He sat up and then saw the clock on the bedside table. It was gone ten.

He hurried downstairs. The house was empty.

Hoping for a note or some sort of acknowledgement of his return, he went into the kitchen. But the table was bare. He slumped against the worktop and clicked on the kettle just as his phone pinged with an email. It was from Mr Frey. A meeting, in an hour.

Sam stared at his contorted features in the kettle's chrome shell. He needed a shower and a shave. Cursing himself for sleeping so late, he hurried back upstairs. He looked for the bags by the door, but they were gone now, of course. As he thought about Helen Seymour again, he reminded himself to buy the girls fish and chips for dinner.

THIRTY-TWO

Zoe would often jog into work. She'd change once she got there, as this gave her an excuse to join in with the locker-room banter that she used to enjoy so much when she was a uniform officer. CID was great and she was proud to have made the grade, but she missed the more visceral, earthy tones of her friends who would soon be out on the streets, facing the world while she would be relegated to a desk and computer. Running in that morning, she'd thought about Lullingdale and the lake. The dull concrete and scattered litter seemed paltry compared with the steep slopes and sliding shale. But she was used to the thundering trucks, the graffiti and boarded-up windows. The familiarity of the drunk with his bottle outdid that towering sky. And best of all was the banter and easy camaraderie she knew was waiting for her. So she ran fast with a light step.

The locker rooms were in the station's basement. The ventilation down here was poor and the air was a little stale and damp. A massive boiler room nearby fed large pipes throughout the building, and these crawled along the basement's ceiling. There were separate female and male shower rooms but the locker room itself was unisex. And here, anything was fair game. It was an age-old maxim, fostered to encourage a sense of togetherness. It was, after all, them against the world.

Zoe threw on the jeans and sweatshirt that she always wore when she had a day without meetings. She needed to write up her report on the case and doubted that she'd talk to anyone besides Sam. She then went through to the large locker room, where big blue metal lockers adorned three of the four walls. The other wall was lined with a long wooden bench. Three male PCs were already there, attaching radios and batons to their belts. She greeted them warmly. They were only a year or so into the job, and while they were laddish in each other's company, they were still fresh-faced and eager to be a part of the team.

Zoe went to her own locker and listened to them discussing television from the night before and a failed date which had ended with an 'early bath'. The jokes were tame and early-morning. But then she heard the door open and a rougher, tougher voice called out to her.

'Bloody hell. There she is. The woman who let a child-killer waltz out the front door.'

Police Sergeant Malcolm Cartmell's voice was gravelly

and came from the back of his throat. He was in his fifties, and while his bulk was softening with age, he was still a big, squat, bruising figure. His hair was jet-black and his neck seemed in a constant battle against his tight shirt collar, although he betrayed no discomfort. His dark eyes were always crinkled, as though he was on the verge of either a joke or a question. In actual fact, the most likely thing on his lips was a curse.

Zoe turned to face him, and gave him a cheery finger. This got a big laugh from the three PCs.

'What happened, love?'

'You heard about the QC turning up out of the blue?' Zoe replied.

'Just because some posh doris walks in, doesn't mean you roll over and let her rub your tummy.'

'The suspect's out on bail. That's all.'

'Yeah? I bet Sam's spitting nails.'

It was cheeky of Malcolm to call Sam by his first name when he himself was only a sergeant, but this was typical of him. He'd been in the job long enough to claim an invisible rank beyond measure. While he might have failed to make the move up to Inspector (and beyond) he was considered the 'eyes and ears' of the place. He called the tune. He opened his locker and rummaged about inside.

'So what are we up to today?' he asked. 'Losing some paedophiles?'

Malcolm winked to the young PCs, who chortled on his behalf.

'Why, have you gone and got yourself caught again, Sarge?'

A whistle from one of the boys, surprised she was up for the challenge. Malcolm turned and faced her square-on.

'Are you calling me what I think you're calling me?'

'Oh I'd never call you anything to your face.'

To which Malcolm roared with laughter. 'This one,' he said, turning to the boys, 'has got bigger balls than the rest of you put together.'

Zoe swelled with pride as he patted her on the back.

'Sam thinks she did it,' Malcolm said, and she wondered if he'd heard this for real or was just reacting to the arrest. 'So you make sure we get her. I don't want that type out. They're the worst. Mums that kill. The worst of the worst. That's a sacred bond they're breaking there.'

The other young men all nodded earnestly.

Zoe looked at their eager faces and felt oddly set apart. They knew nothing about the case, and while she wasn't above casual conjecture on someone else's inquiry, something about this conversation reminded her of those finger-pointing villagers.

'You go get her, Zo-Zo,' Malcolm purred. Then he slammed his locker door shut.

THIRTY-THREE

Sam made it to the police station with five minutes to spare and was a little breathless once he'd raced up to the top floor to find the Chief Superintendent. His assistant wasn't there, so Sam knocked on the door. Mr Frey was sitting at his desk, his pen hovering over a stack of papers. Clearly pleased to see Sam, he waved him inside with a matey grin.

Sam sat awkwardly before his desk as Mr Frey made coffee for the two of them. It seemed to take for ever. Finally he sat down and poured milk into both cups.

'I'm sorry about the case,' he said.

'I moved too fast,' Sam replied, trying to counter what must be to come.

'I doubt it. Doesn't sound like you.'

Sam sipped on his coffee and waited for the second shoe to drop.

'Do you still think she did it?'

'Yes, sir.'

'Hard to prove?'

'Very. Unless we find the daughter.'

'She's alive?'

'I don't know, sir.'

'I've always liked talking to you. You're not afraid to be honest. You can't imagine the amount of smoke that gets blown up my arse.'

Sam just nodded. Behind him, he heard a small shuffle and Mr Frey stood up and went to the door of his office.

'No calls for a while,' he said quietly to his returning secretary. She nodded, glanced in and caught Sam's eye. But then the door was shut and the men were alone together.

'Are you okay to carry this on with just you and your girl?'

'Yes, sir.'

'Good. Wasn't helped by your unfortunate visitor last night.'

'Sir?'

'Helen Seymour.'

'Oh. Yes, sir.'

'What did you think of her?'

'She knows her stuff.'

'That's an interesting way of putting it.'

Sam didn't think it was that interesting, but he nodded and said nothing.

'Did you read the files I gave you?'

'Yes, sir.'

TOM GRIEVES

'Do you understand why I showed them to you?'

'Not entirely, sir. No.'

The answer seemed to irritate Mr Frey, but he simply took a deep breath and broke into a smile.

'Why do you think Ms Seymour appeared so swiftly?'

Sam noted the 'Ms'.

'I was surprised by it.'

'I bet you were. There's something you've missed in the files. Look at who defended every case.'

Mr Frey tapped the desk four times with his forefinger to make his point. *Hel-en. Sey-mour.*

'Every one?'

'That's right.'

Sam considered the coincidence and it made him uneasy.

'Do you know her, sir?'

Again there was that flash of irritation. Sam was asking the wrong questions.

'I know her,' Mr Frey said. 'We've grown up on opposite sides of the track, if you like.'

'And you think that . . .' Sam spoke slowly, hoping the Chief Superintendent would interrupt or finish the sentence for him. He didn't. '. . . her involvement in all of these cases is . . . suspicious?'

'What do you think?'

'I haven't had time to form a proper opinion yet, sir.'

'Come on, Sam, you're not being interviewed here. What do you think?'

'I think she clearly takes a particular interest in a certain type of case.'

'Getting women off murder charges.'

'I suppose so. Yes.'

'And what does that make her?'

'I'm not sure that I understand the question.'

Mr Frey looked up at the ceiling, as if becoming weary of how slow Sam was.

'Do you believe the story she concocted for Sarah Downing?'

'We don't know it was made up.'

'All that, in only a few minutes? After she'd barely spoken in the previous twenty-four hours?'

'It's unusual for a barrister with her reputation to risk inventing a story that quickly. It could easily backfire.'

'Maybe she didn't invent it that quickly.'

'Sir?'

'Maybe she had the story planned.'

'But if that was the case, then she would have needed to know in advance that Sarah Downing was likely to be arrested. She would have needed to . . .'

'Go on.'

'Sir. Are you suggesting that there is some sort of conspiracy here?'

Mr Frey shrugged.

'Because I don't believe in conspiracies. They're for nut jobs, generally.'

'And that's why you're the right man for this case. You're thorough, you're sensible and you're not easily swayed. Look, I don't know what Helen's up to. It may be she's just a perfectly brilliant barrister who happens to have a thing for women accused of murdering children. Are you sure you've got enough resources with just you and the girl?'

'I think so, sir. Yes.'

'Come back to me if you change your mind. A child is missing. And if her mother did this, then there's no way the bitch is getting away with it.'

He stood up and Sam did the same. A firm handshake sent him out of the door.

He walked back to CID slowly. He found Mr Frey strange and unreadable, but the questions of last night bubbled up again. Something about Helen Seymour. Something about her polite, calm professionalism. Something about the way she sat and watched.

Sam started to walk a little faster.

THIRTY-FOUR

Zoe caught up with Sam on his return from the Chief Superintendent's office. She'd gone out and bought a couple of takeaway coffees, expecting him to be brooding in his office after the night before. He was a bad loser. But when she found him, she was surprised to see that he was busy. He had several files on his desk and was working his way though them, his pen circling various facts and details.

'What have you got there?' she asked, placing his coffee on the edge of the desk for fear of it spilling onto the papers.

'Don't worry about it,' he replied, his voice distant.

She waited for him to look up, and when he did, he noticed the coffee she'd brought for him.

'Sorry,' he said a little sheepishly. 'Morning.'

'Morning to you, Guv'nor,' she said, slumping down in one of his chairs and banging her feet on his desk. 'I'll write up the case this morning.'

'Good.'

'Show you a rough draft. But it's all clear enough.'

'I think so.'

'You were right to arrest her.'

'I know.'

'Yeah, but this is me, your mate, backing you up.'

Sam waved his arms in faux worship, showering her with thanks, and they laughed and mocked each other like the old days. Eventually, however, she couldn't resist the itch that had to be scratched.

'What's with the files?' she asked.

Sam sighed, running his hand over the folder and then closing it as though its contents were somehow embarrassing. Zoe recognised their battered exteriors: these were the same files he'd had up at the Lakes.

'I've been asked to see if there's a connection between the Sarah Downing case and some others,' he said.

'It's not the Sarah Downing case,' she corrected him. 'It's Arthur and Lily's case. Sarah's not guilty yet, boss.'

He shuffled the files, a little awkward. 'Yes, you're right, of course.'

'And so what are the files then?'

'Crimes against children,' he said.

By women. She knew the cases. Everyone knew the cases.

'I don't understand,' she said. 'Why would there be a connection?'

Sam shrugged. He was just doing what he was asked. By

216

the Chief Superintendent, he reminded her. Zoe nodded, but she didn't like it. It smelled wrong.

There was a knock on the open door and they looked up to see Adam Brown standing there.

'Sorry to bother you, Guv. Got a little job for Zoe if you can spare her.'

Zoe looked at Sam and could tell he was eager to get her out of the room.

'Sure,' Sam said. 'What's up?'

'Just some thugs on the estate. Damage and whatnot. Uniform have called it in.'

'Right-o. Zoe, you good with this?'

'Whatever you say.'

She got up and followed Adam out. But before she left she turned back to watch Sam. She saw him pull open the file again and run his hand down a page. His eyes were narrow, his concentration utterly focused on whatever it was he was reading. Something about it, something about him, felt too keen.

They reached the Heygate estate by car, but parked a few minutes away on a more suburban road. Police cars had been known to be vandalised while unattended and Adam said he was fucked if he was going to let anyone touch his. The estate was a depressing, tawdry spot. A long run of high-rise towers linked by walkways were all made up of the same dirty grey concrete that felt oppressively hot in the summer and brutally cold in the winter. Kids mucked about on pushbikes and skateboards at the bottom while dealers would whistle and vanish as soon as the police appeared. There was graffiti everywhere. Zoe looked up at the tall buildings and saw a few faces staring glumly down at her. There was a sinking hopelessness about the whole place. Someone should just raze it to the ground, she thought. Knock it all down and start again. If you were born here, if you grew up here, then your future was set.

They passed the marked police car and headed up the concrete steps, avoiding the corners, which stank of piss. More graffiti tags, more litter. On the third floor they followed a walkway along and Zoe looked down at the kids below. They were pointing at the police car.

'Oi!' she yelled down at them. 'Try it! Go on. I dare you.'

The kids looked up at her with faces that were a mixture of defiance and mock innocence. She didn't move and eventually they cycled off.

'Nice one,' said Adam. 'Now they'll do it for sure.'

They reached flat 343 soon after. Adam knocked and the door was opened by one of the PCs who had been in the locker room that morning. Gareth Strivens was blond and tall, with that clumsy mix of someone who knows they're good-looking yet lacks the confidence to do much with it. It meant he could be brash and laddish one moment, then surprisingly diffident the next. Right now, he looked spooked.

'Alright?' Adam asked.

'Yes, Sarge,' the young man answered, standing aside to let them in. 'It's a bit full-on.'

Zoe clocked how pale he was.

'You okay?' she asked.

'Course,' he replied, and nodded a little too vehemently.

Zoe looked past him and saw Malcolm further down the corridor in what must be the flat's kitchen. He was talking to someone out of view, his hands out – placatory, calming.

Adam put a hand on her shoulder. 'I'll go see if the neighbours heard anything,' he said, and slipped out. Malcolm must have heard his voice because he turned and gestured for Zoe to join him. As she walked down the narrow passage, Zoe saw that several framed pictures – some photographs, some children's drawings – had been smashed and now lay on the floor. She stepped over them and entered the kitchen.

'This is Detective Constable Zoe Barnes,' Malcolm said, introducing her to a tall, thin black woman in her early twenties. She was neatly dressed and pretty, leaning with her back against the sink, arms folded. Her eyes met Zoe's and she nodded but barely spoke. Zoe could see that she had been crying and also clocked the shudder in her movements. Trauma.

'This is Miss Jade Adeyobe,' Malcolm added. 'She lives here with her two daughters. There was a break-in while she walked them to school. She doesn't think anything was taken.'

Zoe faced Jade and said all the appropriate things, while trying to work out why CID would be called to a break-in and vandalism case. This was a job for uniform, surely. But she also clocked the sombre tone to Malcolm's speech.

'May I see the damage?' she asked.

Malcolm glanced at Jade, who nodded, clearly close to crying again. He gestured to his right and Zoe followed his direction through the door and into the small living room.

The first thing she noticed was the smell. Then she saw the graffiti on the walls. Some of it was simple tags. But there was more – abuse, sprayed in two-foot-high lettering on every wall. *Slut. Bitch. Nigger. Fuck off. Go home. Get out.*

Everything was overturned. The sofa had had its stuffing ripped out and its yellow foam was strewn across the floor. Chairs had been broken and thrown against the walls – they lay in pieces in the corners of the room. Books had been torn apart, lamps destroyed, CDs and DVDs cast everywhere. There was so much debris that it took a moment before Zoe clocked the dead cat that lay on top of it all. It had been cut open.

'Fucking hell,' slipped from her lips.

She stood still, took it all in again so she wouldn't have to come back in there, and then went back to the kitchen.

'I'm so sorry,' were her first words. And this made Jade cry again.

'Animals,' snarled Malcolm. 'Bloody animals.'

'Do you have any idea who might . . . ?'

Malcolm interrupted her. 'There are a bunch of kids nicking metal, any metal, to sell on as scrap. It's been going on for a while. Yesterday she came home and caught them trying to dismantle the swings in the playground. So she had a word. That's all she did. Gave them a piece of her mind.'

'Okay. Would you be—'

'She knows who they are, alright.'

'And would you be willing to testify against them?'

Malcolm was silent at this and Zoe was given her answer. Jade simply hunched her shoulders, her fingers clutching her sides, digging into her own ribs.

'There are no witnesses,' Malcolm said, a little more quietly, 'and the CCTV hasn't worked for months now. Unless we get fingerprint evidence . . .' Malcolm shrugged. He knew it, Jade knew it. They all knew how this worked.

'We'll have a forensics team over very soon,' Zoe said, trying to hide their painful, obvious impotence.

'The kids will be home at three,' Jade said. She was breathing a little faster, her eyes flicking from side to side as she began to consider all of the things she'd now have to do.

'Do you have friends or family that they could stay with? Until you've had a chance to get things straight?'

221

Jade shook her head. She was all alone.

'Would you excuse us for a moment, Jade?' Malcolm said, and ushered Zoe back into the sitting room.

'Poor cow,' he said quietly.

'Yeah. Chance of fingerprints?'

He shook his head. 'They've done this shit so many times before. They know the game.'

The game. She nodded. They all knew the game. Then she pointed to the tags on the walls.

'Can we nail them for that?'

The tags were signatures. They were blatant admissions of guilt. But even though they said 'This is me, I did this,' they were still not enough to win a case in court. A defence lawyer could easily claim that someone else had copied them. Without the compelling evidence of a witness, DNA or CCTV (and that was often too blurred to secure a conviction), these cases were almost impossible to prove.

Malcolm didn't bother to reply and she couldn't blame him.

'I'll stay with her for a bit,' Zoe said.

'No, it's not your job,' he replied. 'You go do your CID thing, write it up, log it, blah-blah, bollocks. I'll stay with her.'

'Sarge?'

He shook his head, then sighed. 'I hate this. Feeling pathetic. She'll have to tidy it all up on her own. She's the one who won't sleep tonight. We're alright. They're alright. It's just her that's screwed. Because she spoke her mind.'

His radio crackled and he turned it down.

'I can't even start tidying up for her in case we disturb possible evidence. Bloody obvious there won't be none, but still. Can't even turn a table the right way round.'

He seemed too big for his uniform. His hands swung uselessly by his sides.

'And we know who they are,' he added with a hiss. 'You and I know exactly who they are. Eli Robinson and his mob.'

'Probably, yeah.'

'Not probably. Those are his tags on the walls. I've spent enough time chasing him to know it.'

Eli Robinson was known to all divisions of the local police. He was a tall, arrogant lad in his late teens, mixed race, with a history of small convictions that ranged from antisocial behaviour and vandalism to more serious offences such as aggravated burglary. His misdemeanours were a constant source of irritation: a kid out of control who one day would overstep the mark and end up in prison. After that he'd probably come back wiser and quieter, and all the more dangerous for it. But for now he was a wrecking ball of overblown pride and rage, smashing anything he could without hesitation.

Zoe saw Malcolm's anger rising and falling. She didn't

know what to say so she patted him lightly on the shoulder and trod carefully back towards the front door where Gareth stood, a useless patrolman.

'Nasty, eh?' he said.

'Seen worse,' she replied. She had, but she didn't know why she said it. An attempt to alleviate the gloom, maybe. A need not to wallow in it.

He nodded earnestly, his inexperience showing.

'Your sergeant's in a bit of a state,' she added. Behind Gareth, she saw Adam come out of the one of the neighbouring flats. He caught her eye and shook his head. Nothing to work with. As expected. She looked down and saw the kids cycling around the cop car again. One of them had been in that flat, most likely. Smashing and grabbing. The carelessness was disgusting.

'He doesn't like it when they do it to young mums,' Gareth said, and it took her a moment to rewind their conversation and remember what he was talking about.

'Yeah, he can be surprisingly chivalrous,' she said, but the joke was lost on the young PC.

She looked back inside and saw that Jade had come into the corridor and was staring into her sitting room, inspecting the damage. She saw her start to cry and watched as Malcolm put a big arm around her shoulder. Jade leaned into him, but Zoe knew this wouldn't make him feel any better. He wanted to be a champion. He always had been.

She felt a pang of sympathy for him as she noted his grey hair and the creases around his eyes.

'We'll get them, won't we?' Gareth asked. 'We'll catch the cunts, right?'

'Don't say that word,' she said.

'Oh God, it's political correctness gone mad,' Gareth scoffed. 'Cunt say this and cunt say that,' he said, a little too pleased with his own joke. Zoe just shook her head.

'But we will catch them, right?' he said, serious again.

Zoe looked down at the kids below. The ones on bikes rode in long slow, bored circles over and over. Not trying to run, not trying to hide. Slow circles leading nowhere.

THIRTY-FIVE

Sam arranged the six files on his desk into two neat rows of three. He kept everything evenly spaced and ordered. His handwriting was small and neat. He underlined and circled facts and important details as if he were an accountant checking the books. Although he was no slob, he was rarely so fastidious. But this work needed some insulation against the details.

He read again about the nanny and little Melinda, and how the poor young police constable had found the girl drowned in the bath. Then he cross-referenced the details with the death of James Harrison at the hands of his own mother in the local swimming pool. Both times, he found the same name defending them: Helen Seymour.

He opened the third file where Jenny Smeeton, the aunt of a young boy (Leo, eleven years old), had been found shaking and shivering on the kitchen floor after repeatedly smashing her nephew's skull against an old-fashioned butler sink. Blood was splattered across the ceiling as well as the floor and was all over her hands and body. Once again, Helen Seymour was listed as counsel for the defence.

Case four. At first, Lucy Harvey's death was considered a terrible accident. Her canoe had overturned during an adventure holiday just outside of Bolton, and because the incident had occurred on a bend in the river where there had been no witnesses, there had been no initial suspicions. However, the behaviour of Lucy's elder stepsister, Annie, had been noted by the police and by the trip's staff: a strange silence that might have been shock or grief but seemed colder and weirder. It was the small girl who had been sitting on the riverbank who eventually came forward – herself traumatised by what she had seen: a sudden lunge and attack; Annie holding her sister underwater until the little girl stopped struggling, and then letting her drift away, capsized, to be discovered later. Swabs under Annie's fingernails found traces of Lucy's skin.

Helen Seymour defended the case.

Case five found Yasmin Ng suffocated to death by the use of a plastic shower curtain. The prime suspect in the case, defended by Helen Seymour, was her mother, who had calmly phoned the police to tell them of her actions but then never spoke again.

And case six was Sarah Downing, whose son was found drowned in a lake and whose daughter was still missing.

Sam put a simple red line under Helen Seymour every time her name was listed.

No client ever spoke again once Helen had talked to them. Even when the evidence against them was undeniable, she found loopholes and technicalities to lessen their punishments. Both Elizabeth Harrison and the nanny who murdered Melinda were put into psychiatric units after being deemed unfit to stand trial. The evidence found by the police which incriminated Annie was deemed unreliable after Helen contested it. The veracity of the little girl's evidence against her was then derailed in court and a jury was unable to come to a verdict. Annie walked free. However, so traumatised was she by the events that she subsequently had a nervous breakdown and committed suicide.

Yasmin's mother was due to stand trial later that month, but the case had been delayed due to her deteriorating health (she'd been assaulted in prison) and the withdrawal of her previous confession – which Sam assumed was directly related to Helen Seymour's appearance as defence counsel – and the police were in chaos after vital evidence had gone missing.

The case against Jenny Smeeton should also have been cast-iron: blood on her clothes, found with the victim, no denial or alibi. But police were also troubled by the lack of motive, and once Helen was brought on board, a statement was released which claimed that Jenny had found the boy already dead and the blood found on her was only there because she had picked him up, desperately hoping that she might help in some way. The trial was due to begin in three months' time.

Sam took a clean sheet of paper and began writing.

1. Nanny. Bath tub. Drowning. Does not speak. Mad? Helen Seymour.
2. Mother. Swimming pool. Drowning. Does not speak. Mad? HS.
3. Aunt.

He stopped and went back over the file. A boy's head repeatedly smashed against a kitchen sink. He found the pathologist's report and checked it out. The sink had been full of water. A small amount had been found in the boy's lungs. The realisation shook within him: she had tried to drown him first. Clearly he had put up too much of a fight so she resorted to bludgeoning him to death.

3. Aunt. Sink. Drowning attempt? Does not speak. Mad? HS.
4. Stepsister. River. Drowning. Does not speak. Suicide. HS.
5. Mother. Shower.

A shower. Water again. Sam looked through the reports, looking for the connection, looking for water. The girl died while having a shower. But she was strangled, suffocated to death. He reread the files again and again, but there was nothing more.

5. Mother. Shower. Suffocation (??). Does not speak. HS.
6. Sarah Downing.

He stopped there and put the pen down. He ran his finger down the list. Women in a position of trust, brutally killing young children. Water was a key factor, though there was no obvious reason why. And each time, their cases were defended by Helen Seymour QC.

No connection beyond female. No age, no race. No motive in any case.
Children. Murder. Water. Helen Seymour.

Outside his office, two detectives raced past, talking excitedly about a case. They spoke high and fast, laughing with the adrenalin of the moment. Sam watched them and felt trapped behind his desk. All of these cases had been high-profile. They'd created hours of media coverage and reams of press print – the gruesome facts, latest speculation, debates about the monsters in our society, it ran and ran.

The internet had been ablaze with interest. But despite a geographical link of sorts (the North-West) no one seemed to feel there was any real connection. The fever eventually passed. And Sam was now the only one still watching. The connection wasn't just Helen Seymour. It was water. And it was women.

Sam wrote another word on the piece of paper: 'Witches'. Then he crossed it out and ran his pen heavily across the word until it was completely illegible. That bloody lake, he thought to himself. Those fells, that cold water and those silly, ancient fairytales. He was annoyed with himself for considering such nonsense. Why write it down? Why even think it?

He turned the other way and stood up, craning his neck to see out of the tiny window that offered some light and a tawdry view out onto the city. From where he stood, Sam could see cranes and church spires, poking up above dull lines of red tiles. The sky was a uniform grey, low and flat. Sam remembered the thick clouds that soared so high above the fells and the way the sun would make the lake change colour from grey to blue to gold. He remembered the water. He remembered Arthur Downing's body and he worried about Lily, maybe somewhere in the deep. Waiting for him.

THIRTY-SIX

Zoe caught Sam trying to slip out of the back entrance and she grabbed his arm playfully, telling him she was coming along for the ride. Uniform were working themselves up into a lather over the vandalism case, so she was glad to be away from them. She also wanted to keep an eye on him.

They pushed past a stream of PCs who came flooding out of their vans, laden with heavy riot equipment that was battered and scarred, and found Sam's car near the gates. Soon they were out and away. Zoe glanced back at the station in the car's side mirror as they set off: a dirty-grey monolith of concrete, squatting miserably amongst its polite neighbours.

'So where's the adventure?'

'Just checking through the details of an old case. One that got away.'

'I didn't think you ever let them get away.'

'It wasn't my case,' he replied, and she laughed before

he told her the details. A boy who had his head caved in on a kitchen sink. His aunt had been arrested for his murder. One of those damn files, she thought.

They drove for about forty minutes, finally stopping in a middle-class suburban street. It had trees planted tastefully in the pavement and semi-detached houses that cared about their small front gardens. The parked cars were oversize family models with bumper stickers warning of 'baby on board!' and there were Neighbourhood Watch stickers on view in several ground-floor windows.

Sam pointed Zoe towards a house in the middle, a forlorn 'For Sale' sign hanging at an angle outside.

Sam had a set of keys and he let them in. The house had been stripped bare – the parents had taken their other child, a daughter, far away – and there was, of course, no sign now whatsoever that anything untoward had happened here. But still, when they entered the kitchen, Zoe's eyes went straight to the sink, and then to the floor, as though she expected to spot some evidence of the crime. There was, of course, nothing.

Sam walked around the room slowly. Zoe watched him go to the window and stare out.

'What are you thinking?' she asked.

'There were no witnesses to the case,' he replied.

'None?'

'Not one.'

She went and stood next to him, and together they looked out at the overgrown garden at the back of the house. At the bottom was a small child's swing. The wind caught it and blew it ever so slightly, as though a ghost were riding it.

Behind the garden – which was only ten, maybe fifteen metres long – were other houses, flats, most likely. Sam and Zoe scanned the windows. Most were glazed with opaque glass: bathrooms or toilets. It was clear that nearly all the flats followed the same design and layout and that the views were on the other side of the building. But one window caught both their eyes. It was larger than the others, a study or sitting room – you could just make out the shelves and bookcases. It stared straight down into the kitchen. If someone had been in there, they would have seen everything.

They walked over to the next street and rang on the appropriate bell. After what seemed an age, a thin, crackly voice answered the intercom. A man.

'Yes?'

'Police. I'm sorry to bother you, it's nothing to worry about, but we'd like to ask you a few questions, please.'

There was always a pause when you told them who you were. Always that intake of breath and panic, no matter how innocent. Zoe waited for it, got it, and then heard a small mutter before the electronic buzz on the heavy front door let them in.

Sam and Zoe took the lift to the third floor and found the front door open and a small, bespectacled man in his fifties waiting for them. He wore a dull shirt, cardigan and neat brown trousers. He held a battered book in his hands and smiled nervously.

'Hello, sir,' Sam said, 'I'm Detective Inspector Sam Taylor, this is my colleague Detective Constable Zoe Barnes.'

They put on their most polite faces and showed the man their warrant cards, which he inspected carefully. Satisfied, he introduced himself as Arnold Heath and led them into the main room; a straightforward rectangular space which was lined, wall-to-wall, with shelves and books. It smelt a little musty. Arnold, a slightly effete fellow, explained that he worked as a lecturer at the university.

Zoe looked at him and then at Sam. The difference couldn't have been more stark.

There was a comfortable armchair positioned by the window. The cops went and stood by it and saw how it afforded a perfect view into the kitchen opposite. But when Sam asked Arnold whether or not he'd seen anything, they were disappointed to hear that he had only moved into the flat one month after the murder had taken place.

While Arnold fidgeted with excitement, no doubt keen to embellish the adventure for when he later saw his colleagues, Zoe found that she was watching Sam more than him. As her boss questioned and drew polite, slightly breathless answers from the academic, so she saw the way his eyes would always flick back to the window, to the flat opposite, to the sink. It was as though the crime was calling to him.

Zoe stared out of the window herself. The sun was shining into the kitchen and it reflected off the sink's taps. She remembered the paper's excitement at the gore and the now iconic photograph of the boy and aunt together, him wrapped tight in her embrace. In the photograph, it looked as though she was strangling him and the press had delighted in the misinterpretation.

Sam pushed on until Arnold had nothing more useful to offer. They took details of the estate agent who had helped let out the flat and excused themselves. They left him hopping with excitement at his proximity to a real murder. Zoe wished he'd seen it for real, then his ardour would die quickly enough.

Arnold waved to them as they got in the lift, hot and excited by their visit. Once the lift doors closed, Zoe sighed.

'Dead end.'

'Maybe.'

'Maybe? But he wasn't there.'

'He arrived a month afterwards, he said. Say someone moved out, they have to give a month's notice, right?'

'Uh-huh,' Zoe saw where he was heading.

'So if they gave a month's notice, then they'd have left

immediately after the murder. What do you make of that timing?'

The estate agent was a boorish man called Robin Shepherd who was extremely keen to get the police out of his office for fear of losing custom. He found the details of the previous tenant and handed as much over as he could to get them out of the way. They had a name, bank details, references and a mobile phone number. The man's name was Richard Howell. Sam didn't budge when the agent tried to move him towards the exit and instead rang the mobile number he'd been given. The line was dead. They also had no forwarding address. The agent tersely described Mr Howell as a problem. He had often been late on rent, had let the property run down and had then disappeared without any explanation.

'That's all I've got, I'm afraid,' he said, his hands stuffed deep into his red corduroy trousers.

Zoe sighed. This was going nowhere.

'So he just vanished?' asked Sam.

'Yup.'

'So how did you get the house on the market so quickly?' he asked. 'You couldn't just let it unless he'd given you formal notice, surely.'

'Well obviously he did.' Mr Shepherd turned and walked over to his desk and made a show of flicking through papers. But Sam didn't move. He seemed to grow, standing there, dead still in the centre of that office, saying nothing, just waiting. Eventually the agent looked up. He saw Sam staring at him and faltered, blustered something about checking some more and came back with a few more details – a phone call on behalf of the tenant saying that he was leaving and to put the house on the market with immediate effect. Sam pressed for the written confirmation that would be needed for such a request, and the agent, rather tetchy at this point, disappeared into the back room again to retrieve the required papers.

Zoe wondered why Sam was pushing like this, but she was also impressed by his actions. She'd have let this one go by now. But not her boss. It's what made him better than all the others and why she loved to work with him.

The agent returned with the forms, making it clear that he had nothing more to offer. He handed the papers to Zoe, avoiding Sam. They thanked him graciously, just to rub in how unhelpful he'd been, and left.

Sam took the papers off her once they were in the car and flicked through them.

'What a dick,' Zoe said. 'I bet he drives a bloody Range Rover.'

Sam wasn't listening. His eyes were locked on the last page of the papers.

'What have you got?'

He held the paper up for her to read. It was a simple

letter, typed, asking for all post to be forwarded to a specific address. The address was the legal chambers of a certain Helen Seymour.

'She hid a witness,' Sam replied.

'Bloody hell,' Zoe whispered. 'No, hang on, we don't know that for sure.'

'No? How else did her company's letter paper end up in that estate agent's hand?'

It was odd. It was undeniably contentious.

'Maybe, boss,' she said. 'But even if she did, how the hell would we find the witness to prove it?'

Sam didn't reply to this, he was too busy flicking through the papers again. Zoe could feel the heat burning off him. Usually she was the same. They were like bloodhounds chasing a newly laid scent. But this one was becoming special for him without an obvious reason why.

'I want you to find out who's paying the legal bills on Sarah Downing's case,' he said out of nothing.

'Okay,' she said, and he turned the key in the ignition and drove off fast. She watched him as he crunched through the gears, his mind spinning in odd directions. When they got back to the station, they were separated when some of her mates cornered her, trying to cajole her into taking part in a team run for charity, an extreme race involving mud and river crossings. Zoe was up for it, of course, but when she finally caught up with Sam, she found that he'd closed the door and was, once again, poring over the files. Checking, circling, cross-referencing. She watched him through the glass for a while. But this time, she didn't go in.

THIRTY-SEVEN

Sam worked late on the files. He found out little more, but absorbing all the details helped him secure them in his mind. He lost track of time in doing so and returned home later than planned.

He could hear the blaring noise as he walked up to the front door and stepped inside to find his eldest daughter, Issy, doing karaoke with two friends in the sitting room. They screamed hysterically into a tinny microphone and bounced up and down on the sofa, wearing tiny jean shorts and low-cut T-shirts – wannabe popstars. Not so mini, Sam thought to himself as he noticed the way they danced; scarily sexual and adult.

'Hi, Mr Taylor,' yelled Marie cheerfully as she ran her hands through her hair as an actress might do. She was fourteen, Amazonian, and had a cheery, youthful exuberance without which she could easily have passed for nineteen. Sam waved back as enthusiastically as he could. The other girl, Susan, also waved but didn't stop singing the inane pop tune. Issy caught her father's eye and then blanked him. She was sporting a nose-ring and he wondered whether it was a 'present' for him. If he shouted at her, he'd annoy her, but if he said nothing he'd annoy her more. She was pretty, a little heavy, and her clothes looked uncomfortably tight. Sam decided to bite his tongue and went into the kitchen, shutting the door, which did little to muffle the music and girls' voices. He remembered Issy when she was smaller, when she would run to him and cuddle him. Her face had been so open, her eyes so wide and expectant. Time had moved on.

Magda, the nanny-cum-housekeeper, was in the kitchen, placing a casserole dish into the oven as Sam entered. She was twenty-something with a boyish haircut that did not suit her. She wore baggy, shapeless clothes and seemed to move in slow motion; everything was a dull grind for her. Sam liked the lack of fuss she brought to the house, and she never complained or laughed or did anything beyond the exact duties asked of her. At first it was rather off-putting, but soon everyone just got on with life around her.

'Hi, Magda.'

'Hello, Mr Taylor.'

'How are you today?'

She pulled a face that seemed to say, today is just the same as every other shitty day. She never looked at him. Then she went to the sink and started washing up. Sam wanted to slob out at the table, open a beer, go through his reports, but she made him feel guilty. Shortly before she died, Andrea had done up the kitchen, and it felt sparkling and beyond the sort of thing that a man like him could afford. Magda's miserable drudgery seemed to reinforce this sense that he wasn't worthy. He considered asking her about her family back home, but couldn't bear the silence and the next 'whatever' face that he'd get in return. He left her to her duties and went upstairs.

It was tattier here, and all the more homely for it. The money had all gone on the kitchen, and the carpet upstairs was threadbare. He knocked on a closed door and heard the small call for him to enter.

Jenny's bedroom was neat and dainty. His twelve-year-old daughter was sensitive and studious and had buried herself deep in her books after her mother had died. Whenever Sam had tried to talk about Andrea with her, he had always hit a wall.

'It's fine, Dad,' she'd say sadly. 'There's nothing we can do, anyhow.'

It seemed true, but he wished there was a way that he could make her laugh in the way she used to. The way her head would fall back and her body would shake.

Jenny was sitting at her desk, and although her head was bowed over her work, the sight cheered him immediately.

He was also grateful for the small smile she offered. She was still wearing her school uniform and didn't push him away when he kissed her, although she remained seated at her desk.

'What's up?' he asked.

'Geography, then history.'

'Can I help?'

She gave him a look that said, not unkindly, 'Fat chance.' He sat on her bed. Nothing seemed to have changed in years. Small teddies were neatly organised by her pillow, a stack of books lay by the bedside table. Everything was ordered and just as it should be.

'Can I help you?' she said, with a voice and tone that was much too mature for her age. Sam blinked, caught snooping.

'I've hardly had a chance to talk to you in ages.'

'Well, here I am.'

So she was. Sam's mind went blank.

'School?'

'Fine.'

'Your friends?'

'Yeah.'

'Your sister?'

'She's an idiot, Dad.'

He liked that. And she was pleased that he did.

'And how's Gran?'

'We don't see her, really.'

'How come?'

'She's always locked away in her room.'

'Well that's not right. I'll go see her.'

Her shoulders rose and fell, her eyes still on her school books. He sat there and felt stupid.

Sarah Downing popped into his head: her quiet, steely gaze as she was led from custody.

'Dad, I really need to get this done.'

Her words pulled him back.

'Sorry, yes, sorry. Maybe we could do something on Saturday? Go out, do something.'

'I've got netball.'

'Oh. Right. Sunday then.'

Another shrug. He decided to take it as a positive. Then he stood up, brushed down the neat duvet to get rid of his heavy imprint, and left her to it.

He shut the door quietly behind him. Below he could hear Issy and her friends shrieking away. He looked along the landing, but didn't want to go to his own cold, lonely bedroom, so instead he followed the narrow stairs up to the top where his mother lived. The loft was the warmest part of the house, and while they worried about the stairs, his mum seemed happy up there with an ever-burning radiator. Sam knocked, waited for an answer and decided to enter anyway.

Elaine was asleep in her armchair. Her head had slumped to the left and she breathed heavily in her sleep. The television was on. Sam found the controls on her lap and switched it off. He looked at his mother, still wearing a smart, pleated skirt, white blouse and a cardigan just as she'd done all her life. Her hair was a brilliant white. He leaned forward and squeezed her hand gently. It woke her and she looked at him and, for a moment, her face lit up with delight.

'Are you back?'

'I'm back.'

'I missed you, darling.'

'I missed you too, Mum.'

That last word kicked her, he saw it. The sun set behind her eyes and was followed with a gentle nod. She tapped his hand with hers.

'Why did you switch off the telly?'

'Were you dreaming of Dad? Just then, when I woke you?'

'No, why?'

'I just thought . . .'

Elaine pushed his hand away from her as though he'd said something unpleasant, then straightened her skirt. He found that he was kneeling in front of her. She used to read to him like this when he was a little boy. He remembered listening to *Swallows and Amazons*, rapt.

'How have the girls been?'

'What girls?'

'The girls. Jenny and Issy.'

'Oh them.'

'What does that mean?'

'They've got no time for me.'

'Mum, you're meant to be watching out for them.'

'And who looks out for me?'

He sighed and said nothing. Elaine brightened again.

'That Magda girl is a dumpy old misery, isn't she?' she said, and laughed. 'And her cooking's atrocious. I tried to tell her how to do a decent stew and she got all hot and bothered. And have you seen her with the Hoover?'

'Mum . . .'

'When you're away, I'm in charge. Isn't that right? You need to tell her to do what I say.'

'Okay, Mum.'

'What's that racket?'

'That's Issy and her friends. Karaoke.'

'God help us.'

'I know.'

'What's she doing messing about like that? She'll wake the baby.'

'What baby?'

'Her baby! For God's sake, Archie . . .'

He saw her look at him, and then a terrible flicker of doubt clouded her features.

247

'Mum. It's Sam. And Issy—'

'I know who you are. And I know much too much about that daughter of yours. Acting as she is. She's grown up too fast.'

'You said she had a baby.'

'I was confused.' Her voice stung with anger. 'Just a bit confused. Just for a second. Don't jump down my throat.'

'Sure, Mum.'

He tried to take her hand again, or pat it just to show that he was on her side, but she was stiff now and had turned herself away from him.

'And turn the telly on. It's too quiet, locked up here with no bloody visitors. How am I meant to cope when you won't let anyone visit me?'

There was no point answering. He felt so hot in here, his throat was dry and prickly. He muttered an apology and stood up, relieving his cramped legs.

'Have you eaten, Mum?'

'She'll bring it up,' Elaine replied tartly.

'Well maybe we could eat together.'

'You don't need to worry about me.'

'Mum.'

'You need to be worrying about those daughters of yours. The things they're getting up to, Sam. It's disgraceful.'

'Like what?'

Elaine just pulled a face. And then, for no discernible reason, she smiled again.

'You were such a good boy. A little tyke, but good as gold, really. I remember Mr Drayson coming round after you'd smashed those panes in his greenhouse and I wouldn't let him come across the threshold. You hid in my skirt. Do you remember?'

Sam didn't, but he nodded anyway. Elaine switched on the television and it roared into life. Her gaze fixed onto the screen and once again she was lost to him. He shut the door behind him and the corridor outside was cool and gloomy.

He went back down to the first floor. Issy was singing now – he recognised her voice and he could hear the lyrics – heavily sexualised and inappropriate. He heard her begging someone to 'sex her up' and he felt nauseous. Her friends screamed with delight.

He went to the doorway of his own bedroom. Magda had tidied up and it looked neat and proper. A stranger's room. He backed away.

He saw Jenny's door and thought about going in again but found that he was unable. So instead he retreated to the bathroom, shutting the door, then locking it and sitting down on the loo. He put his head in his hands and closed his eyes, slumping against the towel rail. He wondered how long he would have in here before one of the girls came banging on the door.

This was stupid, he told himself. This was his house.

The porcelain was cold on his back but he didn't get up. He looked at the grout that needed replacing and at the tatty shower curtain that was stained brown at the bottom. He listened to a drip form inside the toilet cistern that hinted at repairs, and wondered and worried.

The case slithered around and he took comfort in its escape. And then he remembered Ashley's crooked smile as they fucked in the woods and he felt dirty and stupid. Never do that again, he told himself. Now back at home, such promises were easily made. He resolved to buy a new shower curtain at the weekend. He'd go watch Jenny then let her chose one after the netball. He tried to fix his mind on such matters, but Helen Seymour kept knocking. He didn't want her here, not in his home. Andrea had always guarded the door and kept their home safe. But Lily was still missing and no one could bring her back except him. There was too much to fix.

And then the phone rang.

THIRTY-EIGHT

Barely half an hour after hiding in the bathroom, Sam was once again striding through the police station.

A young woman in her late teens had tried to abduct the two children she'd been babysitting. Things had taken a turn for the worse when she was then spotted leading the boys onto a high bridge. A stand-off had ensued. The police were able to save the children but the woman had jumped, and died.

Woman, water, children. It was all Sam needed to have him racing for the door. He reached the police station and hurried to the soft interview suite. The walls were painted in sickly pastel blues and pinks. It was meant to be calming but Sam always thought it felt like a hospital.

In the interview room – a large space with cuddly toys, wooden train sets and sofas – two detectives sat on the floor talking gently to the two boys who had been abducted. Their parents sat with them, grey-skinned from the trauma. The mother would occasionally pull one of the children to her, as if to reaffirm the truth that her little one was not dead, and hugged him tight to her to banish the darkness. The husband just sat still, listening to it all with that faraway look that people get when they've strayed too close to their nightmares.

Behind a two-way mirror, Mr Frey watched the proceedings. He nodded grimly at Sam as he came in.

'Nasty business.'

'Sir. Just heard about it.'

'They'd used the babysitter several times before, apparently. Had no idea that she had any mental problems of any kind.'

'Is that what this is, sir?'

Mr Frey just shrugged. He turned his attention back to the room. 'Apparently the girl had been eager and keen, they liked her a lot, and then suddenly this. The parents are too shaken up to say much more.'

Sam looked at the two boys in the room. They seemed happy enough. A little wide-eyed with the attention, perhaps, but not fully aware of its import. The elder, Jamie, was seven years old and his younger brother was called Finn. They were still dressed in the pyjamas that they were wearing when the girl had taken them out of the house. They had been barefoot when she led them across the bridge, to the railings and to the terrible drop below.

The older of the detectives, Inspector Philip Bryce, sat on his heels facing the boys. He had grey hair and a worn-in face that made him excellent for such work. It was a face that people naturally trusted.

'You know, I've got five grandchildren,' he told the two boys. 'But no boys. All girls, can you imagine that?'

'Stinky!' shouted Jamie, and Finn giggled. Weary smiles broke out from the parents at this.

'It's a joke in the house,' the mother explained. 'I'm the only girl so I get picked on.'

'You don't pick on your lovely mum, do you?' Bryce asked, wide-eyed.

'Yes!' the boys screamed back.

'You big meanies!' he laughed. The DC with him, a smiley black woman in her twenties called Anne, laughed at this. The room was warm and safe. The children, easily distracted, messed about with the toys in front of them.

'You had a bit of a busy night,' Bryce said. The boys nodded back at him.

'What's happened to Tasha?' Finn asked.

'Nothing's happened to her, she's fine. It's you guys we're worried about.' The boys looked up at him, confused. 'Well, it's not normal for big boys your age to end up on a bridge when it's got so late, is it?'

'Tasha said it was the only way to be safe,' Jamie replied. Finn nodded.

'Safe?'

'Yes, safe from them.'

'Who's them, then?' The cheerful tone kicked against the question.

'She didn't say.'

'Did she seem scared of them?'

The boys both nodded vigorously.

'But you weren't scared, were you?'

'I wasn't, but Finn was. He's a girl. Stinky!'

Finn wailed at this and scratched at his brother, but the chaos was soon quelled. Another cop came in with a tray of hot chocolates and after some chat about this and that, Bryce brought the conversation back to Tasha.

'She's great, isn't she?'

The boys nodded happily. Unfortunately, some bright spark had put little marshmallows in the hot chocolates and Jamie was now more interested in counting how many there were in each mug to be sure that they both had the same and that it was all fair.

'So Tasha was worried about "them", was she? Did she ever mention them before?'

'At bedtime.'

'When she tucked you in?' Bryce asked and Jamie nodded. 'She told you bedtime stories?'

'Not just stories.'

Sam glanced at Mr Frey, but the Chief Superintendent's eyes were locked onto the children.

'How do you mean, Jamie?'

Jamie shrugged, a little bored, and stuck his fingers into his drink to pull out a marshmallow.

'Jamie, why do you think that these weren't just bedtime stories?'

The boys looked shifty and guilty all of a sudden.

'Listen, lads, you can't say a thing that would get you into any trouble. Mum, Dad, isn't that right?'

The parents nodded eagerly behind them.

'You must tell them everything you know, darling,' the mother said, and Sam could hear the worn exhaustion in her voice. 'It's alright, I promise.'

'They wanted to hurt us,' Jamie said solemnly. 'They wanted to eat us. Tasha was the only one who could stop them. That's why she kept coming to babysit. To make sure they couldn't get us.'

'Who were they? Jamie? Did she tell you who they were?'

Jamie shook his head, solemn and scared by the dead woman's words.

'Did you feel safer when Tasha was with you?'

They both nodded immediately.

'But you didn't tell your parents about this?'

'No.'

'Why not?'

'She said they wouldn't believe us. And then they wouldn't let her come over and protect us.'

Finn looked tearfully up at his father. 'I'm sorry, Daddy.'

All of the pent-up fear and emotion suddenly came pouring out of the man and he fell upon his son in a tight embrace, kissing Finn all over his tiny face as tears poured from his own.

'It's okay, my boy, it's okay. Everything's okay.'

Bryce leaned in closer, sitting cross-legged before the boys.

'Can you tell me some of the stories she told you?'

'She said they have claws and teeth like leopards. They look normal, so you can never tell. But they come at you in the night . . .'

'And eat your eyes out,' said Finn, completing the story with an eerie reverence.

'They start with your eyes,' Jamie continued, a little bossily, as though Finn hadn't got it right. 'Then they claw off your face. And eat it raw like sushi.'

'Tasha said that?'

The boys nodded back solemnly.

'They eat you all up, bit by bit—'

'Even the bones!'

'Especially the bones, you dummy,' Jamie scolded. 'They eat all of you so that there's nothing left. No one will ever find you 'cos you'll be all inside her tummy.'

'Her?'

Jamie nodded.

'You said "them" before, Jamie,' Bryce said. 'Now you're saying it's a woman?'

'Not just one. There's a gang.'

'A gang of women? Who eat children?'

The boys nodded eagerly. Bryce glanced at the mirror and raised his eyebrows – he didn't believe any of it and wanted to wind this up.

Mr Frey glanced at Sam.

'What do you think?'

'We need to know what else she told them,' Sam said.

Anne was called out of the room and joined Sam and Mr Frey behind the mirror. She listened to Sam's questions with the politest of frowns.

'She's just a nutter, Guv. Probably schizophrenic. I don't think the parents are going to want to hear more of this stuff.'

'Just ask for more.'

Anne glanced at Mr Frey but he was stony-faced. Confused, but not willing to go up against her superiors, she returned to the room. She talked quietly to Bryce and Sam saw his displeasure at the news. But he did what he was told.

'Jamie,' Bryce said, settling down before the boy again. 'When did Tasha first tell you about all this?'

'Oh, she's always known,' the boy nodded wisely.

257

'And was she scared that they were coming to the house? Is that why she said you should go in the car with her?'

'She said she could feel her coming. She said you can always feel it, but you just don't realise what the feeling is. It's like a cold bit on your neck.'

'On your neck?'

'Yes, at the back. She said she'd felt it and she knew she was coming.'

'Yeah!' Finn, jumped in. 'And she said it was a big one, a really scary one. She was going to chew into my stomach through my belly-button—'

'Is this helping anyone?' the mother interrupted.

'She was going to hurt us, Mummy,' Finn wailed. He was crying now and it set Jamie off too.

'Okay, okay, let's all relax, no one's going to get eaten,' Bryce said, but the boys were not so easily calmed.

'I've felt it, sometimes,' Jamie said tearfully. 'I've felt it when your neck goes cold and you know there's one about.'

Anne stood up, keen to bring this all to a halt.

'I can feel it now!' Jamie suddenly squealed.

'Me too!' shouted Finn and the two boys suddenly huddled together.

'She's coming,' whispered Jamie.

'No one's coming. Just relax, boys, you've had a very late night, but there is nothing to be scared of. I promise.' Bryce stood and laughed loudly, trying to barge the fear out of the room.

'She's coming, she's coming,' they muttered together, trance-like.

They stood back to back, as if this were an action long rehearsed, repeating the words over and over. The mother looked at Bryce, exasperated, and started to complain. The father, taking her lead, snapped angrily in support.

Anne and Bryce went to the boys but they flinched at their touch as though anyone trying to prise them apart would hurt them as a result. No one knew what to do.

'She's coming.'

And, although they couldn't see anyone, the boys looked towards Mr Frey and Sam, staring into the mirror. Sam felt their fear. He wanted to smash through the glass and reassure them that they were safe, that he wouldn't let anyone hurt them. But then he heard her footsteps. He recognised their fast, percussive rhythm as they echoed along the corridor. A moment later, Helen Seymour stepped into the room.

'She's coming,' the boys whispered tearfully behind the glass. But Sam couldn't see them now – he just stared, slack-jawed, at Helen as she quietly closed the door and stared at the two men. She looked momentarily at Sam and then, more heavily, at Mr Frey.

'What are you doing here?' Mr Frey snapped. 'There's no one to defend. The woman's dead.'

'Yes, I heard once I got here. Mixed messages,' she said with a shrug, but made no attempt to leave.

'So go away then,' the Chief Superintendent replied. 'There's nothing for you.'

'But what are *you* here for, Jeremy?' she asked.

They stared at each other, the barrister and the Chief Superintendent. Behind them, Sam heard Anne and Bryce calming the children as they were herded out of the interview room.

Helen was the first to look away. She glanced at Sam again, then walked out, leaving the door open in her wake. He looked back through the mirror – the room was now empty. He turned to Mr Frey, but his boss was lost in thoughts of his own.

Sam slipped out and followed after Helen, letting her footsteps guide him to the front of the station, and outside. She stopped when she got to her car and turned to find him watching her. Neither spoke. Sam found himself rooted to the spot, unable to pursue her across the road. He was stuck on the pavement, transfixed by her.

Her eyes took him in. They stared at each other through the passing traffic that raced between them. They sized each other up. No words, no gestures, no theatricals.

After an age, Helen let her gaze fall. Calmly, coolly, she got into her car and drove away, leaving Sam to stalk the shadows.

THIRTY-NINE

Zoe hung around in CID long after most of the team had gone, hoping to catch Sam, until she realised that he'd slipped away without telling her. While she was hardly his mother, she was disappointed when she tried his mobile and it rang onto voicemail. She hung up without leaving a message. She had done as he asked and investigated Helen Seymour's funding and payment for the Sarah Downing case. Although such information was confidential, she was able to determine that the work was being done pro bono. It seemed that Helen had sought out the case and made it her own. On top of it was the revelation that she might have made a witness disappear. Zoe could certainly understand Sam's interest in the case. But she didn't want him to do it without her.

A little disconsolate, she headed back down to the locker rooms to change into the more feminine clothes she'd brought with her – she was due to see some girlfriends later for a boozy night of nattering. But she'd hardly got round to taking off her trainers when Gareth came running in, breathless and flushed.

'We got him!' he said, hurrying to his locker and pulling out his baton from inside.

'Say again?'

'Eli Robinson. He's only been caught tagging one of our sodding cars! Malcolm's spitting feathers!'

He fixed his belt and charged out. Outside, Zoe heard more footsteps and shouting. She heard one of them banging his baton against the wall as he ran.

'Come on, let's get the fucker!' someone cried, his high voice echoing in the corridor.

Zoe pulled her trainers back on and ran after them. She hurried into the back lot where several uniform officers were piling into a van. She slowed and tried to look casual as she came up to them.

'Alright, Zoe?' called the driver, a squat constable in his late twenties.

'Hiya, Dion. What's up?'

'Nothing. A bit of cleaning is all,' he replied, and the men in the back of the van laughed hard at this.

'Where's Sarge?' she asked.

'Already at it, love.'

The cold November sky was dark and cloudy, lit by the orange glow of the city's street lamps. Behind her, another

PC came charging out of the station and dived into the van.

'About time, Lee. Come on, Dion, let's fucking do it!' screamed Gareth. He tapped his baton against his thigh, pumped and over-eager, then went to pull the van's sliding door shut. Zoe leaped forward and jumped inside.

Gareth paused and stared at her.

'This is uniform business, darling. Off you pop.'

Zoe saw the hard faces that stared at her. But they were young, still puppies, and there was no way that she was going to let them order her about.

'I fancy coming along. Hurry up then, or we'll miss all the fun.'

No one moved for a second. Gareth didn't know what to do, his adrenalin pushing and pulling at him until, with a small cuss, he grabbed the sliding door and ripped it shut with a heavy metallic clang.

'Come on then!' he roared. 'Let's do it!'

The estate was only a ten-minute drive from the police station for a normal car, and only five or six when Dion was at the wheel. No one spoke as the van raced through the streets. Zoe stared out of the scarred windows (scratched and battered from countless assaults) and saw people stop and gawp as the sirens and lights screamed their presence. A group of three kids, chatting together in a huddle, turned and shouted abuse at the van as it passed. Further on, others would glare at them and gesture their hostility with fists and fingers, but they were gone in seconds as they charged towards their target.

When they reached the estate, Zoe hopped out first, getting out of the way so the others could charge off. It only took a minute before they were gone and all that was left was her, Dion and the van's throaty engine. His radio crackled and then fell silent. He peered out into the murky alleyways ahead, expectant.

'Why are we here, then, Dion? Really?'

'Best you don't ask, Zo-Zo,' he said and raised his eyebrows slightly, as if it wasn't something he wanted to be a part of. But she knew him better than that. She looked up at the dark concrete towers above. Inside the flats, television screens flickered in sync from different windows. She could see figures gazing down from balconies while others were busy in their kitchens, oblivious to the police's arrival. On the ground, however, there was no one at all.

'Alright, bored now,' she said.

'Silly cow. I'm not driving you back.'

'Don't worry your cotton socks about it, I'll sort myself out. Laters.'

'Yeah,' he said, but he was staring out again ahead of him, itching to be a part of whatever was going on.

Zoe walked away and then, when she'd turned the corner, broke into a run. She doubled back, slipping lightly through the empty walkways. She knew the estate well from her days back in uniform and she had a hunch that if Eli Robinson was running from the cops, he'd either hide in one of his friends' flats – as she imagined the PCs were guessing (and she heard heavy banging on a door as she ran to confirm this) – or he'd hide in the shadows, laughing as the cops chased shadows and were forced to return home empty-handed. Tagging a cop car was provocative, to say the least. When she first joined the station, she remembered finding him and three mates in a dead-end alley to the south of the estate, giggling together as they burnt an old man's prized possessions in a metal bin, destroying evidence that might have incriminated them. It was the first time Zoe had seen Eli and he stared at her that day with a wild, aggressive confidence – daring her to come closer, itching for a jostle and a fight.

She ran towards that same alley now. The other cops were running above her, across the concrete walkways, noisy and full of bluster. But there was no noise ahead and she slowed, thinking that maybe she was making a mistake. But then she heard the whimper.

Eli was lying on the floor on his stomach, his head twisted to the side, staring out at her. Malcolm was standing over him and as she approached them, neither man moved. But then she noticed that Malcolm was panting from his exertions. As she got closer, slowing to a walk, she caught the reflection of a street lamp in the blood on the concrete floor, and then she saw the bovine, glazed stare of Eli – unfocused and semi-conscious.

'Little tyke went for me,' Malcolm said, a little breathless. 'Self-defence, love.'

She stopped short of them. She could see the wound to Eli's head now. It wasn't the sort of injury you get from a single defensive blow.

'Reasonable force,' he added and winked at her.

Zoe didn't move. She watched Eli and felt sick as his tongue slowly slipped out of his mouth. He twitched and suddenly Malcolm was beating him again with his truncheon, this time around the back and kidneys.

'Don't move, don't you dare bloody move,' he hissed, timing his words to the cruel, metronomic beat of each strike.

'Sarge . . .' she said quietly. But the attack continued. She saw Eli's eyes roll up into his head.

'I said don't move, you little runt . . .' Malcolm grunted and spat.

Behind her, Zoe heard the crunch of boots and turned to see two PCs rushing along the alley. Malcolm saw them too and stopped. He sucked air into his lungs and stood tall and proud over Eli's inert body. The two young cops stared at him, shifting uneasily.

'Little bastard went for me. With this,' Malcolm said

loudly, stepping away from the body and grabbing a metal bar which he held up. 'I'm lucky he didn't brain me.'

Eli's eyes fluttered and closed.

'The kid went mad, totally out of control. Bloody animal,' he added. And then he pointed at Zoe. 'She'll tell you. Our Zoe saw the whole thing.'

All eyes turned to her, but all Zoe could see was Eli and the blood. His unconscious body suffered another involuntary spasm and for a second she thought that Malcolm was going to hit him again. But no one moved.

'Call an ambulance, lad,' Malcolm said to one of the PCs, who hurriedly did as he was told. Malcolm went over and stood very close to Zoe. She could smell his breath.

'Glad it was you that found me,' he said quietly. 'A proper cop. Part of the team. Knows what's what.'

She didn't acknowledge the comment.

'Had it coming, didn't he?' Malcolm said.

'Ambulance is on its way, Sarge,' said the young cop behind them. She heard the words and heard Malcolm thank him in his hearty, confident, blokish manner. And then she felt his hand on her arm.

'Zoe. You saw him go for me. You saw that I had no chance.'

She pulled away from him and walked off. He went to grab her again, but she was too quick, hurrying away. She saw the two young cops look at her, astonished, as she went. A moment later she heard him shout after her.

'So I'll see you back at the nick, then. Okay, Zoe?'

She walked on and away. She didn't go back to the station but did manage to meet up with her friends, where she drank a little fast and argued a little too loudly. They were used to her, and tutted and shushed her when she became too abrasive. She watched them chat and gossip, and laughed at herself when they despaired of her single status.

Later, when they all cried off to bed, with jobs and boyfriends awaiting, she found an ugly bar close to home where she sat in a corner and drank herself properly drunk.

FORTY

Issy and Jenny came downstairs next morning to find Sam burning pancakes on the stove and swearing his head off. The congealed mess in the sticky frying pan made them laugh, and this didn't improve his mood.

'When did we get this stupid thing?' he moaned, waving the pan in the air. The girls both shrugged and busied themselves with cereal and toast. Sam offered to drive them into school and, after a shared glance that made it clear this was never going to happen in a million years, they both declined with a snigger.

Magda had every Wednesday morning off and was enjoying a lie-in, so Sam took his frustrations out on the washing-up. As he beat the living daylights out of a couple of mugs, he wondered again about Helen's appearance that night. He felt calmer now that it was day, but he still couldn't shake the feeling of dread that those little boys had provoked. He stared at the soapy bubbles and wondered what Helen was capable of, and how best to defeat her.

Aware that his daughters were watching him and that he looked ridiculous in the apron he wore to protect his shirt and tie, Sam tried to play the fool to raise a laugh. His antics fell flat. Issy shoved a school form in front of him to sign – a trip to a local museum – and snatched it back off him when he did. Trying a little too hard, he asked them if they needed money. Jenny took some for a new set of files (to which Issy made sarky comments) and Issy ignored the question completely.

'We're out of Marmite,' Jenny said.

'And everything else,' her sister added.

'Like what?' Sam asked. The girls just shrugged as if the list was too enormous to contemplate. Then they dumped their things in the washing-up bowl, muttered goodbyes (Issy was already on the phone by this point) and shot out, slamming the door behind them.

Sam wandered around the kitchen, opening cupboards and peering at tins and jars, trying to work out what was needed. Now fully deflated, he headed off to the local supermarket and trudged miserably round the aisles. As he got lost somewhere amongst noodles and spaghetti, his mind pushed the case back at him.

No one disappears without a trace. There must be a trail, somehow, that would lead back to Helen Seymour. His brain coughed and sparked like a flooded engine as he tried to put the pieces together. It wasn't until he reached the police station that he finally saw a way forward and everything inside him roared.

Helen was clever. She'd have made sure that all mail would be forwarded to her chambers and they would use an automatic post office service to be certain that any other correspondence would be mopped up. There was no way he could find the missing witness that way. But such a service does not cope well with misspelled names and similar anomalies. And that, Sam knew, would give him his chance. But just as he reached for the file, excited by the possibilities, there was a knock on the door and he saw Zoe standing on the other side. His heart sank, but then he noted how pale she looked and he waved her in.

The trouble had started the moment Zoe reached the station the next morning. As she approached the back door, she caught a glimpse of two young PCs heading out on foot patrol , and the look from one of them – that shifty, knowing glance – told her all she needed to know. Sure enough, when she entered the locker room, the place fell silent. She got changed as though she hadn't noticed a thing. Only a few moments later Malcolm appeared at the door, clearly tipped off as to her arrival.

'Morning, Zo-Zo,' he said.

'Hi, Sarge,' she replied with matching jollity, but she wasn't quite confident enough to meet his eye.

He sat down next to her and she was drowning in his heavy aftershave. His thick hand patted her thigh as she pulled on her top.

'Quite a night, eh?' he said.

'Yes it was.' She was standing now, shutting the locker door, getting ready to get the hell out of there. When she turned she realised that all the guys were facing her. She was alone in a room with seven men.

'What I've always liked about you,' Malcolm said, 'is that you're a team player. Remember how I've always said that? It's what sets us apart from the mongrels out there. We work for each other, watch your mate's back, you know.'

'I know.'

'When you buggered off over to CID, some of the guys they were saying stuff about you, honey. Jumped up little something or other, I can't remember the words. Thought you were acting above your station, anyhow. But I saw them right. I've always known you're a good 'un.'

'Thanks, Sarge.'

'Do I need to go on? It's getting a bit stupid now, isn't it?'

There was no air in the room.

'How is he?' she finally asked. She wanted to give in but she could still see Eli's gasping face on the pavement. She imagined that Malcolm's hand might still have flecks of blood on it.

'He's gonna be fine. More than he deserves.'

There was a muttering of approval from the other men in the room.

'He'll say nothing,' the Sergeant continued. 'Come on, Zoe, he knows how it all works. He tagged a cop car. He smashed that poor little girl's house to pieces. He's scum. He got caught. He'll say he can't remember and we all carry on.'

'I suppose I was just being silly,' she said, a little bashfully.

'There you go.'

'Wondering how it would look if I backed up your version of events only to find him saying something else. Like that you went for him and beat him and beat him and beat him.' Her tone was sharp now, but she couldn't stop herself.

'And if he did? His word against mine.'

'His word and his wounds.'

Everyone in the room would know she was right. There was no way that a beating like that could ever be claimed as self-defence.

'We're talking about Eli, here. Remember him? Remember the things he's done, Zoe?'

'Yes, Sarge.'

'It might get messy. Fair call, you're right, it might get a little sweaty. But my boy Gareth's already writing up a statement that backs me up. And when you do too, well, what can they say? They might not like it and some people might wave their hands in the air, but that's all they can do. You know how it works.'

He was probably right. With no evidence and with co-ordinated testimony from the police, something like this would eventually die. The local community would be up in arms, and relations between them and the cops would sink even lower, but Malcolm, most likely, would get away with it.

'It's not like you're exactly whiter than white yourself, is it, love?'

She had to get out of there. But his hand was on her shoulder now.

'See, boys? She's a good girl. She wouldn't do anything to harm one of us.'

She hadn't done anything to warrant this comment and they all knew it. The men carried on staring silently at her. She'd done the same to others over the years, but the familiarity of it all didn't lessen its impact.

'Time I got upstairs, Sarge,' she said as lightly as she could, and tapped her watch.

'Sure, honey, sure,' Malcolm replied. 'You've got to get out there, serve and protect. That's what we do.'

But his hand was still pressing down on her shoulder. He was so tough and thick. She imagined trying to fight him and could only see her puny fists bouncing uselessly off his body.

'You get yourself upstairs, sweetheart. But we'll need your report in today. They don't like it if paperwork takes too long, do they?'

His lifted his hand and she was free to go. She walked towards the door, but noticed that a cop stood in front of it, barring her way.

'Shift it,' she said, but he didn't move.

For a moment she thought it would kick off right then and there. She imagined an arm around her neck, pulling her back, and for these unsubtle innuendoes to turn into direct threats. She stood there and waited. But then the cop stood aside. Malcolm must have nodded to him behind her. She walked past, out into the corridor, which was busy as usual, unaffected by the sweaty antics of the locker room.

Zoe didn't run but she certainly walked fast. She got up to CID and, to her great relief, saw that Sam was in. She barged into his office and crashed into a chair. When she looked at him she got the sense that he was disappointed to see her.

'Hi,' he said.

'You heard about last night?'

He shook his head. 'I've been a bit wrapped up with things. What's up?'

'Really? You've . . . ? Really?'

He was thrown by this. He shrugged at her – so tell me.

'Malcolm went mental.'

'Sergeant Cartmell,' he corrected.

'Yes, Sergeant Cartmell, sorry. The fine and upstanding Sergeant went and kicked a boy into a coma last night. And I was the lucky one to see it happen.'

'Shit,' Sam replied, rubbing his eyes. He looked exhausted. 'What are you doing about it?' he asked.

'I don't know.' There was a slight wobble in her voice as she said it, a release that she hadn't been able to allow herself until now.

'How bad was it?'

'It was disgusting, boss.'

He nodded, but didn't speak for a while. Finally: 'You okay?'

'I will be,' she said, trying to sound strong. It was a job requirement, after all.

'They want you to make up a report, I take it?'

She nodded and listened as he gave her the stock advice: do nothing, weigh it all up, let them think you're doing what they want, even tell them you have if they push. It wasn't the advice she was hoping for.

'Will you talk to him?' she finally asked.

'Okay,' he said, and his head dropped back to his paperwork. The speed with which he seemed to dismiss this irritated her. She still felt a little juddery from the locker room and didn't want to be shoved back out onto normal duties so soon.

'It might need more than a matey chat,' she added.

'It'll be fine.'

He couldn't know this, not for sure, and as she watched him run his pen under a line in a report, she felt increasingly angry.

'Well, thanks, then,' she said.

'Yeah,' he replied, not looking up. She stood and walked out, back into the goldfish bowl.

Zoe flopped into her chair and checked her computer. There were various work-related chores, nothing urgent – mainly HR and new directives. But then two messages popped up that made her lean closer to the monitor. The first was from an anonymous email address with the subject *'DO THE RIGHT THING'* and no content. She knew it would be from one of Malcolm's minions and she knew that there would be more soon. The second was from 'Seymour, Helen'.

She glanced around before opening it.

'Hi Zoe. Do you have a chance to meet? I can come to you if easier. Best, H.'

An email. Not a secretive phone call but an easily copied and forwarded piece of correspondence. It was almost brazen. At the bottom of the email were contact phone numbers, including a mobile. She slipped out into the stairwell before she dialled the number.

Helen picked up after a single ring.

'Zoe, hi!' she said, almost as though they were buddies.

'Yeah. So you wanted to meet?'

'Yes, please.'

'Why?'

'It's easier to tell you in person.'

Zoe bit her lip. She didn't like this. 'Okay,' she said.

'Thank you. I assume you won't want to be seen by your colleagues.'

'Damn straight.'

'How about that cafe on Lyall Street?'

'Fine. When?'

'Now?'

Zoe didn't want to seem too keen. In fact, she was extremely wary of meeting this woman at all, but she was also keen to get out of the station. She hung up before Helen could confirm anything more – her rather petulant attempt at control – and continued down the stairs. As she headed towards the exit she saw Gareth, standing by the door, watching her.

'You alright?' he asked, his voice flat.

'Morning, Gareth,' she replied brightly.

'You done your report on last night?'

'Who are you? My mum?'

'Done mine,' he replied and ran a hand over his hair, flattening it. 'Done it good and proper.'

'Well done you, gold star,' she said.

'Funny bitch, ain't you?'

'Excuse me?'

278

'I said you're funny. Well, always trying to be funny. Must be hard work, all the effort you put in.'

'It's easier than trying to climb up Sergeant Cartmell's arse all day. I'm amazed there's any room, with you all fighting to get in there.'

Gareth didn't have a ready reply to this so he just scowled. She looked at him for a moment. She remembered when he first joined, how eager and fresh-faced he was. He had shaken her hand earnestly and paid attention to everything she said. But now, a year in, he was snide and cold-faced; another faceless uniform, thinking and acting as he was told to do.

She pushed past him. After the claustrophobia of the station's corridors, the city's dusty, polluted air outside seemed wonderfully fresh and clean.

Back in his office, now finally free to get back onto the case, Sam was pleased to see Zoe head off. He noted that her exit was quiet, as though she was hiding something, but he put this down to the trouble she was having with Malcolm. He must talk to the crusty old bugger, he reminded himself. He didn't like the idea of Zoe being scared, especially not in here, a police station.

But soon he was driving again, and the only thing in his mind was a missing witness, Helen Seymour and poor little Lily Downing.

FORTY-ONE

Helen was sitting at a table at the back of the cafe halfway through a bacon sandwich when Zoe arrived. It was a tawdry place, catering for those who had no interest in fancy delicatessens and decaf macchiatos. Helen had to wipe some of the ketchup off her lips and stood hurriedly, grabbing Zoe into a hug.

'Thanks for coming, really. Bacon sarnie? Lizzie does the best in town.'

Lizzie, a tall, sturdy woman, winked at her, and Zoe felt outnumbered by her presence and the unexpected hug. She looked around – an old couple were perusing newspapers in the other corner, but otherwise the place was quiet. It made a surprisingly good meeting place. She ordered a coffee and sat down as Helen cleared papers away off the table, stuffing them unceremoniously into her bag.

Once again, her clothes were simple and understated. It was only by the cut that Zoe could tell they weren't just high-street brands. It was as though everything Helen did was to avoid being noticed.

Lizzie returned moments later with two coffees that she dumped onto the table. She left an arm draped on Helen's shoulder for a moment, before moving on. Helen sipped at hers and then sat back. Zoe waited, well aware of the game being played. She could wait as long as it took.

'I have a small problem with your boss,' Helen said eventually.

'Which one?'

'Your DI. Sam Taylor.'

'So talk to him.'

Helen frowned in a way that made it clear she would if she could. She fiddled with her coffee cup for a moment.

'He came at me, last night, when I was getting into my car.'

'What does that mean? Came at you?'

'I was going to my car, across from the station after some business – he hasn't mentioned this to you?'

'I haven't seen him this morning,' Zoe lied.

'Well, I was about to unlock the door and I looked round, you know, as you do to make sure you're safe, and there he was. He'd followed me. It scared me, Zoe.'

Zoe had seen Sam scare plenty of people. But he did it with lowlife dealers, with thugs and scrotes. Not with women, and never with someone like Helen. She didn't know what to think.

'What do you want me to do about it?' she said.

'I'd like you to calm him down.'

'He seems fine to me.'

'No, Zoe, he's far from fine.'

'Look, you put his back up – steamrolling over his case like that – what do you expect?'

'So this is typical behaviour then, is it? He's "got the hump" and it'll all calm down?'

'Sure.'

Helen shook her head, irritated at Zoe's stonewalling.

'You're the smartest person in that whole department. Don't shut down on me. I know he's your boss and your friend, but don't block me just because of some misplaced ideas about loyalty.'

'Excuse me? I shouldn't even bloody be here.'

'What has he told you about me?' Helen asked, and Zoe was surprised by the abrupt change of direction.

'Fuck off.' It was a stock reply in times of trouble, and it suited her well enough now.

Helen sighed. 'Okay. Stop. Rewind. Let's start this again. I'm sorry, I've come at this the wrong way, but please, don't think of me as some sort of adversary.'

'You're a sodding defence barrister!'

'We're both part of the same system, serving the law. You know that.'

'You're being ridiculous.'

'No, you've just spent too long with your macho buddies.'

Zoe thought of Gareth and his stupid sneer. It shut her up.

'You're not one of them, Zoe,' Helen said more quietly. 'I think Sam's a good guy and a good cop, but I think he's too desperate to get a result on the case. I would be too. A boy's dead and a girl is missing. But he seems more driven than seems reasonable.'

This was a waste of time. Zoe downed her coffee and prepared to leave, pulling at her coat from the back of her chair.

'He was shaking with rage, Zoe. I thought he was going to explode.'

'I don't believe you.'

'So he's not been acting oddly with you then?'

'No.'

But he had. He'd been secretive and angry for months now. Not like that, though, not violent or dangerous. But she could imagine it, even if she'd never seen it. He'd had his moments in the past, before Andrea died, when he was terrifying.

'Why would he be so angry with you then?' Zoe asked.

Helen raised an eyebrow in response. 'You know why.'

'You've been messing with witnesses.'

Zoe saw Helen's fingers tighten on the gingham table cloth and she felt a sting of irritation and regret – Helen had got her to play her hand.

'Why do you think that?' Helen said, and Zoe was pleased to see how uncomfortable she was.

'No, you don't get to pump me for information. You know what you've done. And if you've done wrong, then you deserve to be punished for it.'

'And if I haven't?'

'Then you're not a concern of ours.'

'I think I'm a gigantic concern of Sam Taylor's, even though I haven't been messing with any witnesses.'

'I doubt that. And I have to go now.'

'I fight hard for my clients,' Helen interrupted, her eyes locked on Zoe, 'and I do it by the book. But I pay for it. I used to be a lot brasher than I am now. I thought at first that I should do it like the boys – fight and play like them, be loud and unbending. But that didn't go down so well. Now I'm quieter and they prefer me like that. Quieter, but I tell you, I still fight. And they hate it. They hate a woman like me just because I'm clever and successful and all the other things that women aren't allowed to be in this enlightened age. So I get my share of enemies. You get yourself into trouble when you speak your mind. Don't you?'

'Oh God, are you trying to get me to shit on my boss because of some women's lib?'

'I'm not asking you to shit on anyone.'

Zoe pushed the empty cup away from her. Helen stood, straightening the sleeves of her jacket and throwing her bag

284

over her shoulder. She looked down at Zoe. 'I've done my homework on you, Zoe. You're an exceptional talent. But you're also too loyal to Sam. And it could get you hurt. I just wanted to warn you.'

'I don't believe a word you've said,' Zoe snapped. Helen didn't respond to this. This only annoyed Zoe more, so she continued. 'And the fact that you talk about loyalty like it's some sort of optional extra only makes me think less of you.'

'I love the way you talk. But I bet they bloody despise you back in that cop shop,' Helen said, and walked away.

Zoe remained at the table, her mind whirling. She knew that Helen had dropped a vial of slow-working poison into her ear – seeding doubts against those she trusted and loved. She recognised that Helen had secrets of her own and that she was trying to manipulate her. She should go back and tell Sam now, tell him everything and not let Helen come between them. That's what loyal colleagues do. They're open and honest at all times.

But Sam wasn't being honest with her. And the way he was right now, she wasn't sure if her loyalty wasn't indeed dangerously placed.

The poison was working. She could feel it spreading cancerous tentacles through her, making her shivery and suspicious. Or maybe it was only awakening emotions that were already there.

She got up. Lizzie was clearing a table by the door.

'Does she meet people here often?' Zoe asked.

'I guess.'

'Doesn't seem her sort of place. I imagined she'd eat somewhere fancier.'

Lizzie just shrugged.

'You don't say much, do you?'

'I don't know you.'

'But you know her.'

'Oh yeah. We all know her,' the waitress replied. It sounded, somehow, as though she was describing an army.

Zoe walked back to the station. She had known that visiting Helen would be a mistake. And now she'd done it, although nothing had happened and no deal had been agreed, she felt she'd somehow signed a little bit of her life away.

FORTY-TWO

Sam went back to visit Arnold Heath in his musty, book-strewn flat. The academic prickled with excitement, desperate to help and be a part of the adventure, and Sam was soon able to get what he wanted. Some post had arrived, incorrectly labelled, as Sam had assumed. It was an electricity bill with a large amount unpaid and had sent Arnold into a tizzy. As a result, he had rung the contact number left for him (Helen Seymour's chambers) and had been disappointed to be put through to a temp who was unhelpful and unprofessional. However, Arnold was so concerned that he would be forced to pay the bill himself, that he forced the young woman to dictate the tenant's forwarding address down the phone so that he could ensure its arrival with a recorded delivery. He had even kept a copy of the receipt (with the address included) in case the bill remained outstanding.

Sam thanked him politely for his tenacity and let him ramble on about society and the deterioration of manners until his bulk and the silence did their work and Arnold felt too uncomfortable to speak any more. Sam shook his hand, promised to be in touch with further developments (which caused a flurry of excitement all over again) and left.

The address was in Nottingham, far from his jurisdiction. But that didn't stop him; he drove there straight away. He turned on the radio, then snapped it off, his concentration skittish. It was only as he approached the outskirts of the city, nearly two hours later, that he remembered he'd failed to buy any of the provisions on his supermarket list. What had happened? He'd been in there and then . . . then the case had distracted him and dragged him away. He consoled himself with the thought that he could buy the things he needed on the way back. Right now he needed to concentrate on Lily. And Richard Howell.

The address took him to a depressing part of town. The building itself was a crumbling brick ruin on the corner of two busy roads. Heavy trucks grunted and hissed as they passed, and Sam had to shield his eyes from the grit that they kicked up. He looked at the sky, but there were no rolling clouds here, just a thick, dull blanket of grey.

It was impossible to tell if the intercom worked or not, but it drew no response, and Sam had to wait for a workman to enter, slipping in behind him and heading up to the top floor, the stairs sagging alarmingly under his weight. He knocked on the door, saw a buzzer and tried that as well.

After a few minutes, he was about to give up when he heard a shuffling behind the door. He stopped and listened.

'Open up. Police,' Sam barked.

The shuffling stopped. Busted.

'Come on, I know you're there. You're not in trouble, I just want to ask you some questions.'

After a lengthy pause, the door opened and a scrawny man peered out at him. He was shirtless, with pyjama bottoms that hung loosely over his thin hips. From his research, Sam knew that Ricky was in his late twenties, that he never answered to Richard, and hadn't done a day's work in his life. But on first observation, the pallid figure in front of him could have been anything between twenty and forty. His skin was deathly grey, and a fine line of stubble only heightened the sense of a body in decay.

'Yeah?' Ricky said.

Sam introduced himself and pushed his way into the flat. The curtains were closed, but so thin that the daylight still bled through. Ricky lived in a nauseous half-light. He led Sam across the unopened post that lay thick on the floor and into an awful sitting room which was composed solely of a sofa, a large TV and a low coffee table covered in needles, dope, silver foil, matches and empty vodka bottles.

When he saw Sam looking at all of the drugs paraphernalia, he sniffed.

'It's medicinal, innit?'

He wavered by the sofa, his body swaying slightly. His eyes had a yellowy, nicotine-stained sheen to them, and Sam tried to work out just how far gone he was.

'So what is it, then?' Ricky asked, flopping down onto the sofa. His eyes drifted towards Sam and then away from him as though he were coming in and out of focus. If Sam had stood still for long enough, it was quite possible that Ricky would forget he was even there.

'You used to live at 221 Dalton Street?'

Ricky sniffed a confirmation. He started to fiddle with cigarette papers and rolling tobacco.

'Why did you move?'

Ricky's hands paused at this, then continued. The tell was obvious. Sam pushed for an answer but Ricky just fiddled with his papers, then lit his cigarette and let his head rest against the back of the sofa.

'It was a nice place. Seems a shame to have moved from there to here,' Sam said.

A shrug of the shoulders, but nothing more. Sam asked him more questions, but only ever received the same dull avoidances. He was used to this – this type of regressive, failing man who hides behind a veneer of boredom. He just had to break through the facade.

'I bet you're surprised to see me here. I imagine you thought we'd never find you again.'

Ricky glanced nervously at him and Sam knew he was getting there.

'No one can hide from us, Ricky.'

The trucks below made the window frames shudder. They gave off an ominous rattle and hum each time.

'Did Helen tell you different?' Sam asked.

Ricky gave him a tiny glance, but nothing more.

'I know why you're here, Ricky. I know what you saw.'

'Saw nothing, say nothing,' Ricky muttered, as if by rote.

'Did you see a boy die, Ricky? Is that right?'

Ricky closed his eyes again, as though he was trying to lock the memories away.

'A boy, trying to defend himself, yes? And a woman grabbed him, didn't she? She grabbed him and tried to drown him. And then, when she couldn't manage it, she hit his head against the sink. Beat the little boy's skull to pieces.'

A truck rumbled below and they both shook with it.

'You saw that, didn't you?'

'How did you find me?' Ricky asked.

Sam finally felt as though he was opening him up.

'You witnessed the murder of a little boy and then you ran away.'

'I didn't, I didn't run, I didn't see anything.'

'So why are you here?'

'Because of her.'

'Who?'

'Her. Mrs Seymour.'

Ricky closed his eyes again, but Sam forced them open, snapping his fingers. He had her.

'Tell me about Helen.'

'I can't.'

'Yes you can.' Sam leant over him.

'I can't,' he said. And then he repeated it over and over again. Can't. Can't. Can't. He shook his head, and squeezed his eyes shut again.

Sam cleared a space next to Ricky and sat down close to him. He soothed him with false promises and offers of support. He was a mate, a bloke, a mensch. Slowly, he tried to get Ricky to confirm what he had seen. But whenever he got close, Ricky would wriggle away from the subject. Whenever pushed, he always retreated to the same line.

'I didn't see nothing.'

'Why are you scared of her, Ricky? I'm not scared of her.'

And this got a proper reaction. 'Well you should be.'

And there was the fear again. The fear Sam had felt in those little boys, the surge of dread he'd felt when Sarah had smiled at him outside her bedroom before she fell silent, the same fear now rising like steam off Ricky, like the morning mist at Lullingdale Water.

Sam stared at the table and a freshly used needle, a trace of blood on the tip. Anything could be bubbling in this man's mind, true or false.

The window frames rattled again.

'Why are you scared, Ricky?'

'I need a hit. I gotta have another hit. You've got to go.'

His body shook slightly and Sam felt a similar tremor echo within himself.

'What is it about Helen that makes you so scared, Ricky?'

'Not just her, is it?'

The thin curtains bathed him in a bloody half-light and Ricky started to roll up his sleeve, patting his arm and reaching for a shoelace, a makeshift tourniquet. Sam pushed his arm down.

'Not yet.'

'I have to.'

'Tell me what you meant. Who is else is there, besides Helen?'

'Oh, copper, there's a whole bloody army of them. Can't you see that?'

Blood-red windows shuddered and shook. Sam saw the murderous women's faces from his file, staring bitterly out at him.

'We all know how the world really works,' Ricky said. 'We all know. We just like to close our eyes and pretend it's nice and sweet and kind. But it's not. You know it's not, don't you?'

Hundreds of cases told Sam he was right. The withering flowers on Andrea's grave confirmed it.

Ricky reached for the tourniquet again and this time Sam didn't stop him.

'We think we're special, we think we're the ones in charge,' Ricky said, pulling the lace tight then reaching for a lighter and silver foil. 'You think you're a lion,' he said, and shook his head at how wrong Sam was.

He heated the heroin and they both watched as it melted and then started to boil.

'The world is upside down, copper. Haven't you worked that out yet?'

The syringe sucked the demons up off the foil.

The room reverberated again.

Sam imagined Helen and her army. He heard the man next to him gasp and sigh, and when he looked at him, Ricky's eyes were half-closed, a blissful smile of escape on his lips.

Sam stood, accidentally knocking over the coffee table. The detritus crashed to the floor, but Ricky didn't notice.

'Did you see that boy die?' Sam asked, more frantically this time.

A grin and a sigh.

'Did Helen force you to move?'

Ricky's tongue slipped onto his top lip and his eyelids flickered.

'Who does she work with? Please, Ricky, who is she doing all this with?'

But Ricky was far away now. Somewhere where neither Helen or Sam could get him. He slid onto the sofa, his legs pulled up to his chest in a foetal position.

Sam wanted to grab him and drag him back to Manchester, but he wasn't sure that a word he'd said was credible. But the man was scared of Helen. She had control over people in an extraordinary way. She, and others, had scared him so badly that he'd been reduced to this pathetic husk. And Sam felt the fear by some sort of osmosis. He didn't understand it and didn't know how to fight it. He just felt it seep into his bloodstream, pumped in by an invisible syringe. It rendered him dumb and forced him to leave Ricky where he was. He slipped down the stairs, scared of making a noise for no reason that he could fathom.

When he got outside, he looked around at the grungy traffic and tried to claw back his senses. The sky was still a dull grey, cars drove by as usual. A flashing light above a shop offered kebabs and fried chicken. The world was just as it always was. But then Sam saw a young woman in a suit stride towards him and he felt the fear surge up again. He turned to her, waiting for the conflict, but then felt stupid as she strode past, unaware that he was even there. Angry with himself, he went back to the car with heavy steps, trying to remind himself of who he was and what he could do. The fear retreated. But it swam in tiny circles somewhere in his gut, a cold tickle, ready to come back when the time was right.

It was swimming idly in his stomach, twisting in serene arcs, when Sam got home that night. Magda opened the door to him as he approached. She was dressed differently – gone were the sweat pants and baggy T-shirt and she wore tighter, more revealing clothes now. His eyes took them in and then he felt guilty for doing so, especially when he caught her eye and saw that she was pleased he had done so.

'Hi, Magda.'

'Mr Taylor.'

'You've dressed up. Are you going out tonight?'

'No. I just like to dress nicer sometimes.'

'Well, you look . . . swell.'

Sam stepped awkwardly around her and fled to his bedroom.

He read the files again, checking details he already knew by heart. Issy came to the door but Sam couldn't talk to her. She shouted at him but he ignored her teenage tantrum and ran himself a long bath. He stared at the steaming water and imagined he was Arthur in the lake. He held his breath for as long as he could, then breathed out and watched the bubbles pop the surface. He imagined delicate female hands pulling him down and holding him there.

Later, dry and dressed, he stepped quietly through the

house. Everything was quiet now. The lights were out. He peeked into his mother's room. She was asleep and he sat by her side, watching her the way he imagined she would have done him, when he was her little boy. Her mouth was agape and she shifted uncomfortably in her sleep as though she was in pain, as though she were fighting something. Old age was cruelly dragging her down too.

Issy was on the computer, headphones on and her back to him, and although Sam wanted to make peace with her, he also didn't have the energy. Jenny's door was closed and he let her be.

Magda's door was ajar. He'd never been in her room, not since he showed it to her after giving her the job. Sam noticed that a light was on inside. He didn't go in, but he had to pass it to get to his own room. As he approached, he saw the young woman appear in the shadow of the door. She wore a long shirt, undone and revealing, and nothing else. She stood there and stared at him. Sam stopped when he saw her. He couldn't avoid the provocation: her near-nudity, the stare, the time of night. But he didn't go in. He walked past, entered his bedroom, shut the door and wished that there was a lock to keep her out.

FORTY-THREE

Three young cops, fresh-faced in their neatly pressed uniforms, were waiting for Zoe when she returned to the station later that night. She'd managed to stay away from the station all day with various chores and non-urgent duties, but she had to come back at some point. They stood in a line, arms folded, a barrier between her and the station's entrance.

'I've done the report, alright? Done it, handed it in, so get off my fucking case,' she snapped. They were only there because Malcolm had told them to be, but their bovine obedience was pathetic. She pushed through them, her elbow connecting hard with one of them. He jolted back and said something she didn't catch but also didn't quite have the nerve to question.

When she reached CID, she was informed that Mr Frey, the Chief Superintendent, wanted to see her.

'Who's been a naughty girl then?' came the teasing call as

she turned tail and marched up the six floors to where the top brass lived. It was quieter up here. She passed only one other person as she made her way to his office.

She was shown in and stood awkwardly in front of his desk. Mr Frey was on the phone and didn't look at her as he continued to talk. It was all 'I see' and 'very good'. After a few interminable minutes, he hung up and looked at her with a serious face.

'DC Barnes?'

'Yes, sir.'

'There was an incident, I hear. A young man was hurt.'

Oh shit, it's got all the way up here, she thought.

'Yes, sir.'

'You witnessed it.'

'Part of it, sir.'

'I have a statement from Sergeant Malcolm Cartmell.'

'Yes, sir.'

'He's a good man, Sergeant Cartmell. Excellent officer.'

Right. So that's the message.

'Yes, sir.'

'Is there anything that I should worry about?'

'Not that I know of, sir.'

He gazed at her, and somehow she felt that it was the same leery gaze he would fix on a stripper in a club.

'Good girl.'

She realised that this was her cue to leave.

'Do send my best to Sam when you next see him.'

'I will, sir. Thank you, sir.'

And with that she was done. She headed back downstairs, glad to be out of his gaze. Soon, she knew, they would discover that she hadn't completed the report as she'd claimed and then the monster would come back at her. Emails, texts, abuse in the corridor and worse. But somehow it seemed less scary than that cold man on the top floor and his idle, cruel manner.

FORTY-FOUR

Helen Seymour's chambers sat in the corner of a wonderful old city square. Every building had the same black brick facade and on several were light-blue plaques that commemorated famous artists who had once lived there in centuries gone by. In the centre of the square was an iron-fenced park, for residents' use only. Passers-by would gaze in longingly at the perfectly manicured lawns and plants that blossomed in their liberation from children and ball games. As Sam arrived and walked towards her offices, he admired his surroundings. It was a far cry from the places where Helen's clients lived and worked.

He rang at the door and was ushered inside by an eager clerk, a lad in his twenties in a cheap suit who seemed thrilled to be there. Inside, much had been made of the building's history. The rooms were oak-panelled, with a thick blue carpet that made the place look like an old-time gentlemen's club. Sam sat on a plush armchair and waited his turn, declining a tea or coffee. Fancy broadsheet newspapers and magazines were neatly laid out in front of him, but he didn't touch them.

A few minutes later he was led upstairs. He looked around him as he went, seeing suited men and women digesting massive law books at heavy desks. The clerk led him along the corridor to the far end where he knocked twice, opened the door and ushered Sam inside, shutting the door behind him.

Helen Seymour sat at the far end of her expansive office behind an antique partner's desk with a green leather top (although you could only just make this out, as the desk was covered in papers). Behind her was a large window that looked back down onto the square. The surroundings dwarfed her.

'What a place,' Sam said with a whistle.

'I know,' she replied. 'I think you need a cigar and red braces to work in a room like this. Makes me feel like a bit of a fraud.'

She offered her hand in that same modest but tenacious manner and gestured for him to sit in one of the two arm-chairs that faced her desk. He was too big for it, but tried not to let her see his discomfort.

'So, Detective Inspector, what can I do for you today?'

'I wanted to thank you for not causing a stir with Sarah Downing,' he said. 'I thought I was for the high jump there.'

'Oh?'

'You know, performance tables, arrest rates – it's all about results these days.'

'Join the club, Inspector.'

'Sam, please.'

She leaned back in her desk and waited. Half-librarian, half-wolf.

'May I ask you how you came to represent Mrs Downing?'

'Not really. I don't mean to be rude, but it's private and not relevant to the case.'

'I see.'

Her eyes were fixed on his. Just as they had been the previous night outside the police station. But then she was out in the open, out in the dark. Today, she sat behind a desk, shielded by the finery of her office.

'I suppose I was just wondering,' he continued, 'if you could help me with a series of coincidences.'

She shook her head, as if she didn't understand. But she knew exactly where he was taking this, he was certain of it. She picked up a pen and began to doodle on a large notepad which had the chambers' name printed in an embossed font at the top of the page.

'What coincidences?' she asked.

'Well, ma'am—'

'Ma'am? Behave yourself. I'm Helen.'

'Well, then, Helen, I'm a little intrigued by the cases that you've been choosing recently.'

The pen stopped, choked for a second, then continued. She didn't look at him.

'A series of cases,' he continued, 'in which you seem to have shown unusual interest, involving yourself at stages that wouldn't normally require someone like you.'

'Someone like me.'

'Someone as important as you.'

Her tongue touched the top of her lip and then disappeared. It made Sam think of a snake.

'And in all these cases, there is the violent murder of young children,' he added, waiting for the punch to hit.

Helen feigned a yawn. 'Yes, it's been a strange run I've had,' she said. 'But this isn't really something for a policeman to bother himself with, is it?'

'Well, there's the nature of the cases and also the manner in which you've defended them.'

'Which means what?'

Sam leaned forward in his chair. He faced her full on, there was no point pretending any more.

'I'm investigating you.'

Sam let this comment stew for a moment, then looked around the office and pretended to admire a large oil painting on the wall. But Helen didn't bite. She waited calmly. Like a trap.

He finally looked back at her. He couldn't resist. He'd

come here to face her, to see her for real and let her know that he was going to stop her.

'What do you think you're doing?' she snapped, her bookish pretensions falling away from her. She clutched the pen in her hand like a dagger now.

'Now, now, Helen,' he crowed. 'Don't get your knickers in a twist.'

It was lovely to see just how much the words angered her and how she had to work to hide it.

'You have quite a nerve,' she said. 'Swanning in here, all on your own, with these smears and threats.'

She stood up, silhouetted by the sun that had broken through the clouds and now shone into the room.

'You really should have thought your actions through a little more before charging in here with your empty words and big fists. You stupid little man.'

Sam found that he was standing.

'You come here, into my office,' she continued, 'to do what? You have no questions, you have no facts. Why are you here, Mr Taylor?'

'I was hoping to—'

'We're not in your cosy, beefcake cop shop now. You're not here with your hairy mates, farting and laughing all day. This is my office.'

'I can see that.'

There was a wildness in her eyes that flared and then

faded. She ran her tongue around the inside of her mouth before refocusing on Sam. She pushed her chair back slightly.

'I think it is very typical that a man like you would waltz in with nothing but his dick in his hands and expect a result. You have no power here. Do you get that? You are nothing. No, I'm wrong, scrap that, I know what you are. You are a lapdog – running along to another man's wishes. Sam, you need to go back to your nasty little den and leave me alone. You don't screw with someone like me and not feel the whiplash.'

'Someone like you?'

'Yes. Someone with some real fucking power.'

The phone on her desk rang but she didn't bother to answer it. It rang interminably but neither moved. Then Sam nodded, thanked her for her time and walked out. He tried to do it nonchalantly, but he felt heavy and awkward as he went. Behind him the phone stopped ringing, but he didn't hear Helen answer it and he imagined she was right behind him. He turned, a little spooked, and indeed there she was, standing in the doorway, arms folded, watching him.

She was right. He could feel her power. He knew she had influence and authority, and that ornate office had told him so clearly enough. But that was not all. She wasn't strong because of this. It was her. She was the power. She stared Sam down and he marvelled and feared her in equal measure.

Real fucking power. The words chased him home, spinning amongst the litter that the wind picked up and skittered at his feet. They were coughed from the engines of the cars in the slow rush-hour traffic.

He slammed his front door shut and went straight to his room, ignoring a call from his mother. He spilled the files out onto his bed, going through them all again. Again and again and again.

The fever calmed a little over the hours that passed, but still those guilty women's faces burned out at Sam from the papers. Their cold, emotionless expressions haunted him as their details lay scattered across his bed at home. He looked away from them and saw his wife's photograph smiling at him from the chest of drawers. Magda had laid some ironed clothes in front of the frame, which meant that only Andrea's twinkling eyes were visible. He looked away, back down at the case photographs. Eventually he stacked them into a neat pile and hid them out of sight.

He went downstairs in search of some food and found Magda alone in the kitchen. She was talking to someone on the phone in her native tongue which he couldn't understand. She had a wild, loud laugh and let out a coarse bark of delight just as Sam entered. She turned, surprised by his presence, and for a second her eyes were full of anger. They reminded him of his murderous women.

Magda hung up quickly. 'Hello,' she said.

'Hi. Is there any food?'

'Of course,' she replied, as though he was a child. 'What you want?'

'Whatever you've got. Something easy you can reheat?'

She shrugged and went to the fridge.

'And where is everyone?' he asked. In response he heard a scream upstairs – *Stay the fuck out of my fucking room!* And heard girls' feet stomping and two doors slamming.

'Your mother is not right,' Magda said as he stared uselessly as the ceiling.

'I'm sorry?'

'Your mother. She is . . . going away.' Magda frowned and then nodded as though these words were correct.

'What? Going where? What?'

'Your mother.' Magda tapped her head to make the point more clearly.

'Oh. Yeah.'

Yes, she was going away. Slowly disappearing, inevitably forgetting and fading from somewhere inside herself. Sam wondered what had happened that had made Magda notice, but he didn't want to talk to her about this. He should do something, he thought, but he felt so tired. His mind went blank. And then Andrea was there, laughing as she always did when he told her about his dreary work, jokingly making up her own events where a supermarket shop became a gun-toting heist. And she always saved the day. Sam's eyes welled up with tears and he had to wipe them away.

He sat at the table and a few moments later Magda placed a large plate of stew before him. She returned with a glass of water. As she moved on, she let her hand rest on his shoulder for a moment.

Sam ate quickly then dumped the empty plate in the washing machine. He stared at his glass of water and he remembered the lake, stretching out before him, calm and cold, hiding its secrets deep down in the rocks and mud.

He didn't know how it happened, but the glass smashed and cut his hand. Blood and water mingled and spiralled together down the plughole. He saw beautiful patterns and a seductive dance as these ribbons slipped into the drain. And he imagined a woman's laughter and delight.

FORTY-FIVE

On the other side of the city, Zoe sat at her desk and stared at her computer screen. The inbox for her email was packed with abusive messages. She deleted each one methodically, but couldn't stop herself from reading them first and soaking up the hatred. She reminded herself that all of these messages were, most likely, the work of only one or two men. But they had been busy and the violence and anonymity of it spooked her. She wanted to be stronger and not to care, but it was impossible.

It was dark outside and the office was empty. There would be two duty officers around somewhere, but right now she was alone and she hated it. She needed Sam but he wasn't answering his phone. The door opened at the far end and then slammed shut. She turned around. There was no one there.

Disconcerted, she stood up and walked towards the door, pulling it open and peering out into the corridor. Someone

310

had switched the light off. She reached for the switch, but when the lights clicked back on, there was nothing to see. So this was the new game.

It wasn't too late to write up a report that claimed self-defence and reasonable actions by Sergeant Cartmell. It was all she had to do and she had always prided herself on being part of the gang. But when a door at the other end of the office slammed shut and suddenly the entire CID office was plunged into darkness, Zoe knew that she would never write that report.

She slipped back to her desk. She was lighter and more dextrous than any of her colleagues and she could play in the dark all night. She heard two men slip in by the entrance next to the DCI's office and she knew that they'd come for her. She heard their breathing and saw them peering into the dark, taking slow, tentative steps forward, waiting for her to call out and reveal herself.

Once, an officer called Jared McLean had decided to rat on his colleagues when he believed that they'd stolen some of the proceeds of a post office robbery. They came for him at his home, stuffed a pillow case over his head and threw him into the back of a van. He was found the next morning, tied to a post, waist-deep in the river, screaming hysterically as the tide rose.

Zoe had made no accusations, not yet. And this wasn't stolen money, this was just a cop and a little grunt on an estate. But they were coming for her, nonetheless.

She kept away from her desk and – slowly, silently – she moved to the far end of the office, so that she was near a door if and when they decided to turn the lights back on. She wondered if they'd got colleagues waiting in the corridors, so that if she did run, they'd be ready for her. She even thought about how she'd get out to her car. The tyres would be let down, no doubt. Maybe a key had been scratched across the door or bonnet.

They all look the same, she thought. All in blue, all talking the same, thinking the same, doing the same. All part of the same horrible club. She was angry that she'd been a part of it for so long.

And where the hell was Sam? Why wasn't he answering her calls? She flinched at the sudden idea that he'd turned his back on her. Maybe they'd gone to him and told him their version and he'd bought it and let them go for her. That was why he wasn't here now. He'd told them she was fair game.

She cursed his name silently in the darkness and felt the throb of tears which she stuffed back down inside. She stood in the darkness and watched the thugs stumble forward and, in that moment, she decided that she would find Helen Seymour again.

FORTY-SIX

Unable to stop, Sam worked through the papers once more. He had taken the photos of the female suspects and laid them out at the top of the bed, on the pillows, then started to circle relevant corresponding details and placed them in lines below the head-shots. It created long rows of paperwork that streaked down the bed like some sort of anarchic family tree. He crouched amongst the rest of the files, reading the same facts over and over again.

He'd lost track of time when he heard a knock on the door. He waited, and Magda entered quietly. She smiled a little coyly, but he noticed how her eyes flicked around to the chaos of the room with some alarm.

'Yes?' he snapped.

'You missed a phone call. Your phone, it was downstairs. I answered.'

'Who was it?'

'A girl. Ashley.'

313

Her name jolted him.

'What did she want?'

'She wants you to call.'

She handed Sam the phone and he checked the screen – a mobile number he didn't recognise was the last call listed. He'd given Ashley his card back at Lullingdale. It seemed a lifetime ago.

'She is young?' Magda asked with a teasing tone to her voice.

'She's a witness in a case,' he replied. Magda shrugged that same old shrug and was no less irritating for it. But she didn't leave the room. It was as though she was toying with an idea, and it was some time before she spoke again.

'Was she good?'

'Excuse me?'

'As a witness. I don't think she was very good, was she?'

Sam looked at her, surprised. Magda barely spoke to him normally and would usually drag herself around the house. But there was that moment last night and then, tonight, her hand on his shoulder. And now she talked as though she knew Ashley.

'Say that again.'

'I just say, she wasn't very good.'

'Why? What did she say to you on the phone?'

Her repeated shrugs and face-pulling only annoyed him more.

'Magda, I haven't got time to screw about with you. What did she say?'

'You want to screw with me?'

'No! No, God, no. I'm saying I don't have time for games.'

'But you want to screw with Ashley.'

Sam was on his feet now.

'Magda. What did she say to you?'

'You call her.'

And that was all she gave him. She padded away and he heard her bedroom door shut. Sam dialled the number immediately, but it went straight to voicemail. He turned around, frustrated, and trod on some of the papers, kicking them out of their muddled order. He squatted down and tried to organise them again.

What had Ashley said to Magda? It was as though she had slipped through the phone and into his house. Her scowl and sly laugh were somehow hiding under his bed now, whispering along the corridors, crouching at the doors of his children's bedrooms. And it was as though Magda had let her in.

He rang the number again. This time it rang three times and then clicked to voicemail. She must have seen his number and hung up. He paused, then decided to leave a message.

'Hello, this is Detective Inspector Taylor. I missed a call from you. Perhaps you would like to call me back on this number.' He paused. What the hell was he doing? 'Thank you,' he added a little hastily, undoing the performance. He clicked off angrily.

She wasn't a very good witness. That was what Magda said. It was all too easy to imagine them laughing together on the phone, discussing him, discussing how pathetic he'd been up there, desperate for sex, needy and easily imprisoned by his sickly lust.

He pictured Ashley, lying on top of him, fucking him as his hand pressed against her white jumper, desperate for the feel of her flesh in the freezing cold. He saw the way her eyes stared past him. Now, remembering the moment, it felt as though she was watching someone else, as though her stare was a silent conversation with someone who organised and dictated her actions.

Like a gunshot in the dark, Sam saw Helen Seymour watching them in the night, nodding her approval.

All he had for the Sarah Downing case was Ashley's testimony. Until she'd happened to remember the key facts, and told him about Sarah Downing's dishevelled appearance, he'd had only suspicions. She had made it possible to push the investigation on, made it move too fast in fact, so that it inevitably collapsed once Helen Seymour came on board.

Magda was right. She wasn't a very good witness at all.

He stood up, rubbing his face with his hands, trying to

rub away all of these thoughts. They were nonsense. He was tired, it was late and he wasn't thinking straight.

He rang the number again. It clicked straight to voicemail. He saved the number on his phone so he'd know it was her if she called again. He needed to think logically about all this.

He remembered Ricky and the way he talked about this secret army of women who patrolled the streets, who watched everything. It was impossible to tell who was a part of it and who wasn't. Just like the collection of photos of gaunt women on his bed who stared at the police camera with shark eyes.

His eye drifted to the side of the bed where the photo of Andrea beamed out at him. Her photo shouldn't be anywhere near those monsters who now lay on his pillow. Sam took her photo and placed it delicately in the top drawer amongst his socks. Andrea had always bundled the socks together in neat balls, but now Sam had to flick through to find matching pairs.

He felt the fire stoking again. She was still smiling up at him as he shut her away. He was glad to shut her up.

The women on the bed stared hatefully at him. He left them there, went downstairs, poured himself a drink, knocked it down in one, rang Ashley again, got no answer and didn't know what to do. He sat down at the table and closed his eyes. But all he could see were the women. He blinked his eyes open and poured himself another drink. He imagined Ashley sitting opposite him, facing him, staring at him the same way that Helen had from across that beautiful old desk.

And still, somewhere, out there, little Lily was crying for him to find her.

He pushed the chair over as he stormed back up the stairs. He heard his mother shout something from the loft, calling out names of people who were no longer alive. He knocked twice, quickly, on Magda's door and headed in.

The lights were off and it took him a moment to see her, sitting up in her bed, shocked by his appearance.

'What did you and Ashley talk about?' he demanded.

'Nothing, Mr Taylor. Nothing.'

'No, no, she said stuff to you. What was it?'

'*Nothing*,' she insisted. She clutched the sheets tight to her.

'You tell me what she said to you right now or you'll be out on your arse this second, do you get me?'

'No!'

'Tell me!'

'You call her, you ask her,' she replied, finally angry and fighting back. 'I'm not afraid of you.'

'You should be.'

'Well, I'm not.' She was bolder now. 'When you go away, I'm the one they all need. Not you.'

And there was the fear again, slivering around his waist, tightening around his chest. It was too dark to see her properly, but he could imagine easily enough how she was glaring at him. He could feel the same anger that had poured out of Helen Seymour.

He didn't reply. He peered at her shrouded figure in the dark. He tried to keep his head clear, away from all of the fears that whipped and whirled around him.

'Dad?'

He vaguely heard his daughter's voice behind.

'I am here now,' Magda said, more determined. 'I am not going anywhere.'

'Dad.'

'WHAT DID SHE SAY?!' Sam screamed. He heard a cough of laughter thrown back at him.

'Dad. *Dad.*'

A hand grabbed his. He turned, ready to strike, only to find Issy standing there in her pyjamas.

'Issy?'

'Dad. Jenny's not in her room.'

It took a moment for the oddness of this comment to hit home. Jenny was meant to be locked away doing her homework, then tucking herself in as she always did. Sam hurried along the landing and entered her room. It was empty and the bed hadn't been slept in. He asked Issy questions that she couldn't answer and felt like he was interviewing a suspect.

His phone rang again and he was certain it would be

Ashley. Just as Magda's taunts had ended, so Ashley's would begin. A choreographed attack.

'What?' he shouted at the unknown phone number.

The voice was male. Calling from the Accident and Emergency Department at the local hospital, which had just admitted an unconscious teenage girl. Her ID informed them that her name was Jennifer Taylor.

Sam ran downstairs, shouting at Issy to tell Gran what had happened. He grabbed his coat, finding his wallet and car keys in the kitchen.

When he got to the door he looked up to see Issy crying at the top of the stairs. Magda stood next to her. She had her arm proudly around Issy and stared down at him as his daughter huddled into her for protection. Sam stopped for a second. They stared at each other, enemies within his own home. He didn't know what to do.

He left them there together and charged into the night.

FORTY-SEVEN

Zoe found Sam sitting, ashen, on a small plastic chair in a busy corridor outside A & E. She found a second chair, sat down next to him and took his hand. He squeezed it tight, but didn't look at her. After five minutes like this, she pulled herself free and used her warrant card to elicit some information from a passing nurse.

Unknown to her father, Jenny had found comfort in the company of the cool kids at school who tolerated her because she stole money from her grandmother's purse and bought them all booze. It was a self-loathing pattern of behaviour which had accelerated with each unnoticed outing. That night, Jenny had gone out drinking with these same 'friends'; swigging from bottles of extra-strong cider and being rejected by clubs, they staggered around the streets. A few hours later, she hit her head when tripping on the pavement and fell into the path of an oncoming car. The good news was that the car had squealed to a halt in time.

Less good was that Jenny was concussed and the high level of alcohol in her bloodstream was slowing her recovery. But, ultimately, she'd be fine. Not that you could tell from looking at Sam. His hands were gripped tightly together – a strange mixture of supplication and a giant fist. She sank back into the seat next to him.

'She's going to be fine,' she said.

'I know.'

'So cheer up, you silly old goat.'

He tried to smile, but just couldn't manage it.

'Sam. Sam, it's okay. This sort of thing happens all the time. It's what young girls do.'

Sam shook his head. No.

'You're a great dad, boss.'

If the words affected him, if he felt any warmth from their kindness, he didn't show it.

'She's a good girl, she'll be so ashamed, won't touch alcohol again for a year, I bet.'

'She's a good girl,' he repeated, flat. He turned to look at Zoe then and his eyes were wide. He looked vulnerable in a way she'd never known before.

'I thought she was sweetness and light,' he said, his voice cracking with the emotion. 'I would carry her around when she was little, and she'd hold on to me so tight with her tiny arms. She was just perfect.'

322

She didn't know what to say to this, and they sat together in silence. Finally, he let out a sigh.

'I'm fucking it all up, Zoe,' he said. 'Jenny would never do anything like this if I was doing it properly. Being a decent dad.' Tears welled in his eyes. 'How can I be angry with her? She's my little girl. They're my babies and I love them but they look at me like I'm this stupid . . . stupid . . .'

He ran out of words.

'It was just a couple of drinks,' Zoe said softly. 'That's all. Don't beat yourself up over a couple of drinks.'

'I just want them to be happy. To be normal. How do I do that?'

The question dragged him to his feet.

'I can't give them back their mother, can I?'

His voice was raised, wet with tears. Two nurses looked up and watched him as he flapped his arms uselessly.

'I can't magic her back, I can't stop work. How can I? Jenny should be laughing, she should be watching the telly and doing . . . those things girls do. But I can't make it right. I don't know how. How do I make all this work? How do I fix it?'

She didn't have any answers. Instead she stood up and put her arms out. But Sam pulled away.

'They need their mother. They bloody need their fucking mother!'

And the grief had worked its way into something else

now. The tears were still there but his hands were clenched and his mouth tight, his teeth showing.

'She should be here. She should be here,' he spat. 'I can't fix this. I just need something I can fix.'

And again he slumped into the chair. Zoe looked around, stared down the two nosy nurses and then sat back down next to him. After a while, he looked up and she could see that the fever had passed.

'So tell me something,' he said. 'Are you okay?'

'Not so much,' she replied. 'Did you get a chance to talk to Sergeant Cartmell? About my problem?'

'Sorry. I'll . . . I will,' he said, and then his voice changed and hardened. 'What do you think of Helen Seymour?'

She was thrown by the change in direction. She was surprised that he was thinking about her and she wondered if he knew about the meeting she'd had only a few hours before.

It was in the same cafe as before. Lizzy served the coffee and Helen ordered toast and baked beans. There were the usual pauses and waiting games but the mood now was differently charged.

'I won't do anything that'll hurt Sam,' Zoe had blurted out.

'I wouldn't expect you to,' Helen said.

'But you want things from me,' Zoe said. 'You want me to tell you about Sam and I won't do it.'

324

Helen chose her words carefully. Zoe could tell that she was wary of letting things slip, and this made her all the more unhappy to be there. But she felt she had nowhere else to go.

'I'm going to have to trust you, Zoe,' she finally said. 'This could be some form of entrapment.'

'Why, do you want me to do something illegal?'

'Of course not.'

'So talk.'

Helen bit on some toast and fiddled with the crumbs on her plate.

'I think Sam is part of a plot to frame me.'

Zoe snorted at this, but Helen waved her hand to allow her time to continue.

'I know how it sounds,' she added. 'And I don't say it lightly. Can you tell me where he's got with the investigation?'

'No, of course I can't.'

'Not Sarah Downing. Me. His investigation into me.'

Zoe looked at her as though she was insane. 'He's not after you. We're trying to find a missing girl, remember?'

'You might be,' Helen replied.

Zoe glanced out of the window and saw two PCs stroll by. The men didn't glance in through the window, but Zoe's mouth went dry at the sight of them.

'I need to go,' she said. 'They'll rip me apart if they find I'm hanging around with you.'

'If you want, you can always come and work for me,' Helen said.

'What? Doing what?'

'As an adviser. As an investigator. It will be the same sort of work, but you'll be part of a team you can trust and your pay will be infinitely better.'

'I like my work, I'm not throwing it away on you,' she said.

'I keep trying to tell you, Zoe. I'm the one trying to help you.'

Although she felt the need to get out of there, Zoe didn't move. Helen had always been friendly, and her words were kind and thoughtful, but still she didn't dare trust her. But then she didn't feel she could trust anyone else right now either, and it was this that paralysed her.

'It shouldn't be this difficult, should it?' Helen said, noting her sadness. 'Just being a woman, doing a job, living a life. Why has it become so tough these days?'

'I don't know what you're talking about,' Zoe replied. But she did. She felt it the moment she stepped out of her front door. No, before that, she felt it the moment she stared at her bleary eyes in the mirror, the moment she worried about her choice of clothes. She felt it in the eyes of the men she'd pass as she ran to work, on the way she'd laugh too loud at other guys' jokes, at the constant, pumped-up performance she gave just so she could feel she belonged. It had always been this way. She'd grown up with four brothers who had instinctively pushed her away as they became older, not fully understanding why, but never feeling the same sense of comfort as they did with each other. Plenty of friends had pointed out that her career choice was an attempt to recreate those old feelings, but Zoe wasn't interested in such cod psychology.

'I find it tough,' Helen said. 'And so tiring. I've found that having friends around who understand and who are on your side can make all the difference.'

'I've got plenty of friends,' Zoe scoffed. And she did, it was true. But she had allowed work to consume her so completely that she felt apart from them all now. She had subscribed to the theory that only other cops could understand her because of their shared experiences, and so had pushed away the rest of the world. More often than not, she was alone. She'd grin feebly at herself in the bathroom mirror and pretend she was happy as can be.

'I'm fed up being told how much I can drink, how loud I can laugh,' Helen said. 'I just want to turn my back on all of that. Stick close to friends who don't care about the bits of me that are fucked up, because they're fucked up too.'

'And who are these special friends?' Zoe asked.

Helen caught Lizzy's eye and smiled.

'I guess I have friends in interesting places.'

Interesting places. Zoe could imagine knowing looks all over the city. It felt like she was collecting them.

'I think you would be an interesting friend to have too, Zoe. And I think you would benefit from the friends I have.'

Zoe didn't need to be alone. But she also knew there would be a price.

You don't have to agree to anything yet, she told herself. Just find out the cost. You don't have to hurt Sam. You don't have to do anything wrong. Not yet. Just find out more.

Helen sat patiently opposite her.

'What do you want me to do?' Zoe finally asked.

She frowned as she remembered the conversation, and worried about why Sam, sitting so sadly next to her, had asked about Helen.

'I guess she's probably pretty great at her job,' she replied, tucking her hands under thighs as she spoke. 'Why do you ask?'

'I hate her,' Sam said.

'What's happened?' she asked, alarmed, but he said no more. They felt so far apart. It was as though she'd been 'repositioned' somehow so that Helen was more clearly in focus and it was Sam who was blurred and hard to trust.

'She's dangerous,' he said. She watched his hands twist and his mouth word silent curses. It reminded her of the bad times when he'd appear at her door, drunk and morose, his eyes red with tears, howling his wife's name. She had thought those days were over.

All around them, nurses and doctors marched by with their duties. A patient on a stretcher was wheeled past and Zoe saw a loose hand flop to the side as it went by. A tannoy announced something inaudible.

She left him to stay with Jenny overnight at the hospital and promised to check in on Issy at the house. Sam had rambled on about not trusting the nanny, and she was grateful that he was making it easier for her. She got to his house in the middle of the night, used the key he'd given her and stepped inside without making a sound.

Issy was asleep in her bed, her long hair dragged over her face. Zoe watched her for a moment, remembering days gone by when she would babysit for Sam and Andrea. She used to do 'nail sessions' with their daughters and enjoyed the girliness of her time with them. It seemed so long ago now. Work had dragged her into darker places. She looked around the room, the same way she did wherever she went now – checking, clocking, noting – and then slipped out, glad to be able to tell Sam that she'd checked up on Issy and all was fine.

But that wasn't really why she was here.

She trawled the house, past discarded clothes, tennis rackets and stinky trainers, wondering where Sam would keep the files. Eventually she ended up in his bedroom. The sight stopped her dead.

It wasn't just the papers that were littered all over the floor. Nor was it the heavy scrawls and frantic circles that Sam had drawn on each and every one. It was the collection of photographs – police mugshots – of the women who were laid so neatly on the pillows that made her queasy. Maybe there was some sense in the way Sam saw it all, the way some people know just where things are in piles of junked paperwork. But Zoe knew that Sam was an orderly man, and this was not the way he usually worked.

She didn't touch a thing. She stepped gently amongst the papers and took in every detail. Women, murdering children, connected somehow to water. She remembered the way that the news reports and newspapers had wailed at the dangers of women at the time. And she thought about Helen's words. In this room, they made perfect sense.

It was later when she realised that all of the papers formed a circle and that the effect was rather like a spider's web. And at the centre of all of this was another photo. And the face that smiled serenely up from the bed was Helen Seymour.

Zoe didn't move for quite some time. She knew that the next decisions she made would change everything, irrevocably.

She didn't move. She didn't move for quite some time.

FORTY-EIGHT

Sam returned home with Jenny early the next morning. She was pale and withdrawn, possibly ashamed, maybe just stubborn and angry. He couldn't tell. They drove in silence. He wanted to say reassuring words, but they fell hopelessly into the footwells. Jenny sat still, her hands folded on her lap, her head bowed like a nun.

Eventually they parked up and he stopped her as she reached for the door.

'Jenny, honey.'

She sat back, staring forward, waiting for the lecture.

'I'm not angry,' he said. 'I'm just worried.'

She looked down, but that was as much as he got.

He stumbled on for a bit, made some bad jokes and eventually hated his voice as much as she clearly did. He let her go to her bedroom and change for school. She'd told him she wanted to go back and he'd been keen to show willing.

Tonight, he'd cook them a meal. He'd make a spaghetti carbonara, send Magda off to the pictures, he'd drag Mum downstairs and they could all have a laugh together. Jenny would be fine again. He'd solve this.

Issy was quiet too. He'd expected her to revel in Jenny's villainy, but she just munched on her toast and the only gesture she made was a quick, tight grip around Jenny's waist. She didn't say anything and this short act of solidarity was all the more affecting for it. Sam felt further estranged from his girls. He drank a coffee, standing alone by the microwave, watching them eat. There was no noise beyond chewing and the miserable scraping of cutlery.

Magda came in. She stopped at the door and glanced at Sam, then at the girls. Issy looked up at her and smiled. Magda nodded then turned and left. Sam saw it all and clutched his mug that tiny bit tighter.

He found himself standing by the stairs as the girls grabbed their things and headed off. He had nothing to say as they trooped off down the road and was equally dumb when Magda turned on the Hoover, slowly pushing him towards the door. He wanted to stay, to show some command in his own home, but this was a battle whose rules he didn't understand. He found himself shutting the door and wandering away without purpose.

He stood by the car, keys in his hand, dog-tired, his mind smudged, mistrustful of everyone and of his own cramping emotions. He was about to drag himself back to the station and force himself through the mountainous paperwork that he'd been avoiding since the call to the Lake District, when something popped into his head. Something about the papers upstairs in his bedroom, his addiction to their detail. He hurried back, clocking the wariness with which Magda eyed him as he hurried up the stairs.

He shut the bedroom door and looked at the scattered papers. It only took a moment to realise what was wrong. A file had been moved. To a stranger, all the papers had been dumped in a haphazard disorder. But Sam knew where everything should be, and it was clear to him that the file which housed the details of the witness, Richard Howell, had been touched. It had been moved a few inches from where he had left it. Just a few inches, but Sam was sure of it. He grabbed the case folder and opened it up. Everything was still there, but he felt a little sick as he looked through the details – there, written down for the woman who had spied on him, was the address where Richard now lived.

Now they knew that he had visited Ricky. Helen would have been told.

Magda knocked on the door and he snapped his head around to face her. She saw the aggression and took a step back.

'You want me to clean in here?' she asked cautiously.

He waited for the tell to show that she'd already been in

here and didn't need his permission at all. But her face gave nothing away.

'Don't ever come in here again. Got that?'

She turned tail and vanished. Sam looked back down at the file.

Helen knew about Ricky.

He ran out of the house and threw himself into the car.

He parked outside Ricky's dingy apartment, ignoring the double yellow lines. He sprinted up the stairs, three at a time and hammered on the door. He banged and banged but no one came. He went to neighbours' doors but got no reply. He felt as though they were all hiding from him. Eventually, he made a call to the station, explained that he believed a man's life was in danger and asked to use the necessary protocol to break into the flat. Once permission was given, he kicked and kicked until the wood splintered and he could force himself in.

Sam made his way from room to room, the suspicion hardening to fact as he found each one bare. He stopped in the hallway after his search. Ricky was gone, clothes had been snatched from a chest of drawers, as had bed linen and the television. Once again, he'd been spirited away.

Helen's network had done its job. Sam considered the legal powers he might have to be able to force the chambers to reveal all of its correspondence, but he also felt that such a slow, bureaucratic method wouldn't and couldn't shackle a woman like Helen. And the result was always the same: silence.

She silenced the women and she silenced the witnesses. Whatever was going on, Helen was hell-bent on shutting it up. She got to these women and they never spoke again. Did she know them before they committed their vile crimes? Did she organise these too? Right now, Sam deemed her capable of anything.

He drove to her chambers. He wanted to face her again, wanted to stare her down and tell her that he knew what she was doing and that he was going to stop her. He didn't care if she laughed in his face. He needed something beyond these constant doubts and fears. But when he reached her offices, he was politely told that she had left for business and wasn't expected back for several days.

He imagined her driving Ricky away.

He went back to the station, entered his office, pulled down the blinds and sat uselessly at his desk.

They all fell silent. They killed the children and never spoke again. Every time. Every time, except for Sarah Downing. She continued to act normally. He remembered how she stared at him and swayed when he arrested her, and how cold and 'other' she seemed to him. It was as though something took her over, as though she was nearly revealed to him. But then Helen had silenced her too.

She was free now, and walking among us. Looking like everyone else.

Why was she different? Because she was free? Free to do it again?

Sam thought of Helen again, driving a fretful Ricky away from the city. Far away to somewhere no one would find him. Sam imagined the move from those grotty streets to calmer, cleaner spaces. Open fields, blue skies.

Lullingdale Water swept back into his mind. The waves licked at his feet, the icy breeze bit at his face. Arthur Downing floated before him, just out of reach. And Lily spied on him from the edge of the woods.

Lily. All the other women fell silent once they'd completed their terrible deeds.

Maybe Sarah had been freed because her work wasn't done yet.

And that would be because Lily was still alive.

Lily Downing was alive. Sarah would know where she was, would be waiting for the furore to calm down, and then she would finish what she started. Helen would tell her when. Maybe Helen wanted it done now. And she would have Ashley to help her.

The pieces crunched into place.

Sam hurried home. He packed for several days. He paused

when he thought of Jenny, and of the sly glances that Magda and Issy shared. But then Lily's cries drowned out all of this.

Everything would be fine, but he needed to get up to the Lakes first.

FORTY-NINE

Sam was dumping a bag into the boot of his car when Zoe found him. She seemed to appear from nowhere and made him jump.

'Hey, boss. What's up?' Her voice was strangely cheerful. It felt a little fake.

'Hi. You alright?' He placed the last of his things into the boot and slammed it shut.

'Never better. So what are you up to?'

The sun was setting already and the dull clouds made the day all the shorter.

'Boss?' she asked again.

'Thought I might head back up to the Lakes.'

'You got a hunch?'

'Something like that, yeah.'

'Cool! I'll come with you.'

'You'll need to pack some clothes. I think I'll be gone for a few days, at least.'

'You know me,' she said, holding up a small holdall. 'Always prepared.'

He didn't know what to say. She faced him confidently, then bashed him happily on the arm.

'Come on then, let's get going,' she said. 'Sooner we get there, sooner you can buy me a pint in the pub that time forgot.'

She skipped over to the passenger side and got into the car. He tried to think of a reason why she couldn't come with him. There was something about her persistence and forced jollity that worried him.

It was Zoe, he reminded himself. It was Zoe and she had never let him down. But then darker thoughts crept up and sniggered at his softness.

He went back to the house and returned carrying his heavy boots. He threw them under the driver's seat and got in next to her.

Zoe patted his knee.

'Come on then, let's get the hell out of here.'

Sam grunted and turned the key in the ignition.

No one spoke. The radio wasn't needed. Their thoughts clashed and sparked against each other as they headed away from the city. Black clouds loomed ahead of them, and Sam sped towards the darkness.

PART THREE

PART THREE

FIFTY

Sam drove fast and spoke little. Zoe fidgeted next to him, but the few jokes she tossed his way made little impression. He gripped the steering wheel tight, and the congestion eased as the car sped north. The sky revealed itself, the buildings fell away and for a while the land rose and fell gently around them. But as they approached the Lakes an imposing wall of rocky terrain reared up ahead. It was beautiful and severe, and Sam was struck by the way that the other traffic seemed to vanish, leaving two lonely policemen travelling together, so very much apart.

The low winter sun dazzled their eyes as they headed further into the Lake District. It soon vanished again as they dipped down into a lush valley, empty but for the Jacobs sheep that littered its fields. He glanced at Zoe and was disconcerted to see that she was watching him. She offered him a smile, but he found he didn't trust her face any more. He wondered when this had happened, this divide between

343

them. She had done nothing wrong that he knew of. Why did he feel like this when she had done nothing wrong?

Outside, a doe and her two young bucks looked up from a swollen stream. Sam watched their bodies tense, ready to bolt. The car raced past, and beyond there was nothing but bracken and gorse. He knew that Zoe was still watching him, but he didn't look her way.

Zoe hated the silence. She stared out of the window and admired the great gulf of nature beyond, but always found herself turning back to Sam, wanting to talk to him. His eyes were narrow, shielded against the sun that would suddenly pierce the clouds then be blown away just as quickly. He looked filled with foreboding. Just as he had when they first met. Just as he had when he'd faced down those three drunks with machetes who thought that the cops were fair game in a back alley. Just as he had when a rotting plank of wood had given way and he'd pulled her to safety. He had always been there, always stood firm and resolute before her. A big brother, a line of continuity that couldn't bend or break. She thought this was how it should always be.

The road meandered towards another small peak, and Zoe recognised the small cairns on either side of the road. They would reach Lullingdale in five minutes. It was a short, steep drop down from here. You reached the turn in the road and the lake suddenly appeared before you. It should be a glorious sight, if you didn't know about Arthur and Lily, or witches, or any of those other terrible tales.

She put a hand on his forearm, but he didn't seem to notice. And then they made the turn, and there was the lake and it all seemed much, much too late.

They headed into the village. Zoe had called ahead and secured rooms at the pub. The tourist season had finished some time ago, and there would be little business until the spring. It was dark as they turned into the pub car park, and neither cop was expecting to see a pristine Mercedes parked in one of the 'hotel guest' spaces. A two-seater, fast and sleek.

'Nice wheels,' Zoe said with a whistle of approval.

She was surprised by the look that Sam gave her. He seemed angry. What had she said?

'Who do you think it belongs to?' Sam asked.

She flushed, as though she should know. His stare made her feel guilty.

'No idea, someone richer than you and me. And someone with serious taste,' she laughed back at him as best as she could.

Sam watched her for signs of the lie. He knew who the car belonged to. He'd done his homework and the number plate was etched in his brain. It belonged, of course, to Helen Seymour.

Zoe's laugh was too loud.

'So what's the plan, boss?' she said, pushing her door open. 'Check in, then go see Mrs Downing?'

'Sure,' he replied. The idea of catching Helen and Sarah together seemed delicious. 'Hang on, let's go straight there. Stay in, we'll drive.'

He put the car in reverse and spun right towards the Downings' house. He imagined their faces when he caught them plotting.

'Hey, slow down, Mister,' Zoe said, her voice still sing-song and fake, 'or you'll run over one of those zombie kids. Then again, you probably can't kill them just by hitting them with a car. You probably need to chop their heads clean off.'

But it wasn't Zoe that slowed him down. It was the sight he trapped in the headlights. Fifty yards ahead were two women sheltering in the fading brickwork of the bus shelter. The girl looked up and her eyes widened when she saw Sam behind the wheel. He recognised the surprise in Ashley's expression, but his attention was hooked on the woman stood next to her, stood over her, arms folded. Helen looked different out of her office clothes, now dressed in jeans and a purple coat, her features muffled by a hat. She turned more slowly and her eyes met Sam's with equal, withering hostility.

He was wrong. Helen wasn't plotting with Sarah. She

was plotting with Ashley. No, she was plotting with both of them.

The car crawled towards them and then stopped. Sam stared at Helen through the windscreen. She stared right back at him. His mouth formulated words, but nothing came out.

Inside the car, Zoe was saying something. It took him a while to register.

'Boss. Don't stop here, let's go.'

He felt Zoe's hand on his arm. He felt surrounded.

'Seriously. Not here.'

Her words made sense, but that didn't mean he should trust her. But without another idea in his head, he nodded and sped away, doing a quick three-point turn at an open field's gate some three hundred yards further on. They stopped there for a moment, hidden by the thick hedgerow and the night.

'What do you think she's doing here?' he asked.

'Visiting her client, I'd guess, and checking witness statements,' Zoe replied.

'Sarah Downing was released without charge. She doesn't need a lawyer, let alone a barrister. So how come Helen's here?'

'I don't know.'

'No,' he said.

No. There was no obvious answer. Not one for lawyers and police and everyday people.

He turned the car left and headed back towards the bus stop. When they got there, the women were gone.

Sam cursed to himself. He shouldn't have listened to Zoe. They should have questioned them while they had surprise on their side.

He parked up next to Helen's car and marched into the pub, grabbing his things.

'Hey!' Zoe shouted as he left her behind. But he didn't acknowledge the call.

FIFTY-ONE

Zoe let Sam storm off into the bar on his own. Now they were here again, all of her old fears rose up, and she remembered more clearly Sam's previous sullen silences and avoidances. It made her happier about the decisions she'd made. Helen was right: Sam was out of control. She hated the idea that Sam was just another man who would disappoint her, but then it struck her that these were the kinds of words Helen would use, and she felt a jab of fear that she was being manipulated. Her love for Sam and her fear for him tore at her and she felt herself crumble in the rift. It meant that she stood by the car for a good few minutes before she followed Sam into the pub. She sniffed in the fresh, bitter-cold air. She heard a dog bark somewhere nearby, probably down by the lake.

The lake. It felt prehistoric in its grandeur. Zoe wondered about all of the people who had sailed on it, walked around it, gazed down on it from the adjacent fells. She thought about the very first humans who ever reached the peaks and then gazed down at it. Once again, the thought made her feel small.

She went inside and the first person she saw was David. They almost bumped into each other and the surprise quickly twisted into a stiff, awkward recognition. David did not look down this time.

'Hello, David,' she said, aware of his mood.

'You're back then.'

'I am. We are.'

'So you know where Lily is?'

'You know I can't tell you that.'

He just shrugged. 'Can't do much, it seems. Can't even keep hold of the bitch that did it.' And with that he pushed past her and towards the men's toilets.

Zoe walked on, found Bernie serving drinks and felt a flush of affection for her, and some relief that hers was the next face she saw. She took a key from her – the same room as last time – and was about to head upstairs when she saw a gang of men sitting in the bar. Amongst them, shoulders hunched, was Tim Downing. Zoe watched him with the others and recognised their disposition: angry drunks. A chair was empty at the table which she assumed belonged to David. Normally Zoe would have backed away and avoided the friction, but she couldn't ignore Tim now that he was here in the same building.

He saw her and looked away, making her arrival at the table all the more awkward. David reappeared a moment later and took the empty chair, swigging deep on his pint.

'Mr Downing,' she said.

He was unable to ignore her for long. The basic politeness of the man forced him to look up and acknowledge her presence.

'I'm sorry I didn't call to let you know we were coming,' she said. 'It was all rather spur-of-the-moment.'

'What have you found?' he asked.

'I thought we could come by your house later and discuss it with you,' she said, alarmed by the thought that she didn't really know if they had found anything at all.

He muttered something that wasn't for her or for the stony-faced men at the table. She didn't bother to ask him to repeat it.

'When would be a good time for us to visit you and your wife?' she persisted.

There were angry chuckles at this.

'Mr Downing?'

'You won't find her with him,' David said.

'I see,' she said, intrigued by this development.

'I doubt that,' David added. 'You don't seem to get anything at all. Do you, love?'

'Mr Downing,' Zoe continued, her voice calm and even. 'Where would we find your wife, sir?'

'Where do you think?' Tim replied.

'She's run off with her doggy, Bud, hasn't she?' David added.

So Sarah was now with Bud. This didn't feel right.

'She didn't run off,' Tim corrected David. 'I kicked her out. And he's the only man in this village stupid enough to take her in.'

That made more sense.

'Whose bloody round is it?' Tim asked.

Zoe left them to it without bothering to excuse herself. She knew that any further conversation would only bring more rebukes. It wasn't surprising that Sarah and Tim's relationship had collapsed. Zoe and Sam had probably helped break it. Still, seeing Tim there, soaked in impotent rage, was a depressing sight. A boy was dead, a girl was missing. It was only natural for things to fall apart. But Zoe didn't like the way the men were stagnating and rotting in its wake.

Upstairs, she dumped her bag on the bed and instinctively went to tell Sam her news. But there was no answer at the door when she knocked. Confused and then angry, she listened for any signs of him, but got nothing.

She left her bag unopened and walked down to Bud's house. It was a ten-minute walk, but the exercise didn't calm her down.

When she reached his house, she stopped at the road and proceeded no further. Bud's house was just as she remembered it: sunk forlornly under the cover of thick trees, dank and awkward. His boots still lay by the door, and the curtains stayed drawn and protective. But across the door the letter 'W' had been sprayed in a crazy pink. W for Witch. Someone, Bud most likely, had tried to scrub it away, but had only managed to slur and smudge the letter, which remained as legible as ever.

Zoe stood there for a while, waiting to see if the curtains would move and worried eyes would peer out.

This bloody place, she thought. But then, again, the city was no better. It was odd to think that these ancient prejudices had reached so deep and still held so strong.

Whoever was inside was hunkered down, and Zoe realised that there was no noise inside or out. She kicked a stone, turned and walked away. She saw no one on the way, heard nothing, said nothing. Everything was black.

FIFTY-TWO

Sam found Ashley by the lake, as he knew he would. The water drew them together. When he saw her, she was leaning against a tree, as though inviting him into the wood, with a delighted, almost victorious smile on her face. The expression only irritated him further.

'Miss me?' she asked.

'Who were you talking to back then?' was all she got in return.

'Eh? Some lawyer woman. I dunno.'

'Liar.'

She pulled a 'you what?' face and crossed her arms, then switched emotions and pulled at Sam playfully, her face light and childish again. He pushed her hands away.

'What's your problem, Sam?'

His feet slipped on the pebbles and he had to steady himself slightly.

'You've talked to her before,' he said.

'Who?'

'Helen Seymour.'

'Who?'

'The woman, the barrister, the, the . . .'

The what? Sam's mind spun at words on the tip of his tongue.

'She said there's nothing to the case,' Ashley said. 'That's what she said. So, if that's right, then why are you back?'

The way she said it made it clear that she thought he had come back for her. Her hand snaked out, grabbing at his wrist. Again, he pulled away.

'What else did she tell you?' he asked.

'Who cares? She's boring and old.' Her voice dropped. 'I've missed you.'

She looked up at him and her eyes were wide and needy.

'They're all kids, all the others,' she said quietly. 'They're so dull.'

He wanted to shout. He wanted to pull the lies out from the depths of her throat and dangle them before her. He knew that she and Helen were plotting against him. He'd seen them together. He wanted to drag her to the lake and hold her under the water until she confessed and he had finally, finally, found Lily and killed the case.

'. . . And like, just hang out, you know, miles away from here.'

She rambled on, bashfully. Unable to determine if she was

355

for real or whether this was another elaborate performance, Sam took a deep breath and stuffed his emotions back down.

'I can't talk to you now,' he managed, and trudged away.

He heard her shout something at him but the wind sucked the words away, so all he got was a muffled yell. He didn't look back.

Sam hung a 'Do Not Disturb' sign on the door of his room and pulled a pillow over his head. A little later he heard Zoe pound on the door, but he didn't move. Eventually she went too.

Restless and unable to sleep, Sam got up and pulled back the curtains, staring at his own reflection in the black windows. The ageing, sagging glass warped his features into something monstrous. Beyond his smudged features, there was nothing.

He snapped the curtains shut again and dropped onto the bed. Tomorrow he would go and see Sarah Downing again, sit down with her and make her face all the questions that Helen had stopped them from asking.

He considered calling back home. He was worried about Jenny and the way Magda had been with them, but he also worried about resentful silences in return.

He should keep focused on the job, he told himself.

He remembered Jenny sitting so sadly in the car, and the urge to comfort her was almost overwhelming. He reached for the phone. He needed to hear her voice but he couldn't bear the idea that she wouldn't take his call. His hand retreated and he sat limply on the bed.

He considered the fact that Sarah would be armed with new lies that Helen would have prepared for her, but he'd blast those out of the way, no problem. He only prayed that he could rip the information from her before it was too late.

There was a knock on the door. It wasn't Zoe, it was tentative in a way she could never be.

'Sam?'

He slammed the door open and Ashley instinctively took a step back. She wore her white coat and hat, her witch's costume. The White Witch.

'Can I come in?' she said, and gave the corridor a nervous glance.

'Why?'

'There's stuff I want to tell you.'

'About what?'

'Can I come in or what?'

He let her inside, then shut the door and turned the key in the lock. Ashley noticed this but thought nothing of it. She was in his lair, this time.

'So?' he said, and leant against the door to be sure she couldn't escape.

'I wanted to tell you something. About the case.'

Her eyes were eager, but Sam wasn't biting.

'Since you went, we've had no dealers,' she added.

'I'm sorry?'

'Well, you know how we always used to go down to the lake and meet them there.'

'You said you didn't buy drugs yourself.'

'I don't. But this is what the others said. I've been keeping an ear to the ground. To help you out, like. See? I'm a good girl.'

'What are you telling me?' he asked.

Her hands played with the small silver necklace around her neck as she talked.

'Well, no one was expecting any dealers around while you were here. As soon as Arthur and Lily went missing, we had like a trillion cops all charging round the place. So they steered well clear, yeah? But since you've been gone, no one's been back.'

'And?'

'And isn't that important?'

She tried to grab at him as she always did, but her hand was more tentative this time and his refusal to move meant that she let go and stood there, edgy and quiet.

'Who told you to come up with this then?'

'Piss off.'

She does offended very well, he thought. So Helen tells her to come over with stories about dealers. We chase after them and leave Sarah alone.

358

'And when did this incredible discovery surface then?'

'Eh?'

'Why didn't you mention it when you saw me before?'

''Cos you were being a dick.'

'So what do you suggest, Ashley?'

'I don't know, you're the cop. You do your thing. I guess . . . you could always thank me.'

She unbuttoned her coat. Beneath it was a cropped white top that revealed her midriff. Sam watched her with a trembling rage.

The locked door trapped him in with her, not the other way round.

He pushed her away and struggled with the snagging key in the lock. She started to shout obscenities at him but none made it to his head. He pushed at her and she clawed angrily back.

'Liar, liar, you fucking liar!' he found himself hissing angrily as they struggled on the threshold. He picked her up and dumped her into the corridor.

'What the fuck is your fucking problem?' she yelled.

He slammed the door shut and turned the key again to keep him safe.

Ashley had failed. Helen would be angry when she heard this. When Ashley told her.

The thought of this had him hurrying along the corridor. He could catch them together. And that would prove their guilt. If he saw Helen briefing Ashley now, right now, then there could be no doubts.

Helen had a room at the far end of the corridor. He'd checked when he'd arrived and he ran fast so that he could catch Ashley knocking on the door. But as he rushed past the stairs, he was surprised to see Ashley scurrying down and away.

Confused, he followed, seeing her slip out of the pub via a back entrance near the toilets. It was lucky that she was wearing white.

She trudged away, pulling her coat tight around her.

He followed her down towards the lake.

At the edge she stopped for a moment, then took out her phone and used it as a torch, lighting the path ahead as she turned left and headed for the woods.

Sam heard it before he saw it: the music from somewhere among the trees. He remembered the last time he'd been here. He let her walk further ahead of him. He knew now where she'd be.

The fire curled and flickered higher and higher as two lads stuffed wooden crates onto the flames. The dry wood ignited almost instantly and Sam could feel its heat from the safety of the trees. There were ten, maybe fifteen kids there, all drunk, all wrapped up tight in thick coats and hats, dancing in circles and goofing about.

It took him a while to spot Ashley. She stood amongst

the others with a bottle in her hand, which she guzzled down angrily. Sam realised that she had been crying and a different set of emotions crowded him.

The music got louder. The flames roared and the pyre got bigger. Two lads stripped off to their boxer shorts and, despite the freezing temperatures, danced wildly around as others egged them on. One jumped over the fire and the other couldn't resist doing the same. Others screamed and laughed. Bottles smashed and two girls undressed as well, screaming at the night and the cold.

Sam's eyes flickered with the flames. He saw the kids sway and writhe to the music, their movements in sync with the tribal beat of the heavy bass. They're just drunk kids, he told himself, bored with their little lives. He knew where his imagination wanted to drag him, but he would not let it.

The flames danced and teased. Red sparks rushed to the heavens as cardboard boxes were dumped on top.

Ashley finished the bottle then smashed it into the fire as the others screamed. She didn't dance though, and her coat was tightly buttoned up.

A couple was snogging ferociously near the fire, and the boy pushed the girl down to his crotch. To the wolf-whistles of the other kids she undid his flies and started to give him a blow-job. Even the girls cheered her on, and her only acknowledgement was to give them the finger with one hand while holding his cock in the other. The lad was handed a bottle of beer and he swigged deep, doing a victor's pose to manic cheers. And then, inflamed by his own stupidity and lust, he started to pour beer onto the girl's head. Incredulous and then furious, the girl pulled back and then started punching and slapping the lad, cursing him with a mad fury. He laughed as he ducked from her blows, trying to zip himself up as everyone else crowed and whistled.

But Ashley watched with a forlorn stare, set apart from the rest, her sadness unnoticed. Sam saw a tear, illuminated by the fire, fall down her face.

A bottle of vodka was passed around the circle, each person taking a swig until it was empty and smashed on the fire. Each time someone drank, the others wailed. More of them were naked now. It seemed impossible. Sam's feet pricked with the cold, but they seemed impervious.

Someone was climbing a tree, carrying a burning piece of wood. They tried to light one of the higher branches and Sam watched in horror, imagining the whole forest ripping into flame. A girl appeared in front of him, barely ten yards away, tugging smoke down from a glass bong. She exhaled with a mesmeric gasp and the smoke poured from her lungs like a dragon.

It was too wild. The noise was too much, the flames too high. He took a step back but still his eyes fell back to Ashley. He wanted her to see him, to spy him out in the dark like she had before. But she stared at the floor, hugging a new bottle, unaware. He wanted to step out, and for her to see him, but he didn't know how.

It forced him away from them. He couldn't cope any longer with the madness and he stamped and crunched through the wood, away from the heat, until things made more sense. He stopped and took a deep breath, realising he was lost, but relieved by the cold and the quiet. The beat pumped on from somewhere further back. But here, he felt safe.

It took him a while to find the path back to the village, and as he stepped onto it he heard a foot crack on a branch behind him. He turned and saw Ashley. She saw him and neither moved for a second, but the sight of her stirred the fires again and the beat began to pump and kick against him.

He turned and hurried away.

She followed. She chased him to his bedroom and banged against the locked door.

He found he had to open it.

She stood there before him and her eyes controlled him. He had no choice but to let her in.

He did what she wanted.

'Go away,' he whispered as he pulled her to him.

She made his hands pull the top over her neck, and watched as his eyes took in her skin.

'Why don't you kick me out?' she asked. Her lips brushed his ear.

'I don't know.'

'What did you see? Down in the wood?'

His hand unbuckled her belt.

'Did you see witches?' she whispered.

Her clothes were pulled away and discarded on the floor.

'It was nothing,' she said. 'We do it all the time.'

He nodded. She started to unbutton his shirt.

'There are no witches,' she said. 'You know that, don't you?'

He nodded, mute.

'You let me in because you love me.'

He felt the shirt fall from his shoulders. All he could see were her ruby lips.

'You love me and I love you. There are no witches, there's just you and me.'

She bit his neck and he fell onto the bed.

She crawled onto him and his hands held her tight.

They hid in each other and turned out the lights and wished the world away. When they were done, she snuggled close with her arm wrapped across him.

He did not push it away.

But when he closed his eyes, he found the flames still flickered and danced before him.

Later, when he was sure she was asleep, he got up and

opened the curtains again. His features were lit by the dull light of the bathroom mirror. Despite the girl, maybe because of her, he stared at himself in the glass and he was still the monster.

FIFTY-THREE

Normally, Zoe would have sunk a few in the bar and got over it that way. But tonight she knew that she couldn't go down there, not without risking more scorn. When her phone rang, therefore, and she saw that it was Helen, she was happy to meet up. They met by her car and Zoe let Helen drive her away from the hotel. They parked in a small lay-by that was a popular beauty spot during the day. Right now, all Zoe could see was the vague silhouette of fells under a moonless sky.

Helen pressed a button and lowered the window before lighting a cigarette.

'What are you doing up here?' Zoe asked. 'I wished you'd told me.'

'I would have, if I'd known you were coming,' Helen replied. 'Has something happened?'

'Not that I know of.'

Zoe sat glumly in the car. Helen turned to her. She was too close.

'Come on, Zoe, talk to me. What's the new lead?'

'I don't know. I just thought it best if I was with him.'

Helen nodded and sucked on her cigarette, blowing the smoke out of the window.

'Why are you here?' Zoe asked again.

'I just wanted to tie up the loose ends. After what you told me about Sam, it's clear he's not letting this one go.'

Yes, the things she'd told her. The words sickened Zoe.

'Has he really not told you the reason why he's back up here?' Helen asked.

'No. No, he's not telling me anything at the moment.'

But it hadn't stopped her telling Helen. Leaving his house that night and going back to her with the news that she was right, that her boss was obsessed with her, and that he was trawling through old cases in order to try to hurt her. Now that she'd done it, she felt used and stupid. The horrible thought struck her that Sam knew about her and Helen. It would explain his silence.

'Shit,' Helen muttered. 'I'd hoped he would be more open with you.'

Zoe stared out of the car. The darkness seemed to have wrapped itself around them. The thin line that hinted at the fells had been wiped away and now there was nothing but perfect blackness.

'What's happened with the witness?' she asked.

'Nothing,' Helen replied, and Zoe thought the answer

was a little snatched. 'Why do you think I'd have anything to do with something like that?'

Zoe was about to reply that they'd found paperwork that proved otherwise, but her instincts snapped her mouth shut. Helen had just lied to her. She needed to think very carefully. Helen had lied to her, and no doubt this wouldn't have been the first time. Zoe had made a terrible mistake by placing her trust in this woman. Sam was right to wonder why Helen would make the long journey up here when she didn't even represent Sarah Downing. It wasn't the behaviour of a normal barrister. There was more going on and Zoe shouldn't be in this car.

'I'm betraying my best friend,' she said miserably.

'No, you're protecting him. I told you this. You're here because you're worried about Sam and you're going to stop him doing something very stupid.'

The words didn't feel like advice, more like orders. She heard the tobacco crackle and burn as Helen took a deep drag on her cigarette.

'You're helping him,' Helen insisted, 'and I need you to keep watching him for me. I know you feel torn and you wouldn't be human if you didn't, but it's for the best.'

She spoke so calmly and with such a reassuring tone that it was easy to believe her.

'So you've seen Sarah?' Zoe said.

'I have.'

'And? What did she say?'

'I told you, Zoe. She didn't do it. I was more interested in the witness who came up with all that nonsense about the dress. Ashley Deveraux. She's a piece of work, huh?'

Zoe nodded. At least this was something on which they could agree.

'I almost wish we had gone to court if she was their main witness,' Helen added. 'It would have been quite a circus.'

She was crowing, and Zoe disliked her all the more for it.

'There's something else about her though,' Helen said as she finished her cigarette and stubbed it out. 'I think she's in love with Sam.'

Zoe thought of the way Ashley had sat in the back of the car, and how she'd gazed at Sam in the interview room. Zoe's mind fizzed. How had she not noticed this before? But love? How? When had there been time for this to happen?

'You know, if you're worrying about witnesses,' Helen said, stretching in her seat, 'you might want to look closer to home before throwing any accusations at me.'

'Thanks for the lecture,' Zoe replied.

Helen laughed, apologised, then put the car into gear, steering them back to the hotel. She turned on the stereo and a jaunty song played – country-and-western. It seemed so incongruous with Zoe's spiralling fears. As they drove Helen prodded some more. Would Zoe let her know if Sam did anything strange? Did she recognise how dangerous he was? Did she see that she was on the right side, doing the right thing?

Zoe nodded and made the appropriate replies, but she struggled to maintain this appearance. She hated being here, hated the dark. She wanted it to be light, to throw on some trainers and to run; burn away the doubts and worries and clear her head. But the night wouldn't budge.

Helen let Zoe go in first, telling her she would make a few calls in the car and then wander in later to avoid them being seen together. Zoe slipped out and hurried past the bar. She went back to Sam's room, but stopped when she saw the 'Do Not Disturb' sign. Her hands felt too puny to reach the door and knock. She felt too slight, too small, and yet so pumped full of betrayals.

She went to her room and sat in a miserably lukewarm bath. Sleep didn't come easy.

FIFTY-FOUR

Downstairs, the men huddled together at tables where they muttered and drank, drank and muttered. A loud cough of laughter would punch through, but otherwise all you could hear was a low murmur. Thick, calloused hands, rough from everyday work, grabbed tough pint glasses, and weathered faces flushed red from the heat. They joked the same jokes, just as they had always done. Hands flicked through thinning hair and tales were retold about glory days now long gone.

Someone would mention a girl or a woman and lips would be licked and more jokes would be made. Everything was harmless, everything was just as it always had been. There was no need for it to change or for anyone to take offence.

No one saw Sam slip upstairs, or the girl that followed. But they all saw Zoe when she hurried in and they scoffed at the hasty retreat she beat to her room.

And no one knew what to do with Helen when she strolled into the bar with a small, polite nod to the locals that was somewhat undone by the way she stood at the bar so confidently, ordering a double whisky and daring anyone to come and talk to her. No one did, and as she stood there and watched them all, so the conversation was that tiny bit quieter.

When she left, they grumbled and moaned. Something not quite right about that one. Standing there, so proud and so arrogant. Not right at all.

FIFTY-FIVE

Zoe woke to the sound of driving rain. She got up and stared out at the bleak landscape. Heavy, watercolour clouds squatted on top of the fells, obscuring their peaks, and the wind lashed against the windowpane. A moment later, her phone chirruped with a text. It was from Helen.

'Gone back to the city. Weather coming in. Keep me informed. H.'

The weather was coming in. No shit.

She dressed quickly and went to Sam's room. She knocked loudly, trying to make herself feel as she normally would. A shove and joke to loosen things up. Sam opened the door, a towel wrapped around his waist.

'Morning, boss,' she said, and tried to push her way in, but he barred her way.

'Hi,' his voice was raw.

'Let me in then.'

'Er, no.'

She folded her arms and stared at him. *Explain yourself*.

373

'I'm not dressed, Zoe.'

'So what? I've seen your bits, mate.'

He didn't reply or even offer an excuse of some sort.

'Are you serious?' she said.

Still nothing.

'Fine,' she said. 'Fine. Let's meet in ten minutes downstairs for breakfast. Will that suit you, sir?'

He nodded.

'Great. I look forward to the pleasure of your company.' She turned then chucked an 'arsehole' at him as she walked away. The door shut quickly behind her and she knew immediately why: there was someone in there.

She waited and, sure enough, about five minutes later, the door opened and Ashley Deveraux came out. Zoe made sure she wasn't seen but couldn't help the sting of seeing the case's lead witness slip away from his room.

She watched her hurry out of the hotel room via a back door and then went to the bar and sat numbly at a table. A polite young waitress took her order and poured her some watery coffee. She'd never sat so still in all her life.

Sam appeared soon enough, ordered his food and sat down opposite, grabbing some toast instead of explaining himself.

'What's going on?' Zoe asked. Sam looked up at her and she felt tears flood to her eyes. She didn't want them, didn't want to look weak and emotional, but she couldn't help it.

'It's fine,' he replied, but there was no conviction in his answer.

'We're a team,' she said.

'I know.' He buttered the toast. They were the only people in the room, and a Hoover upstairs was the only counterbalance to this awful intimacy. 'I'm sorry,' he added, much later.

'That's shit.'

'I'm okay, Zoe. Please.'

'No you're not. You've been weird for ages and you won't talk to me and now, you're, you're . . .'

He chewed on the toast and said nothing. Boss, you're fucking the witness. The words were bursting out of her, but she still didn't dare say it. She wanted to throw her coffee at him.

'We should go and visit Sarah today,' he said eventually.

He really was going to pretend that she was stupid and hadn't picked up on anything. He knew her too well for this, but he was bloody well going to do it anyway.

'We go to see Sarah and we listen very carefully for any change,' he continued, then poured himself some coffee and waited for her approval.

'And what do we do if there are no changes?'

Nothing. Another sip. Eyes down. He placed his cup back

on the saucer. His hands enveloped the entire cup. He let out a slow sigh and she waited for the confession.

'After we've seen Sarah, we go back and talk to Tim. He's not protecting her now.'

She kicked him under the table, but missed and the whole table shook. The waitress looked up but then went back to writing the lunch menu on a blackboard.

'Is this how it's going to be? Really, Sam?'

She finally had his attention. He feigned ignorance and this pushed her on.

'You're fucking the bloody witness!' She said it again, more quietly, more sadly, and Sam couldn't meet her eye. You're fucking the witness.

'Why?' she asked after a long silence.

Sam muttered excuses about it being difficult to explain, that he liked her, that he hadn't known she'd turn out to be involved in the case, that he was lonely and sad. But as much as she wanted to believe him, it felt as though he was going through a prepared speech.

'Come on, Sam, it's me. I've always been honest with you, haven't I?'

And then she faltered because her words weren't true either and she knew that Sam would pick up on this. And sure enough she saw him peer at her more closely.

'What's happened, Zoe?'

She tried to answer him with bullshit but the words

made her tongue-tied. The waitress appeared and placed two plates of full English breakfasts onto the table. She warned them about the hot plates with a happy, warm tone and then walked away. Neither ate. Sam watched her and she fidgeted with a napkin.

'Zoe. Tell me.'

'I don't know why you think there's a link between those old cases and this one,' she said, trying to wriggle free.

'What have you done?' he asked. He wouldn't be deflected, not now.

'I think it's crazy. We've got a missing girl here, miles from any of those things. I don't see what the connection is.'

'There *are* connections, Zoe.'

'Which are what, women? Some sort of cabal? Come on, if you did that the other way round with men, then ninety per cent of cases would be linked. It's insane.'

He finally began to eat, but his eyes returned to her soon enough.

'And I don't see why you're so interested in Helen either,' she said, and then fell silent. She'd said too much and they both knew it.

'What do you mean?' he asked. He did it ever so quietly, but she'd worked with him long enough to know that this was the voice he used when he was about to pounce.

'You said you hated her,' she said. 'At the hospital.'

It was a good lie, but it wasn't enough.

'I did, but why are you defending her?' There was a sense of threat in the question.

'I just want to find Lily.'

'Have you seen the files?' he asked. He gazed at her with those powder-blue eyes, and she now knew just how it felt to be on the wrong side of the interview room table.

'Yes.'

'How?'

'I saw them in your room. After I went to check on Issy. Like you asked,' she said, stressing the last bit to make her point. She was his friend. His colleague.

'You went into my room? Why?'

There was no easy answer so she took a different path.

'It scared me. The way you'd arranged it all. The way you'd lined up their faces.'

'They scare me too.'

'Not them. You. I'm worried about you, Sam.'

He chewed on his food, his eyes locked on her, slowly piecing it together, unravelling her betrayal.

'Did you tell her about the witness?' he finally asked.

She didn't know what to say. She wanted to lie, but she couldn't stop herself from nodding.

She saw him grip his knife and fork a little tighter. He stared at her as though she were a stranger, someone to be broken down and taken apart.

And then her phone rang. She grabbed it gratefully, and used the excuse of needing some decent reception to get away. It was from the police station back in Manchester. Mr Frey had demanded to see her. The tone of the call made it clear that this was about Malcolm Cartmell.

She stood in the shelter of the pub's wooden porch and watched the rain howl down. She tried to work out which was worse – the hungry pack waiting for her in the city, or Sam's lies and anger across the table. She was perfectly, horribly trapped. She wanted to run and run, let the rain soak her and wash everything away.

Instead, she went back inside and stood in front of Sam at the table and delivered the news that she was being screwed back at work as well as here. He shrugged her anger off, which only made her come back at him for more.

'You were going to help me with this,' she said.

'You've been helping Helen Seymour.'

'Yes,' she said. 'And you're shagging the lead witness in a case. So we're both fucked, aren't we?'

He stood and threw his napkin onto his half-finished plate.

'You've been lying to me, Sam. Don't turn this all on me. You've not been straight either.'

They stood either side of the breakfast table, close enough to touch, to hug, to scratch or punch.

'Please, Sam. It's me. Come on, mate.'

'Fuck you.'

He said it so quietly she wasn't sure she'd heard him right for a second. Maybe it was because he'd never spoken to her like that before. But she was here to help him, to protect him.

'Sam . . . it's me . . . I'd never . . .'

Words failed her. Her arms hung uselessly by her side. Her mind and body failing in perfect harmony.

'Go talk to Mr Frey,' was all he said before he headed back up to his room. She went to hers and packed her things, then got in the car and didn't bother to look for him to say goodbye. She turned on the engine and wondered how he would get about without a vehicle. How pathetic of her, she thought, to still be worrying about him and his needs after all this. She was about to put her foot on the accelerator when the tears came. She sobbed and sobbed, but the rain hid her tears away and no one saw.

Finally, she drove off, her eyes red and her emotions still raw. She turned on the radio to distract her. A local station warned that the weather was coming in. It confused her for a moment, it was already here, surely. But then she heard them talk about snow.

As she continued, so the rain turned to sleet and then to snow. She made it onto the motorway before it got heavy and managed to escape the worst of it. When she reached the city, a few hours later, all she faced were dull clouds and dusty pavements.

*

But on the fells and over the lakes, the snow fell hard. Sam sat in his bedroom and watched it settle on his windowsill. He looked up at the sky and saw the snowflakes tumble. Whereas that night he had stared out at an impenetrable darkness, now the snow lit everything and swamped it all in a remorseless white. Ashley returned and pulled him back under the sheets, where she teased and played with him, as a cat might play with a mouse.

Later, when they were done, he went back to the window and marvelled as the snow smothered everything. Slowly but surely, the only colours left were black and white.

FIFTY-SIX

The snow fell all day. It wasn't unusual for it to fall like this but it wasn't common to have so much, so quickly. Roads were soon impassable, and as the sheer physical weight of the snow rose, so the power to the village inevitably failed.

There was a small pop, a wheeze and then silence as the lights snapped off. Weary villagers stared at their lifeless appliances and then threw nervous glances at the white storm outside their windows. Common sense told them that this wouldn't be fixed soon. Shrugs followed, then blankets were pulled from cupboards and logs from outside to keep the fires running.

Candles were lit at each table in the Black Bull, ready for the inevitable siege that would follow. In times of crisis, all roads lead to the pub.

Ashley kissed Sam tenderly on the lips. The room was getting colder and they huddled up against each other, enjoying the warmth and the touch of each other's flesh.

Outside they could hear kids throwing snowballs as the sun set. As it fell, the snow reflected an eerie half-light, fighting against the darkness.

'Tell me again about the dealers,' he said.

She kissed his knuckles, one by one.

'Erin was moaning that she was going to have to drive to Penrith or Carlisle to get some decent gear.'

'So the usual dealers just vanished.'

'Yeah,' she said, and began to slip down the sheets. He pulled her back up but she was grinning at him, and he knew she wouldn't be denied for long.

'So there's been no one?' he asked again, and she nodded, bored with it all. 'No one on the day and no one since?'

'Well, Alfie mentioned some woman being in the woods, but I don't think she was a dealer or anything.'

Her hand ran down his chest but he stopped her, sitting up straight.

'What woman?'

'I dunno. He went to the clearing, you know, where the fire is, that's where you'd do business, normally.'

'And?'

She shrugged and sniffed. But Sam pressed her on this. A woman, alone in the woods when the kids went missing. Jesus Christ.

'Why didn't anyone tell the police about this?'

'What, that we were out trying to score drugs? Yeah right!'

383

'Describe her.'

'Kiss me,' she answered.

He did. Then asked again.

'I don't know. He said she was older. Fit, a bit of a MILF, I think he said. Alfie's got a thing about older girls. He dumped me for some Croatian girl who worked at the bar last summer. Like I cared. Hey, you're not going to get jealous of him, are you?'

She wriggled closer to Sam with a playful look on her face.

'I'll try my best. We should go talk to him.'

'You know, he was a great kisser. And the rest. We used to go to the old boathouse. It's the only fucking place around here where you can get any privacy.'

And with that, her hand slipped down to Sam's crotch.

'Can we talk to him?' he asked, ignoring the games.

'Not now. He went down to Morecambe to see his uncle about a job. Snow will keep him out till tomorrow at least.'

She kissed him again and he didn't push her away.

'I love being like this,' she said. 'I feel so safe.'

'Did he say anything else about her?' Sam asked.

'You're so boring!' she laughed. 'How should I know? God. Um . . .' She made a childish 'thinking face', to make him laugh, and he tried to join in. He smiled and pulled the best faces he could, but he had to know more. 'Oh, she was wearing a purple coat.'

He tried to hide the kick he felt. She chatted on about something else, how Alfie had a thing about older women and nearly got himself kicked out of school for making a pass at the art teacher, but Sam wasn't listening. His mind had gone back to the moment that he and Zoe had arrived at Lullingdale, catching Ashley at the bus stop, talking so earnestly to Helen Seymour, dressed in a neatly tailored purple coat.

Helen had stolen Lily away. Sarah had helped, but Helen had done the deed.

'Did he say anything else about her? Hair colour? Eyes? Age?'

'Have you met Alfie?' Ashley replied. 'He can barely remember his own age!'

If she took the children, then why come back?

The room was getting colder, and Ashley pulled the sheets over his head.

'I've made a tent for us to hide in,' she said. 'A sex tent. We can stay here till the snow stops.'

She guided his hand to where she wanted it. And he didn't stop her. But all he could see now was Helen.

FIFTY-SEVEN

Zoe pulled into the police station and parked in Sam's reserved spot. She'd stopped half an hour before to get herself a coffee and it made her shaky. The place was busy as usual and the commotion helped settle her nerves. She strode in, avoiding anyone's gaze, making sure she stayed in busy corridors and areas where everyone could see her.

She stopped when she reached her desk. Dumped in front of her computer, sealed inside a clear plastic evidence bag, was a dead rat. Blood was congealed against the plastic wrapping. She considered dumping it in the bin, but didn't want to touch the thing.

'Zoe,' a female voice behind her made her spin around. It was Angela, a sweet Indian woman who worked as a civilian aide at the front desk. Zoe smiled at her and looked around, expecting leery smiles in anticipation of this cruel theatre. But whoever had dumped the dead animal on her desk was now busy with other things.

'Hi, Angela, what is it?'

'Chief Superintendent Frey has been asking to see you.' Angela was prone to worry, her face was lined with it, and Zoe used to joke with her about taking drugs from the store room to calm her down. But today, her nerves felt justified.

Zoe nodded and turned away from the desk. Angela caught sight of the dead rat and a tiny gasp slipped from her lips.

'It's nothing,' Zoe said and she could almost believe it.

'But, but, but . . .' the small woman's voice trembled. She could never be a cop, Zoe thought. She was too sensitive. She would bake a cake for people's birthdays and be the one to carry a card around to make sure everyone signed it. Zoe went over to her and turned her away from the sight.

'It's fine. Forget about it.'

Angela nodded dumbly and she shuffled quickly away. A tall, scruffy detective barged into the room on the phone and she darted out of his way. He didn't even seem to notice her. Zoe watched her dive away and then out into the corridor. The detective, Jerry, chewed on a chocolate bar as he hung up.

'Hey, Zoe. Who did you shit on, honey?'

'Like you don't know,' she said, and walked away.

'Hey, don't tar us all with the same brush, love,' he called after her, but she didn't have time to flesh out their argument. Maybe he was right, or maybe he was waiting to stick the knife in too. Either way, Mr Frey wanted to see her and she'd be foolish to keep him waiting. She walked out and up the stairs, passing men who had been colleagues and friends only days before. She ignored them all.

She reached the top floor, where a polite personal assistant asked her to sit and wait. She was offered a coffee which she declined. A senior officer, the area's Commander, strolled past. He didn't notice or acknowledge her. She scowled at his arrogance. They're all the same.

FIFTY-EIGHT

Sam and Ashley could only stay in his room for so long before the dark and the cold forced them downstairs. She left first, heading back home, promising to return later with 'goodies'. He watched her sashay down the corridor, listening to the hubbub below, and then came down to find most of the men in the village huddled together, beers in hand, lit by flickering candles and the hissing coal fire. He was greeted warmly and accepted the drink that was offered.

A Blitz spirit had developed, and no one pestered him about the case. Tonight, he was just one of the guys. It was easy to fit in with this lot. They were a kindly, affable bunch, full of bad jokes and big laughs. Sam sat amongst them and fell into their easy patter. He bought a round for the four guys at his table and enjoyed the beers that came later in return. Because of the blackout, the kitchen was closed and everyone was feeding off peanuts and crisps. Without the food to soak up the booze, Sam was soon quite drunk, but it felt okay, he was in good company.

Old Bill Matheson, whose family had lived in the area since time immemorial, had a voice that drowned out others. He started to tell a tale and slowly all other conversation fell away until he was the only one speaking. Lit by the candles, amidst the musky heat and the flowing alcohol, he revelled in the attention.

'I swear on my mother's grave,' he said, although his ruddy grin hinted at less serious intent, 'I swear I saw them down by the lake. First thing you notice is the cold. It's colder near them, like they suck the warmth and the light out of everything.'

There were good-natured chuckles and catcalls at this. Someone asked if they could change the channel, but Bill waved them away.

'I tell you, I saw them. I was only a kid, but I saw them and it's stuck in my heart, the sight of them. They were beautiful, the most beautiful things I ever saw. But their skin was grey and wet, like fish. And they turned to me and touched me. And I felt terrified and excited all at the same time. She was there, right there in front of me, and my heart was racing like a stallion.'

He had the crowd in the palm of his hand.

'I'll never forget her eyes. Glacier-blue, they were. And her breath was like morning dew. And she stood there, right there before my eyes and I felt this shudder go right through me. So I said: "'Ta very much love, but I've come now so you can get your hand out of my pants!'"

And the room erupted. Old Bill gave a theatrical bow and was bought a double whisky for his troubles.

Sam laughed loudly with the others and the chatter continued until the voices fell away and someone else played to the room. This time it was Elliott Johnson, a tall man in his early fifties, his jet-black hair flecked with grey. Elliott owned most of the cows in the area and had a fancy pad on the other side of the valley. Despite his Land Rover, the snow had trapped him in the village for the night. His tale was colder, and as he spoke, it became clear that there was no punch-line to follow. He talked about a little child he'd seen on the fells, a boy, no more than six, who he'd chased after, worrying for the kid's safely. The boy had led him to the edge of a steep drop just as the clouds had come down, and had it not been for good fortune, Elliott would have slipped and broken his neck.

'I tell you, I was being led to my death. I found out later that a boy had been found at the bottom of that ravine, a hundred years before. And I bet you if they showed me a photo of him, it'd be the lad I saw on the fells.'

People muttered and turned away. But then another story started, where a young woman had beguiled a man into the lake. He'd jumped onto rocks and punctured his lung in the process.

An old woman watched a teenage boy – now a fully grown man – whenever he stepped outside the house, wherever he went. A little girl's footsteps could be heard as she played hopscotch every night in a man's house until he was forced to call in the local priest. A woman with fingers like twigs and hair like winter gorse would rise up from the shale and attack passing walkers. A teenage beauty turned herself into a deer during the day, and into a vicious wolf at night. The mood was playful but edgy. The alcohol swirled within, and the snowflakes twisted and twirled without.

Sam noticed David and Tim sitting at a far table. They raised their glasses to him and he returned their salute.

Inevitably, it was his turn.

'You must have seen some terrible things, in your line of work.'

He had, but there was always an explanation. And sometimes that made the horror much worse.

'But there must have been some grim old crimes that you could never explain?'

There had been. Plenty. He'd often get a result, but that wasn't the same as an explanation.

Like the woman who had seemed so sweet and kind, but carried poison in her purse. She appeared to be just like any other woman, no, sweeter than that, kinder than that. She came into your life and stayed for a while and made you think that everything was perfect. But all the time she was dropping slow, cruel drops that were tasteless and invisible. And then, when she disappeared without explanation or notice, the drug would begin to do its work, staining and throttling. Slowly but irresistibly it crushed and strangled everything she had touched until all that was left in her wake was broken beyond repair. She tricked you into loving her and then she abandoned you, leaving only the poison behind to rot and corrode.

She was his wife. The case Sam could never solve. The woman he could never find. The perfect crime. He had invited her in and had not seen the danger she posed. He had been played. And he would never let a woman play him again.

Sam stared down at the table, unable to say any more. There were no tears in his eyes. Instead he gripped the table between his hands, and no one in the room would have been surprised to hear the thick wood snap. This wasn't grief, not any more.

Someone shoved another pint in front of him and he drank deep. Another man began a story about a young girl who turned into a tree, but no one was interested and, embarrassed, he fell silent and stared with interest at his empty glass.

The mood had changed. Sam didn't look up but David

and Tim watched him intently. David went to the bar and came back with three large whiskies. He left one at Sam's table without a word and sat the other in front of Tim. Outside, the night was white. Everything was backwards and anything was possible.

Bernie, the barmaid, poured the drinks without a word. Sensing the mood, she excused herself from work with stories about small children. The landlord let her go. She stumbled away through the heavy snow, glad to be away from there.

Inside, the men drank on.

FIFTY-NINE

Mr Frey made Zoe wait for a very long time. His embarrassed secretary, unaware of the circling politics, knocked twice on his door to remind him of his waiting visitor and was given such short shrift on the second occasion that she didn't knock again. Zoe sat still, watching the way a flashing neon light illuminated the metal framework of a large building site opposite, soon to be a shopping mall.

Eventually the door opened and the Chief Superintendent stood at the door, tall and stiff. He gestured for her to enter with a jerk of the head. She stood up and followed him in. She'd changed at the petrol station earlier, but still felt that she should be smarter. He didn't offer her a seat so she didn't take one.

'How's Sam?'

'Well, sir. I think.'

'You only think?' he scoffed.

'Yes, sir. I only think.'

She felt quietly proud of the double meaning in her words and wondered if being clever mattered to this man. His criteria more likely involved wealth, a loud laugh and tickets to the big game.

'So, we talked before about Sergeant Cartmell, yes?'

'Yes, sir.'

'What's happening with that?'

She gave a stammering reply about having been away in the Lake District and therefore not being entirely certain of the latest developments. Mr Frey leaned back in his chair and watched her as she did so. Eventually she ran out of words.

'There's a dead rat on your desk,' he said, and waited for her reaction.

'Yes, sir,' was all she could think of to say.

'Doesn't bode well, does it?'

The floor felt uneven. He was endorsing it. There was no air in the room. This must be how it feels, she thought, when the prison door opens and the guards come in with truncheons.

'What should I do, sir?' she heard herself say.

'I can't stop an entire police station from hating you, Barnes. Especially if you show no interest in pulling your neck out of the noose.'

'He beat him into a coma, sir.'

'Shut up!' Mr Frey snapped. 'I don't want to hear about any of it. Not one word.'

She didn't know what to say. The sun was gone and she saw her insipid reflection standing awkwardly in the dark glass behind him.

'So what do I do?'

He straightened files on his desk, for effect she assumed, as he considered her words.

'Sergeant Cartmell isn't going to pay for his actions. Let's get that straight. He's a good man and even good men do terrible things sometimes.'

He shifted in his seat and then gestured for her to sit down. The offer surprised her and she meekly accepted.

When Zoe had first signed up to become a cop, she had sat at the desk of a senior officer who had joked and enthused about the opportunities ahead of her. She had lapped up his words, giggling on the edge of her seat. And now she sat before a similar sort of man, who held no interest in right or wrong, in the law, and especially not in her. She realised that all of the previous discussion was just foreplay. The real, awful deals would begin now. Most likely, she thought, she would leave the room having resigned.

'Sam speaks very highly of you, by the way,' Mr Frey said.

She nodded, scared to give anything away.

'It's a shame when the good ones are thrown to the wolves. The police service can be very excitable when it comes to protecting itself.'

Here it comes.

'You need to prove your own value, Detective Constable.'

I'm all alone in here, she thought. He could do anything and no one will come running.

'You were seen,' he said, and suddenly there was ire in his voice. 'With her.'

For a moment, Zoe didn't understand who he was talking about, but then suddenly her stomach rolled and she realised that he meant Helen Seymour.

'I'm not sure I follow you, sir.'

'Yes you do. What are you doing cosying up to a QC?'

'She asked to meet me, sir. I agreed. The meeting was brief and we haven't met again.'

She waited for him to blow her lies out of the water. The silence that followed didn't tell her anything.

'What did she want?' he asked, and still she didn't know if he'd bought her story.

'She felt intimidated by DI Taylor, sir.'

Nothing. He just waited. He was sly and clever, she thought with grudging admiration. The silence forced more out of her.

'She wanted me to feed her information about him. I refused and left immediately.'

'Who did you tell about this?'

'No one, sir.' The raised eyebrow flustered her more. Her lies were going to unravel. 'DI Taylor had told me about his distaste for Mrs Seymour.'

'Good man. And she's not married. It's Ms Seymour. Even if she married, I bet she'd remain Ms Seymour,' he said and she noted the bitterness in his tone with surprise. He looked away from her for a moment, and it struck her that they might once have been lovers. Mr Frey and Helen Seymour. She felt so revolted by the idea she decided it couldn't be true.

'I don't understand why you wouldn't tell him about her approach,' Mr Frey said.

'I thought it would inflame the situation. He didn't trust her and knowing about it wouldn't change that.'

'You were protecting him, were you?'

She told the Chief Superintendent that she had only been interested in an easy life. Self-deprecation, she had learned, was the easiest way to sell a lie. He gazed at her and she felt like prey once again.

'She's dangerous, that one,' he said, and she nodded. 'If she's worried about Sam then he should know, because she'll come for him. I've seen it happen. I've seen her take men apart.'

Zoe could believe it. Had it not been Mr Frey behind the desk, she would have asked for the grisly details.

'What do you think of her?' he asked.

'She seemed very determined,' was her wary reply.

'But she clearly thought you were like-minded, or else she wouldn't have contacted you.'

Each time she felt that the sword had been put away, suddenly it was unsheathed again.

'I think she just thought I was stupid and easily bought.'

'She offered you money?'

'She didn't get the chance.'

'Shame. We could have used that against her.'

Zoe nodded as best she could.

'You're a good girl, Zoe,' Mr Frey said, and she dared to believe she had passed a test.

'Thank you, sir,' she said.

'Poor old Malcolm's problem is that he thinks you're not part of the team.'

Her mind raced back to this old line.

'You're loyal, I can see that. You need to make him see it too.'

'By writing a false report on what happened?'

Mr Frey waved his hand as though this was no longer an issue.

'I've told you, men get over-eager. Sam gets over-eager. It happens. I'm here to be an umbrella for them, an umbrella against the shit that others want to throw at them. It's not the most pleasant of jobs, but I think I do it rather well.'

He pulled some gum from his pocket, took a small tab and offered some to Zoe, who politely declined.

'I'll protect you and I'll protect Sam and I'll make sure Sergeant Cartmell falls in line.'

'And what do I do?' she asked. It was meant to come out meekly, but Zoe just needed to know the facts, however good or bad.

'You bring me Helen Seymour's head on a plate.'

He said it with no obvious pleasure, but she knew it was there.

'I'm not entirely convinced by your rendition of events, but I'm willing not to press too much harder if I see that your loyalty really is to us. She clearly thinks you can be trusted too.'

Zoe didn't know who she trusted, but she could feel the knife being turned.

'And that's useful for us. As you're part of our team. One of us.'

She nodded.

'I bet a clever girl like you will be able to get under her skin, find her weaknesses. She'll never see you coming.'

Zoe thought of the intimacy she'd felt with Helen. He was probably right. If she did what he said.

'Oh, and if you don't? Well, we'll all know whose side you're on for real then, won't we?'

He continued to smile and chew, but his eyes were ice-cold. She stood up and nodded.

Destroy Helen Seymour and all would be fine. Follow Sam and his mad obsessions and join the male brigade that wants another mouthy woman silenced and then you can breathe again.

Zoe didn't know what she thought of Helen Seymour. At the very least she was tough and exploitative, but her failings felt slight compared with the monster in front of her. Unless she allowed him to abuse his power then she would drown. Malcolm and his rogues were waiting downstairs with more than just dead rats. And she loved this job. She bloody loved it. She loved the physicality, the sense of action, of doing, of immediate effect. And she was good at it. Who was one man to stop her? Who was one woman?

'Thank you, sir,' she said and turned and left. She waited for a parting shot as she walked out of his office, but he didn't say a word. She wondered, as she walked past his secretary, whether he was on the phone now to the thugs downstairs, telling them to put down their cudgels.

The corridors below were quiet and she was able to find an empty office – an incident room which was unused after the successful conclusion of a case. Zoe was able to work at a desk without anyone knowing about her.

She began with the cases that Sam had investigated. The terrifying women and their infanticide. The details made her feel sick. She turned the facts over and over, just as he had done.

In time, she saw the connection that he had been led to – Helen Seymour's involvement in each case. She discovered it with a gasp. But she worked on, through it and out to the other side. And it was here that she found the second connection. The connection that Sam hadn't yet discovered. One other person was connected to each and every case. Just as Helen had made sure that she was introduced to each woman, so another figure made sure that they were the Senior Investigating Officer's first port of call, every single time. And that person was Chief Superintendent Michael Frey.

Zoe didn't know what this meant. She didn't know why Helen would want to be involved in every case either. But Mr Frey was right about one thing. She would be able to get Helen to tell her.

She made photocopies, making sure that no one saw her. And then she dug deeper into the cases. Her work took her hours. Once done, armed with what she needed, she headed out, well aware that she was unlikely to sleep any time soon.

SIXTY

The village was muffled and gagged in white. Inside the pub, the men drank and the mood corroded further.

David stoked it up. Without him, the men might well have just grunted and growled, but the strangeness of the night, the booze and the lust of the mob got things going.

'She's laughing at you, you know that don't you?'

The question was easily dismissed, but it still buzzed about in the crowded room.

'There's a woman who's killed her kids and she's got away with it.'

Sam sat still and stared David down, but he could feel the heat that the words generated.

'Are we seriously going to let her get away with that shit?'

People tried to calm David down, and for a while he was willing to let them. But memories of Zoe meant that he couldn't leave the itch unscratched. He brought it up a little later and noted the way men said less against him this time.

Five whiskies later and they were nodding.

It only needed a little more. And then a glass smashed on the floor and soon chairs were upended.

David ushered Tim towards the door, and somehow this kind and gentle man found himself swearing and encouraging others. Men burst out through the back doors, suddenly high on the freezing air, giddy and overexcited. They marched together with grim purpose, not really sure if they were going to do this or not, not really sure what 'this' even was.

'Let's fucking show her!' someone had yelled, and that was the fuzzy mission.

It was a ten-minute walk to Bud's place, but the booze made it feel like a thirty-yard stroll. As they got there, a few men slowed, the realisation dawning that the words now had to be translated into action. But Tim, David and four others marched ahead, not willing to entertain doubts. As they got to the house, Bud opened the door and stood there, shiftily. They'd made plenty of noise on the way and Sarah had, no doubt, shoved him out to face them. No one had any truck with Bud.

'What is it?' he asked meekly.

'Send her out,' Tim said. His voice was set with rage.

'Don't think I should, Mr Downing,' Bud replied.

'Give me my wife,' Tim countered, and Bud faltered under such authority.

'Get her out!' David screamed in agreement.

Bud shook his head. 'I don't think you should be here.'

'Get out of the way!' David yelled, but Bud didn't move. And he was such a big lump that no one was quite sure how they'd get past him.

'Bud, you dumb shit—'

'Give me my wife!'

'Get out of the way!'

The abuse rained down but Bud stood firm. It seemed like the more they screamed, the firmer his resolve. It might have remained like this, but there was a momentary pause and someone heard Sarah's voice call out from behind Bud.

David and another man ran at Bud, and while he pushed David away with ease, the other was able to knock him to the floor. Tim and two others were right behind him, barging into the house, tripping over his heavy boots, crashing into the corridor.

Sarah stood in front of Tim, and he slowed for a second until he saw that she was wearing the silk pyjamas that he'd bought her for Christmas. The top buttons were undone and hinted plenty at the flesh beneath. She'd worn them in their home, in their bedroom, in their bed.

Tim reached out to grab her. Sarah pulled back but he had a hold of her arm and he dug his fingers into her flesh. She yelped with pain. He needed to hear that and he wanted to hear more. He was about to slap her in the face when something pulled him up and away and he found himself outside the door with a new barrier between them. But the barrier was not Bud, but Sam.

'I can't let you do this,' he said.

David was up in his face, shouting that Sam was one of them, and to get out of the way. But Sam was immovable. He looked at Bud and offered him a hand. But as he pulled him up, he saw the cut above Bud's eye open up and blood spurt out. It hit the snow and suddenly everyone was silent.

'You should all go home,' Sam called out. 'Everyone. Go home now.'

Those at the back were happy to be directed and immediately began to trudge away. A straggle of men remained.

'There's nothing here for you,' Sam called out. 'Go home now, please.'

He spoke so calmly, his words were undeniable. Eventually they all left. David and Tim were the last to go, muttering to themselves, but mollified nonetheless.

Bud smiled shyly. 'Thanks,' he said.

'You're hurt.' Sam's voice was painted gentle. 'Is there someone who can help? It might need stitches.'

'Sarah could fix me up,' Bud replied.

'No, she won't be up to it, not after what just happened. It's not fair to ask her.'

The words seemed sensible. Bud frowned and then nodded.

'Mrs Pascoe will sort me out, I bet,' he said.

'Great. You go see her. I'll stay with Sarah.'

'Okay,' the big man happily agreed. He grabbed a coat and then bounded off.

Sam watched him all the way to make sure he didn't turn back. Then he went to the door and quietly closed it. Inside, Sarah watched him from the small distance of the living room, retreating when she saw the way he looked at her. She saw that the mob was still there, now distilled into one man. Its purpose, its violence, its deafness and blindness; it was all still there.

Sam turned and checked that the door was locked and that no one could disturb them. Then he walked back towards the living room, ready to finish the job once and for all.

SIXTY-ONE

The men walked away from the house, the mob dispersing into smaller groups, then petering out into individual, shamed journeys home.

For a while, Tim and David walked together until a fork in the road forced them into different directions. They paused momentarily, but neither could think of a thing to say. Tim walked on, head down against the falling snow, blood still pumping, but now with nowhere to go and nothing to do. Slowly the usual drain of tiredness and misery sapped his anger and left him fumbling with the key in the door like the sad, lonely drunk that he was.

He went inside, but didn't bother to turn on the light. He didn't want to see the unwashed dishes dumped in the sink, or the rooms where nothing had changed because there was no one to change them. But then he tripped on something and slipped on the floor. And when his hand went out to steady himself, he realised that the floor was covered in other things. Confused, he found a switch and turned on the lights.

The house had been trashed. While he'd been in the pub, someone had come in and ransacked the place. He went from room to room, and in each he was greeted by the same sight – debris and carnage. His first thought was to call the police, but then he remembered the deluge of snow and knew it was a waste of time.

And then he wondered why.

What had he done?

What did they know, whoever they were?

He went to his bedroom where the drawers' contents spilled out across the floor. His wife's jewellery was gone. But somehow, this didn't feel like the work of common thieves.

He went back downstairs. There was no clear sign of how the burglar, or burglars, had got in, so he double-checked all the windows, pushed latches across doors where he could, and heaved the heavy fridge across the back door.

He grabbed some blankets and sat down on the sofa, swamped by the exhaustion of fading adrenalin and the spiky fear that something worse was about to come.

When he finally slept, he did so upright.

SIXTY-TWO

Sam walked into the sitting room, and there she was, waiting for him. Sarah stood behind an armchair, tightly gripping its tatty fabric. The room was lit by the flickering fire, well stocked and burning brightly. She didn't move but the flames seemed to make her shimmer.

'Go away,' she whispered.

'Where's Lily?' he asked.

'I don't know. How could I know?'

He took a step further and saw her flinch.

'It's okay,' he said, and neither believed him. 'I got rid of that lot, didn't I?'

She didn't have an answer for this.

'I just want you to tell me the truth. About everything. If you do that, I can end all of this. You must be so unhappy, living like this. Am I right?'

411

She looked around at the shabby room and shrugged a little miserably.

'I'm here to help you, believe it or not.'

Bud's dog stumbled in from the corridor. It stared at them both with a mournful look then collapsed in front of the fire and promptly fell asleep.

'Everyone hates me,' Sarah said.

'Yes.'

'But I haven't done anything wrong.'

'Yes, you have.'

'No, I'm just, I'm not right for here.'

Was that it? No. She was out of place, for sure. But it wasn't just this village where a woman like her was out of place.

'Where's Lily?'

'I told you.'

'No, you've said nothing. You've hidden behind lawyers and rules. But there are no tapes here. We don't have to do things by the book tonight.'

Sam threw a log onto the dwindling fire. The dog rolled onto its back and stretched.

'Please, Sam,' she said, and she gave him her widest eyes. 'Please believe me.'

It was a mistake, to try to win him over like that. He'd been expecting as much.

'You're good at getting men to do what you want, aren't you, Sarah?'

She frowned at the question.

'Tim, now Bud.'

'I do what I have to,' she said after a moment's thought.

'I think you do a little more than that.'

'If you were a woman, you'd do exactly the same.'

'I doubt that.'

A shove in the street can easily deteriorate into something worse. It's a short leap from kissing to killing.

'Where's Lily, Sarah?'

'Stop asking me that.'

But he wouldn't be deflected. Not now when he was so close.

A woman's eyes, the sway of her hips, the pull on her lip to force a smile. Sarah lied with every movement of her body.

'I will make you talk,' he said.

'You're a cop. You can't make me do anything.'

Sam rolled his heavy shoulders as though he was warming up for something.

'How long do you think the snow will last? I heard them saying in the pub that we'll be snowed in all night. It'll melt tomorrow, sure enough, it's only November after all. But tonight, no one can get to us. I don't think I need to be a cop, not tonight.'

The snow began to fall again outside, as if to make his point. Sam saw the flakes, illuminated by the fire inside. They seemed to glow red, like it was raining fire.

'If you touch me,' Sarah said with a slow, clear calculation, 'then Bud will kill you.'

She smiled after saying it. Sam just rolled his shoulders again, looser and looser.

'He'll come after you if I tell him to. You have no idea how much he loves me.'

'You have a way,' Sam said.

'I have a way.'

'Just like your lawyer.'

She just shrugged.

'Where's Lily?' he asked again.

And again, she just shrugged. The casualness felt so cruel. He took a step forward and saw her retreat again.

'You killed your son, didn't you?'

He thought of the little boy, smothered in his mother's embrace, floating like jettisoned cargo in that empty swimming pool.

'How did it feel?' he asked.

Maybe she and Helen did it together, maybe they smashed his head on the rocks, before dumping him in the lake, just like Jenny Smeeton – her nephew broken to pieces against a kitchen sink.

'Is she still alive, Sarah?'

Nothing. A blank stare. Maybe it was too late. The thought made his hand shake. He grabbed for her, but she was quick and pulled away. He pushed over the armchair that she hid behind and heard the wood crack as it fell.

'Where is she?'

She couldn't run now. He could hold her by the throat, he could tear her apart. Where is your daughter? What did Helen Seymour make you do? Why did you kill them? Where is your daughter? The questions burst upon her but she wouldn't answer.

He stepped forward and she screamed with terror. But he was trying to save her. Why didn't she see that he was trying to save her? He had to rip the truth from out of her, but she wouldn't let him. He just wanted to save a little girl. He just wanted to find Lily and stop this. Stop it all. Bring everything to a halt so that people could be people again. So he could be his old self, a cop, a dad, a good guy. She had to stop fighting him. She had to stop the lies and tell him where Lily was. It was so simple, so fucking simple.

He went for her again, and as she ran from him she slipped and tripped on the upturned chair, sprawling onto the carpet.

'Why won't you help me, Sarah?'

He should grab her and shake her, but she seemed so small, so frail, and he found he couldn't do it. Outside the snow had stopped falling. The window was now just a black rectangle, a leap to the stars. He looked down at her again, forcing his resolve.

'You never loved them, did you?'

The question brought a miserable cough from her.

'You were a terrible mother. They were better off without you.'

And finally, she spoke.

'Yes.'

Good girl.

'You let this happen.'

'Yes.'

'You let Helen manipulate you and sent them to their deaths.'

'Yes.'

Yes. Finally. Yes. The truth made him feel sick. He noticed a smear of blood from her nose.

'You killed your son.'

She nodded, tearless.

'And your daughter?'

But she didn't reply to this one.

'She's alive, isn't she?'

There was nothing there. He was talking to a shadow. She slowly got to her feet, but she wouldn't look at him.

'Sarah. Why did you do it?'

But then he heard the front door open and feet kick the snow off boots on the mat. He and Sarah turned, expecting Bud to return, but instead it was her brother Jed who walked in. He wore the same bedraggled clothes as before and his appearance, if possible, seemed more dishevelled. He stared at Sam in shock, then saw the blood from Sarah's nose.

'What the fuck's going on?'

Neither Sam nor Sarah replied. Sam found himself slipping his warrant card from his back pocket, like it was some sort of free pass.

'I'm Detective Inspector—'

'Yeah, we met before, I remember. What's happened to my sister?'

'It's nothing, Jed,' Sarah said, her accent thicker now, adjusting to her brother's presence.

'You've come to visit, have you?' Sam asked.

'Piss off,' was all he got in return.

Sam turned to Sarah, but he knew he could do nothing now.

'Jesus Christ,' Jed said, his arms waving up and down. 'She's the bloody victim, here. What is all this?'

'Jed. Don't.' She seemed so calm despite everything.

'In bits, ripped to bloody bits, she is,' Jed continued. 'Smashed to bloody pieces by it, aren't you, Sis?'

Sam looked at her, but there were no clues in the look that met his.

Lily was alive. She'd admitted as much, and now she knew that he'd worked it out. He needed to act fast.

'And the way everyone else treats her, Jesus!' Jed went on, but neither Sam nor Sarah were listening to him. Their eyes continued their silent conversation.

Sam trundled through all of the appropriate words to mollify Jed, then made his polite and professional goodbyes. Jed continued to protest as Sam made his way to the front door, where he stopped long enough to allow one last look between him and her. This wasn't over.

Back at the pub, a few men still lingered around the bar, but Sam went straight to his room. His phone was crammed with messages from Ashley, but he ignored them all. Three hours' sleep. No more. He needed to be ready for whatever Sarah did next.

SIXTY-THREE

Zoe sat in the dark and waited. She had parked at the end of a smart road where the cars had their own drives and the houses were tall and white. Ten minutes earlier she had sent Helen a text message, and she saw its effect as lights snapped on in the house opposite, starting on the top floor and slowly working their way down. A lamp above the front door clicked on and a moment later Helen stood in the doorway, wrapped in a dressing gown. Zoe got out of the car, walked across the road and entered her house. She noted the way that Helen glanced out behind her before she closed the door, as though spying out the enemy.

Helen led Zoe along the corridor and down the stairs into a long, open-plan kitchen that took up the entire length of the building's basement. A wooden floor stretched out before her – oak or beech or something well beyond Zoe's reach. The kitchen was large, too large for one. The countertops were bare but for a folded newspaper. To Zoe, it felt lonely.

'Tea, coffee, something stronger?' Helen asked. Zoe shook her head. Helen nodded, fair enough, but put the kettle on for herself and then busied herself with a mug and teabags from a cupboard. Eventually she turned to face the young detective.

'I was summoned by the Chief Superintendent,' Zoe said.

'James Frey?' Helen asked with a smirk.

'You know him.'

'I do,' Helen replied.

'I know. It wasn't a question.'

The kettle boiled and Helen made herself some tea.

'He's going to get me fired,' Zoe said.

'Shit. Really? I'm sorry.'

'So, I wondered, if the offer, you know, of me coming to work for you, if that was still on.'

Helen nodded before she spoke, as if trying to frame the sentence right.

'Yes, of course I can help find something for you.'

'Something?'

'It's the middle of the night, OK? But I won't let you down.'

'I can trust you?'

'Of course. Of course you can.'

She smiled at Zoe and put her hand on her shoulder, then turned back to the tea, dunking the bag in and out of the mug, and finally dropping it into the bin. Zoe watched and waited.

'Because, the thing is,' Zoe said, stumbling a little, 'there are things that worry me. About you.'

She had Helen's attention now.

'Sam will never forgive me if I sign up with you. It'll kill him. And I need to be sure, Helen. You do understand that? I need to be sure of you.'

Helen nodded, making all the right faces.

'I'm not a fool, Helen.'

'Of course you're not. I never thought that.'

Zoe let Helen lead her to a bare kitchen table. She could imagine Helen sitting here, working her way through cases in the dead of night. She placed her briefcase on it, between them.

'The reason you got me to go after Sam,' Zoe said as she sat down opposite her, 'was because he'd worked out that you were fiddling with a witness.'

'No.'

'Yes. Sam was right. He's a really good cop, Helen. He worked out what you'd done.'

Helen was staring at the briefcase, trying to discern its significance.

'I've got the details here. The case, the witness's name and original address, the police's inability to find him and all the problems this has caused for their investigation. You have perverted the course of justice. Sam knew it, but didn't have the proof. But I'm more thorough than him.'

Zoe tapped the bag.

'You lied to me, Helen.' Zoe watched her flounder. 'How do I trust you?'

'It's not what you think.'

'Oh God, don't use words like that.'

'Let me explain it to you.'

'You broke the law.'

'It's not as easy—'

'Yes. It is. To me it is.'

'Jesus, Zoe . . .'

Helen ran out of words and Zoe saw how rattled she was. She sipped on her tea, put the mug down, then picked it up again and clutched it tight to her.

'What else have you lied about?' Zoe asked. 'How about Sarah? Did she do it? Really?'

Helen drained her tea. When she spoke, it was fast and quiet.

'It was you guys, not me, who cocked up the case by jumping in without enough evidence. I don't think Sarah did it. Actually, I'm sure she didn't. She has a history with the police and she'd got it in her head that saying nothing was the only way to deal with you. Her brother's a dealer, so the whole family gets a little touchy when it comes to the boys in blue.'

'But you fed her that story, about being stoned in the woods.'

'No, I didn't, I promise. I get people to talk because I tell them that I'll do anything to protect them. And I back that up with results. Sarah was desperate to unburden herself. She just didn't dare talk to you. Listen, this witness—'

'Do you think she knows what happened to Lily?'

'No, and I don't really have anything more to tell you about the case. Zoe, let me explain myself and this business with Ricky Howell. Please.'

Zoe sighed and waved a hand as though she were being generous.

'Ricky Howell is a drug-dependent fantasist,' Helen said. 'Six months before, he'd been used by the police as a witness in a GBH case. The cops were desperate to nail some thug and they knew Ricky had been in the vicinity. So they picked him up and scared the shit out of him, locked him up and intimidated him. He took the stand and told the jury a whole host of details that he simply didn't see. Wasn't my case, by the way, but I know the barrister involved and he was steaming. So when I saw that Ricky could be a possible witness on this one, I knew that James Frey and his chums would be back to their old tricks. So I moved him, before they could mess with his head. He's an incredibly sensitive and vulnerable man.'

'You just did the same as them. Just the same!'

'No, I was protecting him from them.'

'Did he see what happened?'

423

'No. No, that's the point – I didn't bloody tamper with a witness because he didn't see a thing. I moved him to stop the cops using him. Do you see?'

It was plausible. But then again, a barrister as good as her would expose a fantasist like Ricky Howell in court with ease.

'You've broken the law, Helen. You are a solicitor, you know how important that is, you know exactly what you've done.'

She watched Helen sag and nod.

'Say it.'

'Yes. Yes, I've broken the law. I don't need a jumped-up copper to tell me that.'

It took Helen a little longer than Zoe had expected, but suddenly her head snapped up as the thought struck her.

'Why did you ask me to say that? Out loud?'

In answer, Zoe pulled out the small recording device from her pocket and placed it on the table. It was new and sleek and fitted in perfectly with its lush surroundings. Helen stared at it, ashen. Zoe pressed a button and a small beep announced that the recording had ended.

'Mr Frey said he would destroy me, unless I got you,' Zoe said, with a shrug that was less apologetic, more matter-of-fact. 'At first I was livid, but then I thought about the way you've been using me and it felt pretty even. This case, all the cases, they're just one long fight between you two. That's all any of this is. The cases, Sam, me.'

'It's more than a fight.' said Helen, low and quiet and angry.

'You kept saying "trust me" and "I'll look after you", and you were lying to me all the time. All the time. You're just like them!'

Suddenly Helen reached across the table and grabbed Zoe by her wrist. 'Delete it, please. Wipe it out.'

Although Helen was panicking, the movement was still intimate. Zoe looked away, uncomfortable. On the fridge were dozens of small magnets, collected from her travels. Rome, New York City, Beijing, Malibu. She felt the heat of Helen's breath and when she turned to face her, they were close enough to kiss.

'That man uses these cases, he uses everything to his own ends. He's a cunt. I've known him practically all my life. He hates women. Hates them. And each time a case comes up like this, he makes sure he splashes it as loud as he can. To hurt us.'

Zoe thought about the way the stories had leaked to the press and the media and the fuss they'd caused.

'Why does he hate women so much?' she asked.

'I don't know. Maybe his mother screwed the milkman, who cares?' Helen said. 'I saw what he was doing and it made me angry. So I made it my business to take on those cases and make it an even fight.'

Zoe gently pulled her wrist away, but the women remained close.

'Don't you see where this goes?' Helen said. 'He takes every broken woman and pushes them into the spotlight – turns them into monsters and witches, and suddenly we're all like that. We're all part of the gang. Don't trust women, they're all potential child murderers. Don't trust your wife with your kids, don't leave your nanny alone with your loved ones. Beware women. Beware. Turn your back on us and we'll stab your babies. That's what he wants.'

Yes, those are what the headlines were saying until they got bored and moved on to something else. And yes, Zoe had felt the effect, felt guilty by the simple association to her sex. Maybe there was a tipping point, a crime that would break men and women for ever.

'You have to destroy that, Zoe.'

Zoe looked down at the recorder.

'If you hand that in, he'll use it to destroy every case I've ever defended. He'll kill me. And in a few years' time he'll find a way to get you thrown out – whatever he says.'

This was true, Zoe conceded to herself.

'You're a clever girl,' Helen said. 'You've met that man, seen him face to face. Are you really telling me you'd put more faith in him than me?'

'He told me you were bent and told me to get you. You are, and I have.'

426

'And he's told Sam that Sarah Downing is guilty and to nail her. And he will. But she didn't kill her kids.'

No motive, no evidence. But still Sam stalked her. Was this really because Mr Frey had told him to?

'If you hand that in,' Helen said, 'they'll get Sarah. She won't have me to watch her and all of those fucking men will make sure they send her down. And then they'll go after all the other women I've defended. Yes, I screwed with a witness, but I only did it before they did. One bloody witness. That's all. Are you really going to have me burnt for one man?'

'If I don't hand this in, then he'll burn me too.'

She had been so certain as she planned this all out. But now the choices were too great, the outcomes too uncertain.

'Zoe, you don't have to hand that in tonight. You don't have to do anything right here and now.'

Another hand on her wrist.

'Please. Please don't go to Mr Frey with this. They are working together against us. You know it's true, don't you?'

Zoe thought about how much pleasure Mr Frey would take if he finally managed to bring Helen down.

'I'm not going to tell him,' Zoe said after some thought.

'Thank you. Thank you. You're doing the right thing, you are.'

'I'm going to tell Sam.'

Helen's mouth fluttered open for a second. Zoe saw her shake her head as the momentum of this hit her.

'But Sam works for him. It's the same. You tell Sam, you tell your boss.'

Maybe. Maybe not.

'Zoe, please, think about this.'

But that was all she was doing. She was thinking so hard her head was spinning.

'You've got Sam wrong,' Zoe replied. But then she thought about him and her that morning, facing each other over the breakfast table, so angry and far apart. But then again, if Sam were right, then it was Helen who shouldn't be trusted. The women she had defended were guilty at best. At worst, Helen commanded and orchestrated their crimes. But something inside her turned away from this.

Too many variables. Too many choices. Too much to go wrong.

'Sam's one of them,' Helen said. 'He'll go running to his bosses. You know he will.'

He had lied to her. He had lied and hidden things from her. And worse.

'He's desperate to hurt me. You can't. You mustn't. You know what these men are like, Zoe. If they get me, they'll rip me apart.'

Zoe turned away, grabbing the recorder, but Helen pulled her around to face her. 'What are you going to do?'

Zoe felt Helen's arms holding her tight, and she wished she could say words that would make it all alright. Square the circle, magic a happy ending. But she simply didn't know how.

'I have to talk to Sam,' she stammered, and stood up.

Helen pulled at her, desperate. 'Zoe – for God's sake!'

'I have to go,' was all Zoe could say. 'I have to.'

Helen stared at her, finally empty of words. Zoe hurried up the stairs to the front door. As she did so, Helen came after her again.

'But why?' she called. 'Why trust him? Why?'

Zoe pushed through the door and out into the cold. The question charged after her.

'Why?' Helen cried out, as Zoe got to her car.

Zoe turned on the engine with a shaking hand. She pushed the car forward and saw Helen framed in the doorway, staring out at her like a ghost. She drove much faster than she should.

All the traffic lights seemed to turn green for her. The streets were quiet and she was flushed out of the city in no time. The roads shone wet as she progressed, and signs flashed weather warnings from the side of the motorway. The fields on either side went from a dappled coat to a thicker blanket, and slowly, inevitably, the dusting on the road turned to a slush that thickened. Cars slumped into the sludge and slowed, and stopped. The jam stretched for miles.

It would be easier to turn back.

Zoe's fingers tapped out an uncertain rhythm on the steering wheel.

The fields beyond were an endless blur of white. The side windows steamed up. Zoe pushed the car on, inching forward, yard by yard. Slowly, slowly, slowly. As the sun rose, she saw snow glint on the top of the fells. She was getting closer. Slowly, slowly, slowly.

At one point she thought that she saw Helen at the wheel of the car behind her. It shocked her, the idea that Helen would come after her, chasing her all the way back to Lullingdale, but she also believed it possible. She was a woman who got what she wanted, after all. Zoe wondered if she should have believed any of the things she'd told her, but as she considered this, so she looked again in the mirror and Helen was no longer there. Maybe she never had been.

By the morning she had reached the far side of the lake. The road died here, and there was no way forward. She parked her car with the others, next to a line of vehicles that had not found shelter and were now white humps among the frozen deluge. A local explained that some farmers were planning on clearing the roads themselves, using their tractors, as it could often take the council ages to clear a way through. Zoe asked how long this would take and the men sighed and pulled faces. With luck, Adam and Chris would be through by lunchtime. On the other hand, Clarky had been moaning about problems with spark plugs all last week and if he couldn't get his one going . . .

They advised her to stay put. The weathermen said it would all be melted by the end of the day anyway.

She thanked them and turned away. Three geese flew above her, so low she spun and ducked as they passed. She heard the wings beat against the air and watched their graceful, effortless journey over the lake with both envy and delight. Three kids nearby were building a snowman. She listened to their giggles while her heart beat fast.

She looked to the lake. At the far end, hidden by thick mist, was Lullingdale village.

Zoe noticed a small red dinghy, turned upside down, only visible from the snow because half of it was sheltered under a crumbling jetty. She trudged down to inspect it. The kids mucked about behind her and when she turned to them, she was wearing her friendliest smile.

'Hi guys!' she said, beaming. 'Any idea who owns that boat down there?'

SIXTY-FOUR

Sam was surprised to hear that Helen had left the village. He received the news from Bernie with mixed emotions; part anger that she had slipped away again, but also intrigue as to why, and what she had left in her wake. There was still no power in the village and all the pub could offer in the way of breakfast was juice and cereal. Sam politely refused both. He needed to be watching Sarah.

He made his way back to Bud's place as the day broke: the sky was still a deep-purple bruise as he crunched through the snow. It was like one of his old surveillance jobs back in Manchester where he'd sit in a car, the engine off so as not to attract attention, slowly freezing away as he watched rubbish-strewn alleyways. Today he was on foot, accompanied by a plucky robin redbreast that bobbed on nearby branches, and breathing in air that was pure and clear. But it didn't change a thing – the job was the job.

It made more sense the more he thought about it. If Helen had been involved, then she would have been the one who stole the children. It would have been impossible for Sarah to move them on her own, and police and witness statements showed that she hadn't left the village that day. But Helen could easily have slipped in and out without anyone knowing. And, if this was true, then she would have been the one who would have kept Lily alive.

There was a light still on inside Bud's house. Sam wondered if Sarah had been awake all night, just as he had. He saw a silhouette pass a window for a moment, but nothing more. It didn't matter, he could wait for ever. His toes were numb, but he stayed put, watching the house from the safety of a small copse. Eventually the sun broke above the fells, and the snow made everything brilliant and dazzling. Sam heard a slow drip as water fell from branches, and where it landed he noticed small pools of green appear. Colour was battling back against the monochrome. Slowly the sun climbed higher and the sky was lit into a beautiful powder-blue.

Sarah had confessed that Lily was alive. She knew this. But there was no way that she could have had any contact with her since she disappeared. All eyes had been on her. The only way she could know for sure would be because Helen had told her.

Just as Sam wondered again why Helen had chosen to visit and then to leave so soon after, he saw the front door open and Sarah Downing step outside. She was wrapped in a thick black coat and wore heavy boots with a chunky woollen hat, pulled down low to obscure her features. She strode away from the house and Sam was able to follow her easily from some distance as she trudged along a footpath, towards the lake. Hers were the only footprints in the snow, and so he was able to let her get some way ahead, just to be sure she wouldn't see him.

If Helen had Lily, maybe the reason she came back was to return her to Sarah. To finish what they'd started.

The thought made him quicken his pace. Sarah reached the lake, but didn't even stop to look at it. Instead she marched on, past the spot where Arthur's bike was found, heading into the wood. The same woods where she'd disappeared before and returned covered in blood, grass and mud.

Blood. Sam's throat was dry. He followed her deeper into the woods, and thought about the bonfire and the kids and the drugs and the dealers, but all he could imagine was a poor little girl waiting alone among the trees for her mother to come and kill her.

It was easier among the trees to follow her more closely. They walked on for some time until Sarah stopped and sat on a fallen log. Sam watched her carefully as she reached into the pocket of her coat and pulled out a packet of pills. And then another. She placed them delicately by her side and then her head fell. It took Sam a moment to realise that

434

she was crying. She reached into her pocket and pulled out two more pill bottles, and then a bottle of vodka. She laid them all in a line on the log next to her and continued to weep.

The noise of melting snow, dripping from the trees' branches, made it feel as though it was raining. But the sun poured down and the lonely woman cried her heart out, alone in the wood. Sam saw her rip the top off the bottle and take a long, deep swig. But when she reached for the first bottle of pills, he could watch no longer.

His appearance startled her, but once she realised who it was, she just drank again, her eyes never leaving him as she glugged the booze down. He walked over to her and she gripped the bottle like a club.

'You going to go for me again?' she asked.

He shook his head, no. 'What is this?'

'What do you care?'

She reached for the pills again, but he kicked them off the log. 'Do you really think I'd let you kill yourself in front of me? You think I'd let you escape that easily?'

A smile pushed its way through the tears. A bitter laugh.

'You told me, Sarah. Last night, you told me what you did.'

She shook her head, laughing at the empty weight of his words.

'You said it,' he repeated. 'I heard you say it.'

Again, she shook her head. She didn't know where her

daughter was, she hadn't killed her son. She had just said yes to a violent man when alone in a room with him. What had he expected?

'So where were you then?'

Stoned in the forest, she told him. Hiding away from this shitty little place with its snooty women and lairy men. She was brought up in a world where you would shout what you thought, face-to-face, and everything was done up front. Her brother Jed had laughed at her, reminding her that as tough and vicious as their childhood was, it was nothing compared with the cold, hurtful barbs that came with money and manners.

She had tried to be maternal, but it didn't come naturally, and she envied the way other women would play with children so easily. She yearned for the company of adults and found her children's needs suffocating. One day she'd pushed Arthur angrily in the road and someone had seen. From that moment on, everything had taken a terrible lurch downhill.

'I love my children,' she said mournfully.

She loved her children, but often she didn't like them. She hated the constant demands and incessant drain on her time. She wanted to be like the mums in the adverts, but it was a world she couldn't reach, a performance she couldn't master.

'Everyone does it behind closed doors, I bet.'

But no one could forgive her. She wasn't a proper mother. Her clothes were wrong, too short, too tight. She wasn't a proper woman for a life up here. And the only way to escape was to get drunk or stoned.

'I would go to the forest and lie on the floor. I could see the sky through the branches and watch the clouds drift by overhead and in the summer it could rain and I'd still be dry. I'd stare up at the clouds and imagine I was up there, far away from here. I fucking hate it.'

When stoned, it would all go away. She'd take more and more, buying pills and other stuff from the local kids. Sometimes, when they couldn't buy them locally, she and Ashley would drive off to a local town and she'd wait in the car while the girl would trawl the alleys for dealers. But the high never lasted, and each hit worked less and less. Her flights to freedom barely made it over the treetops. And afterwards, the return would feel all the more painful. Each return to Tim's dull, drab, polite home would make her skin crawl.

'I didn't like them. But I loved them. And I never hurt them.'

But they were gone, and so was her husband. And it was time for her to go as well.

'Turn around and let me go, Sam,' she said. 'I'm so tired. Let me go, please.'

Ever since she was a little girl, no one had thought much

of Sarah. She was a pretty girl but always sneering, and no one realised that she was merely reflecting the scorn that she saw in their expressions.

'Oh Arthur,' she sobbed. 'My gorgeous little boy, what did they do to you?'

A bird flapped its wings as it landed on a branch, causing a small avalanche of snow to crash to the ground beside them. Sarah saw none of it, her body rocking with grief, contorted with loss.

She came here to repeat the act, to lose her mind to drugs and let the cold steal her body. She had tried to live with the loss, but it had overwhelmed her.

'Everyone said I was a shit mum. I guess I thought they were right. But if I'm so bad, then why does this hurt so much? Why can't I stop crying?'

Her hand pulled again at the pills, but Sam held her back. She had confessed, he'd heard the words. This was a lie. But then she told him how happily Arthur would sit in her lap as they munched on Kendal mint cake at the foot of the fells, how Lily's face would light up when Sarah let her paint her face with make-up, and of the terrible, clawing ache that woke her every morning, and her grief poured into him.

'Where's my little girl?' she cried. 'Where is she?'

When Andrea died, the grief had licked at him, over and over like the tide. It had caused him to rage and fight, to drink and punch and kick at anyone and everyone. It had made him a stranger to those who loved him most. And it had wounded and winded him, slowly dragging him down, making it hard to stand, to fight, to care. And here was Sarah, just the same.

'She's dead, isn't she?' Sarah said. 'I think they're both gone and it's all too late. And I just want to go too. Let me go, please, Sam. Let me go too.'

No, not just the same. Because he had helped drag Sarah down here. It wasn't grief and loss alone that had sucked her to the bottom, it was him as well. And the sad, broken look she gave him and the pleas for him to leave her to her fate only confirmed this.

He scooped her up in his arms. She fought him for a while, but gave up the struggle as he marched back through the wood. He didn't look at her, he couldn't.

Bud was standing by the door, having seen them approach, and he let Sam enter and settle her on the sofa. Sam told him what had happened, fudging the facts a little to explain his presence. He made Bud swear that he wouldn't let her out of his sight.

Jed had disappeared and Bud didn't know where he'd gone, but this wasn't important. Sam walked away, making empty promises before he left about finding Lily no matter what. She wasn't dead, he insisted. She wasn't dead and he would find her. He felt the urgency and believed in his mission, but he knew that he was walking without direction. The case was crumbling around him.

But if not Sarah, then who?

Much of the snow had turned to slush now. He passed a forlorn snowman who had tipped over, crippled by the thaw.

Helen will have taken her. But not alone.

Sam's head spun with Sarah's grief, and he felt the same sickening impotence he'd felt at his own loss. He couldn't let this happen again. For a split second, he imagined a scenario where Lily was never found, but the idea was too terrible and he shoved it away.

Helen was the ringleader. She was the source. If not Sarah, then who could she have used to help her?

His phone buzzed again in his pocket. He saw the message: '*wrud? Ax*'. It made no sense, but then another appeared: '*wrud = what are you doing! Old man! xxx*'.

Ashley. Since he'd been here, she hadn't let him out of her sight. He remembered that she was the one who had pushed him towards Sarah in the first place. He thought about the shock on her face when he'd seen her talking to Helen and of the way she'd sought him out at the lake that first night. It was as though she'd stalked him. And even though she'd told him she didn't know what the woman with the purple coat looked like, or who the dealers in the woods were, because she never scored herself, Sarah had just blown her lies wide open. Ashley had bought drugs. Ashley had lied. He couldn't trust a single word she said.

He stabbed a message back on the phone: '*Down by the lake. Come now.*' Then he turned the phone off and looked out over the water.

It made sense that it was her.

'Hi, Sam.'

He heard the voice behind him, sooner than expected, and turned with his face pulled to the appropriate expression. But it wasn't Ashley and he was startled by the surprise.

It was Zoe.

SIXTY-FIVE

Zoe had been searching for Sam all morning. With stories of 'essential police business', she'd managed to persuade the owners of the half-sunk boat (a polite, taciturn couple who ran the only convenience store on that side of the water) to let her take it across the lake, and promised to return it as soon as she could. They had helped to right the vessel, attached its outboard motor with many frowns and head shakes, and warned her to be careful out in the middle. The phrase 'seaworthy' was bandied about and made her want to laugh, but her need to get back to the village and her worries about Sam held her back. Thanking them and gratefully receiving a thermos of coffee (they had a small camping gas stove), she steered the boat out into the water.

There was a time, as the boat chugged forward, when the mist fully enveloped her and she could see neither end of the lake. She was all alone and it was a wonderful feeling. But it could not last, and as she saw the shore approach, so her shoulders naturally hunched in anticipation of what was to come.

Sam wasn't in his room. Bernie mentioned that he'd slipped off early. Zoe took her aside, engaging her as an ally, whether she wanted to be or not. How had her boss seemed? Bernie told her breathily about the march on Bud's house and the news that Sam had stopped it all. Zoe's heart leapt at the news, but something about Bernie's tone told her that Sam wasn't quite as heroic as the story made out.

Wondering what this meant, she went to Tim's house and found him cowering behind the front door. When Tim saw who it was, his confidence returned and he squawked angrily at the break-in.

'This sort of thing doesn't happen here,' he said. 'We all know each other – there's no way.' But then he realised that this had happened before, and worse. His children were the awful proof. Instead, therefore, he complained angrily about how useless Zoe and her colleagues were – nationwide. Zoe took in the damage and wondered about the timing. Tim looked ragged, as though he was coming apart, and she made a hasty retreat.

Walking along the road, she inevitably saw David. He was shovelling snow off the small drive of his house and he glared at her as she approached, holding the spade tight in his hand. Like Tim, there was a wildness in the way that he stared at her. She had heard that he was one of the ringleaders and it felt as though he was still searching for a suitable ending. She was happy to get away from him.

Lastly, she visited Bud and found Sarah stretched out on the sofa, her eyes fixed to the window, red and unseeing. Bud told her how Sam had saved her, and once again she felt a flush of pride and relief, but then he told her that Jed had found him in the house alone with Sarah the night before and her heart plunged again. She was surprised to hear about Jed being there. He was gone now – it was his way, apparently, to come and go as he fancied.

Everything felt as though it was breaking apart. She went back to the lake because she could think of nowhere else to find him. The sun was high now and big patches of open fields revealed themselves from under the snow. She turned down the path and saw how the lake sparkled in the light, and how different it looked from earlier that morning. And there, staring out at it, his back to her, was Sam. She was so pleased that she almost ran up to him before he turned and the mistrust in his eyes stopped her dead.

'I didn't expect you back,' he said.

'We're a team,' she replied, rather weakly.

He didn't even bother to nod at this. She struggled on, regardless.

'I have something, I think it might be useful.'

'Go on.'

'I talked to Helen again . . .'

She saw his eyes narrow, but there was nothing she could do about this.

'I saw Helen and she told me that Sarah's brother Jed was a drug dealer.'

'And?'

He stared at her so coldly, like she was a stranger. She couldn't bear it. They had been inseparable in the past.

'And, come on, Sam. We always wanted to know who the dealers were in the woods. Well now we know.'

'Jed was in a police cell in London when Arthur and Lily vanished,' Sam replied, his voice drenched with contempt. She stammered slightly as she continued, taking in the stains on his clothes. He looked terrible, jagged and raw, just like the others.

'Yes, I know. But I thought we should explore it. And did you hear that Tim Downing's house was broken into last night?'

Sam hadn't, but he couldn't see the relevance to their case. And neither could Zoe. Yet there were pieces here that had to fit together, somehow. But she couldn't do this on her own. She never had.

But then Sam walked past her and she saw him striding towards Ashley Deveraux, who approached with a coy smile. Zoe cursed silently as she saw him grip Ashley by the arm and lead her away.

She didn't follow. She just stared out at the lake, trying to take everything in. But then she realised that Sam was shouting.

Ashley pulled her arm from Sam's grip, twisting away from him.

'What the fuck are you talking about?' she snapped.

'You've been lying to me,' Sam said.

'No. Never!'

'What did Helen Seymour really come here for?'

'FUCK OFF!'

He tried to grab her again but she sank her nails into him and he pulled away sharply as thin lines of blood sprang up across the back of his hand.

And then Zoe was there on the other side of him, asking again about the break-in and other leads, while Ashley coughed up theatrical anguish.

'Okay, shut up a second.' He tried to clear his mind. 'Just shut up!'

He faced Ashley, trying to turn his back on Zoe.

'You said you never bought drugs yourself.'

He saw her eyes drop as the lie was exposed. But now Zoe was trying to distract him.

'Sam, she's a kid, she's nothing to do with this.'

'Not now, Zoe,' he said, trying to maintain his focus. 'You lied, didn't you? You know those dealers perfectly well.'

'Piss off,' the girl replied. It was a truculent mutter, a confession of sorts.

'Why did you lie?' His voice came out louder than he meant it to.

'Jesus, Sam,' Zoe said, tugging at his sleeve, but he didn't bother with her.

'What did Helen tell you to say?' he continued.

Ashley's eyes bored into the ground with shame.

'Sam . . .' Zoe's hand was on his arm again and he wheeled around and pushed her. She slipped, not expecting this, and fell backwards onto the floor. She didn't get up, but just stared at him in shock. He felt a wave of shame pour over him. Another wave to add to the ocean. He couldn't look at her so he slammed back to Ashley instead.

'What did she make you say?'

Nothing. The girl was crying.

'Don't fucking cry. Just tell me. Why did you lie?'

He grabbed her shoulders, and she answered in a tiny voice, without pride or cunning.

'So you'd want me.'

She shrank slightly after saying the words. 'If I'd told you I was a user,' she said, 'and you knew I scored and loved to get high, you wouldn't have stuck with me. You'd have screwed me and gone. You know you would have. I remember how you looked at me, when we started. Like I was nothing.'

She pushed the hair away from her face and wiped her eyes.

'I just wanted to keep you here. 'Cos I love you so much. You have no idea, do you?'

'What did Helen say to you?'

'Nothing! God, you're stupid. I don't know anything about Lily. No one does. I hope you never find her.'

She shrank at her own words.

'That's terrible, isn't it? Saying that. But it's true. 'Cos if you never find her, then that means you'll always be looking. And you'll have to stay here, with me.'

She put her arms out and pulled him tight, and he didn't know what to do.

'I'd tell every lie in the world to keep you, Sam. I don't care. I don't care about anything except you.'

He looked around. Zoe was still lying on the ground. He felt Ashley kiss his lips, but there was no connection, it was as though he wasn't there. The snow was too bright.

'Sam?' Ashley asked.

'Sam,' Zoe countered.

Nothing made sense.

He had to find Lily.

'I love you. You love me. You know you do.'

Zoe got back to her feet. He felt outnumbered again as Ashley reached for him once more. But he held up his hands, trying to protect himself, trying to work it all out.

How can they all be innocent? If a boy is dead and a girl is missing, then how can nobody be to blame?

The water lapped against the shore and offered nothing.

He had been certain it was Sarah, but now this seemed wrong.

He was sure Ashley was deceiving him, but her words rang true.

He had been so sure about it all.

Stop. Think. Take it all in.

If Lily was still alive, then where would she be? If she was here, in the village, then they would have found her. If she was in the lake, then that final trawl would have discovered her body.

Why had Helen really come back? If she was at the heart of this, then she must be pulling the strings. She must still have Lily. It's the only possible answer. But where could she hide her?

Water, a woman, a purple coat, a little girl.

He stared out over the lake and let his eyes follow a line of geese that beat their way through the sky with heavy wings. They passed over the old boathouse, halfway along, its crumbling jetty more visible now that the trees had shed their leaves.

Sam's eyes gazed at the boathouse. The place where the kids went because no one would find them. The only place in the village where you could go and not be seen.

Something glinted; metal, reflecting off the sun. He looked again. It was the bonnet of a silver car.

He started to run.

SIXTY-SIX

Jeremy Durrant's old boathouse was surrounded by woodland. A car could get down there if it knew where to turn off from the road, but the uneven path was steep and hazardous. There was little reason to drive there anyway, as it was easier to launch a boat from the other side of the lake, and the locals had scoffed when it was first erected in the late fifties. Although he was rich and well liked, everyone used to laugh at Jeremy, telling him that the boathouse was a folly and he might as well throw a suitcase of money into the depths of the lake itself. It turned out they were right. No sooner had the work finished and his chic white motorboat been happily stored there, than Jeremy's wife announced that she was leaving him. His house was soon put up for sale, and although he still owned the land and the boathouse, no one ever saw him up in these parts again. Someone said he now lived down in Cap Ferrat with a *Playboy* model, but it made no difference to the villagers.

Bitter winters and storms ate at the wood, and time did its inevitable damage as the building developed an unfortunate list towards the lake: a drunk diver, ready to take that final plunge. In this state, unloved and abandoned, it was inevitable that eager young couples would seek its shelter for amorous adventures. A tree had grown up through the platform on one side, splitting it apart, and much of the wood had crumbled and splintered, but it was still a place of sanctuary, a feeble attempt at escape.

Sam sprinted through the snow. He heard Zoe shouting from behind him, but nothing could stop him as he charged on amongst the trees.

He slowed slightly as he approached. There was, indeed, a silver car parked just in front of the dilapidated building. Zoe was suddenly by his side and they walked forward together, inching towards the truth. From the trees, still some two hundred metres away, he saw a flash of purple. A purple coat. A woman in a purple coat, her back to him. She moved into the shelter of the boathouse and out of sight before he could see more.

The snow dulled the noise of their steps and they pushed on fast. Nearly there. Sam prayed that he wasn't too late. It felt all too horribly appropriate for Lily to be found here, floating where the motorboat was once housed, all alone, with Helen standing next to her, her work finally complete.

Four wooden steps led up to the faded platform where the car was parked. It creaked slightly under the weight. The two cops paused before heading up. And then they heard a woman's voice call out.

'Are you fucking kidding me?'

And then a woman appeared – thin, thirties, with a gaunt face and expression that was sharp and severe. She wore the purple coat, buttoned up to the neck against the cold, but her jeans and shoes were unsuitable for this place and the weather. Too fashionable: city dress.

She walked straight to the car and didn't see the cops nearby as she pulled open the car door. Inside, asleep on the back seat, was Lily Downing. She still wore her school uniform – white ankle socks, a simple blue skirt and matching top with the school's crest emblazoned in yellow. It was as if she'd stepped out of her own photo. Sam was about to lunge for her when he heard another voice. A man.

'It's all they had!'

'You said they were *loaded*,' she replied.

'It's all I found, Jesus. You think I didn't try? I've tried everything. I mean, breaking into your own sister's house and robbing her, bloody hell, that's low, isn't it?'

Jed walked out and stood next to the woman by the car. They stared in at the sleeping girl.

'I was told not to let her go unless you had it all,' she said.

453

'I've tried, I've told you, I don't have any more. This whole thing . . . there was no need.'

Sam's leg was shaking and cramping – he wanted to run at her now, grab her and pin her into the snow.

The woman was angry. He watched her red lips purse.

'It wasn't my idea,' she said. 'I told him it was stupid. I'm sorry about the boy, everyone's sorry about the boy, but he's on your conscience so shut up about it.'

She had a regional twang, and when she spoke the darker and harder tones were more pronounced.

'He was just a kid,' he said.

'Don't go on about it, for God's sake.'

'You sure she's okay?' Jed asked, staring down at her.

'Yeah. She's fine. Been out of it most of the time, so might take a bit to come round proper.'

'What? So, she could be, like, brain-damaged or something?'

'I said she's fine, didn't I? We didn't want any chance of her seeing anything though, did we? Then we'd all be fucked.'

'Instead of just me.'

'Yeah, Jed. Instead of just you. Jesus, we fed her and cleaned her clothes and shit. We're not monsters. And it wasn't my idea to take the kids in the first place. I thought it was fucking stupid. But you created the problem and he wanted to make a statement. And this is where we end up.'

'You killed Arthur, you stupid bitch.'

'Do you have any idea how hard it is to get a needle in a kid when he's wriggling about like crazy? No wonder he ended up getting too much.'

Neither of them moved for a moment, a little crushed by the tragedy.

'So what do we do?'

'I don't know, I'll have to call. But I just want rid of her.'

Sam felt something ripping and tearing away at the top of his head. He couldn't hear anything. His eyes watered with the cold.

You are wrong.

This is no witch.

There is no conspiracy.

You are wrong about everything.

You stupid, ignorant, foolish man.

It felt as though bubbles were prickling up inside him, bursting out of his skin. He couldn't breathe.

Zoe watched the woman smooth Lily's hair back behind her ear. It was an incongruous gesture. Sam suddenly exploded next to her – charging out at them without warning. He charged towards Jed, twigs snapping under his weight as he ripped forward.

'Stop, police!' she screamed, sprinting after him.

Jed turned and ran, jumping off the platform and flying through the trees, much faster than expected, and Sam went after him.

The woman was too stunned to move and Zoe didn't even bother to cuff her.

There was a scream from the woods, then silence.

SIXTY-SEVEN

Mary-Ann Porter was thirty-three years old, with a string of convictions, starting with petty thefts and, perhaps inevitably, ending up with drugs. Once a drug user but now clean, she had noticed the easy exploitation of addicts and so hadn't strayed too far, returning as a dealer. She refused to answer questions about associates and said nothing about Arthur and Lily Downing, but Zoe didn't care. She'd caught her with the girl, she had her.

Zoe handcuffed her into the front of the car, then checked on Lily, whose breathing was shallow but regular. They waited in silence for her to awaken, sitting in a hostile silence as the boathouse creaked in the water. Sam hadn't returned with Jed by the time Lily opened her eyes. She stared blankly at the two women before Zoe took control and explained as best she could to the child that she was safe and that she was going to take her back to her mother. She didn't mention the inevitable intrusions that would follow: from the police, from child psychologists, from the press and the public.

Lily listened wide-eyed and nodded when asked if she was okay and understood. Then Zoe rang Bud, who passed her straight to Sarah Downing. Zoe told her the news, feeling a slight pang of guilt as she decided not to ring Tim Downing and do the same. He'd get his turn, she reasoned. Then she rang in to the local police station and told them that the girl was safe and the case was over.

Zoe worried that the car would slip on the snow as they made their way up the steep bank, slipping slightly on the tight bends until they made the main road. She didn't ask Lily any more questions, and whenever she glanced at her as they headed home, she saw the little girl staring out of the window, up at the sky.

Zoe headed into the village, slowing because some of the melted ice had now refrozen. She noted a car ahead had spun and slipped off the road and several locals were out, trying to force it out of a ditch. Zoe carefully eased around them, but inevitably someone peered into the car and saw Lily. And so the cry went up.

By the time Zoe had got to Bud's place, half the village was rushing to catch the moment. Zoe parked, got out and opened the passenger door to help Lily out. She was wearing simple black, strap-on school shoes and she gazed down unhappily at the slushy snow.

'Come on,' Zoe said. 'It's just a little snow. You're okay. Yeah?'

Lily looked up at her and nodded. I'm okay. Zoe fought the urge to burst into tears. Lily seemed unharmed. She wondered if this could be true.

The front door opened and they turned and saw Sarah stumble into view. Lily ran away from Zoe and she smiled as the little girl charged into her mother's arms. Sarah hugged her tight, letting out an ecstatic, guttural moan as she wrapped her daughter up tight. They didn't move for ages and Zoe noted more people appear and witness the scene. David was there and Zoe clocked the shock and confusion in his face. He turned away, shorn of his righteous anger. Someone patted him on the shoulder, celebrating the good news, and he found it within him to smile and shake their hand.

All around him the village united and rejoiced. It was a happy day.

Behind David, Zoe saw Ashley approach. As people cheered and hugged each other, so she stood aside, her hands stuffed deep into pockets, searching for Sam amongst the crowd. Zoe wondered if she should warn her that he would not be back, but then she saw the girl turn and storm away and Zoe knew that this was another disappointment, heaped on after the last. The girl didn't need telling of men's fickleness. She wondered if she would ever see her again. Maybe on a corner, maybe in a cell, maybe on a slab. Why such unhappy endings? Zoe wondered. This was what her instincts predicted, that and the angry, empty stare of the girl. She watched Ashley walk away, her head down, shoulders hunched, angry at everything. Walking, as always, in the opposite direction to everyone else.

Zoe turned back to Sarah. She hoped she would catch the woman's eye and offer her a silent nod, maybe receive a thank-you. But then she saw Sarah yank Lily inside and slam the door shut. There was a pause and then a collective moan from the crowd at this anticlimax. It seemed a fitting revenge, Zoe thought, however small.

She got back into the car and called the local station again. Officers were on the way, she was told, and she was directed to bring Mary-Ann in for questioning. Good work, the senior officer had barked before he hung up.

She drove her prisoner in without asking questions. She'd let her stew in her cell for a while. This was an easy one now. It was only a question of pulling in the others, however many there were, and making sure that Mary-Ann was wrung dry of information. Whatever happened, Lily was safe. Zoe parked her car in the small backyard of the local police station, and a young constable charged out, overexcited at the result. She regarded him coolly. He was like a young crocodile, harmless enough for now. But what would he grow into? She thought about Mr Frey and suddenly the colour of the day faded. She had a result, she'd fixed the case. But still they would come after her.

She let the young constable babble on about his first few months in the job, then led Mary-Ann inside. She listened as the custody sergeant processed the prisoner, but her mind pulled her back to Malcolm. She heard the cell door bang shut and turned around, wondering what the hell she was going to do next.

Her mind spun to Sam. She made a few calls and learned that he hadn't returned and that there was no news of Jed.

She ran to the car.

SIXTY-EIGHT

Jed was faster than expected, and fitter too. Sam had charged after his slight frame, expecting to pull him down within moments and drag him back to the car. But he had been drawn across the craggy terrain and out of the forest before he finally caught him near a small stream, crashing him down onto the snow, feeling the sharp elbow of a tree branch in his ribs as he tumbled onto the floor himself.

Sam hit him first. A heavy piledriver straight into Jed's eye that broke the skin and sent blood spurting across his face.

Jed shrieked in pain and spat at Sam, who hit him hard in the stomach, sinking his weight into the punch so that Jed was left gasping and coughing.

'Tell me,' was all he said. As Jed rabbited out his pathetic excuses, he was unable to stop more blows from raining down.

Jed was always in debt, but had never worried about

it much. However, when the stash of drugs he'd bought was stolen from his flat, he found himself in real trouble. Thinking he was clever, he bought more drugs from a gang he didn't know, telling them he'd be able to pay in full the next morning. But when he went to his old contacts and tried to flog the drugs off onto them, he found that no one was buying. And suddenly he was out of his depth.

A kick in the kidneys left him coughing and breathless. A stamp on his knee made him howl in pain.

Although the debt was huge, Jed believed he could blag his way out of anything. So he strolled back to meet them the next day, some loosely prepared lies ready for them.

But when he went into that basement and saw the hammer on the table, his stomach turned and he knew that he'd misplayed his hand very badly indeed. The weapon had remained unused, but he'd been warned: find the money – twenty-four hours – or we'll hurt you in ways you cannot imagine. How was he to know that these guys had been ripped off by another grifter only a week before? They told him they weren't going to let it happen again – that if he failed them, they would make an example of him. Send out a message.

He'd gone to friends, thieves and grifters, hoping to start the see-saw game of debt again, but they all laughed in his face, aware of his debts and knowing he could never pay them back. He'd sat on the pavement, head between his knees, knowing that there was nothing he could do. He had no money, and while he might be able to do stings and deals to raise the money in a month or two, the day was closing and so was his luck. Desperate now, he followed a man in a suit home and then tried to barge his way in as he opened the front door, hoping he might find cash or valuables inside. Instead he found five other men and was easily caught, arrested, and banged up in a cell. He was bailed the next day by a magistrate and returned home, expecting to find men in his flat, ready to smash him to pieces. He couldn't stop thinking about that hammer.

Sam hit him hard and fast about the face – three sharp punches that sank him back into the bloodied snow.

But when he returned home, the flat was empty and untouched. Jed stared out of his window, amazed that everything was normal. Foolishly, he'd wondered whether they had been empty threats. He wondered idly about the other part of the conversation, the chatter at the front which had duped him into thinking there had been an easy way out of that basement. The talk of his nephew and niece and of the extravagant presents he'd bought them. He'd told the story to show he was a good guy, that they couldn't blame him for frittering some of his money on children. He'd overdone it a bit, for sure, going on about how great they were, how rich their parents were and what a dutiful uncle he was. He had no one else in his life, after all. But he had just been trying to play them by giving them a sob story.

Mary-Ann had laughed at his stories and encouraged him to tell more anecdotes about them.

We'll hurt you in ways you cannot imagine. They were words from a bad film, he thought, and chuckled to himself.

Punch followed punch and Jed's skin broke and bled.

Then the news came in. Arthur and Lily had vanished and he knew that all of his stories were just information so that they could do the job properly. He went to the loo and puked until his stomach was empty, then puked some more.

Yes, they'd made their point alright. But it didn't matter that they had Arthur and Lily, he was simply unable to find the bloody money. He did all he could, slowly scrimping and dealing away, but by the time he had anything like enough, the news came through that Arthur was dead. Every night he curled up and sobbed alone in his caravan.

A kick, a stamp, a smashed fist. Over and over.

When he was told that he had three more days to find the cash or the girl would disappear for ever, he decided that the only chance he had was to break into Sarah and Tim's house and take what he could. He'd remembered rich trinkets and fancy jewellery, and arranged to pass them on straight away to a fence in Newcastle. But when he got in and searched the place he realised that posh paintings and sofas were not going to solve this, and that Tim had safely hidden his most valuable belongings. And then the snow came down and trapped him.

He was trying, willing to do anything to save his little Lily, he sobbed.

Sam punched him again.

He punched him and felt a rib pop.

He pulled him up to his feet then knocked him back down again.

A dead boy, utterly innocent, because of his stupidity and greed.

Jed tried to get away, clambering across the stream, and it gave Sam the excuse to hit him again. His fists crashed into his nose and jaw, shattering it.

This stupid man, this disgusting clown. He hit him with a combination of punches and felt Jed's body soften as he lost consciousness and flopped down, out.

Sam stood over him, panting.

He was the cause. He had started it all. Sam had done his job. The girl was safe. He had Jed. It was done. It was over.

A thin line of white cloud had drifted across the sky and enveloped the sun. Sam stared down at his fists and slowly unclenched them. His arms hung at his sides but the blood had congealed and clung tight to his skin. He felt it on his face and neck, and saw the mud that stained his clothes from head to foot. He was a monstrous sight.

He was lost and empty. Finished.

Sam stared up at the bare sky, his feet wet from the stream, and howled.

SIXTY-NINE

Zoe found Jed handcuffed against the rails of the boathouse, and her emotions lurched. As she approached, she saw blood smeared against the metal railing where he sat, redolent of a butcher's shop. He sat sagging on the steps, crumpled and broken like the building itself. He heard her approach and started to shudder, clearly thinking she was Sam. He recognised her and calmed down, but still he was still unable to speak or make eye contact. His right eye was so swollen and his right cheek so badly sunken that he looked ghoulish.

He reminded her of Eli Robinson.

Jed had no idea where Sam was and muttered feeble, barely comprehensible words. She left him where he was, calling in once more to the local station and letting them know where to pick him up. Instead of waiting, she followed the neatly marked footpath signs, each carved into sturdy wooden posts, which pointed to the fell above. She looked around, called out for him, but saw no one.

She took the path out from the forest and up a steep incline. It was extraordinary, the way the land could rise so suddenly, almost vertically, from nothing. Her legs hurt, but she pushed herself up, hoping, ever hoping. Ahead of her, a little higher, were two giant boulders through which walkers would have to pass in order to continue their way to the top.

She thought she spotted something, and when she pulled herself up, Sam was indeed there, sitting on one of the rocks, staring out at the view below. He had blood all over him, but she knew that none of it was his. He was a terrible sight.

She thought of Malcolm and of the matey jokes that he and Sam would share. She thought of Helen, waiting for her to destroy her career. All of them, all pushing her, all using her to their own ends. Even Sam.

He looked at her and opened his mouth, but nothing came out.

'Come on, boss. Case closed. Sun'll be going down soon.'

He said something else – a hoarse croak that made no sense.

'Say what?'

He shook his head and she went over to him and dropped down by his side.

'What is it, boss?'

She took in the view: Lullingdale to the right, picturesque like a model; to the left were the woods with steep hills opposite, and in the middle, pride of place, the lake. As always, it was majestic, immovable, and utterly unaffected by man's progress and intrusions. The wind swept waves across it.

Zoe spotted the roof of Bud's bungalow. A small plume of smoke billowed from the chimney. She was about to tell Sam that this was where Lily now was, but she felt him move and realised that he was crying. He looked at her and tears poured down his bloody, mud-stained face.

'I'm sorry,' he whispered.

I'm sorry. The clouds danced above him and he remembered his wife.

I'm sorry. The wind shook tree branches and he thought about the way he had grabbed at Sarah. He remembered the cruel intentions and desires that he'd let fester.

He noticed the tiny cracks and etches in the stone below him, thousands of years old, and he wept for his daughters and the ways that he had failed them.

Andrea, his heart yelled, Andrea I love you and I'm sorry, I'm sorry, so, so sorry.

He thought of his betrayal of Ashley, of his murderous rage at Helen Seymour, and he wept at the poor, broken women who he had demonised into witches and demons. A put-upon housekeeper, a schizophrenic nanny, all re-imagined as monsters.

He put his hand on the boulder, it made him feel weak and tiny. Zoe, next to him, felt like a mountain.

'I'm sorry, I'm so sorry,' he said again and again.

Zoe pulled him to her and he crawled into her embrace like a small child. She hugged him tight and stroked his hair and soothed him.

The sun slipped downwards through the sky, but Zoe held Sam firm. Clouds darkened overhead. She held Sam close to her, kissed his cheek and whispered promises in his ear.

Eventually she helped Sam stand and led him down to the car. They drove to the hotel, where she managed to get him inside via the back entrance without anyone seeing. There, in his hotel room, she washed the blood away and helped him change. They left together, her leading the way.

And then, last of all, she drove him back to the lake.

Although it was dark, the full moon lit the water. It remained just as it always had: remote and imperious. They stared at it together for some time before Zoe left him, going down to the lake by herself. It seemed right that she was alone here now. She gazed over the still water and took it all in. It held no fears for her now.

Zoe reached into her bag and pulled out the tiny tape that had recorded Helen's confessions. She ran her finger over it, and then hurled it out into the water. The lake swallowed it whole. The tiny ripples soon vanished, and order was restored.

470

Zoe watched it all. She saw everything now.

A little later she left the lake behind and drove Sam back to the city, leaving Lullingdale for the last time. Up the steep hills, through the valleys and out again, back towards the electric light of the city.

She sped forward, ready for the fight.

As she drove, Sam stared out at the sky above. Before they had set off, Zoe had called home and told the girls that their father had finished the job, before handing the phone over to him. He had heard laughter and delight at the news of his return. He wondered if it had always been there. He shared the joy and made new promises that he now knew he could keep. He was going home. He stared out of the car window, and for the first time, as his eyes scanned that vast, perfect black canvas, he finally saw nothing but the night.

ACKNOWLEDGEMENTS

Huge thanks to Jane Wood and her excellent colleagues at Quercus Books, but especially Katie Gordon whose editing skills finessed the novel at every stage. Thanks also to Jonny Geller and all at Curtis Brown. Last, but never least, my beautiful love, Ceetah, who is my first reader, sternest critic and finest inspiration.